MW00887106

Leave the Little Light On

Book I: Windsor

Sonia Palleck

◆ FriesenPress

One Printers Way
Altona, MB R0G 0B0
Canada

www.friesenpress.com

Copyright © 2023 by Sonia Palleck
First Edition — 2023

All rights reserved.

This is a fictional memoir. It reflects the author's present recollections of experiences filtered through time. Any references to historical events, real people or real places are used fictitiously. Other names, characters, places, and events are products of the author's imagination, and any resemblance to actual events or places or persons, living or dead, is entirely coincidental. Some names and characteristics have been changed, events compressed and some dialogue has been recreated.

No part of this publication may be reproduced in any form, or by any means, electronic or mechanical, including photocopying, recording, or any information browsing, storage, or retrieval system, without permission in writing from FriesenPress.

ISBN
978-1-03-916239-6 (Hardcover)
978-1-03-916238-9 (Paperback)
978-1-03-916240-2 (eBook)

1. FICTION, FAMILY LIFE

Distributed to the trade by The Ingram Book Company

One person's truth is another person's fiction.
Truth implies an entirety that cannot be told here.
It has to be lived.

This is not my truth.
It is my story.

For Me

Chapter 1

Athena took the grey-painted stairs one at a time. She was going to fetch her father, her *tata*. She would have to venture across the road to the variety store. She was strictly forbidden to leave the sidewalk but her mother had given her very specific instructions: "Go to Fred's and tell Tata it's time to go, please."

Athena stepped down—*one foot, two feet*. Her pudgy hand guided her along the wall. She had tumbled down the bare flight of stairs not long before and so was careful to pay attention. Upon reaching the bottom step, Athena moved through the small entryway quickly, careful not to look back toward the basement. Her tata's tool shop was there, with the dungeon door.

It was late summer and the back door was open, leaving the screen. Athena ran her fingers across the mesh where it was warped. She reached up to the flat metal handle and banged the button with her palm.

The air outside was humid, but it wasn't much different inside; it only smelled sweeter because of the dirt and grass. Having made it out of the house, Athena felt satisfied. She jumped out of the way as the door swung shut. The familiar slam made her fear that her tata would be alerted, and she would miss her opportunity for adventure.

The sidewalk beside the house rocked under her bare feet as she stepped from one concrete slab to the next. She paused to lean over and inspect a line of ants streaming from a sand pile. The ants flowed in and out, climbing over one another. Athena wondered what the inside of their house looked like. A car drove by, and the revving of the engine made her look up. It wasn't far to the road.

Athena's house had wide plank siding that was dusty rose. It was the prettiest house on the block. Fred and Freida lived next door in a two-storey, but it had horrible green awnings. A chain-link fence separated their houses. It felt grimy on her sweaty palm. From where she was, Athena saw her tata standing across the street at the corner store, speaking with another man. His black car was parked in front.

Athena stood for a moment to catch her breath. She could hear the faint buzzing of mosquitoes, and she ran her fingers across the back of her neck. Her hair was cropped close, like a boy's. Her mama wouldn't let her grow it long; she said it would take too much to comb it. Athena had to cross the street. She puffed out her chest. Her pot belly hung below the tight T-shirt, and her shorts were falling slightly, twisted.

Athena watched for green bits of glass as she stepped off the curb. She peeked around the family car, looking both ways. After crossing, she sidled up to her tata, who was becoming more animated as she approached.

"You don't know what yer talkin' about," he said.

The man who didn't know what he was talking about didn't look too happy. "Drag, look, you gotta consider . . . it's the seventies now, man."

"I don't gotta consider nothin'. The union is tryin' to muscle in and is only gonna make it harder for regular guys when these companies move to Mexico—'cause it's cheaper."

Athena came up to her tata's knee. She put her hand on his pant leg and tugged, even though she knew not to interrupt.

The man retaliated with a wave of his hand. "Aw, you don't know what's good for ya."

"I don't know?" Her tata's voice changed in pitch. Athena became determined to tell him to come home.

"Tata!" She tugged harder on his pants.

Without looking down, he brushed her away. His hand, holding the cigarette, swept her backward. There was a small hiss. He extinguished the butt on her wrist, just below her thumb. Athena gasped and shrank back. The salt of her sweat stung the burn and she cried out.

"Jesus!" Her tata grabbed her arm, and he brushed the ashes roughly away.

Athena started to cry.

"Whaddaya doin' here anyways, kid? You're not supposed to cross the street."

Athena pulled her arm free, the skin puckering around the burn. "You gotta come home now. Mama says." Her voice was thick with hurt pride.

"Yeah, sure. Get home now and tell your mother I'll be right there." He lifted her hand up and inspected it. "Why'd you put your hand there, peanut? Didn't you see my cigarette? Geez." He brushed it again and she winced. "Hey, stop cryin'. You're okay."

Athena wanted to be okay. She wiped her eyes. She glanced back up at her tata's face, his black hair falling across his forehead, his nose broad, and his sharp green eyes framed in thick, black-rimmed glasses, squinting down at her.

She turned and ran across the street. A car horn blared and tires screeched, combining to disturb the heavy summer air hanging over the oily street. Athena felt her feet leaving the ground, her arm hoisted above her head, and a strong slap delivered to her backside through the thin shorts. Her tata plunked her down unceremoniously on their side of the street. His hand gripped her shoulder; she dared not move.

"You can't run into the road, Athena!" He accentuated each syllable with a shake of her small three-year-old body.

She nodded. All of the pain flooded in, and she was grateful he let go of her, even if it was with a shove toward the house as tears spilled over her hot, embarrassed cheeks.

Her tata turned to look at the other man, already disappearing into the air-conditioned variety store, and said, "I gotta go now." The street was empty.

Athena ran into the house through the side door.

"Hey!" Tata shouted. "Don't bang on the screen door like that! Yer gonna break it."

Chapter 2

With a frown, Mama looked down at Athena's hand. She lifted the cold cloth she had placed over the burn and peered closer. "It wasn't Tata's cigarette."

Athena pleaded her case softly. "Yes, it was, Mama."

"Well, it was an accident."

Athena said nothing. How could it have been anything else?

She turned at the sound of her tata's steps coming up the back stairs. He filled the kitchen doorway. He pushed his hair off his forehead and adjusted his glasses.

"She's all right. Aren't you, peanut?" His hand fell on top of her head and ruffled her damp, pin-straight hair.

Athena could taste the saltiness of her snot and tears and just nodded and smiled. Of course it was an accident.

"What were you doing?" Mama asked.

"Ahh . . ." A dismissive sound came from her tata's lips as he went into his room.

Athena took the washcloth from her mama's hand and moved to the kitchen nook.

"Get ready," Mama said toward the bedroom door. "We're going in ten minutes and I'm helping in the kitchen, so I don't want to be late."

She sighed as she turned toward the sink. She continued washing the dishes and placing them in the rack. Athena loved the sparkly pattern in the countertop; it looked like silver stars and snowflakes.

Mama turned to Athena, who was sitting quietly dabbing the red-ringed burn. "Hey, don't play with that. Go tell your sisters to get ready. I laid your dresses out on your beds." Mama reached out to inspect her hand again. "Let me see."

Athena admired her mama's beautiful face. Her soft brown eyes were gazing down at her. She leaned forward and the scent of cold cream and floral perfume floated through the dust-filled late-afternoon air, the sun pouring into the bay window.

Mama kissed her boo-boo without actually kissing it. "Come. Let's put a Band-Aid on that first."

Athena smartly followed her mama, who was careful not to let go of her wrist. Athena felt important.

Her sister Danica saw them entering the bathroom. "What happened?"

"Oh, it's nothing," their mama answered.

As Danica crawled out from under the dining room table to see, her sister Lejla looked up. Danica was already marching to the bathroom, so Lejla followed. Athena's sisters crowded the doorway to the narrow room.

Danica asked again, "What happened?"

"Tata's cigarette—" Athena started to explain.

Mama interrupted. "It was an accident. Athena got a scrape, but it's going to be all better."

Lejla leaned closer to watch her mother cover the injury. "But how did it happen?"

Mama acted as though she hadn't heard the question, and Lejla and Athena exchanged a glance as Danica said, "It's no problem, right, Mama? It'll be fine."

"That's right." Their mama smiled down at them. "My three little angels. Now go get ready. We're going to be late, as usual." Her easy smile was chased away.

The two older girls skipped through the living room with Athena close behind them. On the beds were three matching outfits: red-and-white smocked dresses their *baba* had made for them. Athena didn't like the elastic bands on the arms because they dug in and left marks.

Mama appeared behind them with a wet towel that she moved vigorously over Athena's face, neck, arms, and hands. Her mama rooted between her fingers. "Your nails!" Athena tried to distract her by showing her the troublesome elastic bands. Mama ran her finger underneath them but dismissed her concern. "Your arms are just a bit too chubby." Athena looked at the dresses hanging loosely on her sisters. She saw Mama coming toward her with the nail clippers, so she went to run out, but her tata intercepted her, picking her up.

"Noooo," Athena wailed, struggling to get down.

"Her nails, Drag."

He inspected her hand, not mentioning the bandage, and nodded. "Look at those nails. Mama's gonna fix those. We can't go to the hall with dirty nails like that."

"What will people think?" her mama asked solemnly. "There's no excuse for being dirty. We might not have all the money in the world, but we have manners and we're clean." This she recited as she deftly trimmed and cleaned Athena's nails. Her tata was holding her tightly, and she was too hot. The bandage was starting to peel up. Athena held as still as she could so she could go run outside.

"Don't go outside. You'll get dirty," her mama said the instant her feet hit the ground.

Athena believed she could read her mind.

Once assembled, the Brkovichs piled into the car. The girls fought over who got the black leather seat that scorched your backside if you weren't careful. Inevitably, it was Athena. It was the natural order. She sat down in the wheel well behind her tata's seat. It felt a tiny bit cooler there.

"Roll down the windows, please," Danica and Lejla begged.

Their tata did, but not before methodically taking a cigarette out of the familiar packaging. Blue-tinged smoke filled the steamy car. The engine started, and Athena plugged her nose and held her breath, waiting for air. She had to let go and choked on the smog before the car picked up enough speed, creating a breeze. She wasn't excited to be going to the hall. There were always so many people.

The tires moved slowly over the stretch of gravel from the main road to the Serbian community centre. The hall was a long rectangle, low and lined with windows. Standing at the front door, you could see all the way to the kitchen at the back. This was where Athena's mama would be. To the right was the bar. This was where her tata would be.

Tightly packed tables, draped in white tablecloths and surrounded by folding chairs, filled both sides of the hall. Woven baskets, two to a table, held fresh bread. The air smelled of cigarette smoke, perfume, and onions. Everyone knew everyone.

Between the two lines of tables, people moved in a snake-like pattern dancing *kolos*, bouncing on the balls of their feet while holding hands. A man leading the *kolo* was waving a handkerchief in a circle above his head and letting out sharp whistles that punctuated the loud music. When the tempo ramped up, it infused the line with an infectious energy. Athena skipped to the accordion and bass as she ducked under the singing, smiling revellers and ran toward the kitchen, following her mama. People hugged Mama as they moved along.

Athena grabbed her hand and shouted, "Who are all these people?"

Her mama laughed. "They all know you, Athena. They know *us*." This was oddly comforting but confusing at the same time. Athena didn't know anyone here.

"Tilley!" A large woman wearing a hairnet and a butcher's apron covered in brown grease waddled out of the kitchen, her arms extended. She had to turn sideways to fit between the counter and the wall. "Oh, I'm so glad you're here. And who's dis?" The heavy accent came from lips covered with black hair and small beads of sweat.

Athena recoiled behind her mama's legs. The woman reminded her of the witches in her big storybook.

Her mama retrieved her and held her firmly by the shoulder while pressing her other hand into her back. "This is Athena. Yes, the little one."

"So pretty—like you Mama." She turned to Athena. "I knew her ven she vas your age."

Athena didn't smile. Had her mama been afraid of her when she was small? The woman held up one finger, winked at Mama, and disappeared into the kitchen.

Mama took the opportunity to examine Athena, who looked up at her, displeased. Mama frowned, licked her thumb, and cleaned Athena's face. "Theenie, please. Use your manners."

"But she has a moustache."

Mama looked as though she would laugh for a second but recovered. She put her hand to her mouth, and Athena copied her. She wanted to be just like her beautiful mama.

The woman returned with a big pastry for her. The icing sugar was melting. Athena took it and looked back up at the woman. *It must be hard to be ugly like that*, she thought, *but it probably helps to be nice*. Her mama was pretty *and* nice.

Athena ran off with the treat in her hand. Two children chasing one another were fast approaching. Their eyes widened. "Where did you get that?" they shouted.

Athena just pointed at the kitchen a few feet away and they were gone. Outbursts of laughter, swearing, and arguing came from the bar. People were lined up to buy tickets for drinks and plates of food.

Athena was free to do as she pleased. Trying to get past tables without getting her cheeks pinched or kissed was nearly impossible, so she slipped under the table closest to her. No one could see her. No one even knew she was there. Athena studied the people's legs near her and the red ink impressions stamped on the underside of the table. She hummed to the loud music as she enjoyed the pastry and licked her fingers. She should find her sisters.

Athena lifted the white tablecloth and peeked out. Halos of smoke surrounded the lightbulbs. She tried to look past the tight clusters of people, for her sisters. She saw her tata and remembered she was thirsty. He was talking like he had at Fred's.

Athena pushed her way up to the bar and tugged at his pants. She needed to be higher up so she could see. "Up, Tata!" she called. "Where's Dani and Jaja?"

Her tata put his cigarette in his mouth and set his beer on the bar, which stretched out about twenty feet. He hoisted her up on his hip.

"This is Kum Danny." He pointed to the large man with smiling eyes in front of her.

"Aw. So beautiful, Drag."

"All my girls are. But even better, they're smart. This one's the smartest."

"Yeah? That's good. But you know the smart ones can also be trouble, eh? Girls don't need to be so smart."

"Listen to this one. Theenie, say the alphabet."

Athena was listening but wanted to go play. She spotted her sisters by the wooden doors, about to go outside.

"Tata, no. I see them. Hey!" She felt a squeeze.

"It's okay if she doesn't want to."

"No. Say it now."

Athena looked in her tata's eyes. She knew by the way he spoke that he wouldn't listen. She started to sing, softly at first.

"Hey, c'mon. Louder. Sing for Kum Danny like you do at home."

Both men were looking at her, and now another turned around.

"She's a baby, Drag. She doesn't know her ABCs yet."

"I'm telling you, this one's a genius. Louder. Now." He squeezed her to emphasize that he meant what he said.

Athena tried harder to be loud. She saw the approving nods of the people at the bar. *"L, M, N, O, P . . ."* Tata was smiling proudly, and she was happy for that even though she didn't like everyone's eyes on her. "Now I know my ABCs, next time won't you sing with me?"

A round of applause broke out and her tata ruffled her hair, laughing and acknowledging the men on either side. He put Athena down and she faced a sea of black and brown pants. She pushed her way past them and ran for the front doors.

She soon found her sisters. Danica and Lejla had wandered to the red picnic tables along the front patio. The farmer's field that stretched to the road in the distance was covered with crumpled yellow cornstalks. There was a slight breeze, but the overhang didn't afford any great shade. Even the setting sun was hot.

Lejla was swinging around the poles. "This is fun," she said to her older sister. Danica took up the game and the two girls giggled as they exchanged places.

Two boys, Tommy and Niko, flew around the corner and stopped short when they saw the girls. Tommy and Danica knew each other.

"Hi." Danica stopped swinging and held up her hand to wave.

Tommy smiled. He had dirty blonde hair, freckles, and had failed grade one. Niko was different; he had white-blonde hair and pale green eyes. Lejla kept swinging and running.

Tommy took up what she was doing and motioned to his younger brother. "C'mon."

Niko swung on the first pole, flung himself to the second, and then headed down the line of poles. Lejla squealed as her game expanded down the length of the building. She followed. So did Danica and Tommy. The children weaved in and out. Athena listened to their panting, their fingers hitting the painted metal poles, their feet tapping on the cement, and the music filtering through the thin-paned windows. They went up and back a few times. She watched her sisters with delight and respect because they were playing an important game with the boys. She wanted to join in.

"You can't play." Tommy's words came flying in her face as he propelled himself wildly around the last pole.

Lejla, immediately behind him, came to a dead stop, planting her scuffed blue cloth sneakers. "She can *so* play!" she shouted at Tommy, who no longer seemed to care one way or another. Lejla snatched Athena by the hand and flung her around the pole.

When they had all nearly gone to the other end, Athena, her heart pounding, ran in and out to catch up to them, but she was too small.

"Get out the way!" Tommy shouted.

Athena jumped off the patio. She slouched forward, doing her best to look sad, but no one took any notice. Athena was distracted by a leaflet taped to the window in front of her.

Tommy came up behind her and startled her, exclaiming, "You can't read that!"

"Yes, I can!" Athena got a small jolt of power as she saw the confidence fade from Tommy's eyes. "It says, *Carousel of Nations, Food, Dancing, Music, Cash Bar*."

Tommy stared.

Lejla had stopped to catch her breath. "Yes, she can read."

"Who cares?" Running away, he looked back and yelled, "No one!"

Athena wanted to catch Niko, but the sun was stinging her burn, so she decided to go back into the hall.

The coatroom had a doorway and a countertop, like a restaurant. It was empty. Athena was sticky from the heat. Her throat was dry. She had forgotten to get a drink. A stack of brown wooden chairs sat in the corner. She crawled underneath them and sat with her back against the cool concrete block wall. She fingered the stripe of thick paint that had run down, pooled on the floor, and dried there. Athena imagined it was a palace drawbridge with a moat. She slid her feet out in front of her; the floor was smooth and polished and felt nice on the back of her legs. She wasn't supposed to sit on the ground, because Mama said it would give her pimples on her bum. Athena was singing one of her mama's lullabies when two boys came upon her, grabbed her shoes, and dragged her out from under the stack of chairs.

"Hey!" Athena frowned, jumping to her feet and smoothing her dress down. She didn't want anyone to see her underwear.

"What were you doing under there?" asked the younger-looking boy. He was about her size. He peered under the chairs as though trying to find something he'd lost.

"Nothin'."

The two boys looked at each other and grinned.

Athena felt nervous. "What's so funny?"

"Your face!" said the bigger boy.

Athena felt a knot in her throat as she glared back at him. "No, it's not!"

"Yeah, it is," insisted the older one. "C'mon, let's get away from this stupid girl."

"I am *not* stupid!" Athena hardened with confidence.

"You are!"

She balled up her fists in her stress and confusion.

"Ha, ha, ha!" chuckled the older one, stepping forward and leaning close to her. He wasn't much bigger than Danica, so he really didn't scare her that much. He looked in her eyes and something in his demeanour changed and he said, "No, maybe not, but you still look like a boy with that haircut." At this, the younger boy laughed hard and disappeared around the corner.

Athena crawled back under the chairs and tucked her feet up against her bum so she couldn't be pulled out. After twenty minutes or so, with the background hum of unintelligible conversation and music, she fell asleep.

A white lightbulb was swinging above Athena's head as her eyes cracked open. She heard the clatter and clang of the stack of chairs being lifted.

"Here she is! Here she is!" rang out in chorus.

She could see the countertop. Someone was lifting her over, her tata grabbed her arms and she flopped onto his shoulder. His breath had the sour smell it sometimes did when he sounded funny. He slapped her once on the back of her legs. She winced and he said, "You can't go disappearing like that, peanut. We have to know where you're at." He smelled like him, a combination of Old Spice, beer, and cigarettes. She breathed in, roused by the slap but too deep in her slumber to fully wake up.

"C'mon now, enough." Mama's voice was muffled. Athena was passed to her mama's arms for the car ride. She smelled much different from Tata. Somewhere in her mind, Athena knew it would be safer to stay fast asleep, so that's what she did. When she was rolled into bed, she heard some talk about her disappearance and how they had searched for her everywhere.

Lejla climbed into bed, clutching at the bedspread as she heaved herself up and over Athena. "We were all looking for you. Mama was crying."

Athena smiled, imagining how she mattered to Mama and Tata and her sisters. She loved her little house and her family, and how they loved her.

"I would look until I found you. I'd never let you be lost." Lejla kissed Athena's forehead and picked up her hand, looking at the red burn and blew gently on it.

Mama reached down and pressed the black button under the small lampshade. The amber light fell between the double and single beds, competing with the moonlight. From the kitchen, Athena could hear the cupboards opening and slamming shut. Mama looked up and tiptoed quickly out, gently closing the door to the girls' bedroom.

Chapter 3

The church stood alone like a Byzantine monument. It was striped with dark red and golden-yellow bricks that made it look like a layer cake. The domed copper roof had turned green. It looked ancient and true. The church was next to the tire centre and across from the fish and chips place, the record shop, and a gas station.

The Brkovichs pulled up into the already crowded parking lot. "We're late," Mama noted. Athena didn't like getting there earlier because the services were so long and she had to stand the whole two hours.

She was trying to climb the long flight of stairs to the front doors as quickly as her sisters. It was always hard for her eyes to adjust to the dark gloom of the church. The nauseating incense hit her when she walked in, so Athena pinched her nose and opened her mouth to breathe. As she bumbled in behind Danica and Lejla, Mama swiped her hand down, then stopped to get candles. Her baba hadn't been feeling well and Mama wanted to ask the angels to keep Baba safe. Tata swung into the office just before the entrance to the nave. Her tata was the church treasurer; he looked after the treasure. He had been for years—going to church without actually going to church.

"Dragan," the provost said, greeting him in a whisper.

Tata swung his briefcase up on the desk and asked him how he was. "*Kako si*, Milos?"

His Serbian was slow and methodical, like most things about him—except his temper. Mama said that was quick and you had to get out of the way quicker, or better just listen to him and avoid it altogether.

The girls followed their Mama to the sandbox that held the candles just outside the office. She crouched down. They leaned in. Mama's eyes welled up with tears, and Athena pressed her hand to her Mama's cheek as she whispered, "Bless Baba and make her well. Amen." Then she stood up, kissed the beeswax candle, held the wick to another flame, and shoved the candle into the sand to stand it up. Mama passed each of the girls one. Athena closed her eyes tightly and prayed very hard that her mama wouldn't be sad. Mama grabbed Athena's hand and helped her light her candle. When she went to bury the candle in the sand, her mother caught her arm and lifted her up. "We put the candles up on top if people are alive. When they die, we put the candles down below." Athena wondered what would have happened if she had done it wrong.

"Okay, girls, I have to go sing. Go downstairs quickly. You're late, but it's no worry."

Athena watched their mama tiptoe gracefully up the stairs. Golden light cascaded from the window on the landing, lighting her way. Everyone told Athena what a beautiful singer her mama was. She had been singing like an angel in the choir loft when Tata looked up and saw her and fell in love. His parents had been killed—that's why he went to church. Athena wanted to be a beautiful singer, too.

Going up the stairs was like going to heaven. Going down was like going to hell. At the bottom of the stairs, the air around Athena's brown dress shoes felt distinctly cold. To the left was the Sunday school room. To the right were double doors that led to where formal functions were held. All sorts of interesting things happened there involving folding chairs and coffee percolators with stacks of Styrofoam cups.

Lejla cracked open one of the double doors to peek in. "C'mon. No one's in here."

Danica glanced at the Sunday school door and then slipped past her sister. Lejla held the door open, waving her in. Athena followed without question. The three of them played lines, jumping into the big squares made by the mortar joints on the floor. Soon they could hear the children coming out of Sunday school. Athena's heart jumped, afraid they would be caught and punished. But they simply walked out and joined the other children to go back upstairs. No one even noticed.

Men and boys were separated from the women and girls by a red velvet carpet down the middle of the church. The carpet led up to the giant carved and gilded altar, which hid all of God's secrets. Women and girls were strictly forbidden to go behind the altar. Even if you were trying to look, you were reprimanded, as Athena had found out. You had to stand still, not fidget, and face the front so you wouldn't turn your back on God.

The children marched to the first icons. Athena watched and realized that she hadn't quite grasped how to cross herself. There was something to do with three fingers; she raised them to her forehead as if in a salute. The teacher patiently formed her first two fingers into a triangle with her thumb and traced the path of the cross from her forehead to her navel, and her right shoulder to her left. She lifted Athena up to kiss the dark, gothic painting, but Athena looked away. The teacher didn't make her do it like her mama would have.

Athena ran into line on the girls' side. She rocked on her feet and inspected the dark mahogany altar. The swinging doors on either side of it were quite busy with men going in and out. The middle doors were reserved for the priest. Rows upon rows of angels and saints adorned the three arches of the looming structure.

In the centre, at the very top, was a cross with Jesus nailed to it. Athena tried to avoid looking up at it but she found it irresistible. Jesus had never done anything wrong and people hammered nails through his skin. She didn't go to Sunday school like her mama told her to. Athena rubbed her palms anxiously, fixated on the crucifix, until she wept.

"Athena's crying," one of the Sunday school children pointed out.

The teacher stepped quietly. "Athena? What's wrong?" She bent down and whispered in her ear. Her breath smelled bad and it made Athena try to pull away. "What is it?"

Bewildered by guilt and fear, Athena looked at her as she pointed up to the cross with the man's body nailed to it. "He . . . he's *bleeding*." Athena's sobs grew louder.

"Shhhhh," the teacher said as she picked her up and quickly carried her out to her tata. "Hi, *Chico* Dragan." The young woman wiped Athena's face as her chest convulsed.

"Hey, peanut. Whatsa matter?"

Her tata's kindness melted Athena, and she sank her head into the teacher's shoulder, crying harder. "Jesus, Tata! *He's bleeding!*" Her words carried her despair with absolute conviction. "He's bleeding! They pu-put nails in his hands!" She felt wild as she tried to configure who had done this, how it had happened, and if it could happen again. This wasn't the first time Athena had to be consoled about Jesus. Danica and Lejla didn't seem to notice.

"*Theenie*, he's okay now. He's in heaven."

19

"He died for our—" the teacher began, setting Athena down, but Tata's voice stopped her.

"Not with the baloney right now, 'eh?"

The teacher's face turned red in front of the small audience of men, and she left the office.

"He's okay."

Tata got up from behind the desk and sat Athena on his lap. He went back to discussing the papers and ledger in front of him with the men.

Athena lifted the lapel of her tata's suit jacket and looked inside. She tried not to think about Jesus. Christmas Jesus only showed up once a year. Easter Jesus was always in church. The cruelty and uncertainty of it always overwhelmed her. In a small pocket inside her tata's coat, she could feel the outline of his wallet. Athena could hear her own breathing. She started to sing, "Jesus Loves the Little Children," softly until she felt better.

"There she is." Danica pointed to Athena. She was holding her mama's hand.

Athena wanted to stay on her tata's lap, but she wouldn't be allowed. He lifted her off and continued talking to the men. They had already handed out the bread; Lejla got her a piece.

A few pockets of people were still milling about, kissing each other three times, alternating cheeks. Athena followed her sisters around the mostly empty church, as the rector put out candles with his bare fingers after licking them. Lejla was going to try it, but Mama caught her before she got a chance and dragged her out. Athena skipped along the benches on the perimeter of the room and read the weird names, wondering who they all were and trying to remember not to look up. Petra Markovic. Stanislava Popovic. Djura Maric. Ljuba Lalic. Athena wondered if one day she could get her name on one of the benches too. They all probably went to Sunday school like they were supposed to.

"Theenie! C'mon! We're going to the hall!" Lejla called to her.

Athena glanced up at the crucifix and a jolt of fear went through her. She turned and ran as fast as she could. "Wait, Jaja! Wait for *me*!"

Chapter 4

Athena sat on the top step of the front porch and cried into her hands. "It's not fair!" She shrieked, banging her heel into the back of the riser. She sputtered from the injustice.

"You're too little," Lejla said, only to be met with a scowl.

"I can read better than you!"

Lejla didn't flinch. She had a new lunch pail and a white sweater with small pink flowers dotting the collar. "You're just jealous, Theenie."

"Arghh!" Athena drove out her frustration, screaming until she was out of breath.

"Hey! Stop! We have neighbours." And with that, Mama picked her up. Athena believed adamantly that she belonged at school. She'd listened to Danica describe the big classrooms, the long hallways, and the gold stars on the big chart paper. Athena coveted the children's Bible that Danica had been awarded for reading. She was certain she'd receive her own if she were given the chance. Her attention was brought back by her mama's voice.

"Don't get off anywhere but at school, and then right here on the way home. You have to pass Fred's store, then get off. Tell the bus driver," Mama said to her sisters.

The city bus passed by every fifteen minutes. Athena had never been on one. She was burning with envy as they crossed the street. Her sisters were beaming and erupted with tiny squeals of excitement as they spotted the blue and yellow of the mythical chariot lumbering around the corner in the distance.

"Behave like young ladies. We don't want any bad reports from the school. Do you both understand?"

Danica and Lejla nodded solemnly as Mama reached down and placed a shiny new dime in each of their hands. The bus drew close, its dust and exhaust surrounding the cluster of girls. The driver pulled the handle back to open the doors. Mama bent down and kissed each girl on the cheek. Athena turned her face away; she couldn't bear to watch her sisters' pleasure.

"Please make sure they both get off at the school." Mama smiled.

The bus driver tapped his index finger to the black patent bill of his blue cap. "Sure thing, ma'am. So, your first day of school, girls?" His voice trailed off as he swung the door shut and the bus revved away.

The morning sun had already leached the colours out of Athena's surroundings. Through her tears, everything looked a pale yellowish-grey, even her mama's eyes. Mama wiped her tears with a balled-up Kleenex from her pocket and put her down. Taking her hand, they walked across the intersection to the store.

"I have to pick up some eggs, Theenie. Now that it's only you, you get to come with me everywhere."

It was as though Athena had drowned in her sorrow and washed up on the beach of dreams come true. She stopped dead and smiled with elation.

"I didn't want your sisters to realize that it would be only us, or they might not have wanted to go."

Athena bubbled through and through with satisfaction. She wandered into Fred's behind her mama.

Fred always stood behind the glass counter at the back. He usually had a short-sleeved shirt on, the kind all the men wore, her tata included. The buttons pulled across Fred's belly, which hung out over his belt. He had thick auburn hair parted to the side and a handlebar moustache. Fred didn't care for kids touching the glass counters. Athena stood close to her mama as she paid for the eggs. She didn't ask for anything, because that was rude. Her mother looked down at her and Athena smiled.

"One caramel, please, Fred."

Fred chuckled at Athena's reaction and reached under the counter to scoop the candy, then added an extra penny to the bill.

"Thank you!" Athena sang as her mama handed it to her right away. She put it in the front pocket of her navy shorts and placed her hand over it.

"Aren't you going to eat it?"

Athena squinted up at her mama. "No, I'm going to save it. It's special." Mama laughed.

After putting on her pyjamas, brushing her teeth, and saying her bedtime prayers, Athena lay quivering, waiting for everyone to fall asleep. She found the caramel under her pillow as she lay on her side. When Lejla's breathing grew deep and slow, Athena pulled the caramel out to examine it, turning it around and around. She peeled the plastic wrap off, smelled it, and then wrapped it back up. She wanted to keep it at least until Lejla's birthday later that month. Athena opened it again and nibbled the corner off; she couldn't resist having a taste. After rewrapping the caramel three times, she ate it whole, sucking it through her baby teeth and licking her sticky, sugary lips and fingers.

Athena had completely forgotten the pain of being left out of school. She stared into the darkness of the room thinking about her day. Her mama was everything to her, and she had her all to herself. She got a caramel no one else got, and no one knew about. She and her mama had secrets they kept together. She closed her eyes, smiling, convinced that the world had finally found a way to give her exactly what she wanted.

Chapter 5

November came quickly. Everyone squeezed around the table in the nook, singing "Happy Birthday." Mama, the loudest of them all, winked at Athena as she placed a chocolate cake in front of her. Plastic flowers held the four pink candles that were melting onto the frosting. Athena inhaled, ready to make her wish come true. The singing subsided. She pressed her eyes tightly together, wishing to always be her mama's baby girl. They did everything together. She blew out the candles. Then there were presents—the usual dress her baba had sewn, which matched the other two dresses her sisters had already received for their birthdays in August and September. There was also a Slinky and an orange skipping rope. But Athena was hoping for something else, something extra, because she was special to her mama.

"There's one more present!" Mama announced, beaming from ear to ear.

Athena's heart skipped a beat, and she searched for a brightly wrapped package to surface from somewhere. With strained anticipation, Danica and Lejla looked from their mama to Athena.

Mama looked at Tata and he said, "Now you're going to be a big sister."

Danica and Lejla clapped and cheered as Athena processed this information. Every cell in her body was reeling. She started to cry, "No! No!" Mama's face dropped and Tata's jaw tightened. Athena ducked under the table, and ran to her room. She flopped on her bed and cried herself to sleep. No one came to check on her.

***

Mama couldn't play on the carpet the way she used to because her tummy was so big, but Athena didn't understand why the doctor was at their house to check on her. She listened as the gray-haired man spoke gently.

"We think it would be best, Dragan, if Tiljana was admitted in June so she can be observed. She'll stay a couple of months after that because she'll need some help with the babies at first."

Dragan looked at Tilley with a questioning lift of his brow. "Well, what are we gonna do with the girls?" Athena's ears pricked up.

"I don't want them split up Drag. They can't be split up," Tilley said this softly, averting her eyes. Athena thought her mama looked worried. She bit her lower lip, like her mama did, but she wasn't worried. She was going to be with her sisters. No one else said much about it so Athena went back to her puzzle.

***

The woman was standing over Athena. Her bare legs were tanned and she was wearing fuzzy slippers. Athena hadn't heard her come in. She was saying something, but Athena was busy placing shapes into the matching holes of a plastic container. She wanted to do this without having to try any of the pieces twice. She had almost accomplished her goal.

"Hey, honey." The voice was gentle enough but sounded annoyed.

Athena was used to this tone. Her mama had taken her for a hearing test since she didn't always respond when spoken to. It wasn't that she wasn't listening—she just couldn't hear over her own concentration. Mama told her it tried her patience, as Athena was almost always concentrating on something.

"Where's your mommy, sweetie?"

"She's in the hospital." Athena felt that she had delivered all the information required and went back to her game.

"For how long?"

"I'm not sure. She's going to have two babies, twins, so she has to stay in the hospital."

"Well, where's your daddy?"

At this, Athena looked up to see the confused look on Mrs. Murphy's face. She wore a red-and-white polka-dotted halter dress, so when she reached down to pick Athena up, Athena had to touch the woman's bare shoulders. She smelled like smoke and her skin was sweaty. Athena didn't struggle, though, as Mrs. Murphy said, "Well, I got your sisters over at my place. They were playing out in the alleyway. This is unbelievable. Goddamn unbelievable."

They made a circle of the front room and she peeked past the doors of the three bedrooms. Athena proudly smiled when Mrs. Murphy flicked the light on in hers. Then off. The middle room now had two cribs set up in it with a tall dresser. Athena loved the look of the round brass knobs on each drawer. She wanted the dresser for her few things, but Mama said it was for the new babies.

Mrs. Murphy didn't turn the light on in her parents' bedroom; she only tapped the door open slightly. "Well, for Pete's sake. It's the middle of the day. Looks like you're going to be coming over, too."

The screen door at the bottom of the stairs slammed, and the jingling of keys made Athena's body stiffen, loosening her new caretaker's grip.

"That's my tata! Tata! Tata!" Athena jumped down and ran to the back stairs in time to meet her father pushing against the wall.

"Hey, peanut," he said, his words slurred.

Athena stopped and looked back to see Mrs. Murphy standing there.

"Where the hell are my girls? Jus' who do you think you are?"

A loud and long exchange followed between her tata and their neighbour. Athena knew that everything would be handled according to what her tata wanted and wouldn't involve her. She sat down and focused intently on placing the plastic shapes—squares, rectangles, triangles—into the appropriate holes without having to rotate them. If she made a mistake, she would stop, pull out the shapes, and start over. The background blur of voices was no different today from the other days her father didn't feel well. Athena moved from the hallway outside the bathroom door to the wooden plank underneath the dining room table. Pots clanged. More yelling, more talking.

All the while, Athena played until Lejla pulled her out. "C'mon, Theenie. Tata wants to go."

"Let's take a drive, girls." Tata's voice wasn't as slow as before.

Athena's father loved to drive his car and smoke. Doing the two at the same time made him especially happy. Since Mama was gone, both of her sisters were in the front. Athena stood on the hump in the back, holding onto the top of the bench seat. Swaying and jumping occasionally, she tried to get a word in about Mrs. Murphy and what had happened.

"I don't know what that broad was thinkin', walkin' into *my* house. Why, she was damn lucky all you girls weren't gone when I got there. Man, I woulda lost it on that dame."

Athena smiled and felt safe knowing that her tata would have been upset if she hadn't been home when he got there.

"What would you have done, Tata?" Lejla asked.

"What would I have done?" Tata's eyes widened and he bumped his glasses up on the bridge of his nose as he held a dwindling cigarette. "Why, I woulda bulldozed her door down like a truck with no brakes. I woulda knocked down every house in that neighbourhood to find you. You're my girls. My *princesses*."

The girls twittered with glee. If they were princesses, their tata was the king.

"Yeah, but you know she was just checking in, was what she said. So we're gonna go see your cousins for a visit."

This meant a longer drive than normal. The cousins lived in the country. Athena got carsick, especially when Tata smoked and only opened the window a crack. She didn't want to throw up, so she lay down in the wheel well with one of the bags that Tata had packed, using it as a pillow. The droning sounds massaged her to sleep.

She was roused by a cheerful "We're *here*!" from her sisters, who were running up the driveway and being greeted by their cousins. Tata picked her up out of the back seat and ran his big hand over her head, smoothing her hair.

"It's gonna be okay peanut."

Chapter 6

The cousins' house smelled. It wasn't a bad smell, just very different from her home's smell. Maybe it was from using different laundry soap. Or maybe they just needed to open the windows like Mama always did. Athena winced when the smell engulfed her.

The house was long with a garage on the front of it. The street had no sidewalks. No one was ever allowed in the front room unless they were practising the piano. The kitchen filled up the centre of the house and had a big window with a view into the backyard, where a rectangular inground pool sat. Beyond the fence were farmers' fields. The house had four bedrooms and two bathrooms. There was a big one with a tub and a small one with just a sink and a toilet by the back door off the kitchen. The basement was filled with neat things like a pool table and a chalkboard on the wall like at a real school. Her uncle Milan, her *Stric,* was a schoolteacher. Like Mama, her aunt Kristina, her *Strina,* didn't have a job. There was a flurry of running around.

"All right, shut that door now and stay downstairs," Strina instructed them. No one would have dared to disobey her.

A lightbulb with a chain and a long string tied to it hung just over the first step. Athena couldn't reach it. There were only four small windows in the laundry room, partitioned from the main room. It looked scary but Mira was there and that made Athena feel safe. The green chalkboard was in a small area off the laundry room filled with baskets, boxes, and miscellaneous piles of toys.

The eldest of all the Brkovich cousins was Novak. He was handsome, tall, and athletic. Tata favoured him with special attention because he was a boy. All of the girls looked up to him. He was eleven years old and gave his sisters nicknames, which Athena envied; she wanted a nickname too. She wanted her cousin with his perfect white teeth to notice her. He didn't.

Fortunately, there were three girl cousins too. Jelena, Mira, and Vesna were all older than Athena. Jelena was the oldest so she and Danica played together. Vesna and Lejla were the same age and played together. Mira was Danica's age but played with Athena. They paired up based on their temperaments. It made for very harmonious visits, except that Vesna was always whining and crying about something to her mama. She always had a headache. Strina would hold her like a baby and talk about it a lot. They always had to pack up and leave early when they were visiting after church because Vesna didn't feel well. Athena couldn't imagine Mama ending everyone's fun for one person's headache.

Mira wanted to play school, and this suited Athena perfectly well. The chalkboard was so beautiful, and there were sticks of coloured chalk—pink, green, blue, and yellow—in a brand new box. "Don't take any new ones out. Use the ones on this ledge," Mira said. Shorter pieces were lying along it.

Athena took a seat at the red fold-out table, happy to be a student to Mira's teacher. Her lesson on animals was so engrossing that she didn't realize it was time to go until Novak burst through the door, yelling, "C'mon! We have to say bye!"

Athena dropped her pencil. She ran quickly through the basement and took the stairs, her hands on the steps and her feet following in a rhythmic motion. She emerged into the kitchen's bright light. Athena rubbed her eyes. The house seemed too quiet. Where was everyone? She felt a small panic.

"Tata?" Her voice was rising.

"C'mon, Theenie. They're outside already." Mira ran by and shot out the back screen door.

No one was allowed to use the front door except company. Athena ran in her sock feet behind Mira, catching the screen door before it closed. Her heart was pounding heavily as she wondered if they had left her. The tightness in her chest unwound when she saw the black family car in the driveway.

Stric and Strina were talking to Tata. He held Danica in one arm and stroked Lejla's blonde hair with his other hand. She was hanging around his leg.

Athena turned and hugged Mira. "Bye." It was customary to hug and kiss everyone hello and goodbye; Mama said it was rude not to. Athena approached her cousin Novak. "Bye, Novak," she said shyly, reaching up for a hug.

"You're not going home, Theenie. You're staying here with us," he said.

Athena didn't grasp the concept of not going home. She looked up at Tata. "I don't want to stay here. I want to go with Danica and Lejla." Athena's throat tightened as she moved from her cousin's arms and rushed to her family. Tata put Danica down and wrapped the three girls together in a hug.

"It's going to be better if you stay here, girls. You listen to Stric and Strina and do as you're told, okay?" Tata wiped the tears from Danica's eyes.

Athena was relieved that her sisters were going to be with her, so she didn't cry.

"That's my brave girl. Look at Theenie. She's not crying."

Everyone approved overwhelmingly, and Athena stood proudly under Tata's gaze, wondering why her sisters were in tears. They were going to have a sleepover at their cousins' place and play school.

"Please don't go, Tata," Lejla cried. She had to be peeled away and held back as Tata climbed into the car.

He methodically brushed his hair from his forehead and adjusted his glasses. He tilted the rear-view mirror and started the car. For a split second Tata stared at her; he was sad, but there was something else, something Athena couldn't identify before he turned away. Everyone stood in the driveway. After Tata backed the car out slowly and put it into drive, Novak ran alongside it, crossing the green lawns and poured concrete driveways of the neighbours' houses, waving and laughing frantically. Two honks came from the car as it turned right at the end of the street, the tail lights beaming red. Novak lightened the mood, and the family watched him trot back toward them, grinning.

"We have to see where everyone's going to be sleeping and then wash up for bed." Like her voice, Strina's smile was strained. Her hands were on her hips, her apron still tied around her waist.

The older kids cheered and exploded with ideas as to who should sleep with whom and where.

"Me and Lejla sleep together. Me and Lejla sleep together," Athena insisted.

But Lejla didn't want to sleep with Theenie; she and Vesna had plans. Mira offered to let Athena sleep in her bed. Athena didn't want to show how hurt she was that Lejla preferred Vesna over her.

As their aunt pulled bedcovers from the linen closet and distributed them, Athena was hit with a wave of homesickness for her cozy little room and her beautiful mama. Her chin started to tremble, and Lejla saw this.

"Theenie, don't cry. It's fun. We're having a sleepover and then we'll go home. Don't be sad." She squeezed Athena's round head tightly and wiped her tears like Tata had just done. "Don't be sad," she repeated.

The final arrangement found Jelena and Danica in one room and the other four girls together. Lejla and Vesna were on the bunk beds; the top bunk was Vesna's. Athena would be with Mira in the double bed. At least she would be close to Lejla.

Athena looked outside. It was almost dusk.

"Everyone has to wash up," Strina announced.

At her house, Athena had to brush her teeth. Mama would use a warm, wet washcloth to wipe down her face and then her hands and feet. Usually, she would play "This Little Piggy." Then Mama would floss her teeth. This was her favourite part. Her head would be on Mama's lap. She enjoyed the slippery feel of Mama's housecoat and the soft scent of her night cream. They would recite the Lord's Prayer, which she was learning line by line in Serbian. But this wasn't what Strina did.

The bathroom was right outside the children's bedrooms at the end of the hall. The girls were assembled in the hallway, and water was running in the tub.

"Okay, everyone get in. You girls first," Strina said to her nieces. "C'mon." She leaned over the tub, checking the temperature with her hand and adjusting the hot and cold handles. She placed the white rubber stopper into the base of the tub.

Athena, Lejla, and Danica looked at each other.

"Don't you guys take baths before bed?" Mira asked in disbelief.

"We wash up, but we don't all take a bath together," Danica answered.

"Well, you will here, and I don't want this to take all night, so let's go," Strina said, striding toward them. She took hold of Danica's T-shirt and lifted it over her head. Danica covered herself, folding her arms over her exposed chest. "Let's go, girls. No time for this." Strina's voice was high. Danica hustled into the bathroom and started to shut the door. "Whoa, whoa!" Strina's hand caught the door before it closed. "We don't close any doors here." Athena felt uncomfortable; this wasn't how Mama treated them. "You three, get in this tub quick, and make sure you come out clean or I'll scrub you down myself. There are washcloths on the counter."

There was no point in arguing. The three sisters were in and out of the tub quickly because the tepid water was getting colder by the second. They washed each other's backs. Danica went over Athena's feet, as Jelena advised that Strina would check there first. Three towels were set out. No one helped them dry off.

Athena's nightgown was on Mira's bed. When they got dressed, they could see their cousins going into the bathroom.

"Get in bed, and I don't want to hear a peep out of anyone," Strina called. She was busy cleaning the kitchen.

The familiar sound of pots and pans and cupboards banging came down the hallway and soothed Athena. Her eyes were heavy. Even though the lights weren't off yet and she hadn't brushed her teeth or said her prayers, Athena gave into sleep.

Chapter 7

Athena opened and closed her eyes a few times. Everything looked greenish-grey. Mira was asleep, facing the wall. Athena watched her, remembering yesterday. She missed Mama, but today she would be going home. Athena propped herself up on her elbows. Lejla was sleeping on the bottom bunk. Her arm was hanging off the side, her mouth wide open and her pillow marked with a puddle of drool. Athena couldn't see Vesna, but she would be way up there. Athena didn't like heights and didn't wish to sleep anywhere that required climbing a ladder. She lifted the covers. It was a bit chilly in her bare feet. She crept out into the hallway, peering around, holding her breath, and went to the bathroom. She snuck back into bed.

It wasn't ten minutes before Strina announced, "Time to get up, please. Let's go. Today is starting."

Her aunt drew the roller blinds up with the silver beaded string on the side, and the room was instantly brighter. Happy to get on with the day, Athena hopped out of bed and looked for her clothes from yesterday.

"I put your things in the bottom drawer of that big dresser there, Theenie."

For a second, Athena thought she had heard her wrong. But Strina had already walked away. Athena turned slowly toward the dresser. There were her clothes in the bottom drawer, folded in four neat piles like she kept them at home. She stared at them, unable to make sense of what was happening. Her stomach felt sick and her throat tightened up. Athena sprang up to Lejla, who was a deep sleeper.

"Jaja! Lej-la!" Athena tried to control the panic that seized her.

Lejla seemed unaware that there was a problem.

"Our clothes are here," she whispered fiercely in her sister's ear. "They're unpacked. Like we're living here." Athena grabbed Lejla's face, trying to get her to focus on her words.

Mira matter-of-factly confirmed her suspicions. "Yeah, you three are staying here 'cause your mom's having the twins and your dad needed help with you guys." She dressed quickly, pulling her T-shirt over her head.

Athena didn't want to stay. She would talk to Tata later and sort it out. She put on the same clothes she'd worn the day before and followed the other kids into the kitchen.

Strina was busy at the sink. She turned as the children filed in. After four children, Kristina Brkovich was slim and sinewy. Her features, although beautiful, created an angular profile. She had a thin nose with a small tip and thin lips that she often pulled back to bare her teeth in a disingenuous smile. Her blue eyes alternated between wide-eyed disbelief and sinister scrutiny. She was like an actor playing a spy on television. Athena didn't trust her.

"Where is everyone? Get in here, children. We need everyone in here," she muttered as she tied her apron on. Pink foam rollers, covered by a gauzy kerchief, were in her hair. "Is everyone here?" Her voice trailed off, holding the last word like a note she didn't want to let go of.

The children assembled at the table and turned their heads, looking around, counting. Lejla wasn't there.

"Go get Lejla right now."

Vesna slipped off the bench and ran down the hall, running into Lejla as she came out of the room.

"Hurry," Vesna whispered to her and took her hand. They skipped quickly to the bench. Athena felt a wave of anxiety.

Strina turned to look at them. "Okay, now. We're going to go over some rules so we can all get along here."

They nodded. Athena sat completely still, riveted by the fear in her heart.

"You children are going to listen and do as you are told." Strina strolled the length of the table, her hands on her hips, her voice suddenly low and menacing in its sweet tone. "I am not going to have to repeat myself, am I?"

They shook their heads. Athena could see them, but she didn't take her eyes off Strina.

"Good. That's good."

The children looked around at each other, smiling. Jelena rolled her eyes behind her mother's back, but Athena didn't feel reassured.

"Breakfast here is at seven thirty, and you'll be sitting in these places."

Athena was happy because she was next to Danica.

"You have your choice of these two cereals." There were two big clear bags. "Puffed Wheat or Rice Krispies. These are the only two choices."

Athena didn't know what she would pick. Strina started with Novak and took the orders going clockwise.

Athena paused when Strina got to her. Her stomach was in knots and she didn't have any appetite. "Strina, I'm not hungry."

She had barely finished her sentence when Strina said, "You will eat breakfast because there's not going to be any more food until lunch, and that's that."

"Rice Krispies, please."

Strina placed a bowl of cereal in front of her, filled to the top with milk. The spoon she plunked down next to it was large.

"Do you have a small spoon?" Athena was certain that this was an oversight because the kids were older and not used to little spoons.

"No, we don't have any small spoons," Strina said mockingly in a baby voice.

The Rice Krispies crackled, and the lump in Athena's throat grew larger. Danica was on her left and Mira was on her right. Danica got Puffed Wheat.

"I can't eat this," Athena whispered urgently into her sister's ear.

Cupping her hand over Athena's ear when Strina was busy, Danica whispered back, "Don't cry, Theenie. Just eat it."

Athena looked at the bowl in front of her. The other kids were starting to eat.

"Quick, before it gets soggy." Danica scooped up a spoonful and raised it, as if to show Athena how it was done.

Athena thought of Mama asking her how her tummy felt before making her poached eggs on toast or oatmeal with milk and sugar. Her little bunny bowl and the small spoon that was scalloped around the edges were always hers. She picked up the unwieldy spoon and started to eat.

Some of the older kids, Mira included, were already finishing. Mira jumped up and took her bowl to the sink. Athena had had enough, so she started to slide out of the bench.

"Where do you think you're going?" Strina was standing at the end of the bench. "You're not done."

"I can't eat anymore, Strina."

"I can't eat anymore," Strina sneered. "Well, you will eat it. If you take it, you eat it."

"But I can't eat that much."

Danica said, "She can't eat early in the morning, Strina."

Strina leaned her face close to Athena's. Athena looked at her eyes and could feel her malice as she said, "You *will* eat it. Now get going."

Athena missed her mama so desperately. She picked up the spoon, but before she could take another bite, she threw up what little she had eaten—all over the bowl, the tablecloth covered with roosters, and the big spoon.

Strina's response was immediate. There wasn't so much pain but shock as her aunt grabbed Athena by the hair and lifted her out from behind the table. "Get out of here!"

Athena hit the ground running.

***

The next morning, Athena saw a bowl of cereal with a big spoon next to it.

"That's for you. You will sit down and eat, and I don't want anything coming out of you like yesterday."

Athena doubled down, making a concerted effort to eat after seeing the sad looks on her sisters' faces when they saw the bowl in front of her. She started out okay, but her eating was interrupted.

"Well, well, well. It looks like we have a problem we need to fix."

Athena's heart rate tripled. The way Strina smiled so widely, so pleased when she said the word problem, alerted Athena to danger.

"It appears that someone here is a baby and doesn't know how to be a big girl."

Athena's face flushed as her eyes went to Lejla. Lejla sat still, her head down, her eyes focused on the centre of the table at the napkin holder Novak had made for his mother.

"And that baby is you." Strina prowled around the table and her hand landed on the top of Lejla's head. She delighted in describing the situation. "I had to clean the dirty sheets from your bed last night, and there they are, hanging in the yard." She pointed out the window. Two bedsheets were clothes-pinned to the line. She gripped Lejla's head and turned it toward the window. "What do you think we should do?" She bent Lejla's head back and sank close to her face, hissing out her words like a snake. "What do we do with a *baby*?"

The cousins laughed and jeered.

"Lejla's a baby. She peed the bed." Strina's eyes were sparkling. "Do you think we should put a diaper on her?"

All of the cousins cheered.

Athena could barely breathe. It was unthinkable.

"She just has to get used to a new bed!" she shouted above everyone.

There were more shouts from the cousins. "Yes, diapers!"

"No!" Athena cried. It was very loud, and Lejla sat quietly.

"Well, I think that's what babies wear—diapers. I can't have babies peeing the bed. Enough! Enough! It's decided. Now eat your breakfast."

Lejla's cheeks were red, and all the children gulped down their cereal. Enraged and horrified, Athena sat there. She gazed at her cousins' cold, stupid faces. She thought they were pigs. She stood up, holding the spoon in her right hand.

Strina was staring at her, smug and powerful. "Sit down and eat, Athena. I'm not going to say it again."

Danica pulled on Athena's shorts, and she plopped down onto the bench. She already felt like throwing up. There was no way she could eat. Four spoonfuls later, she covered her mouth, trying to keep the cereal down, but it was no use.

This time, Strina did something Athena never knew was possible. She picked her up by her ears. Athena clamped her hands over Strina's vise-like grip. Her legs dangling, she kicked as her aunt carried her down the hallway into Novak's bedroom and threw her against the wall.

"You will stay here until you are told you can come out."

The pain hit Athena minutes later. The gouges behind her ears started to sting. Athena's ears were small and lay close to her head. Many times, Mama had told her how pretty they were. The impact of the wall had knocked her breath out. There were rug burns on her left elbow and knee. But worst were the bitter tears of loneliness as she wondered if she would ever see her lovely mama again. Athena allowed her tears to plunk onto her scraped knee. She spread them out over the cuts, even though the saltiness hurt. She tasted her tears. Athena spoke gently to herself and sang songs Mama liked to sing when they were at home alone together, a time and place that seemed distant and unreachable now. She kissed her hands and counted as high as she could. She dreamed of playing hopscotch and rolling coins with Tata, and she fell asleep in the corner, exactly as she'd been thrown there.

***

"Here she is."

Athena's eyes opened to semi-darkness. The street light was glowing though the bedroom window.

Jelena was holding the door open. "C'mon, Theenie. It's dinner."

Athena rubbed her eyes, following her big cousin into the kitchen where a table full of children were chatting and laughing.

"She was in Novak's room," Jelena reported to her mother.

"Why didn't you come out today, Theenie?" Strina asked. Her demeanour was different.

Athena wondered if she really didn't know. "Because you told me not to come out until someone said I could."

After a second's pause, Strina led the cousins in laughter. Athena ate very little but ate everything she took; she was careful not to take too much. She was relieved to see that Lejla and Danica were okay. She hadn't forgotten her aunt's words that morning, but everyone acted as though they had. Athena felt a little hopeful. Strina was washing dishes. Stric was helping pick up plates and clean the table. Athena wanted to get to sleep. She wanted to go home.

She was watchful as she brushed her teeth. Everyone was doing the same, or combing their hair. The girls flew back and forth into each other's rooms. Everything seemed to be happening without Strina taking note.

Athena wanted Lejla to hurry up and get into bed, but she was sitting with Vesna in Jelena's room.

"Go to sleep, Theenie. Everything's okay."

Athena waited by her sister, guarding her.

Stric and Strina were suddenly standing in the doorway of the bedroom. Everyone got very quiet. Stric held the end of his leather belt, hanging like a noose, in his right hand. In his left was a brown plaid woolen blanket.

"We have to get the baby ready for bed," Strina said, standing behind her husband. Her eyes were glittering.

"Okay, let's go. Lie down here, Lejla," her uncle said firmly.

Danica, Mira, Jelena, and Vesna were gone from the space before Athena understood what was about to happen. Everything went into slow motion. From where Athena stood, just behind Lejla, she saw a double bed to her right and a long dresser to her left. On the floor in front of her was Lejla. Stric had

38

grabbed her arm and pinned her down. He kneeled before her. Strina stood with her hands on her hips, glaring down with a twisted smile and nodding.

The roar of indignation inside Athena was so loud, it was deafening, but no sound escaped. Lejla started to cry, her eyes squeezed shut. Athena looked at her beloved sister's face and rage enveloped her, heat flushed her cheeks from the devastating shame they were subjecting Lejla to. Lejla was five years old, a big girl, and Athena's voice was useless.

Lejla tried to get up, but their uncle pushed her down by the shoulders and lifted up her legs to slide the blanket under them. She rolled to one side to resist him. He picked up the belt he had laid next to her and shook it in her terrified face. Athena watched, her hatred blazing at this injustice.

"Do you want this?" he shouted, his face nearing Lejla's. *"Do you?"*

After an interminable pause, the life seemed to leave her sister's body; she was limp and defeated. Athena collapsed on her knees next to Lejla and clasped her hand, her arms outstretched. *Like lying on the cross*, she thought. Athena's big tears fell, splashing on the carpet. Her lips were parted, but she couldn't scream the horror out.

"Babies don't wear underwear. Put her in the diaper. That's what she needs," Strina said.

On cue, he removed Lejla's underwear and placed her back down on the thick, scratchy blanket, spread her legs, and pulled it up between her thighs. He slung the belt underneath her and cinched it tightly. The blanket was huge and awful.

Athena's saliva formed a gob and fell out of her mouth. She couldn't swallow. She wanted to vomit. Athena bent down and started kissing Lejla's hand. She looked up past Strina to the jeering faces of her cousins, who cackled and pointed. The shame and humiliation Athena felt for her sister engulfed her completely. Her entire being was filled with an unwavering certainty that Stric, Strina, and her cousins were evil, like the people who'd nailed Jesus to the cross, and that this is what it must have felt like to watch—helpless.

On legs like wood, Athena followed Lejla. The girls climbed into bed. Lejla sobbed into her pillow, her back to the room. Athena lay with her eyes wide open, her heart pounding out of her chest, blood pouring into her ears, reverberating with outrage. After a minute, she started to focus on her body, trying to separate her soul's pain from her physical self. But her body was in a state that resembled her feelings, and what she felt was true—her body told her so.

Athena climbed out of bed after an hour had passed. She tiptoed to the window and lifted the roller blind. A huge full moon stared back at her. Athena gazed at it, looking at the craters all over the perfect marble. The North Star hung low, twinkling.

"Star light, star bright, first star I see tonight, I wish I may, I wish I might, have this wish I wish tonight." Athena whispered it, breathing in and out slowly and carefully. She spoke distinctly, so as to be very clear to God. "I wish Stric and Strina would die." Athena wished for that more than anything, even more than seeing Mama. With her left hand, she helped form her three fingers the right way and then crossed herself. "Amen."

Athena stood for a while, wondering how Lejla could sleep, or anyone. She turned and lowered the blind but the room's darkness overtook her. She turned back around and folded a corner of the blind. A narrow shaft of light fell on the floor, and it widened to touch Lejla's back. Athena followed the moonlight to her sister. She kissed her blonde hair that gleamed on the pillow, comforted that Lejla slept so deeply. Athena's heart ached in her chest. She kneeled beside Lejla's slumbering body, put her head on the bed, and wept bitterly.

**

Athena came to the kitchen in the morning exhausted. She encountered Strina in the kitchen moving among the sink, the fridge, and the cupboards with a hardness Athena recognized now.

She stared Strina in the face, with a directness she knew her aunt wouldn't like. Athena felt guilty that she hadn't stopped them from hurting Lejla. Strina poured a big bowl of cereal and grabbed a big spoon as soon as Athena sat down, and set them in front of her.

"This is the third and last time, young lady. You are going to eat this cereal, and don't you dare throw it up or I'll shove it down your throat." Her jaw was tight the whole time she spoke.

Athena knew that she couldn't do it. Danica and Lejla were now sitting on either side of her. Lejla grabbed her hand, and Athena wanted to cry but remembered what her sister had just endured; she wished it had been her and not Lejla. She lifted the metal spoon to her mouth, her chin quivering. Athena hadn't swallowed three spoonfuls when she felt the familiar contraction of her stomach. She clamped her hand over her mouth, trying to alert someone that the inevitable was coming, but Strina pounced.

"I told you what I was gonna do, didn't I? You keep making a mess!" The woman's voice escalated as she lifted Athena up by the hair with one hand and grabbed the cereal bowl with the other.

Athena was carried like a sack of flour to the sink in the small bathroom, where her aunt pinned her to the vanity with her knee. She couldn't touch the ground. The pressure on her chest as Strina pressed her head over the sink forced her arms back. Although she tried, she couldn't grab anything. She cried in protest, but her words were met with the big metal spoon filled with milk and cereal. It rattled against her teeth. Strina forced it in and pulled it out, cutting the corners of her mouth. Athena tasted blood. She couldn't breathe. She *could not* breathe. Strina rammed the spoon in over and over. She choked and vomited, desperate for air. The cereal came out of her nose. Athena shut her eyes, feeling the incredible will to live. Was she being killed for wishing her aunt and uncle would die? The force-feeding suddenly stopped. The cereal blew from her nose and mouth as she hacked and coughed. Athena opened her eyes and saw her reflection in the mirror: her aunt holding her by the hair, blood dripping down the corners of her mouth and chin. Her eyes were red and puffy, her skin tinged bluish-purple.

The voices became sharper. "Leave her alone! Don't! Stop it!" Danica and Lejla were crying and pulling on Strina's arms. Their aunt dropped Athena with a shove.

Danica jumped down to help her, but Strina stopped her. "No, Danica. Get back to the table," she said, smoothing her hair. "This is your sister's problem." Strina turned to Athena. "Now clean this up. You are never to come to breakfast again. Is that clear?"

Athena's breathing seemed to ricochet around the food particles trapped in her mouth, nose, and throat. She spluttered and nodded. Strina's last command brought exquisite relief.

None of the cousins had watched, Athena noted, as she saw her sisters being led back to the kitchen. Athena took the bowl that was on the bathroom floor, turned it upright, and set it down. She picked up each Rice Krispie, counting it as she placed it in the bowl. She recited the numbers, liking the order of them and the sound of her own voice. There were 117. Athena searched the tiles to make sure she hadn't missed any.

"Are you alright, Theenie?" Danica snuck in and threw her arms around her. She frowned as she inspected the cuts on Athena's lips.

"It hurts there," Athena confirmed.

Danica just frowned. "You'll be okay, though." She said this in the optimistic kind of way Mama would, and Athena knew that the right answer was yes, so she nodded. Danica smiled, albeit weakly. Her eyes filled with tears.

"Don't cry, Dani. I'm okay. Really. It just hurts to smile." Athena raised her eyebrows and made a silly face, her laughter escaping past the tears.

Her older sister picked up the bowl and kissed Athena's head, then placed the bowl in the kitchen sink.

Athena kept to herself, even away from her sisters. She was thinking. It took her the entire morning to develop a plan to rid Lejla of the grotesque diaper. She simply had to stop peeing the bed.

Athena approached Lejla with her obvious solution after lunch. At the mention of it, her sister became very agitated. "No, Theenie. I don't want to talk about it."

"But you have to stop. You can't—" Athena couldn't even finish the sentence before Lejla ran away.

At bedtime, Lejla was again forced into the diaper, but Athena couldn't go in to be with her. Instead, she scolded her cousins for watching her sister, grabbing and pulling them away from the door of Jelena's bedroom. At least Athena had a plan now, and she took solace in knowing that this wouldn't continue. She lay down and tried to will herself to stay awake. She told herself that if she fell asleep, someone would shoot Mama in the head. Her eyelids were growing so heavy, though. She could hear Stric and Strina talking in the kitchen. She had to wait. She needed to stay up.

Athena awoke with a jolt in the night. Everything in the house was still. The shock of adrenalin made her sit upright, and she sprinted to get to work. On the balls of her feet, she noiselessly made her way to Lejla.

"Get up, Jaja, get up," she coaxed while lifting her sister from under her arms. She was younger than Lejla by just over a year, but she was stronger than her. Athena swung Lejla's legs down off the side of the bed. She patted her cheek. "Jaja. Jaja, wake up."

"Noooo," Lejla moaned and tried to lie back down.

"C'mon, we have to go to the bathroom."

Athena removed the belt and the blanket and let her sister's nightie fall down. Athena felt the blanket. It was dry. She slung Lejla's arm around her neck and found it surprisingly easy to lift her up on her hip and walk to the bathroom. She didn't turn the light on. Moonlight filled the tub with a silvery beam that came through the top half of the window. Lejla peed. Athena couldn't understand how she didn't wake up. She wiped her sister with toilet paper from behind, the way their mama did with Athena when she was a baby, then lifted her back to bed. She didn't put the diaper back on.

Athena didn't sit down at breakfast and was happy not to. She made a point to pass her uncle, who was sitting reading in the front room. "Lejla didn't pee the diaper last night, Stric. You see, she just had to get used to the new bed." Strina was outside hanging clothes.

That night, when bedtime crept up, Athena waited anxiously.

"If you're a good girl, tonight will be the last night," Stric said from the other room.

Athena was mortified to contemplate what was happening and had happened since they'd arrived. The hope that her plan could work moved her to such joy that the meaning of all they had gone through and her longing for her mama were dampened by it. Athena's vigilance paid off that night and Lejla was not required to wear a diaper.

Every night afterward, Athena would awaken with absolute terror that she had overslept, allowing her sister to wet the bed and subjecting her to their relatives' degradation. Every night she was relieved to find that she hadn't failed.

Chapter 8

Strina's meanness diverted back to her own offspring for the next few weeks. She would often rap one of them on the head with her knuckles, pull their hair, yank and twist their ears, or breathe fire into their faces like a dragon. Although Athena never wished this on any of them, she didn't suffer as if it were her two sisters. She tried to remain as cheerful and as positive as she could around her aunt, and this produced the desired effect of being overlooked.

The long summer days in the country seemed eternal. Athena and her sisters weren't allowed to leave the property—the front and backyards including the driveway—unless they had specific permission. On days when Stric was in a good mood, he took all the kids to the baseball diamond behind the community complex. They would all pile into the long station wagon. He'd put the rear window down and Athena would feel as though she was venturing into an unknown world of gravel roads and dust clouds.

Stric was Tata's older brother. Athena saw the word "streets" in her mind when she said his name. He talked a lot more than Tata, but about things she couldn't quite understand. It was important that he had gone to a university in the United States. He mentioned this many times, and also that Novak would go there as well. Athena once asked if girls went there. Stric pinched her cheeks and didn't answer her; he just chuckled and shook his head. He also stressed the importance of baseball. Athena could see that if you were a better baseball player, you were treated nicer. Mira was better than her sisters and Stric favoured her. Knowing that Mira was most connected to her gave Athena some comfort. Vesna was Strina's favourite because she looked just like her. Athena worried about Vesna being with Lejla; she didn't trust Vesna.

The family fell into a routine of running into the house for meals but mostly being outdoors. Because Mira was older, she participated in sports and attended camps and lessons. Athena missed her when she was gone. Danica and Lejla didn't want to be stuck watching her if they could go do other things with the bigger kids, so Athena retreated further into her own rich imagination. There were no clocks or calendars, simply long, hot days and restless, vigilant nights.

After sitting on the driveway stacking pebbles, Athena, sunburned and weary, slept deeply one night. She forgot the dangers of not being watchful. She awoke as daylight peeked around the edges of the roller blind, begging someone to raise it. She forgot that there could be anything wrong and yawned and stretched, feeling her body tingle as she wiggled her fingers and toes and took stock of herself. Athena rubbed her eyes, then saw Lejla plucking her wet nightie from her leg. Vesna was stirring above. Mira was asleep.

"Lejla," Athena whispered with authority, shoving the blankets aside. In one motion, she grabbed the nightie and peeled it off over Lejla's head. "Quick! Get new clothes and go wash in the bathroom!" Athena grabbed Lejla's underpants, which were heavy with urine. Lejla scooped up some dry clothes and scampered out of the room.

Athena moved quickly underneath Vesna, mentally ordering her to stay up there. She pulled the covers back and speedily—just as she had seen her mama do—pulled the four corners of the fitted sheet back. There was a big round stain on the mattress. Athena grabbed the wet bundle, shoved it underneath the bed, and whipped the bedcover over the stain. She made sure that no part of the mattress was visible. Athena dropped down on the floor and shoved the sheet as far back as her arm would go. You couldn't see it, but you could smell it. Athena boldly went to the tall dresser and, standing on her tippy toes, reached the bottle of body spray Mira used on special occasions and pumped it twice.

"Hey! What are you doing, Theenie?" Vesna asked sleepily.

Athena placed the bottle back carefully. "I want to be like Mira," Athena replied and marched out of the room.

She had a window of time in which to fix her mistake. Athena lingered until everyone had moved to the kitchen for breakfast. She crawled under the bed to pull out the single fitted sheet that held all the evidence. She shoved the sheet under her shirt and then grabbed the giant stuffed dog on the bed and gripped it tightly around her belly. She marched through the kitchen to the basement and shut the door behind her. She paused at the top step to let her eyes adjust to the dark. She was too short to reach the light, so she made her way carefully down the stairs. It was almost pitch-black. Athena felt her way to the pool table, taking tiny steps with one hand out and clutching the dog with the other. She ran into the table and then guided herself to the corner of it. It would lead her straight to the laundry room door. When she opened the door, a flood of light hit her from the window wells. The washer and dryer were facing her.

This was a dilemma! If she started the washer, Strina would hear her and likely come down. She realized that it was hopeless to try to wash the items, so she stuffed the sheet, the nightie, and the underwear behind the washing machine in a tiny space you could barely get to. The children played hide-and-seek in the basement for hours, and Athena hid in that space because no one ever found her there. Once she had stacked enough items in front of the area, she studied it until she was satisfied that nothing looked out of place. All the while, she admonished herself; her predicament was only partially solved. She had to make the bed.

Athena knees weakened at the thought of crossing through the kitchen at breakfast, but she reminded herself that the consequences were such that she couldn't waver. She was going to make the bed. No one would see her. All would be well. Athena enveloped herself in the protective knowledge that she would become invisible. She glided up the stairs toward the strip of white light at the top. With every step, Athena felt herself dissolving.

Gracefully, with complete authority, she moved through the kitchen, smiling inside with a peaceful aura, knowing that no one saw her. They busied themselves with the usual banter and activity, which she didn't fully grasp; she only knew that all was well. She slid on her stockinged feet across the kitchen linoleum, feeling the ridges of the dimpled pattern under her toes. She hit the brass strip that separated the floor from the carpeting and padded onto the plush hallway.

Athena opened the door to the linen closet. She reached up, and stretching her middle and index fingers as far as she could, she grasped the corner of a sheet and tugged it from the shelf without disrupting anything. She picked up a blue towel from the first shelf in front of her. She paused as she stood exposed in the hallway, looking at almost half of the kitchen table; she was in plain view of the others. Athena stared at her family then crossed the chasm from the linen closet to the bedroom. She was safe; no one had noticed her. Athena paused, surprised she could hold her breath for as long as she had.

She now went to work remaking the bed, first laying the towel flat on the wet spot that was still visible. It took a few tries to put the fitted sheet on, as it kept springing off and curling up. Athena's heart sped up, but again, the thought of what she faced if she were to fail spurred her on with a steely determination. Athena figured out how to manoeuvre the sheet. She tossed the covers back over the bunk and was just laying the pillow down when she heard Vesna's voice.

"What are you doing in here, Theenie?"

"I was tired, so I lay down again for a bit, but I'm okay now."

"We're all going strawberry picking, and my mom's going to be making pies and tarts later, so we have to go now."

Athena jumped up and down and clapped, which satisfied Vesna.

On the car ride, Athena stared out the window at the cloudless blue sky. The breeze lifted a piece of her hair and put it down again and again on her forehead, tickling her. She let it and and pretended it was her mama. She imagined when she would use her invisibility power again. Or maybe, she wondered, it could only be turned on when you were super certain of something and your life depended on it.

***

Strina was a very skilled baker. "You children are like flies. Now, shoo!" She waved her hands to move everyone along and outside.

No one could answer back or know just from her words quite what her meaning was. It could be just what it seemed, or it could be twisted up and mean, making the child she was talking to go from happy to sad or from calm to angry. Athena studied her, trying to understand.

"Come on, Theenie. We're going to play catch outside. Put your runners on. I'll toss it to you." Mira was smiling, wearing her glove and tossing a tennis ball into it. She pitched it into the pocket of the glove and locked it up.

Athena went to the back hall and dug through the mountain of shoes heaped in a pile to find the two smallest.

"My feet are already size six ladies," Mira said.

Athena glanced at Mira's feet. She looked at her own. She loved the way her toes marched down in a line. Mira's second toe stuck up in a weird way. Athena's eyebrows pinched together. "Why are your feet so big?"

"I don't know. They just are. It's what makes me fast."

"Well, I'm fast and my feet are small."

"You have wide feet."

Athena shoved her bare feet into her runners. The laces were fraying, and the shoes, which should have been off-white with red stripes, were dark grey. Two holes had formed where Athena's baby toes were; the flesh peeked through the openings.

"Can you tie them for me?"

Mira obliged and expertly snugged the laces.

"Who doesn't know how to tie their shoes?" Strina was standing at the kitchen entry. "You're starting school this year, Athena. You can't go to school without knowing how to tie your shoes."

It was true, and Athena nodded.

"Did your mama never show you?"

Athena hesitated before answering. "No." She blushed, having betrayed her mama, and suddenly missed her intensely.

"Well, here, let me show you how I learned." Strina got down on the floor and sat cross-legged. She lifted Athena's foot with the shoe on it and explained, "There's a little bunny that lives in your shoe, Theenie. You make ears with the laces. You cross the ears to make the head, and you tuck one ear through for the nose and pull tight."

She said all of this in a voice Athena had never heard. It was almost kind, and she sat watching Strina, trying to figure out why she wasn't always like this.

"Now you try."

Athena hadn't followed the directions, but she would now. "Can you show me again, please?" she murmured.

Strina undid the shoe. "You see, just pull on one of the tails and, poof—it all falls apart."

Strina showed Athena three more times before she got it herself. She tied up both her shoes, now ready to be at school with all the other big kids. She hugged and kissed her aunt, convinced that all the problems at the beginning were just because she hadn't listened so well, perhaps.

When she smiled at Athena's delight, Strina's blue eyes looked quite beautiful.

Chapter 9

There were often nights that Athena dreamed of her mama holding her close to her soft neck, stroking her hair. It was as though Mama woke her gently to check on Lejla and take her to the washroom. Athena would lie awake afterward and wonder where her mama and tata were, if they were ever coming for them, and she would cry herself back to sleep.

One day, a rumble of excitement spilled unexpectedly through the house, and out to the back where Athena was pulling the grass up one blade at a time. The wave of energy carried the news that her tata was there.

"Tata!" Athena ran blindly to the front to see the beautiful black car and Lejla and Danica already claiming him, each holding onto one leg.

"Well, I couldn't stay away all summer." His voice trailed off as he lifted Lejla up into his arms.

"Tata! Tata!" Athena pushed past all the legs cluttering up the driveway until she reached him. His hand dropped to her head and she started to cry tears of joy. Athena felt rescued. They were leaving! "When, Tata, when?" Athena shrieked to be heard over the clamour.

Stric and Strina stood on the driveway, watching all of the kids surround the girls and their tata.

"Well, let's not spend all night out here," Stric said. "Come on in, brother. You look good."

"Well, hey, I'm keeping all right. But, boy, did I miss you three." Tata crouched down. "Dani! Jaja! Theenie!" His voice broke. "You girls have grown bigger."

"I have, Tata! I'm bigger!" Danica crowed, standing up as straight as she could.

"I'm almost as big as her!" Lejla said, without lifting her face from his neck.

Athena knew that she was still rather short. "I think my *tummy* got bigger!" She rubbed her hands all over her belly, sticking it out as far as she could, making her tata laugh.

"When are we going home?" The girls spoke in unison.

"Well, I mean, I miss you girls so much, but . . . I just came to visit. I can't take you home right now. I have to go to work on Monday, and it's Friday. There's not really enough time."

"You could bring us back Sunday," Danica said. "We could go—"

"We don't go to church in the summer, sweetie." Tata spoke gently. "It's too much driving."

Athena moped as they headed back to the house. She wanted to tell him how mean Stric and Strina were, but they were right there. And the way Lejla was clinging to him, she didn't know if she would get a chance. The family moved into the kitchen as dusk rolled around. It would be bedtime soon. Her tata said he wasn't staying, that he couldn't. Athena went to the bathroom to brush her teeth. She had tried to kiss and hug him, but he was busy talking to his brother about things she wasn't allowed to hear and he was still holding Lejla.

"Don't leave without saying goodbye, Tata," Athena had warned him before she went to the bathroom.

"I promise."

But when she emerged from the bathroom, everyone was already outside. Her tata was in the car, and Lejla was with him! Lejla! *"Tata!"*

Dread and disbelief enveloped her, and she was sprinting for the car when Strina grasped her arm tightly. "Where do you think you're going?"

Screaming for her father, Athena was in no mood for this. Her aunt picked her up, and pressing her hand over Athena's nose and mouth, she said, "You will be quiet now." Danica was crying as well. Lejla's blonde head was leaning on her tata's arm. She hadn't let go of him the whole night.

Maybe she told him what happened, Athena thought as she lay in bed. If Lejla had, then Tata would have taken only her. He hadn't wanted to take anyone, but he took Lejla because it was her they'd hurt the most. This explanation satisfied her and she hadn't gotten one from anyone else.

Only a day later, Lejla appeared on the front porch. Before Athena could give him a hug, Tata left. His car rolled down the street, Novak chasing it.

"It's best he doesn't upset you girls like he did yesterday," Strina explained.

Lejla told Danica and Athena how she'd got to go to their house and Tata made her eggs. She slept in her own bed, got breakfast there, and then they drove back.

"Did you tell him all the bad things?" Athena said. She wanted to know why he hadn't come to get them all.

"No, I didn't. Stop talking about it, Theenie." Lejla was comforted—Athena could tell. She had been singled out by their father, whose attention was rare.

"Did you see Mama?" To alleviate her agony, Athena cried into her hands, pinched her upper lip, pulling it away from her teeth, and jumped from one foot to the other.

Danica saw her suffering. "No, Theenie, she didn't." Athena realized that Danica didn't get to go home either and was sad too. "But you know what Mama would say." It was as though Danica had read her mind. They were both crying but started to laugh. "Life ain't fair, kid." Athena now understood what her Mama had meant by that.

For Athena, there was no end to the sentence she was serving. The notion that they were being held against their will crystallized in her. Because she couldn't see beyond what was happening now, the concept of a future with her mama again was lost on her, and the grief palpable. Wanting to see her mama, who certainly wanted to see her, grew like an obsession in her chest.

The rules seemed to be relaxing, and with the exception of Novak making problems when his sisters went into his room, the house was more pleasant. It was moments like this that people like Vesna waited for.

Vesna walked into the living room with a satisfied look on her face and a book in her hand. "This is the autograph book I got for my birthday." She plopped down next to Athena and opened the hardcover book, exposing a rectangular stack of tightly bound writing paper with crinkly vellum in between each sheet to keep them from sticking together. "This was from my teacher. It says, *All the best this summer, Vesna. Love, Mrs. Mitchell.*"

"I can read it." Athena reached for the book, but Vesna twisted away from her.

"Don't, Theenie. It's very special. I'd have you sign it, but I don't want you to ruin it."

Athena was insulted. She knew how to read, print, and write, which Vesna knew since Mira loved playing school downstairs.

"Here's one from my ball coach. *To a great athlete and an even better girl! Always keep your eye on the ball! Coach Larkin.*"

Athena was envious. She wanted the small book with its signatures, but Vesna wouldn't let her touch it.

"You're too little, Theenie." Vesna flipped through the pages.

There were tons of empty spots. If only she could sign her name! She thought about it all day. Athena was lying on her bed, reading, later that afternoon when Vesna walked in. She took the book out from under her pillow and read from it, lying on her top bunk, and, satisfied again, slid it back underneath.

"Dinner! Dinner's ready!" Strina called.

There was a chorus of feet. This was the moment to go, but Athena didn't go. She was preoccupied with having her name in Vesna's book. She was convinced that once Vesna saw how well she could write her name and how clever she was, she would be extra happy.

Athena took the black pen on the dresser and climbed up the ladder to Vesna's bunk to retrieve the prized possession. She thought carefully about what to write. *If I write my own name, she'll know it's me.* But Athena wouldn't be denied. She wrote, *You're so nice. From anonymus* on a clean page near the middle of the book. When she looked at her entry, though, something didn't seem right. It was on a slant, and she was uncertain if she had misspelled her clever word. She tore the page out, regretting instantly what she had done. Athena tucked the book back in its spot. She ran to dinner.

That late-summer night was magical. It smelled like a campfire. They ate fresh peaches from the basket and sticky juice dripped down everyone's faces. They were hot and desperately thirsty from playing hide-and-seek across two yards. The sun didn't seem capable of setting, as if it were too happy painting the sky pink and orange. The air was warm, so lingering in the cool areas behind the bushes and lying in the tall grass felt like being in an oasis. The children ran in pairs and helped search out the others still hidden. Novak and his friend led the charge, but the others created the most laughter when they burst out with a scream when getting caught. Mrs. Jacobson, a neighbour, brought a pitcher of lemonade out, and its tartness made the inside of Athena's cheeks tingle. Athena felt safe and included. Novak picked her up and even carried her around on his shoulders for a bit. But the street lights were coming on, and that meant bedtime.

Athena's hair was wet, and Danica brushed it smooth. It was growing a bit longer and her bangs were almost in her eyes, so her sister pinned them to the side with a small pink barrette. Athena admired herself in the bathroom mirror. Her skin was tanned and much darker than her sisters'. Her big brown eyes reflected her own admiration. She had a round button nose and rosy cheeks. Athena loved her pink satin quilted housecoat, which matched the barrette. She was preoccupied with herself when she heard a bloodcurdling scream from the bedroom.

The entire family came to the source. It was Vesna, flying into hysterics. Stric and Strina spoke in low, hushed tones to her and each other.

Athena looked up at all their inquiring faces, knowing exactly what had made her cousin upset. There was no yelling. Strina wiped Vesna's tears as the other girls got into bed.

"What happened, Ves?" Lejla asked, but Vesna only answered Lejla's question with a dismissive hand as Strina enfolded her and led her from the bedroom.

It's only a book, thought Athena. She waited. As time ticked by, her reassurance grew that everything would be okay.

"Everyone out here, now! Everyone to the living room," Stric said.

Stric and Strina herded all of the children to the front room.

A long couch sat underneath the big bay window dressed in fancy sheers. Athena's mama had said she liked them the last time they were all here together. She remembered Strina telling her mama that they were expensive. The cousins sat on the couch. Danica, Lejla, and Athena sat in front of them on the floor.

Vesna stood facing the audience, shattered. Her voice broke as she tried to explain what she had discovered. She looked up as if pleading to her parents. "It's ruined. It's all ruined!"

Strina consoled her, then Stric spoke. "Who did this?" he demanded, holding the ripped pieces of paper up.

Fear paralyzed Athena.

He started to unbuckle his belt. "I mean it. Whoever did this is going to get it."

Athena dropped any notion of admitting her actions.

"Well?" His voice rose as he lifted the belt.

"I told Theenie about my book." Vesna pointed directly at Athena, but she protested vehemently out of an incredible hatred for Vesna. Couldn't Vesna see that her father had a belt? Couldn't she see that she would be beaten?

"Whoever it was wrote the word 'anonymous,'" Stric said. "I don't think it could be Theenie. She doesn't know that word."

"Yes, she does," said Vesna.

Athena just stared, her eyes wide.

"Well, whoever wrote it didn't spell it correctly, so we'll see who did it, won't we?" Strina sneered. "You're all going to come into Vesna's room and spell this so we can narrow it down. One of you did it, and you're going to be in big trouble now."

Everyone looked at each other. Athena writhed inside with remorse and guilt. Worse was how to admit it; she couldn't bring herself to. She hated Vesna and her book.

Vesna and her parents went into the bedroom and called Novak in. You could hear muffled words through the door. Theenie went closer. He came out and Jelena was next. Athena could hear her cousin spell the word.

"That is correct," Stric said.

She hadn't caught it all but recited the first part in her mind: *A-n-o-n-y*. Mira went in and said loud and clear, *"A-n-o-n-y-m-o-u-s." Like Mickey Mouse without the* e, Athena thought. She ran to Lejla and Danica to spell it out quickly for them. It was Danica's turn next, and she too was released. Lejla went in and spelled it out.

And then it was Athena's turn. *"A-n-u-n-y-m-o-u-s."* Athena spelled it wrong, but differently from what she had written. She didn't want them to catch her.

Everyone was instructed to sit back down on the couch and await the verdict. Strina and Vesna came out of the room. Then Stric marched in and moved swiftly to where she sat. Athena raised her hand to shield herself from him, but he grabbed Lejla instead. To her complete horror, her uncle quickly pinned Lejla between his knees, her bum facing all of them, and raised his thick leather belt. She screamed. So did Athena.

The second clap of the belt hit so hard that Athena sprang on top of her sister when Stric raised the belt again. She slid underneath it before the belt landed, taking the next blow. "I did it! I did it! I wrote it!" she screamed.

Stric stopped, confused, and shook Athena by her arm. "You did it? Why?"

"I'm sorry! I'm sorry! I just wanted to be in her book and she said no!" she blubbered.

Stric wiped the sweat from his brow and dropped his arm, still holding the belt.

Athena fell on Lejla, sobbing, "I'm sorry, Lejla."

Lejla pushed her off bitterly, and Athena wished Stric had beaten her instead so she would have suffered more than her sister.

"Say you're sorry to Vesna, not Lejla," Strina said.

Athena looked up mournfully, and smoothing her nightgown and wiping the snot bubbling out of her nose, she said, "I'm sorry, Vesna."

"Yes, well, you should be," Strina hissed into her ear as she tugged angrily on it. Using it like a handle, she dragged her to her room to send her to bed. Athena's ear, though sore, could still hear the belt and Lejla's scream.

***

The next time Lejla got the belt was because Vesna tattled on her for crossing the street—although it turned out she hadn't and Vesna had lied. Vesna didn't get the belt, though, because Strina stopped it. Danica called her sisters together for a secret meeting downstairs.

"We have to go home," Danica told them, saying what they were all thinking.

Lejla's eyes were puffy from crying. Athena felt wretched because she hadn't intervened this time and simply let it happen. She had been too afraid.

"Maybe if we call Tata?" Lejla said with a whimper.

"Yes! Call Tata!" Athena said. "But how? Do you know our phone number?"

Lejla and Athena looked at Danica.

"Yes, but we can't let them hear us. We're not allowed to use the phone."

They sat anxiously in silence, contemplating how to get to it. There was only one. It hung on the wall in the kitchen.

"Okay," Danica said. "We have to call now. Everyone's outside. Theenie, you watch the front door, and Jaja, you watch the back."

The prospect of reaching their tata was almost too much. The girls crept up the stairs. No one was inside. In an instant, Danica picked up the receiver and started to dial. Their tata would have to be home, would have to pick up the phone. Athena stood in the hallway at the door to the living room. She could see through the sheers on the front window. Lejla stood in the back hall near the small bathroom. Two . . . Danica put her index finger into the dial, pushed it around to the silver stopper, and released. Five . . . Six . . . Each number seemed so loud and long.

"It's ringing!" As quickly as Danica's face lit up, it clouded over. "It's saying it's a long distance number," she relayed. She didn't know what that meant. Danica hung the phone up, dejected. She put her head down on the table and cried into her arms. Lejla and Athena crawled in around her and hugged her, crying.

"Could we run away? Do you know the way home?" Athena asked.

"No." Danica lifted her head. Her face was breaking out into a red rash, her eyes inflamed from her tears. "Lejla got the belt for crossing the street."

"I didn't cross," Lejla said with vehemence.

"No, I know that. But if we did and got caught . . . Besides, it's too far. We just have to stay." At this conclusion, her voice broke.

***

Stric brought home a giant watermelon and a huge bag of delicious cherries. To save time and get more cherries before they were gone, Athena decided it was easier to swallow them with the pit. Their smooth purple-black skin was firm and succulent. Athena played at taking small bites and exposing the pit first. It looked as if it was made of wood, and she wondered if it was cherry tree bark and if cherry trees would grow inside her. When her stomach was sore, she stopped eating. Her fingers were sticking together.

"Okay! Everyone in. Let's get cleaned up," Strina said.

Athena fell into line behind everyone else. She stomped and hummed to a sugary song in her head, one that matched her love of the cherries. As she was waiting to use the bathroom sink she crouched on the cream-coloured rug and began drawing with her red fingers.

"*What*—" came the spell-breaking exclamation, "*are—you—doing?*" Each word was a loud and unmistakable declaration of trouble.

Athena froze and looked up. Her mouth hung open. Strina was shaking. Everyone looked at Athena. No one had stopped her, but now it was too late.

Strina lifted Athena by her forearm and swung her onto the kitchen counter. She grabbed the wet dishcloth and attacked her hands and face, scrubbing the residue off. She was angry. Athena waited. The flyswatter was on the counter. It had a twisted metal handle with a flat rubber head covered with small holes. It was flexible and a pretty teal colour.

"You don't make a mess like that in this house!" Strina spoke in staccato. "Put your hands out."

Athena had seen her cousins receive this form of punishment, and she and her sisters had been lucky to avoid it. Until now. Athena knew she had messed up the rug. She lifted her freshly washed hands, palms up. Strina lifted the flyswatter and brought it down like a whip. It stung so terribly that Athena gasped silently and instantly pulled her hands behind her back. No noise escaped from her.

"Put your other hand out," Strina demanded.

Athena just shook her head, unable to breathe.

"Put your other hand out!"

Strina's insistence grew, but so did Athena's defiance. Air filled her lungs, forcing tears to her eyes, and blood rushed to her cheeks. She could no longer contain her contempt. Athena howled back, *"Noooooo!"* and with her hands firmly behind her back, stared into her aggressor's eyes.

Strina dipped the flyswatter into the sink filled with soapy dishwater, then struck Athena across the face. "You will go to bed this instant, young lady! Shame on you. I'm going to tell your mother how you've behaved here."

At the mention of her mama, Athena cried pitifully into her pillow. She felt the indentations on her face and studied the pattern on her hand as she lay in bed. She knew they would fade because Mira had been hit with the flyswatter once and they went away. Athena didn't understand the cruelty of it all.

Chapter 10

The day of emancipation came soon after. Unannounced, the black Chrysler pulled into the driveway, and the honk of the horn sent a ripple of hope and fear through Athena. She didn't leave her tata's side during this visit.

"Am I going home with you too? Please don't leave me, Tata."

"I'm not going to leave you."

You did before, thought Athena, but she didn't say this. It was no time to make accusations; her tata was there to save them.

During the car ride, her sisters were in the front, while Athena stood on the back seat behind her father, her arms around his neck. The smell of smoke and his Old Spice cologne filled her with joy. The windows were open and the sun was shining.

"Mama can't wait to see you girls."

"Tata, it wasn't good," Athena began, but stopped when Lejla and Danica turned around, frowning and shaking their heads. Athena worried that she could be returned.

"Okay, let's just be happy and excited when you see Mama. There's a big surprise waiting at home for all of you."

Athena bounced on the seat. With one hand, Tata both managed the steering wheel and his cigarette. Fields of yellowed cornstalks whipped past them. Athena delighted in the idea of a big present for herself. Yes, it made a lot of sense to receive something after being treated so harshly. The notion of her own ordeal always brought tears. She wondered if Danica and Lejla also suffered from this; they didn't seem to. With these thoughts, her heart constricted, then expanded with joy when she saw the familiar street signs, Fred's Variety, and their front porch. She heard the bang of the handle on the screen door, sniffed the wonderful smell of their home, and saw the long set of grey wooden steps leading up to the landing behind the kitchen.

At the top of the stairs, a golden beam of dusty light illuminating her angelic eyes, stood their mama. Athena hadn't forgotten what her mama looked like, but when she saw her again, it was like seeing her for the first time ever. She felt overwhelmed, unable to understand the beauty that befell her. Mama's hair was set in perfect brown curls that accentuated her sparkling brown eyes. Her clear skin was glowing, her face open and honest. She held her arms out wide, and her songbird voice exclaimed in a joyous outburst, "Oh, my angels!"

The interminable distance to reach her was almost too much for Athena to bear. The three girls stampeded up the stairs toward their Mama, who enveloped them. Tears streamed down Athena's face. All of them squeezed and kissed their mama everywhere—on her hands, her face, her hair. It was never going to be enough.

"Oh, my little angels! Oh! Let me look at you! You've grown so big! Oh, I missed you so much! Oh, my precious dearests, my angels!" Again, she planted a round of kisses on their foreheads and cheeks.

"Okay, c'mon. Let's go in," Tata said.

The reunion with their mama aroused more emotion than Athena could contain. When she felt the presence of her mama, her arms around her, she knew she was safe. Like hot water to sugar, it melted her ability to conceal her unthinkable despair.

"Mama, it was horrible!" Athena grabbed her mama's face between her hands and stared into her eyes. The anguish started pouring out as she recounted the wrongs done to her. "We got the belt, and Strina hit me with a flyswatter and . . ."

Athena couldn't hold her mama's gaze, so she immediately moved to look at Tata, at each of them. Danica and Lejla were speaking as well, but Athena couldn't hear what anyone was saying other than Tata, who said, "Enough! Enough right now." He led Mama into the kitchen, all of them trailing behind her. Danica and Lejla had stopped talking, but not Athena.

"Athena!" Tata bent over, his face in hers. He shook her by the arms. Athena was still trying to get her words out. He pulled her back to the landing. "Athena!" he repeated, and she paused long enough to hear what he needed to tell her. "Do you want to make your mama sad? Do you want to make her cry?"

Athena slowly shook her head. The consequences of doing so terrified her.

"Do you want her to send you away again?"

At this suggestion, the blood drained from Athena's head. The force that had carried her monstrous need to tell Mama and the enormous love for her went away, as if the sun's rays had suddenly been blocked by a cloud and put her in the shade. A barely audible whisper escaped Athena's lips. "No."

"Good. Then we're not gonna speak about any of this again. We want Mama to be happy, and we want to be happy now."

Athena knew what she was being asked to do, and she knew it was possible. She'd seen it in her book, *The Five Chinese Brothers*. Her tata was asking her to swallow the sea. Her tears stopped as she crossed the threshold back into the kitchen. She wanted her mama more than anything in the world. Truly. Mama never asked her about what happened that summer, so they never spoke of it again.

***

The surprise, as it turned out, were the twins, Mitzi and Max. There were no presents. Two baby blankets with satin trim were laid out on the living room carpet, and the girls were instructed to sit in a row. Athena was in the centre.

Tata disappeared into the middle room and came out carrying a laundry basket. He gently set it down in front of the receptive audience. Inside were two babies, swaddled in blankets, with caps on their heads.

"Can we hold them?" Danica asked her tata who, looking at Mama, received thoughtful approval.

"Be careful to hold his neck," she said. Tata lifted Max out and passed him to Danica.

"Me too! Me too!" Lejla chirped. Quickly, upon receiving the same instructions from Mama, she took Mitzi into her arms.

Athena whined impatiently. "I want to hold one. Give me one of them."

"You're too little to hold them," Mama said.

Athena struggled in her own skin to remain seated, to care at all about these stupid babies, to avoid crying, but then realized that if she didn't behave . . . and suddenly she could again focus. She had to be the best little angel. She had to be good. Athena trusted herself to do this. She knew she could behave so things would be well. It didn't matter if she couldn't hold the babies. It didn't matter if she couldn't tell Mama what had happened. She was home, and this was her family. She loved the blue-green carpet and the way it was woven. She loved the collection of old paintings on the wall, including *Pinkie* and *The Blue Boy*.

"Mama! Tata! Mitzi is like Pinkie and Max is the Blue Boy!"

"Yes! Yes!" Her parents laughed, and Tata grabbed the camera off the top of the fridge to snap two pictures. Athena sat there, studying everyone in this moment, happy that everyone else was happy.

Chapter 11

"Athena, this is the most important day of your life."

Athena stood in the kitchen, her tata crouched in front of her. The words were for her alone. "Nothing you ever do will be this important and you must try your absolute best, always. Do you understand?"

The message was delivered in the same slow, methodical way he had of speaking. He rarely spoke only to her, except to say, "Good night, I love you" from behind his newspaper. He wasn't sick today, so his words were clear and direct.

Athena stood at attention, filled with pride in herself. She was wearing a brand new white turtleneck with a tiny Winnie the Pooh stitched on it. Her fingers kept twiddling it. Her hair was almost touching her shoulders. She wore jean shorts and her dirty runners, but that didn't matter—she was going to school today with her sisters.

Athena met her father's green eyes and he looked surprised. He stood up and patted her on the head after tapping a cigarette from the package in his front pocket. The orange circle radiated and receded.

"All you girls do good." He pointed to them and blew a cylindrical cloud toward the wall before leaving down the stairs for work.

Athena was going on a city bus to the big school. Finally! She wasn't little anymore. The summer had prepared her for this.

"I want you to hold your sisters' hands," Mama said, placing a shiny dime in Athena's palm.

She held a metal lunch box with *Scooby-Doo and the Mystery Machine* on it. Inside was a sandwich wrapped carefully in waxed paper, an apple, and two cookies in tinfoil.

"How can I hold their hands when my hands are full?" Athena grinned at her mama.

"Hold hands, girls," Mama said.

Waiting at the bus stop, Athena worried that, because of the excitement running through her body, she might be sucked under the bus after falling off the curb. The bus sidled up to the stop, and the door made the familiar sound as the driver pushed the handle that opened it. Athena lunged up the first step, suddenly unsure, then excited again.

"Bye, Mama!" She looked back. Danica was pushing her up.

Athena reached up to drop her dime into the coin box. The driver clicked the change belt around his waist and handed her a nickel, which was for the ride home. There had been a long discussion about Danica holding it for her, but Athena refused. She pushed the nickel into her front pocket.

She turned to face the tube-like interior. Metal poles were everywhere. At the front, two benches faced each other. According to the sign above them, these were for women, small children, and old people. They were unoccupied, so Athena sat down and was joined by Danica and Lejla a moment later. Overhead, ads ran the length of the bus. Tires. Insurance. Pizza. Athena was reading them, but when the bus turned the corner she felt a wave of nausea.

"I don't feel good, Dani."

"Face forward and look out the window. Like in the car."

Athena looked outside, but the bus was rocking to and fro. It lurched forward for the next three blocks. Athena took a deep breath.

By the fourth stop, Athena was quite green. "I'm going to be sick, Dani."

Danica stepped up to the driver. "Mr. Bus Driver, excuse me. My sister is going to throw up."

He glanced back at Athena, who was holding her hand over her mouth. He swung the big vehicle to the curb and opened the door. Danica and Athena jumped out, and Athena bent over and threw up into the grass. They got back on the bus and sat down. Finally, the bus pulled up to a stop sign in front of a church.

"Here's our stop," Danica said.

"Where's the school?"

"You have to walk down the block, silly."

Athena thought she might not remember how to get back.

"If you can't find us after school, walk back here and catch the bus with us. We meet here."

Athena was anxious at not being with her sisters. "Where are you going?" she asked. "Aren't you going to be with me?"

"No." Danica laughed. "For someone so smart, you don't know a lot of things."

"Yeah." Lejla shook her head. "You go to your class and we go to ours."

The girls were walking and talking. Past the next side street where the trees ended, the three-storey grammar school came into sight. It looked huge from up close. Athena had only seen it from the car. It was magnificent and official. Just like her tata had said, this really was the most important day of her life. She was going to be perfect.

***

"My name is Mrs. Cowan, and I am your teacher."

Mrs. Cowan had short brown hair and cat eye glasses. She wore bright red-orange lipstick that Athena liked very much. She was heavier than her mama, but Athena decided she still liked her because she explained everything in the classroom so wonderfully. Each child wore a big sticker on their chest with their name printed in black magic marker. The best part of the room was the wooden kitchen, which had cups, plates, and bowls just like a real kitchen, only it was sized down. Athena couldn't wait to play in it. All of the kids, about twenty of them, sat in a circle on the ground, and Mrs. Cowan sat in her chair in front of them.

She was going to read a book about the alphabet. "How many of you children know your ABCs?"

Only about half of the children put their hands up, and Athena looked over those who hadn't.

"Well, we're going to learn all the letters this year. We're going to start with *A*."

Athena was already bored. She stood up and walked over to the kitchen.

Mrs. Cowan called, "Sweetie? What's your name?"

Athena turned to show Mrs. Cowan her sticker.

"You have to come sit in the circle, Athena. We're working here, and you don't get to play now."

Athena frowned, saying nothing at first. "I don't want to sit. I know the letter *A* already."

"Well, that's great, but come sit over here, please."

Athena remembered her tata's words and jumped back to the circle. But the call of the kitchen was too much, and she meandered over after a few more minutes.

"Athena. I need you to stay in the circle."

She shuffled back and let out a heavy sigh. She sat down cross-legged and rested her head on her hand. Mrs. Cowan read the page she was on and, turned the book to show it to everyone. Some of the boys were moving their feet back and forth as they stretched out; Athena did it too, since it looked like fun.

"Now we're going to go find a seat at one of the tables. I'll hand you each a piece of paper and three crayons and we'll do an exercise."

Athena sat in a plastic bucket seat. The table was just the perfect height. The paper was thin and grey with one side glossier than the other. The crayons were big and had no paper on them. Athena had orange, purple, and green.

"Now I want everyone to watch me up here." Mrs. Cowan took a piece of white chalk and showed them how to print a capital *A* over the solid and dotted lines painted on the blackboard. She then drew a small *a* next to it. "We're going to practise these, but first we'll fold our paper into four sections."

Athena was irritated with Mrs. Cowan for going so slowly. She saw so many books on the shelves at the side of the class. And a map and a real spinning globe! And an actual kitchen! Athena kept trying to refocus on folding her paper extra slowly and drawing pictures and letters in the boxes as she was asked to. When she finished the fourth box, she pushed her chair back to go to the kitchen.

"Athena, dear, we're not going to be in the play area of the kitchen today."

Athena didn't understand what she was supposed to do. "But I want to."

"Yes, I can see that, but you must sit down like all the other children."

There were snickers from a couple of boys and disapproving nods from some of the girls. Athena decided that she learned much more at home. When the children were told to put their papers in their cubbies at the back, Mrs. Cowan had to help a lot of them find their own names. Athena left to go home.

It wasn't that she had given it much thought—she just knew that she preferred being home. She was missing *Sesame Street* too. Athena padded noiselessly down the empty hallway. She looked in the open doors as she passed different classes. Sometimes teachers were at the front speaking and glanced at her. Other times children were around tables and some of the kids noticed her and smiled. No one stopped her.

Upon arriving at the bus stop, Athena sat on the bench, swinging her feet. It would only be six stops until her house. Cars went by once in a while. After a minute or so, a woman came and sat down. She had a blue brocade coat and a fancy hat with black netting.

'Hello,' Athena said. "I like your hat." The woman smiled and nodded. Athena thought that she must not speak English.

"I'm going home." Athena counted the cars and noted the colours.

In a couple of minutes, the bus came. The woman climbed on slowly. Athena followed right behind. She dropped her nickel in. The woman took the first seat opposite the driver and Athena sat down next to her, exactly where she'd sat in the morning. The bus pulled away. Athena was reading the signs and ads over the tops of the windows. Only a couple of people got on and off. She didn't notice when the woman stood up to leave.

"Hey, kid," the bus driver said. "Hey, kid, your mom is leaving."

It took a moment for Athena to realize that he was talking to her and that she didn't recognize anything from the window. She approached the driver. He wasn't the one who'd driven her that morning.

"That's not my mama. I'm going home, but I don't know where I am." A tightness in her chest developed.

"Well, where do you live?" He pulled away again.

Athena grabbed the pole behind his chair, which had a colourful pompom fringe. The chair bounced up and down a bit as he manoeuvred the two huge paddles on the floor and the stick to his right. He never stopped moving but glanced in the big mirror above him to look at her. Photos of three children were taped to the plastic panel on the change box.

"Albert Road."

"It's okay. We'll get you home. I know where we're going. You got on going the wrong way, I think."

"The wrong way?"

"The bus travels in a big circle"—he motioned with his arm—"and there are different stops along the way."

She frowned, not quite understanding.

"You'll see. Enjoy the ride, kid. I'll let you know when it's time."

Athena liked him very much. She sat down in the very first seat, as more people were getting on and off at each stop and she didn't want him to forget about her. The bus went all the way up near the market. Athena's family only went to the market on Saturday because Mama didn't drive. The bus rambled along and the motion didn't affect Athena; she was too busy watching for familiar landmarks. She wanted to know where she was, so that if she ever got lost, she could find her way home, like Hansel and Gretel.

"There's where you got on, kid," the driver told her. "And here's where you get on to go home. Across the street."

It was a very good thing to have ridden the bus route. Relief spread through Athena's body as the bus turned into her neighbourhood. It was one of the poorest sections in Windsor. The railroad tracks caused a hump in the road, and Athena's tummy lurched when she went over it too fast. That is how she knew she was close. The butcher shop. The Salvation Army. The Europe Tavern. Just before the underpass was the big driveway to the car plant. The bus turned onto Richmond Street and Athena felt triumphant.

"I can see Fred's!" she exclaimed. She jumped up and stood behind the driver. "There's my house! The pink one!"

He stopped right at her corner. "So you gotta get off back there next time, okay, kid? But I'll let you off here."

Athena was so happy, she forgot to pull the cord to ding the bell. "Thank you!" She took the giant steps. *One foot. Two feet.* A cloud of black smoke bigger than her plumed up over her head; she watched it swirl up out of the exhaust and climb into the air. Athena ran past Fred and Frieda's and into her house through the side door. "Mama! Mama!" she called.

Mama was in the kitchen. Mitzi and Max were in their playpen in the living room.

"What on earth?" Mama looked at her in confusion. "How did you get here, Athena? Why aren't you in school?"

"I took the bus home. I didn't want to stay. I already knew what they were doing today."

"Well, you are not allowed to just leave the school, young lady."

"Yes, I am."

"No, you're not."

"But no one stopped me."

Mama's face looked worried. "And you just caught the bus?" Incredulous, she raised her eyebrows as Athena recounted the details of her adventure. "But something could've happened to you. Someone could've taken you."

Athena didn't think that was possible.

"Your tata is not going to be happy about this."

It was fortunate that Tata came home after work that day. When he did, Mama was happy and everyone ate dinner in the nook.

He didn't yell right away when Mama told him. "Theenie, you can't just leave school. If you do that again, you're going to get the belt."

Do not leave school again, Athena told herself.

"So what was your teacher showing you?" Mama asked.

"The letter A."

"Well, shit, she was bored, Till."

"But what can we do about it?"

"I dunno, but someone has to be told she's not like the others."

Athena felt very special that they were talking about her. Danica and Lejla were listening as well.

"I'll go to the school tomorrow. Before work. I'll just go in a little late," Tata said.

After prayers, Mama sang, "You Are My Sunshine."

"Leave the door open, Mama," Athena reminded her. She didn't like the dark. She had had nightmares since the summer, and the living room lamp glowed in a soft golden tone.

"Theenie," Lejla whispered, rolling over to face her. "You're smart."

Athena nodded and took Lejla's hands into hers. "So are you, Jaja."

"No, I'm not smart like you. You can read all the signs on the bus."

"You can read too."

"Not like you. And you can do adding and subtracting and times tables."

Theenie saw the look on Lejla's face and felt sad. "It's easy. I can help you. You just remember the answers first—two, four, six, eight . . ."

"No, not now." Lejla shut her eyes so she couldn't see Athena, who put her hand on her sister's cheek.

She couldn't love anyone more. Like Tata's, Lejla's green eyes crinkled up when she smiled, and she had big dimples. "You're so pretty, Lejla. I wish I was pretty too."

Lejla's eyes popped open. "You *are* pretty!"

Athena knew that wasn't exactly true. She knew because people always told Mama and Tata how pretty Lejla was. "And you're smart!"

They paused as they each absorbed their own truth. They giggled into each other, rubbing noses and holding hands.

"I love you, Theenie." Lejla smiled.

"I love you too, Jaja."

Chapter 12

The next day, the girls didn't take the bus to school. They drove in Tata's car and parked in the lot where the teachers did.

Athena sat in a hard chair outside the principal's office. Her tata was talking to him about why she had left school. When they emerged from behind the frosted glass pane, they shook hands.

"Athena, you're going to promise Mr. Keeswick that you won't leave school again, okay?"

"I promise."

Mr. Keeswick laughed and addressed her. "We want to keep you busy, Athena, so talk to your teacher, or, if you need to, come and see me before you just leave again."

Mr. Keeswick walked Athena down to her classroom. He knocked gently on the door and motioned with his index finger to Mrs. Cowan to come over. "Athena needs a bit more to do," the principal told her.

Athena wasn't interested in anything they were saying. Immediately upon seeing the kitchen playset, she ran straight for it. Today, no one stopped her. She was there for a couple of hours when another knock came at the door.

"Athena Brkovich?" The voice was loud and direct. The woman at the door wore her black hair coiffed into a beehive piled high at the back of her head. She had a purple pantsuit on, and a ruffled top spilled out from under her chins.

"Athena, please go with Mrs. McGinty," her teacher said.

Athena didn't want to go, as she was having the grandest time. She stood staring at the newcomer.

"Okay, Athena. Let's go. I can't wait all day." Mrs. McGinty looked down at her watch.

Remembering her tata's words, Athena ran to the door, deciding it was better to listen. "Can I come back here?" she asked Mrs. Cowan. Her teacher's face broke into a smile.

Mrs. McGinty dispensed of all pleasantries and walked quickly down the hall. She held a clipboard in one hand and swung the other to propel her at a pace Athena could barely keep up with. She spoke as her bell-bottomed pant legs slapped against each other. "We're going to be doing some testing." She glanced at Athena to see her reaction. There was none. "It's nothing scary. It's just answering some questions."

"Why?"

"Why what, child?"

"Why are we doing the testing?"

"Well, we'll find out the answer to that once we do it."

This made no sense to Athena, but she was intrigued. At least it was exciting. "So it's like school questions?"

"Yes, exactly."

Athena beamed and inserted a quick couple of steps and a hop between strides to keep up with Mrs. McGinty, who, despite her cumbersome polyester pants, showed no signs of slowing.

"We'll be meeting every morning this week. I'll get you myself and you'll return to your own classroom afterward. Once we get your results, we'll determine the next course of action."

The tests were a series of timed exercises conducted in a tiny office up on the third floor. They had to climb two winding sets of stairs. There were no windows, just a desk and three chairs. One sat in a corner as though it had never been used. Athena felt sorry for it.

The questions covered everything Athena had ever learned at home and other things she knew nothing about. These things fascinated her, and she was sometimes allowed to ask questions about them and discuss them; at other times, speaking was strictly forbidden. She was never really sure what was okay until Mrs. McGinty would brusquely say, "No talking. No questions." These were Athena's cues to carry on. The teacher didn't like to repeat herself and rarely smiled. Athena had seen her smile twice at other teachers they passed.

On Thursday, there was a marathon in spelling bee format. Mrs. McGinty said the word, used it in a sentence, and then repeated it. If she had read them before, Athena could see the words in her mind when they were spoken. As Mrs. McGinty formed the words in the sentence, it was as if a typewriter was punching out all the letters in sequence, making it easy for Athena to recite them. It was nearing lunch and she was hungrier than usual.

"We're almost done. Let's just get through it," Mrs. McGinty said firmly. "Magic. Pulling a rabbit out of the hat is a magic trick. Magic."

For some reason, Athena couldn't visualize the word. She tried sounding it out. In her mind she tried to place the letters in sequence and frowned. It was a simple word, and Athena was dismayed that she couldn't recollect the correct spelling.

"Okay, give it a try."

"Magic. *M-a*-" Here she paused and then decided to just say what she visualized. "...*j-i-c*. Magic." As soon as she said "magic" it changed to a *g* in her mind. "No! *G*!"

"Too late." Mrs. McGinty was marking her answers.

"No! I know it's a *g*! I'm just tired and couldn't."

"Too late." Mrs. McGinty wasn't going to budge and Athena felt crushed. "Don't worry. Everyone makes mistakes."

But Athena couldn't be consoled. She spelled "magic" in her mind and out loud for the whole afternoon and couldn't sleep that night as she relived her stupidity. She knew the right answer. Athena knocked on her own forehead to stop the painful memory. It seemed to help a bit.

"What's the matter, Theenie?" Lejla asked that night, concerned.

"I spelled 'magic' wrong."

Lejla's expression changed to one of confusion. "So? So what?"

"So what?" Athena said sarcastically. Her mind raced around for the answer and couldn't find one. She was sure there were consequences, and that they could be severe.

***

It was two weeks before the results of the testing came through. Mr. Keeswick had another sit-down meeting, this time with both of Athena's parents; Mrs. Murphy was watching the twins. Mrs. McGinty was there.

Athena both liked the attention she was getting these days and didn't like it. She felt special that everyone was so interested in her. Her tata had even asked her to sit on his lap at nights so she could read the paper with him. There was a lot of bad news.

Mama and Tata sat in the guest chairs in front of Mr. Keeswick's desk. Above it were windows that went to the ceiling. Brass bars separated the big rectangles into eight smaller rectangles.

She was counting all the ways she could make rectangles when Mr. Keeswick addressed her. "What do you think, Athena?"

She looked at her parents for a prompt. None came.

"About what, Mr. Keeswick?" Athena swung her legs back and forth. She liked the way it felt—like running, except she was seated.

"Look, I don't want her to skip grades. She's too small. If she went to grade three she'd be a year ahead of her oldest sister. Naw, that's not gonna be any good. She won't have any friends," said Tata.

"Mr. and Mrs. Brkovich, Athena's IQ score is at the genius level. She needs opportunities to develop, and staying in kindergarten will hold her back," Mrs. McGuinty explained.

"Just pile on the work. She'll be fine. She's not jumping ahead of her sisters." Tata was enjoying telling the teachers what to do.

Mama just listened, and no one asked her what she thought.

"Well, then, at the very least I think we should put her in my enrichment program. It covers gifted children across all the grades. Of course, Athena would be the youngest. The classes run all morning from nine to twelve. She would spend the rest of the day with her classmates and Mrs. Cowan, but we'll make sure she's aware of Athena's abilities."

"Yeah, sure, if that keeps her mind busy. Yeah, let's do that."

"Did you see the shadows from the leaves on the floor, Mama? Weren't the windows beautiful?"

"Yes, my love." Mama held her hand in hers as they walked down the empty school corridor. Mama glanced down at Athena. "I think you got your brains from Tata."

"Of course she did. You're just like me, kid."

Athena smiled up at her tata, but her heart sank. She wanted to be just like her mama.

Chapter 13

The three hours in Mrs. McGinty's classroom were filled entirely with learning. There were eight children, including her, out of the over three hundred students in the school. All of the students in Mrs. McGinty's class were bigger and older than her. Talking was frowned upon by "McSquinty." While the students were silent, one soundtrack didn't seem to stop: the clip-clop of Mrs. McGinty's heels as she marched up and down between the rows.

Once in an odd while, Mr. Keeswick would join the class, but everyone had been specifically warned not to look at him or address him; he was simply there to watch how Mrs. McGinty taught. Athena noticed immediately that when he was there, her teacher's voice was lighter, her mouth curled up into a smile, and she laughed occasionally with the students, which was forced and strange. None of the children ever laughed back. The phony way she acted reminded Athena of Stric and Strina when they came to their house.

At first Athena relished walking to the new class. It meant a long trip to the third-floor classroom. All the half-wall bookcases were filled with resources separated into subjects like astronomy, physics, archeology, and other things that didn't exist in kindergarten. But when Athena returned to Mrs. Cowan's classroom and the kitchen, her heart filled with relief. What troubled her was that she was never there to play in the kitchen with the other kids. The plates and cups had been moved from where she had left them.

"Mrs. Cowan, I don't like the way that all the bowls and cups are messy. Can I fix them?"

"May I."

Athena wanted to fix them herself. "No. Can I fix them?"

"It's '*May* I fix them?' not '*Can* I fix them?' I know you *can*. 'May I' is the proper way to say it."

Athena registered this piece of information; they said "can I" at her house.

"And, yes, you may, but please do it quickly because I want you seated on the carpet in ten minutes with everyone. We're going to start our star challenge."

The children's attention was brought to a giant piece of chart paper that Mrs. Cowan hung near the windows. Down the left-hand side were all of the children's names printed in block letters. Along the top of the chart were numbers from one to twenty, one in each square. All of the children sat at their teacher's feet as she explained.

Athena almost couldn't breathe when she saw the small plastic box filled with shiny gold stars, the ultimate prize. If you licked the back of a star, it stuck to the paper.

"There's one star to be earned for each activity. I've written the activities out here." Mrs. Cowan held up laminated cards. They had a big numeral on one side and a description of what needed to be mastered on the other.

Athena wanted all of the stars immediately. Mrs. Cowan read the list of activities to the children. Athena knew how to do all of them. Spell her name. Say her ABCs. It would be so easy to get stars.

"I can do all those things!" Athena shouted, jumping up with excitement.

"Thank you, Athena. Please sit down and let me finish talking." Mrs. Cowan continued, but Athena was carried off to the place in her mind where her row of gold stars was complete.

"So you'll be allowed to do one activity per week, and you don't have to go in order."

This was a catastrophe! "Why do we have to wait if we know how to do everything?" Athena complained.

Mrs. Cowan looked at her kindly and patiently explained, "It's so everyone gets a chance. You see, we're all going to watch while someone does their challenge."

Athena's heart soared. She loved playing school, and all the other children would see how clever she was and want to be her friend.

"Now, is there anyone who thinks they can complete one of—?"

The words hadn't finished coming out of Mrs. Cowan's mouth before five or six in the circle shot their hands up, grunting to attract attention.

"Well, you need to be sitting up straight."

It was as if a vacuum had sucked all the children's bottoms to the ground. Vibrating but motionless, Athena strained her arm skyward, willing Mrs. Cowan to select her.

"Okay, Athena. Why don't you start?"

Athena floated to the front of the circle. She was so excited. She wanted to impress Mrs. Cowan, as well as the other children. She flipped furiously through the cards until one caught her eye: *Count to a hundred using the abacus.* She held the card high in the air. Mrs. Cowan brought the abacus front and centre. Without hesitation, Athena deftly slid the beads in rows of ten on the metal lines, one at a time from left to right. "One, two, three . . ." Each polished wooden ball made a satisfying smack as she moved it. "Thirty-five, thirty-six, thirty-seven . . ." Athena was in a rhythm, singing the numbers to a beat, swaying as she slid the beads over. "Fifty-eight, fifty-nine, sixty!" She was picking up speed, wanting to go as fast as she could. She fell into a stunned silence after she counted "Sixty-eight, sixty-nine . . ." and realized that there were two beads still on the bar. There couldn't be! Snapped out of her own demonstration, Athena looked up at Mrs. Cowan.

"All right, well, it looks like you missed a number, Athena."

"I know them. I was just going too fast."

"That's okay. You can try again."

Athena slid the last row back and started over "Sixty-one, sixty-two . . ."

"No. I don't mean now, dear. Everyone gets a chance."

"Noooo," Athena recoiled at her own carelessness. Some of the children clapped, happy that she didn't get a star. All would get a star before she could and Athena fell into a desperate outburst. "You have to let me just start here, Mrs. Cowan. You know I know how to count to one hundred. It's just one. I just missed one!"

"Yes, but that was the exercise, Athena. You have to be careful and not rush through. And you have to wait your turn now. Please sit down."

Athena's blood boiled and hot tears filled her eyes as she stepped over the cross-legged obstacles to the very back of the carpet. She cried into her hands. She was very angry with Mrs. Cowan at first, but her teacher wasn't wrong, and although she didn't want to have to wait, wait she would.

Athena replayed it in her mind. She could still feel each bead—sixty-one, sixty-two—under her fingertips, and in her hurry she wasn't even sure which number she'd skipped. Was it sixty-four? Sixty-five? When she got to the end of the row and visualized the two beads, her tummy ache started again. She twisted the fingers that had moved the beads until they hurt. Athena noted her physical pain and didn't like the repeated suffering. But she was helpless to escape.

When she told Danica, Lejla, and her mama at dinner what had happened, her sisters seemed to enjoy her failure.

"So you're not as smart as you thought?" Danica said.

Mama made a face.

"It's no big deal, Theenie."

They clearly didn't grasp the situation. It wasn't just a silly mistake; it cost her so much.

Athena sat with her grief and anger over the abacus for hours, thinking of never going back to school. This only made her cry tears of self-pity since she loved it so. Or she would feel reckless, thinking that she would go out into the world and find her own way for herself. But she realized that she didn't know how to do that either. Athena decided the only way was to be as perfect as possible in the future.

Chapter 14

Sunday rolled around, and the Brkovichs were late for church again. They put on matching coats and tams because a chill was starting to fill the autumn days. Athena was to formally start Sunday school. She followed Danica and Lejla downstairs. When they knocked on the door and peeked inside, the teacher, a young lady named Lisa, smiled and waved them in. They were speaking about the story of Noah's Ark. Athena liked this one because of the animals. It had been a while since she'd heard it.

Lisa read from a big picture book and showed the children the illustrations. After removing their coats, the girls had just found their chairs when the door opened again. This time it was three boys—Tommy, Niko, and their cousin Georgie. They were dressed up and their hair was combed neatly to the side. They looked shy, so different from at the hall. Athena stared at Niko; he was different. She thought he was handsome and caught his eye.

"Here. Sit here," she whispered, motioning to him to take the seat next to hers. He did, smiling at her. "I'm Athena."

"Yeah, I know."

Athena made sure Niko had all the crayons he needed to colour in the picture they had been given—the ark with a big rainbow in behind.

"There's no brown in rainbows," Athena said, examining his picture.

He looked over at her. "I don't care. There is in mine."

She liked his directness. He was definitely fun. She broke into a big smile, "Well, here, maybe you want to add some black?" She laughed.

"Maybe I will!" He committed heresy, colouring one of the lines in black.

She giggled with delight, and this pleased him.

"You're silly!" she said.

"Yep, I am," he replied, grinning.

Athena was sad when it was time to go upstairs. "My dad is the treasurer," she said.

Niko's eyes got wide.

"Come on, we can go in the office."

They ducked past Lisa, and Athena grabbed his hand as they ascended the stairs. They passed the candles and snuck into the room that was off limits. They stood listening to the men argue in Serbian. While in the corner, Niko dropped Athena's hand and wrapped his arms around her, hugging her. She felt dizzy with electricity.

"*Hey*—you kids, go on out of here," Tata said as more men vied for space in the cramped room.

Athena sprang forward. "Tata, I just came to give you a kiss."

"Oh, okay, Theenie." He leaned down. "Now go on out of here."

Lisa was looking for them, and when she saw them she put one hand on each of their shoulders and directed them to go to the appropriate sides. But first they had to cross themselves and kiss the icon. Niko went first, and Athena made sure she kissed the picture exactly where he had.

After church ended, Mama brought the girls back down to the basement. "You're going to join the junior dance group," she told them excitedly. "You're going to learn all the *kolos* and even perform at *Sveti Sava* and at the hall for picnics and carousel."

Athena's heart flew open wide. She adored dancing and longed to join the big circles of people all holding hands, moving with strange steps and motions. Athena was a natural, but she was so small, no one wanted to allow her in, except Mama. Now she would receive instructions directly. Athena scanned the room and her heart jumped again when she saw Niko.

The teacher's name was Sasha. He was spry, bouncing and clapping as he spoke in a sharp, staccato manner. His accent was very heavy; Athena had a difficult time understanding him. He was not very big, but he had a big voice.

"Dancing! Is in your blood!" His right index finger shot toward the ceiling as he exclaimed this with the flourish of a matador. "Ve are gonna learn da steps and make everyone proud. Understand?" All heads nodded as he placed a cassette recorder on top of the upright piano. He opened a shoebox of tapes and popped one in. "Now! Line up! In von row." Accordion music filled the basement and the snare drum echoed.

Sasha spoke loudly over the music. "Ve gonna start vit our right foot. *Gledaj ovde.* Look here. Step!" He stepped right. "Over!" He stepped over his right foot with his left foot. "Step!" He broke down the dance steps, and then the children lined up and tried them.

After almost an hour, when the murmuring was getting louder than the music, Sasha ordered everyone to line up from smallest to tallest. Athena was the smallest. Niko stood next to her.

"Ve gotta pic-a-nic in two veeks!" His fingers made the peace sign. "Ve gonna dance dis *kolo*!" Sasha gazed at the lineup. "Ve gonna lead vit da little ones—*mala deca*."

Athena would lead the *kolo*! She could hardly contain her excitement. Sasha walked down the line. He placed a girl in between two boys standing next to each other. When he came to Athena's end, he grabbed Niko and put him in front of her. Her face darkened.

"Boys gonna lead da *kolo*!"

Athena wanted to protest, but she was happy to be next to Niko and hold his hand in his position as the leader.

"Remember vere you are. Dis is how you vill line up next veek! Let's go!" Like a gun to start the race, the last two words ignited movement as the tape started again. "Hold hands!"

Niko took Athena's hand and watched her feet as he led. Athena confidently went through the dance in her head. It was just a repeating pattern. *Step over step hop. Step hop. Step hop.* When Niko stumbled, he watched Athena and got back on track.

After the class ended, Athena approached Sasha. "May I lead the *kolo* sometime?"

"Girls don't lead da *kolo*. Better you are behind da boy. Den people gonna vatch you. Da man in front."

Athena wanted to hold the handkerchief. She knew the dance better than he did.

***

"Mama, why can't girls ever lead the *kolos*?" Athena asked as her mama was putting her to bed.

"Oh, girls lead them all the time. But in the dance group, the custom is for boys to lead. They go first and we're behind them—you know, cheering them on and helping them. But they don't help in the kitchen. Only Chico Dusan is ever in the kitchen—when there's a pig roasting." Mama laughed. "Why do you worry about these things, Theenie? It's just the way it is."

"Sometimes I wish I were a boy."

Mama frowned. "Why would you say that?"

"Because they get to do what they want."

"No. They have rules too, just like you." Mama tapped her on the nose to emphasize her point.

She perked up at a banging sound in the back hall. There was a loud clatter from the kitchen. Tata threw his keys on the table. Mama jumped up. Her voice lowered and sped up. "Good night, now. Go to bed." She turned off the light and then crept rapidly out of the room, closing the door noiselessly. It felt too dark but Athena was afraid to open the door.

There was nothing at first. Athena waited, listening. It always started with Mama's voice. She could never hear exactly what she said, but Tata was easy to hear.

"You stupid . . . idiot . . . I'm sick and tired of this bullshit. . . ."

Athena wondered what her mama said that made Tata so angry and yell at her. If only she wouldn't say anything. Then maybe Athena could sleep. She pulled the pillow over her head. Lejla was already asleep next to her.

"Dani?" Athena pulled the pillow back and whispered, "Are you awake? Dani?" She slid out of bed and tapped her sister's back.

"No, I'm not." Danica was crying, facing the wall.

"Are you okay?"

"Yes. Now get to bed. Get to bed!" She turned with an urgency that frightened Athena, who leaped back into her own bed. She covered her head again with the pillow. Hopefully, Mama wouldn't talk back and it wouldn't last long.

***

There was an Abbott and Costello classic on the local Detroit channel. They weren't bad, but Athena really loved Shirley Temple.

"Fix the antenna," Lejla said, and then she got up and played with the device to try to get rid of the static and lines. The girls were dressed for church, waiting for their tata.

Today, the twins were going to be christened and there would be a big celebration at their Kuma's house afterward. Mama looked drawn and tired. She wasn't smiling and said very little until they got to the church. In the back seat, Danica held Max and Lejla held Mitzi.

"Watch their heads, girls. Careful—hold them under the neck," Mama said.

Athena felt she would never get to hold them, but she didn't say anything today. Important things were happening.

Her *kum* and *kuma* were godparents to the Brkovich children. The Lalovichs were older than Mama and Tata, but not old enough to be their parents. They were there to guide them in all things Serbian. Kuma Andjelka was the expert. She was from the old country. Athena wondered if Kuma was happy she was in the new country now. Athena was her favourite because she had been christened Andjelka. Mama said this was done out of respect but she preferred Athena because it meant "wisdom".

Kuma saw her. *"Andja!"*

Athena knew to go straight to her. Kuma hugged her so tightly that her back bent the wrong way.

"Oh, my goodness, you girls—look at how big you get-ting! Can't believe it!" She held Athena by her shoulders at arm's length, studying her.

Athena smiled. Kuma looked like a gypsy. She had thick black hair and a broad smile. Golden ducats on woven gold chains hung on her expansive chest. Despite high heels, she was still short. Kuma was the president of the circle of Serbian sisters and prided herself on her cooking and baking skills.

"Look, Andja." Kuma steered her to the table where she had laid out the *kolac* and *zito* she'd made for the service.

"You gonna learn how to make it one day. Kuma gonna show you." She squeezed Athena's cheeks. Athena caught her mama's expression and could see that letting Kuma do this pleased her, so she just smiled.

The kids in Sunday school were just coming out of the small room. Athena ran down just to walk up the stairs with Niko.

"Where were you?" he asked.

"We have to christen my new brother and sister today."

"That's good. Lisa said that if you don't get christened and you die, you go to hell."

Athena climbed the stairs, thinking. "But what if the baby just died too soon?"

"Too bad, I guess."

Athena was very happy that the twins wouldn't go to hell. According to the pictures, it was a gruesome place.

"Then we're having a party at my Kuma's. She's going to make pizza." Athena broke into a smile.

Niko walked to the boys' side. Athena watched him. He kept looking over at her, and he smiled when he saw that Athena's attention was on him. The service always finished faster when he was there.

The christening ceremony was long and boring. Athena and her sisters sat on the red-carpeted step going up to the altar. Athena tried to look nonchalant as she leaned back, straining to see what things were forbidden. It all looked like stuff girls would like. The vicar shooed her off the step and closed the swinging altar door. It had a big picture of Saint John the Baptist. Athena didn't like most religious paintings. The people's noses looked as if they couldn't breathe through them, but John the Baptist seemed more fun than the rest. And he was Jesus's best friend. He looked quite dirty and his clothes weren't fancy, so Athena knew that if her nails weren't clean or if she grew up and didn't want to wear dresses, God wouldn't mind. But you had to have clean hands and wear a dress to church. Mama was always saying, "People will see you," an obvious statement that explained nothing.

The highlight was when they took the babies out of their blankets and dipped them three times into the giant silver basin filled with water. Athena gazed at these new siblings in her life, wondering how this kept them out of hell. Max cried and turned bright red. Mitzi didn't make any sound at all, and Athena liked her very much.

***

Kum and Kuma's house was on a street with a boulevard. They had three floors. On the second floor, you opened a small door to reveal a narrow set of steps to a landing, and, once there, you continued up. This brought you right into Kuma Mileva's room. She was Kuma's mama, who lived up there. She didn't speak any English but she always gave the girls ten cents, so it was worth the climb. She had a walker that she used to move around. The roof had a steep pitch, making her room look like something out of a storybook. She had a bedroom and a bathroom with a tub. Like a crib, the bed had rails. Lots of crocheted items were lying around. The most interesting to Athena was the Barbie doll; her lower half was a crocheted skirt that covered a roll of toilet paper. She didn't understand what good the doll was without legs, but because she didn't have a real doll of her own yet, she liked to imagine that this was hers.

The day was spent climbing stairs to the third floor, then down, down, winding through the kitchen past people coming in and out of the side door, then down again to the basement, where there was a mirrored bar with black swivel stools. Kum was serving drinks to all the guests while Serbian music played on the turntable. Different sets of crystal glasses and goblets lined the wall above the bottles. Lights glowed up from underneath, making everything sparkly.

Danica and Lejla turned around, all ready to run back upstairs. Tata caught Athena by the shirt. "Hey, peanut, c'mere. This is my genius, Kum." She wanted to go with her sisters, but he dragged her back, slurring his thick, sour words over her shoulder. "Show Kum how you do your times tables, Theenie."

"Food's ready!" came a cry from the kitchen. "Come on up, everyone!"

"No, Tata. Let's go." Athena squirmed, but the weight of Tata's arm around her made it impossible to escape. *"Tata!"* Athena tried to lift his arm.

"Hey!" He grabbed her arm and lifted her up to face him. He was *not* happy. "Don't—you—dare," he said in a low voice, and she watched him carefully. "Did you hear me?" His voice was rising, and he shook her to emphasize his question.

"Hey, Dragan." Kum reached across the bar and tapped his arm. "Come on, food's ready."

This was too much. Her kum's soft, kind voice made Athena's tears well up.

"Stop that right now," Tata said. He marched her up the stairs and brought her out the side door. "Are you gonna cry? Eh? You're gonna cry like that in front of your kum?"

He brought his hand across her backside with such force, it lifted Athena off her feet. He held her by her arm.

She let out a cry. Athena didn't understand what she had done wrong.

"Are you gonna stop?" He hit her again. He shook her in frustration.

The air couldn't get into her lungs fast enough, but as her tata lifted his hand again, she pushed out her plea. "Plee—please," she said, huffing and sucking in air, "I'm—*hic*—I'm t-trying to stop. *Wait.*" Athena put her hand out like a traffic cop. She wiped ferociously at her tears and tried to breathe past the clamp on her vocal cords.

"Don't you look at me like that. When I tell you to do something, you better do it."

If Tata were an animal, he would be a black bull. His hair fell messily across his forehead and he pushed it back, sick as he was. He let go of her to take his cigarettes out of his front shirt pocket.

Athena stood there, angry with herself. She repeated the word "stop" until it was a soothing mantra. She didn't think she had done anything but was learning that sometimes it didn't take much to make her tata upset with her.

"Hey, food's ready." Mama looked at him and pressed her lips together like she did when putting on lipstick. "Get in here." She motioned to Athena, holding open the screen door.

Athena sat alone in the front room on the piano bench. She imagined she was playing because she didn't want to make noise. Mama came and sat next to her, giving her a kiss on the head.

"Mama, why does Tata hit me when he said no one better hit Mitzi?" Her voice broke.

"It's just that she's so little, sweetie."

"Dani never gets hit either." Athena's voice was strong as she looked up into her mama's face.

Mama's eyes were big like Athena's, and love poured out of them as she spoke in the gentlest voice. "Dani is too sensitive, Theenie. Her whole face breaks into a rash when she cries."

Athena sat still, realizing her fate, her place.

"You're all different, Theenie. All of you."

"But I listen!" Athena pleaded, not sure how to get to the bottom of it and clear things up. "Lejla doesn't, but I do!"

Mama's face clouded over and she said, "Okay, that's enough, Theenie. You're okay. This is a party, and no one wants to see you being sad or mopey." Mama patted her face and got up to rejoin the party, which had moved downstairs.

Athena wanted to be happy. Maybe she could find a way to start a rash on her face. She went to the bathroom and checked her eyes. They were puffy and red. No rash. She scratched under her eyes and watched the skin redden as the blood flowed to the surface. The skin was tender. It was no use. Mitzi was little. Danica was sensitive. She was solid. Lejla was . . . Lejla. No matter what, Tata would always find a problem with Lejla. It was okay, then, to get hit. If Athena didn't get hit once in a while, Lejla would get hit more. It was the least she could do for her sister. And at least Tata didn't say mean things to her like he did to Lejla. She told Lejla, "Just because he says so doesn't make it true." She didn't think Mama was stupid and she didn't think Lejla was a loser. Her tata only said these things when he was sick—that was the real problem. Her eyes had calmed down, but there were two small scratches on either side. She stared hard at her reflection, instructing herself to stop crying. She would have to practise this because she almost hadn't stopped herself today, and crying just wasn't smart.

"Theenie!" It was Lejla. "There you are! We're going to play in the park!" She spun around and ran to join the larger group heading out.

Athena glanced at herself as she ran out, strong and solid. *Just don't cry from now on*, she told herself.

***

The drive home was so late that Athena could barely climb out of the car. She wished someone would carry her in, but Mama's arms were full with the babies.

"Girls, go change and brush your teeth quickly," Mama said.

She disappeared into the twins' nursery and then popped back and forth into the kitchen. Already in his chair, Tata was snoring loudly, like a sleeping bear. After tiptoeing past him, the girls climbed into bed, too tired from all the excitement and fresh air to say their prayers.

"Dani," Athena said, then repeated it a bit louder. "Dani."

"What?" Danica rolled over to face her, lying on her side.

"How do you get a rash on your face when you cry?"

"I don't know," Dani said, annoyed.

"Mama said Tata doesn't hit you because you're too sensitive." Her eyes had adjusted to the darkness, and it was quite easy to see everything, even Danica's face.

Her sister was quiet for a minute, and Athena thought she shouldn't have brought it up. Then Danica said, "When I was your age, Tata came home like he does, not feeling so good. He yelled at Mama, but then Mama was screaming, so I went to see." She paused and collected herself. She spoke in hushed tones, like someone telling a ghost story. "Tata was strangling Mama with his tie. I was so scared, I ran down to the basement and hid. When Tata tried to get me out of the cupboard, I was crying so hard, he started crying too." She didn't look scared now, just tired and annoyed.

Athena's breath came in short gasps as she pictured her sister, frightened and huddled in a cupboard in the awful basement.

"I think that's why he never hits me now. I don't want to talk about it anymore."

Athena lay in the dark room. She couldn't fall asleep. She couldn't imagine Tata crying. When she did, she felt incredibly sorry for him. She felt the panic and fear of running down the stairs, all by herself, to open the dungeon door and hide. The veins in her temples throbbed and her heart pounded beneath her hand. She pictured her mama being strangled, not being able to breathe, and then forgiving Tata and staying with him. Yes, her mama must really love her tata.

Chapter 15

The school was hosting parent-teacher interviews. Athena couldn't wait to show her mama and tata all of the gold stars she'd accumulated, and she was hopeful that her teachers would tell her parents how smart she was and make them as proud as she felt.

Mama left the twins with the neighbour and, having put the girls in matching dresses, she took the bus with them to school. There was no one home to drive them.

"Mrs. Brkovich, it's such a pleasure to have Danica this year. Her work is always neat and tidy," the first teacher told her.

"Lejla is doing wonderfully. She needs to make a little more effort to be less social during class time, though," said the second.

Then she spoke to Mrs. Cowan, who said, "Athena is exceptional. She—" She stared past Mama to the door of her classroom.

Athena had been waiting all day for her mama to hear what Mrs. Cowan would tell her. Surely she wasn't going to stop now! Athena's eyes followed Mrs. Cowan's gaze, but she heard Tata before she saw him.

"Naw. What the hell? I'm here to see ma girls." Tata pushed a man's hand from his arm. He swayed back and forth on his feet.

Mama went immediately to him and whispered something in his ear. She motioned to the girls. *Move*, she mouthed. Her cheeks were flushed. "I'm sorry, we have to be going."

Tata pushed past Mama, knocked into a desk, and fell back into the chalkboard, upsetting the items on the small wooden ledge. Athena jumped down to pick up the chalk and eraser and replaced them.

Tata was arguing with someone. "No, now . . . Who're you?"

"Tata! Tata!" Athena tugged on him to get his attention.

"Oh! There's my little genie-us. This one's a genie-us." He looked at the retreating parents, leaving Athena's family in an open space.

"That's enough," Mama said.

"I'll tell *you* when it's enough." He pointed at Mama's face.

"Let's go, girls. Come on. We're all done. We've seen all the classrooms."

Athena felt hands on her shoulders, turning her around; it was Mrs. Cowan, kneeling in front of her. Her eyes were filled with tears. Athena put her hand to her teacher's cheek the way Mama did to her. "It's okay, Mrs. Cowan. My tata is just sick. Sometimes he gets like this, but he's really nice all the other times."

Mrs. Cowan let out a soft sob and pulled Athena to her chest. "I'm so sorry," she whispered.

What does Mrs. Cowan have to be sorry for? Athena wondered.

***

Long days at school were good for Athena. The work kept her occupied but recess was lonely because the girls and boys in her classroom knew each other well. She tried to join in on hopscotch, but she wasn't welcome, so she wandered out into the field beyond the paved playground. Here she would sing or speak to imaginary friends.

She didn't see Mama as much as she used to because Mitzi and Max were always there. But over the first year, they began making more appearances in the living room—sitting, standing, and then walking. Athena could tell that her tata favoured Max. He always mentioned it and would step over Athena to pick up her brother and carry him around. Athena asked to read the newspaper with him, but he had less interest in doing that than he used to. She tried to include herself in the games Danica and Lejla played, but they would often run away, laughing and calling her a baby. If she offered to help them with math, they shunned her.

"No one likes a know-it-all," Danica informed her when Athena suggested she could mark her sister's homework instead of Mama.

At Sunday school, she didn't see Niko very often anymore. And her questions seemed to annoy Lisa. "If everyone died in the flood, doesn't that mean everyone's related to Noah? Why do babies who die before they're christened go to hell? That would be mean of God. Who did Cain and Abel marry? There were no other girls."

Athena saw her cousins once a month after church for Sunday dinners when her family didn't go to see her *baba* and *deda*. Mama's parents lived about five minutes away by car and on a prettier street than Athena's. Their house had a big corner lot that was fenced in on all sides. Rose bushes surrounded the entire yard in every colour. In between the ring of roses were fruit trees: plums, peaches, pears, apples, and cherries.

Athena adored going to visit. The visits were always the same. Mama would start by asking, "How are you going to act?"

The girls would answer in unison, "Like little angels."

The first order of business was to kiss each grandparent three times and hug them both. After the greetings, each of the girls would step into the living room. Baba sat in a swivel rocker next to a built-in bookcase that held small knick-knacks. Athena's favourite was the brown-speckled shell. Baba inspected each girl's dress, which she had designed and made, while they twirled and walked for her. The others would lift the shell to their ear to listen for the ocean. When Danica and Lejla said they could hear the waves, Athena agreed, even though she never actually did.

Plastic covered the couches and a chair in the living room, except Baba's chair, and no one was allowed to sit there but her. She baked small *pogaca*, and her house smelled like a bakery. Athena's mouth watered when they came fresh out of the oven. Her baba would giggle watching Athena devour them.

"Stop eating now, Theenie," Mama then turned to Baba. "I don't like that, Mama. She's being a pig."

"*Jedi, jedi*," she would say, giggling. She was telling her to eat and nudged Athena toward the pans on the counter.

Baba didn't speak English, but she did understand Athena's body language. Athena would stare at one of the roses in bloom and keep smelling it until her baba noticed and cut it for her. For whatever reason, Mama took offence every time Athena was gifted a rose.

Deda would give them each a nickel, and they would run out of the gate at the front walk to the variety Mrs. Hutch ran just two doors down. She would get three small brown paper bags ready. Hers had a silky feel to them; Fred's were rough. If you couldn't decide between two pieces of candy, Mrs. Hutch would just give you both and fill the bag to the top: mojos, black babies, red ribbon licorice, maple syrup waffle cones, caramels.

After eating dinner, the girls were dismissed to the basement, and they ran around the metal poles. The rule was that no two could be at the same pole.

Downstairs was a Singer sewing machine with gold printing. This was where Baba sewed all the pretty dresses and made Mama's to match.

When it was time to go, Deda blew up one of his cheeks and the girls all kissed it. He made the peace sign when they drove away.

Mama didn't have any brothers or sisters. That was okay with Athena. Tata didn't have any parents. They were killed by a drunk driver, but when Mama told her this, she spoke in a very low voice, then put her finger to her lips so Athena knew that they didn't speak about it. Athena studied the patterns and habits of the people in her family, and she was starting to feel as if she understood her place and her role in it.

Chapter 16

"Athena Ber-ko-vich?" Some kids sniggered at the stumbling pronunciation.

"Brkovich. Yes. Here."

Ms. Simpson was her new grade one teacher. She wished she had a normal last name like Simpson. Athena looked up in awe; she thought Ms. Simpson was dazzling. She had red hair that she wore in a big bouffant with the ends flipped up; they rested on her shoulders. She wore miniskirts and shiny high boots. She even drove a silver Corvette Stingray.

"My mom says she got a divorce! That's why we call her Ms. and not Miss or Mrs.," the girl sitting behind Athena informed her before class.

When Ms. Simpson asked, "Does anyone have any questions?" Athena raised her hand.

"Do you have any children?"

Ms. Simpson smiled. "No, I do not. But I have all of you."

Athena wished she was her daughter.

She soon discovered that being in Mrs. McGinty's classroom gave her special privileges.

It was reading hour, and Ms. Simpson called for her. "Athena."

"Yes?" She looked up.

"Can you take this to Mr. Brennan for me?"

Athena nodded, unsure where to go, but she was afraid that if she didn't know, her teacher would ask someone else to go.

"Do you know where his classroom is?"

She nodded. Her stomach sank. She left the room and turned toward the other end of the school. Luckily, an older student happened to be approaching her. "Excuse me. Do you know where Mr. Brennan's classroom is?"

"Yes, I think it's at the end of this hall on the left."

Deliverance! Athena skipped in her stocking feet down the polished corridor until she reached Mr. Brennan's room. An attractive man was writing on the chalkboard, as he spoke about cell biology to an attentive classroom of grade eight students. One of the boys in the first row saw Athena and put up his hand.

"Yes, Arthur?"

"We have company, sir."

Everyone laughed gently.

"Well, hello, young lady. Come in." After putting down the chalk, he dusted off his hands on his pants. "To what do we owe this honour?"

Athena smiled shyly but then remembered to look Mr. Brennan in the eye and speak up. "I have a note from Ms. Simpson for you."

The class erupted with "Oooooh," although Athena didn't understand why.

"Well, my young friend, what's your name?"

"Athena."

"Ah, Athena. The goddess of war. Why don't you wait right here?" As he spoke, he swooped down and picked Athena up, then plopped her down on top of the filing cabinet in the front corner. The children laughed. Athena enjoyed this very much.

Mr. Brennan read the note, then scribbled a response. "Thank you for your patience. I'd be very grateful if you could return this to your lovely teacher."

Another round of oohs ensued, and he lifted her off the cabinet and sent her back.

Athena delivered the message exactly as Mr. Brennan had asked, and she became the class messenger. Although most of the messages went to Mr. Brennan, every once in a while she was asked to go to Mr. Keeswick's office.

One sunny day, Michelle, one of her classmates, was pouting on the playground as Athena approached. The other girls were skipping rope. "It's not fair." Michelle stuck out her tongue at Athena.

Athena frowned and thought about walking away, but Mama had told her that to have friends you had to include yourself. "What's not fair?"

"That you get to be the messenger all the time!"

Other girls nodded, also disapproving of Athena's appointment. Apparently, they preferred Michelle.

"Well, I can't help it. She asked me to do it."

"You could say no," Lillian chimed in.

Athena didn't think that was possible. The girls moved closer to her. They were bigger than her.

"I bet you think you're great because you get to do that, don't you?" Michelle leaned in closer, her anger rising.

"No," Athena said clearly, "I don't think I'm great." It was the truth.

"Yes, you do. You think you're *so* smart." With both hands on Athena's chest, Michelle pushed her back.

"I don't *think* I'm smart," Athena said plainly. "I *know* I am."

"Beat her up, Michelle!" said one of the girls.

"Fight!" some others cried.

Two nearby boys jumped up from their game of marbles and scrambled over to make sure they didn't miss anything. "Michelle and Athena are fighting!" they said.

"Don't!" Athena protested as Michelle swung and punched her in the arm.

"Athena Burp-a-witch! Ha, ha, ha! Burp-a-witch!" all the kids sang.

When Athena covered her arm, Michelle pushed her again and she fell down. Michelle jumped on top of her. "You're a stupid witch!" She spat the words in Athena's face.

Athena felt rage well up inside of her. She wasn't afraid of Michelle. She wasn't stupid, but she was angry. She grabbed Michelle's hair and, with incredible strength, pulled her off herself. In a flurry of kicking and punching, she climbed atop her attacker and set out to destroy her. She couldn't see anything but red as she swung down, chanting, "Me-shell, you smell! Me-shell, you smell!" She was pulled from above by the yard lady, and the girls were sent to Mr. Keeswick's office.

"If this happens again, I'm going to phone your parents. We take fighting very seriously, and I'll give whoever doesn't follow the rules the belt." He brought out a brown leather strap from the bottom drawer of his desk.

Both girls nodded. Michelle was crying and sniffling. Athena loathed her.

"Michelle, you can go back to class now. Athena, stay here for a moment." She watched coldly as Michelle left.

"I don't expect this kind of behaviour from one of my best pupils. You're too smart to be fighting."

"She started it. She's jealous 'cause I get to be the messenger. And then she called me Burp-a-witch in front of everyone. Am I supposed to let her beat me up?"

Mr. Keeswick pondered her words. He reached down into his bottom drawer, and for a moment Athena believed she was going to get the strap. Instead, he produced a purple lollipop. Athena was baffled.

"Here you go," he said, chuckling. "Try not to get into any more fights."

Athena took the sucker and popped it into her mouth as she exited the office, then took her time heading back to class. What were the rules for if you could break them? Why were they applied to some and not others? It must be her intelligence that had earned her this privilege. Tata was right—crying and being a suck doesn't get you a sucker. Having privileges also doesn't make you popular. Danica and Lejla didn't get to do the things she did, and they had all kinds of friends, especially Lejla. Athena might have preferred it that way, but she didn't know how to change it. For now she was just happy that Mr. Keeswick didn't call her house. She would have certainly got the belt, as Mama was against fighting and violence of any kind.

Chapter 17

The Sveti Sava church celebration was being held at Walkerville High School, which was nice because it was so close. Mama could push the double stroller and pack what the twins needed, and she wouldn't have to worry if she couldn't arrange a ride. Athena listened as her mother explained this to Kuma, the phone tucked between her shoulder and her chin. The long, winding cord stretched across the kitchen as she moved between the high chairs, feeding Mitzi and Max.

"Theenie, feed your sister."

Athena took over the bowl of carrots. Mitzi turned her head quickly to one side, then the other. She didn't like them.

"She doesn't want them, Mama."

Mama took the receiver away from her mouth. "Play the train game," she said.

Athena looked at her little sister. She was so tiny. Her fingers were perfectly dainty. When no one was looking, Athena would stick Mitzi's whole hand in her mouth. The baby was spreading remnants of food around the plastic tray. The seat was way too large for her, so Mama had tucked a blanket around her before doing the plastic seat belt up. Max was chunky, solid, like Athena. He didn't need a blanket to keep him steady.

Athena lifted the spoon of carrots high in the air. "Mitzi! Look! The choo-choo is coming! *Chugga chugga choooo choooo*." As she imitated the train, she bounced the spoon closer to Mitzi's mouth, which opened as she watched Athena opening her own mouth wide. "And num num." She scooped the spoon in.

"Pfft." Mitzi stuck her tongue out and gave Athena a raspberry, spraying carrots all over her.

"Mama!" Athena shouted.

Mitzi got startled, and Mama cuffed the back of Athena's head. It never hurt physically when Mama hit her.

Sveti Sava was the patron saint of the Serbian people. All the children at Sunday school spent weeks learning and practising their pieces. Athena could recite hers immaculately. It was very long, which impressed all the adults. Athena didn't know exactly what it meant in English, but she didn't have to. What was important was speaking slowly and loudly so everyone could hear you and understand you. No one liked it if you went up there and mumbled— Tata had told her explicitly.

The children in the show had gathered in a classroom-like area just backstage. The energy was high. The choir director raised one hand straight in the air and put a finger to her lips and just stood there. Her message caught on like a virus.

"Okay, children. It's very important that you're ready to go when those ahead of you are done. We don't want the show to take three hours. Watch for Lisa here to tell you who's next, and she'll send you out. Littlest ones, when you're done, go to your seats in the first row."

Athena bubbled up with excitement inside. Sometimes it paid to be little.

Niko and Tommy came in just as the instructions were finishing. Niko headed for Athena. He was nervous. Athena explained everything to him.

"I'm not sure I'll remember it all," he confided anxiously.

"Don't worry. Watch my lips if you forget. I'll go slow."

He smiled at her and she hugged him, feeling her joy triple inside.

As they stood waiting to go on, holding hands, Lisa looked down at them and gushed, "Oh, you two are such an adorable couple!"

Niko dropped her hand. Athena felt her face flush hot with embarrassment. Of course he wouldn't want to be coupled with her. He was so handsome; she was just smart.

As they walked toward the stage entrance, Athena turned and said, "Just watch me." She winked.

Niko didn't reply. For a split second when the group of four went on stage, Athena thought of not trying—or, worse—acting as though she couldn't remember the words. But there was no excuse. Her parents were waiting to tell her she was the best girl there.

The spotlights were blinding and you couldn't really see the audience. Athena did what came naturally; she poured out the quatrains in Serbian in a slow, articulate way so everyone would understand her. She didn't once look at Niko. There was a cheer when her voice rose, and then she held hands with the others and bowed once, then twice. Athena felt a surge of power and adrenalin as she galloped off the stage.

The older children leaned forward and congratulated her. "Good job!"

Athena pulled the theatre seat down and hopped into it. Niko sat next to her. They had a song to sing later.

"You were good," he whispered to her.

Athena didn't look at him. She just smiled.

After the high school portion of the event was finished, everyone drove to the hall. The bar was open and the tambura group was tuning their instruments. The end-of-year performance for the dance group was about to begin. The group had been practising weekly for months leading up to it. Niko went to dance practice more than church, but he wasn't there every week either. When they were at the hall, he would mostly run around with the boys, but he always made a point of coming over to Athena if he saw her. He would never kiss her in greeting, even though this was customary.

"Look at these two, Dragan." Niko's dad Marko pointed to Athena and Niko dressed in their Serbian costumes.

"Maybe they'll get married one day and have beautiful Serbian babies," Tata said, and he gestured grandly to the scene in front of them.

Niko led the *kolo* farther and farther into the crowd. Athena's heart soared with pride in her costume. The audience loved them. The folk music filled her with excitement, and she remembered Mama's directions to stand tall, lift her chin, and keep her upper body very still.

The comments from the tables were easy to hear because people had to shout over the loud music.

"What a beautiful little dancer."

"That's one of the Brkovich girls,"

"So precious, these two."

Niko swung her arm and checked his steps against hers. Athena wanted to lead the dance herself, but she didn't mind it if Niko did, because boys were the leaders anyway. She watched his handsome face smiling and wished she could be prettier rather than smarter. Niko squeezed her hand. At least he made her feel pretty.

Chapter 18

Mrs. McSquinty was in a harsh mood. She was walking up and down the rows in the classroom, hammering home her point. "You think because you're smarter, you don't have to work?"

Athena wondered during the long pause if anyone was going to offer an answer.

"It means you have to work *harder*, people."

Again there was a confusing pause. Athena didn`t understand who wasn`t working their hardest. She gazed around the room.

"It's all of you. Every single one of you."

Athena took exception to this and was about to raise her hand to object when the teacher brought the metric ruler she was swinging beside her down with a sharp *thwack* on the desk in front of her. The boy sitting there jumped. Athena decided to say nothing.

"I want everyone to work this entire morning, and I don't want to hear a peep."

Athena's project was on Japan. She was reading about their culture and customs. The cruel ways that they bound the girls' feet made her realize that she didn't have it bad at all. The morning disappeared as Athena immersed herself in geisha girls. She drew a kimono and coloured it carefully, then wrote about a tea ceremony.

When she stood up, Athena realized suddenly that she had to go to the bathroom. She walked quietly to Mrs. McGinty's desk. "May I go to the washroom, please?"

Mrs. McGinty looked at the clock on the wall. "No, you may not. There are only ten minutes left."

Athena returned to her seat, feeling the urgency increasing. She sat down at her desk and tried to distract herself by tapping one foot down, then the other. When the pressure became a steady pain, Athena raised her hand.

"You can hold it," Mrs. McGinty said dismissively. "Five minutes. Clean up and line up here, please."

Athena hopped from one foot to the other. The bathrooms were practically on the other side of the school.

"Mrs. McGinty." Athena pushed her way to the front.

Mrs. McGinty exhaled in exasperation.

"Maybe I could go now so I can beat everyone coming out of class?" Athena could barely hold it and bent over, grabbing herself.

"It's only two more minutes."

Athena didn't know what to do. She looked at Mrs. McGinty with absolute desperation, and the woman returned her gaze with disdain. The bell rang. She bolted. Big bodies poured out of doorways toward lockers that lined the endless hallway. Athena tried to run and hold it, but she was losing. She ran as fast as she could—all the way down the hall, dodging and pushing people until she arrived at the girls' washroom. Athena let out a wounded howl. Her legs were soaking wet.

"Are you okay?" a girl's voice asked.

Horror-stricken, she wondered how to escape without being found out, her mind racing. Agony and shame filled her, and she sat on the toilet and wept into her hands.

A soft knocking sounded on the door. Feet appeared. "Hey, little girl. Are you okay?

Athena answered the gentle tone. "No."

"Here, let me help you."

"You can't," Athena whimpered, humiliated.

"Everything will be all right. *Really.* I can help you."

Athena felt hopeless. She would be spoken of as one of the kids who peed their pants at school, a relentless label that never went away.

"But I pee my pants," Athena said, sobbing.

When she quieted down, the girl said, "Well, we have an hour for lunch, so let's get you cleaned up and we'll both be on time for class."

Athena unlocked the door and peeked out. The much older girl wrapped her sweater around Athena's waist and washed her socks, underwear, and pants in the sink. She held each one in front of the hot-air hand dryer while the other items hung on the radiator, awaiting their turn.

The girl had heard how Mrs. McSquinty could be mean. "You should have just left. Teachers aren't experts. Adults don't know everything. Kids still have to think for themselves." This confirmed what Athena had long believed.

"Your pockets are a little damp, but it should be alright." The girl handed the pants to Athena and she slipped them on.

"And you won't tell anyone?"

"No one will ever know." She had golden curly hair and beautiful blue eyes.

Athena had never experienced gratitude more acutely. She entered the classroom as the children were running in from outside, and no one realized she hadn't joined them.

The next day, she walked up to Mrs. McGinty and told her that it had been an emergency and she should've let her go.

"Well, how was I supposed to know that? You should've gone, then." That was all.

Athena thought about it as she kicked rocks on the playground and swung on the swings when it was her turn. It didn't make sense to listen to adults who thought they knew better. You had to listen because you were supposed to, but a lot of adults were mean people who took their anger out on others. Athena thanked God for sending her an angel. It was nothing less than a miracle that no one found out she had peed her pants. Not even her family.

***

Ms. Simpson stood at the front of the room. She wore a pink tunic dress and tall white boots. Athena had fallen very much in love with her and imagined her teacher might take her home and raise her as her own. Probably no one would even miss her.

"Today we're going to talk about jobs. My job is being a teacher. I want to know if your parents have jobs. Most of your dads will, and maybe even your moms, which is great. So I'm going to write down your name, if you want to share that with us. Who wants to go first?"

Hands shot up in the circle.

"Okay, Christopher."

"My dad is a carpenter and my mom stays at home."

"Wonderful." She wrote *Dad* and *Carpenter*.

"Who's next?"

Another round of hands.

"Stella?"

"My dad works at the car factory."

"Do you know which one?"

"Yes. Ford's."

"Okay. Do you know what he does there?"

"I'm not sure."

"And your mom?"

"Oh, she doesn't work."

This went on for another couple of rounds. Athena sat listening, unimpressed that her classmates' parents were just like her own. She wasn't sure exactly what her tata did at the car company he worked for. She wanted Ms. Simpson to think she was special, so she put up her hand.

"Athena?"

"My dad is a doctor and my mom is a nurse."

Ms. Simpson paused and smiled. "Really?" She turned and started writing it on the chart.

"Yes, they met at the hospital." As Ms. Simpson wrote the words, Athena started to feel nervous—even more so when the children looked over at her enviously, or doubtfully.

Then one of the boys said, "That's why she's so smart."

Athena's heart rate slowed, but the sinking feeling stuck with her.

The next day, the paper was still up. And the next. When Athena lay down to go to sleep, she prayed to God to forgive her, and if He did, she wouldn't lie ever again or He could send her to hell. She would picture the ultimate punishment for wanting to impress Ms. Simpson. On the third day, it was too much and Athena couldn't wait.

"Ms. Simpson?"

"Yes, darling?" Ms. Simpson wasn't as young as she looked from far away. Up close she had a lot of grey hair and small wrinkles at the corners of her eyes and mouth.

"What are you going to do with the chart paper with the names and jobs on it?"

"Well, I hadn't really thought about it. Why?"

"Could I have it? I'd like to keep it and show my mom and dad." Athena smiled.

"Oh, well, sure. Come after class today and I'll fold it up for you."

Athena counted down the minutes. She sprinted outside with the paper when the bell rang. She had to make it to the dumpster behind the school and then get back to the bus stop. She tore the paper into pieces. With every rip she cried, ashamed of how her tata and mama would feel if they thought she wasn't proud of them. Athena had lied again to get the paper, knowing that she risked going to hell.

"First things first," she muttered to herself. She had to throw the bits into the dumpster. She climbed the side and, standing on her tippy toes, tossed them in.

"Hey, kid! What're you doing there?" a voice yelled and a man in coveralls started walking toward her.

Athena said nothing. She jumped down and grabbed her lunch box. She had to run all the way around the school to avoid the janitor. Her lungs felt as if they were on fire when she caught sight of her sisters. She stopped running, but when they turned and waved wildly, she made herself run the remaining distance, arriving just in time. Panting, she slumped down next to Lejla.

Lejla asked, "Where were you?"

The bus pulled away. Athena thought about it and decided it was better not to share it. "Mrs. McGinty gave me some extra work to do and made me late." Another lie.

Her sister nodded and patted her leg. "Well, you made it," she said, smiling.

Athena tilted her head up to get more air. Above her was a picture of a woman with bouncy hair, holding a skinny cigarette. The ad read, You've come a long way, baby! Athena thought it was a long way from working at a car factory to being a doctor. It was also a long way from lying to going to hell. She would revisit her deal with God. Now that she thought about it, she may have promised Him more than was fair.

***

Athena walked down the empty hallway with the piece of paper in her hand. It always surprised her that she was the only one around. No one else. Not one other student. Everyone was where they were supposed to be and she was alone.

Ms. Simpson had given her directions to wait for Mr. Brennan's answer and then return.

"Well, class, I see a little birdie has come to deliver me a message. Hello, Athena."

The class spokesman told his classmates that Mr. Brennan had a girlfriend.

"Enough of that, please." Mr. Brennan sat down at his desk. Athena stood at the front. The students started to get restless. Mr. Brennan looked up and said, "Oh, pardon me, class. This is going to take a few minutes. But you all remember Athena?"

She smiled as lots of the students said, "Hi, Athena."

"Yes, well, this little girl is in grade one. Is that right?"

Athena nodded.

"And I'd like you to listen to her read to you aloud."

Her heart skipped a beat.

"Your teacher tells me you are quite the reader."

Athena was often asked to read to the class. She would forget that anyone was in the room and use different voices for all the characters, as well as sound effects. When she read to Mitzi and Max, it delighted Danica and Lejla too; there was always some laughter.

Mr. Brennan walked to the bookshelf at the side of the room. "Please pay attention, class, and decide for yourselves if you can read as well as this young lady or if you should be polishing up your literary skills." He ran his finger over the titles until he came to an old book and handed it to Athena. "Will this be okay?"

Athena read the title *Rumpelstiltskin* and nodded.

"Don't be nervous. Just read." He picked her up, swinging her atop the empty desk at the front of the classroom. Athena looked at everyone, and as they were sitting silent already, she didn't have to wait for them like she did her classmates.

Athena calmly opened the book and began to read, "Once there was a miller who was poor, but who had a beautiful daughter." She glanced up. Right away she imagined that she herself was the beautiful daughter. "Now it happened that he had to go and speak to the king, and in order to make himself appear important he said to him, "I have a daughter who can spin straw into gold."" Athena wondered if she wasn't more like the miller; not exactly a liar.

Everyone was drawn into Athena's storytelling. She read effortlessly, with an unabashed enjoyment of the story. Mr. Brennan finished writing his reply and allowed Athena time to come to a natural pause. When he interrupted, the whole class groaned and argued that she be allowed to continue.

"She'll come back again, I'm sure, and we'll pick that up. Well done, Athena. Thank you."

Athena sauntered back to her classroom dreamily. She was engrossed in the story she'd been reading. Was it possible to spin straw into gold? If she knew how to do that, then she would have so much money that Tata would never yell about it again.

Chapter 19

"She got the prize for best student in her grade," Tata explained to Stric as he poured the bag of charcoal briquets into the barbecue. He placed the round metal grill over them and sprinkled them with lighter fluid.

"Yeah, lots of the kids have gotten those over the years—"

"Not like this one, not like this one." Tata was intent on making his point heard. He took a matchbook out of his pants pocket. He continued, "I mean, they wanted to skip her three grades—three grades!" He tossed the match on the charcoal and it ignited with blue flames and an explosion of heat. Tata waved the smoke back and forth to get the flames going and put the lid on.

"I tell you, this one's going to be a doctor. Right, kid?" Tata turned to Athena.

She smiled and nodded. Athena could see that Dani and Jaja didn't like that she won the award, but she had Mira to play with.

"Enough of that talk," Mama said, coming out with a steaming plate of fresh corn on the cob. Two big bricks of butter sat on the table. "Kids, careful, they're hot."

"So when is building going to start?" asked Stric.

"In a couple of weeks. We got the design done. John is the builder and we've met a few times. I like him and I'm gettin' a good price. We need the space. It's just too small here."

"I can't wait for an extra bathroom," Mama chimed in.

"I'm going to have my own room!" Danica shouted, and Mama smiled, nodding at her.

"Me too!" shouted Lejla.

Athena wasn't certain what everyone was talking about but she repeated what her sisters had said. "Me too!"

Instantly, Danica corrected her. "No. No, you don't get your own room."

"Yes, I do," said Athena.

"Okay, enough, Dani. Don't worry, girls, who gets their own room," Mama said.

Athena munched on her corn, making patterns in it as she ate. She made sure she had cleared one section of niblets, then sucked the juice out of the cob before spinning it around. She couldn't imagine why she would want her own room. She was perfectly happy in her beautiful pink house with her sisters right next to her. She knew that Tata's parents had lived in the pink house and Tata had grown up here, and now he owned it and she was growing up here. Then one day she would own it. It was her family's for all time.

They took lots of drives to the country to see the new house. There was a turnoff where new brick houses lined the street on both sides. Then after one block there was a winding road that made a big circle. In the middle was a park with a hill. Two lonely houses sat on the big circle and there were soybean fields as far as the eye could see.

Athena would get out of the car and roam around the big pile of dirt and stare into the big hole with everyone. Soon, there were wood piles, then a house with no walls that the girls chased each other through, screaming and laughing. Then there were windows and a roof. Every time Athena went to see the house, it seemed so disconnected from where life happened, where people lived, and where they belonged. It was like a strange dream.

***

Grade two started, and, once again Athena was given extraordinary privileges. Her teacher asked if she wanted to instruct the class in grammar, actually standing at the front of the room. Athena used the long wooden pointer to guide the students through the sentences. She got to ask children to come up and write on the blackboard, and she made a special effort not to pick Michelle.

Bus fare went up to thirteen cents, so Mama gave them each thirty cents. Danica and Lejla quickly figured that if they got off the bus at the engine plant and walked up the block, they could duck into Fred's and, with the extra four cents, get a bag of candy. But only once a week. One of them would say that the bus driver didn't give them the change. The girls split the haul and hid it in their room. Life was about as perfect as Athena could imagine.

At the end of a regular Thursday, Athena was packing up her supplies like all the other kids and going to collect her lunch pail when Miss Vandeven, her teacher, announced, "Everyone! We have a student leaving us, so I want you all to sing with me and send her off with good luck."

Like her classmates, Athena looked to see who it was.

"Athena Brkovich." Extending her arm, Miss Vandeven guided everyone's attention to Athena. Athena was about to answer that she must be mistaken when her teacher continued, "We're so sorry to see you go, Athena. You've been a lovely student for me. All the best at your new school."

Everyone started to sing, "For she's a jolly good fellow, for she's a jolly good . . ." Athena couldn't take her eyes off Michelle, who sang with robust sarcasm, bursting with joy and pumping her fist like Popeye at the start of each chorus.

Athena let them all finish. She had a feeling there was something she didn't understand. Athena left her big-city school convinced that there had been some mistake. They would all be embarrassed when she returned the next day.

***

When the moving truck showed up and three men started to dismantle Athena's sacred space, there was a lot of confusion for everyone. Mama wondered how random items kept moving out of boxes and crates back into previously emptied cupboards. Danica and Lejla plainly rejected tiny remnants of their pasts, like a hand-me-down shoe, not understanding Athena's desire to fish it from the trash. They blocked her from returning to the empty bedroom, pulling her by her feet and laughing as she struggled to get back in and curl up on the floor.

Mama found the strainer she had packed back in a drawer. *"Athena!"* Her footsteps approached loudly, where out on the porch she found Athena grieving. Her arms were folded and her head cradled in them as she cried.

"I don't like this. Stop putting things back. You're being silly," Mama said.

"What's happening? I can't believe we're moving!"

"Honey, we've been over this. You've seen our new home being built."

"But this is our *home*! This is where we belong! I didn't know we were leaving here."

"This is *not* where we belong. We're moving to a beautiful new neighbourhood and will have lots of space—a big backyard for all of you to spread out. And the park. The park is fantastic." Mama gestured as though she was showing Athena the park, but her arm moved from one end of the street to the other. Her street. Her bus stop. Her front porch.

Athena sobbed. "I'm not moving!" She felt it in the core of her being. How could her parents even want to move?

Mama threw up her hands in exasperation. "Things change, Athena." Mama waited. "Everything changes." Again, silence. "Get used to it." Mama didn't wait this time. She turned and walked toward the house, saying, "If you don't want to move, then don't. But no one else will be here."

Athena had her head down. She imagined the possible outcomes: leaving her beloved pink home, or living there all alone while her entire family happily unpacked into their big new house. Mama's words rang in her ears. *Get used to it.* Athena felt offended. She would never get used to a new house. When her baba or deda cut a rose for her, even if they wrapped it in foil and put it in a vase as soon as they got home, it wilted and died. Athena would take the rose petals before they started falling off and press them in the pages of the big children's Bible she kept under her bed. Roses needed roots to live. So did she.

Chapter 20

Athena slumped into the corner of the back seat and pressed her mouth against the small triangular window that she'd opened to escape the cigarette smoke. She felt as though she had suffered an amputation. Athena kept hearing Mama's words. *Everything changes.* When they turned onto the street leading to the new subdivision, Athena realized that Mama was right.

The house on Woodridge Drive was a side-split three-level home with an attached two-car garage. Mama and Tata sounded like the salespeople they had dealt with as they described its features to everyone. The pale orange brick and tan siding were stylish and modern. The dark brown storm door that fronted it had glass panels, not just cheap mesh.

Inside, Mama floated from room to room, admiring the colours of the rugs and the paint choices. "I love this green!" The stairs going up were covered in a kelly-green carpet that extended throughout the living room, dining room, and hallway. Branching off from the hallway were three bedrooms and a large purple bathroom with two sinks. Everything was brand new. The stairs going down from the foyer were covered in orange carpet that matched the family room rug. The bedrooms downstairs had dark, panelled walls.

"This is *my* room!" declared Danica, taking the red shag-carpeted room.

"This is *my* room!" Lejla said, mimicking her. Hers had a bigger closet and orange shag.

Athena simply watched. There was another bathroom with a shower but no tub. There was a laundry room and a toy room, but that would also be Tata's office.

When the movers had unloaded all the boxes into the garage and placed some mattresses on the floor in the rooms, Tata called everyone into the family room. "This is our new house. I wanna make sure you're gonna be careful with everything in here. We're gonna go to the furniture store tomorrow and get new things for the new house. But if anyone is careless or ruins things"—Tata paused, and his eyebrows rose as he wagged his finger—"then there's gonna be a problem. Understand?"

Everyone, including Athena, nodded.

"Now your Mama's gonna tell you where things go, and I want everyone listening and helping out, okay? I don't wanna hear that you're not listening." Tata slowed down his words and spoke to Athena. "You're gonna start your new school on Monday, and we got a big day tomorrow, so let's get to sleep."

Athena followed Danica and Lejla downstairs. Her sisters were happy.

"I love the big globe in my room with the crystals," Danica said to Lejla.

"Where's my room?" Athena asked.

"Theenie, you're upstairs," Danica told her.

Lejla added, "Yeah, with the little kids. Crying like a baby today! What's wrong with you? Look at this big house! It's like we're rich!"

Athena didn't understand the last part, but she took offence to being upstairs with the twins. "I'm just as old as you, Lejla."

"No, you're not. You're younger. That's why you're upstairs. Now go."

Athena had to remember how to get through the maze that was the giant house. She walked upstairs and followed her parents' voices to the end of the hallway. The three bedrooms had the same carpeting and lights but in different colors: purple, blue, and yellow.

"Mama, where's my room?"

"Right here, Theenie. Next to me!" Mama bent down, hugged her, and showed her to the yellow room. It had a huge picture window, but it was black outside, so all Athena saw was her and her mama standing in the empty room. It was so big.

"Tomorrow we're going to pick out a beautiful new bedroom set." Her voice undulated as she tried to sell Athena on the excitement. "And then Mitzi is going to stay in here with you."

Athena's nose crinkled up in response.

"You'll be her favourite," Mama whispered, looking over her shoulder as if pretending to keep it from her sisters.

Secretly, Athena was pleased, as she coveted the attention of her brother and sister.

"She'll look up to you and listen to you."

She would give it a try.

Athena got up in the night and walked to the window. She put her hands to the cold glass and peered out into the black space. There was nothing to see. It was a moonless, starless night and the farmer's field out back seemed an endless abyss. Athena went to Mama's room and asked if she could crawl in with her. She kissed her mama's neck and fell asleep.

***

The next morning was unlike any other. Tata was laughing and excited before he'd had his first cigarette and coffee. He even made Mama laugh. She was making Pop-Tarts for breakfast.

Athena didn't know why going shopping for all new things was considered so much fun. Danica and Lejla were done trying to convince her that brand new furniture was better than all the "old junk," as Mama and Tata now referred to it. The only thing that remained was the dining room table and chairs that had belonged to Baba and Deda Brkovich. Athena sat there under the table, wondering if there was a chance of returning home.

"Cut that out," Mama said. "Your tata has worked very hard to buy this new house, and now we're going to the furniture store. He wants the best for you— for all of us—and you should be grateful."

Athena didn't know what to say. Her deep feeling was that none of it was necessary. They'd had a beautiful home. Why didn't anyone else think so?

Tata went out for an errand. They were going to select the appliances that day, as well. Mama wanted the green series. According to all the design magazines, it was in style.

"Eat at the dining room table, please. And don't get any crumbs anywhere," Mama said.

There was honking outside. No blinds or drapes covered the front windows, which Athena likened to two big bug eyes.

Danica was closest and peeked out. "Who's that?"

A station wagon pulled into the driveway, honking again. As the children ran down the stairs to see, Tata opened the driver's-side door. Wood-grained panelling ran the length of the car. While everyone cheered, Athena's heart sank. Danica and Lejla opened the doors and climbed over the back seat.

"Oh, Dragan!" Mama gushed. She held her hands to her face and then placed one on her chest. "Oh, my, really! What's going on? This is too much!" she protested, although she was beaming through her words.

"With the twins, the black car was too small. We needed it," Tata said.

Mama looked at him adoringly.

"Hey, I got you. Right, kid?"

Mama giggled. They hugged and she kissed him on the cheek.

"Okay, have they eaten?" Tata asked.

"Yes, yes, we're all ready."

But Athena didn't eat her Pop-Tart because there was no milk and her stomach felt nervous. Now she had to climb into the car, and the new smell made it impossible to breathe. When Tata lit his cigarette, she said, "Mama, I don't feel good."

"It's only about twenty-five minutes to the store."

"We'll open a window," Tata said.

"You don't have to crank the windows, girls. You just push a button. Hey! Don't play with it. Don't break it in the first five minutes! And don't pull up on the locks—just hit the button." *Pop. Pop.* The door locks opened and closed on Tata's command.

"Wow. This is too much," Mama said.

"Nuttin's too good for my girls." Tata grinned at everyone. "My prin-ces-ses! Ha, ha, ha, ha. Only the best!"

Tata had to pull over for Athena to get out and throw up on the side of the road. Mama held her forehead.

When they finally arrived at the furniture store, Tata told them to go look around for the bedroom set they wanted. Mama was going to take Max, while Athena was in charge of Mitzi. She trailed behind Tata, who said he was going to find a very lucky salesman. He informed the first salesman that he was no ordinary customer, but it seemed the man didn't agree because he left. The second salesman seemed very helpful.

"Look, I'm outfitting our new house, so I want to see what you can work out for me on the prices."

"Well, sir, what were you looking at purchasing?"

"I said we're here to outfit the house. The entire house."

Tata never just said things quickly or plainly. Some people got annoyed, like the first salesman. But some people knew how to play the game—letting Tata speak, making a big deal about things he said. The salesman must have been very good at this because Tata was laughing with him.

Taking Mitzi by the hand, Athena wandered around the store. She saw where the bedrooms were set up. Danica was lying down on one of the beds. Lejla was jumping on another.

Danica encouraged Athena to be happy about the new home. "We get to pick a whole new bedroom! We're not moving back. That house was too small and now we'll have our own rooms. And look, you wanted to share a room, and you'll have Mitzi."

"I'm–getting–this–one!" Bouncing, Lejla let out a word each time she landed on the bed.

Athena strolled along and came upon the perfect suite for her and Mitzi. It was white with gold trim. It had a four-poster bed like in the books she'd read. The desk had a hutch with a pretty chair to match.

"Yes, I think the white will look lovely in the girls' room," Mama said.

She approved everything they bought. Tata let her point at and pick things out as though that was the way it always was. Her mama looked as if she was in charge, and she fully embraced her role, which only pleased Tata more.

"This is going to be one beautiful home, ma'am." The salesman turned to the children. "Your father obviously loves you all very much. You're very lucky." He turned to Tata. "We're going to be able to make a really good deal with you today, Dragan, because no one shops like this." Everything he said made Mama and Tata very happy, and apparently the saddest guy in the place was the first salesman.

"He didn't know what he was lookin' at," Tata told Athena as they strolled again around the store. "You don't judge people by the way they look. I got money, but he don't need to know that. *And you don't ever tell people that.*" His eyes widened.

Athena nodded fervently in agreement.

"It's nobody's business what we got. But you gotta be smart with money, peanut. You don't buy stuff on credit." He grimaced at the very mention of the word. "You save your money and you buy the best. You understand?" Tata took out a fat envelope full of cash and disappeared to the back of the store with the salesman.

All the goods were delivered to the Brkovich family home the next day and set up. Athena's parents laid out rules about all the new furniture. Unless you covered everything in plastic wrap, you had to be extra cautious even sleeping in the bed or there would be consequences.

"Athena! Take your brother and sister outside and watch them, please."

Athena wandered through the maze of boxes and found the twins.

"You're not to go far. Is that understood?" Mama said.

"We're going to climb the mountain in the backyard, Mama," Athena replied.

They went through the garage and out the back door. Athena took in her new surroundings. There was dirt—to the left was a mountain as high as the house that rose on a gradual slope and had many flattened areas. It was dirt, not sand, so it was safe to climb. There were two other houses on their side of the street, and two other mountains of dirt, but those didn't belong to them.

The wind was blowing strongly, but it felt warm. Athena led the climbing expedition to the top of the mountain. They had to defend themselves from bears and lions. They had to build a shelter in a cave and find food. Athena foraged for scraps of carpeting and the ends of wooden planks and collected them for their game.

It was hours before Mama called them. "Okay, come in now, please, wash up. It's lunch. C'mon."

The twins started to slide down. Athena climbed to the top of the mountain and looked out in all directions. They lived in the country now, the earth solid beneath her feet. They were guarded by the huge, rustling trees and the flowing fields. Athena breathed in the sweet air and raised her hands slowly with the wind, conjuring the gusts to raise her up so she could fly. She felt an incredible surge of energy in her body. She was so powerful and perfect. She scampered deftly down the dirt pile and came inside, filled with new hope and acceptance.

"It's like the wilderness!" she said at the table.

Everyone laughed. Athena couldn't wait to go back outside.

"Well, it's not the wilderness. You still have school on Monday," Mama said.

Athena optimistically anticipated resuming her special place in school. She wasn't scared like Danica and Lejla. All they talked about was what if they didn't make any friends. They didn't like Athena's solution: "We've got each other." Her sisters rolled their eyes and stared at Athena, but she couldn't follow the thread of the conversation. All she knew was that she wasn't worried.

Chapter 21

The morning routine was much different on Monday. They all had to drive Tata to work and then Mama had to drive the girls to school to register them, as there were no city buses. Athena didn't even realize that Mama knew how to drive a car.

"They'll be taking the school bus, Drag. We can get by with just this one."

"No, we can't, Till." Tata was agitated. A lot was happening, and although he'd been all smiles, his happy-go-lucky mood was evaporating quickly. He didn't let Mama drive him.

When he got out to go to work, Mama moved behind the steering wheel and turned to them. "Okay, ladies, here we go."

"Mama's driving!" Athena announced.

Danica and Lejla, who had jumped into the front seat, cheered, "Go, Mama, go!" until she laughed, which was a beautiful sound.

Athena's day wasn't off to the best start because Mama had insisted she wear a fancy red dress. It had a gingham apron with ruffles around the hem and on the shoulders. Athena had protested terribly but lost. The compromise was that she was allowed to put shorts on underneath. "Dress up for Sunday" had been a scourge at her other school, and she had tormented some of the girls with it, especially Lillian, who had to wear dresses every day.

Athena knew it wasn't entirely bad to wear a dress because at first glance lots of people thought she was a boy. It was her hair. Mama cut it by laying masking tape across her bangs and using it as a guide. If it was crooked, Mama would simply reapply the tape and move it up slightly. By the third try, she had usually evened out the bangs. She would cut straight back across the ears and then close to the neck in the back. Even though Danica and Lejla had hair down to their shoulders, Mama said she didn't have the time for hers. Athena didn't see the value in arguing, except that sometimes people called her a he. The dress would let everyone know.

Mama pulled into the parking lot of the school and announced, "We're here."

"Where, Mama"? Athena asked.

"Now, girls, you will listen and try your best. Do you all understand?"

Athena was struck by how different the school was. It was a one-storey shoebox. There was definitely no upstairs. It barely looked tall enough. The school ended so quickly that the soccer field out back seemed to swallow it up.

"This is it?" Athena shrieked. "Where is it? Mama, this isn't a proper school!" Everyone got out of the car.

"This is a smaller school because it only goes to grade four. And I don't want to hear that kind of talk, Athena. Do you hear me, young lady?" Mama was being very stern and speaking close to her ear. "I'm going to tell your tata if you don't behave yourself."

Having good manners and making good first impressions were of paramount importance. Athena struggled to regain her composure. Mama opened her purse and took a stick of Juicy Fruit out of the yellow package. The shiny silver foil glinted up at her. "Here, keep this for recess, okay? Be my good girl now, please." Athena took the gum and put it in her dress pocket.

The office near the front door was small, the size of their new kitchen. One woman sat at the desk. "Hello, there. You must be the Brock-o-viches?"

"Brkovich," Mama replied.

"Oh, I'm not good at those types of names. Such strange spelling." Mama smiled.

"Well, aren't you all so pretty?" After picking up three file folders, the woman stood up and walked around the glass partition. "You girls are going to love your teachers. My name is Donna. If you need anything, you just come find me."

The woman walked ahead with Mama, who held Mitzi, and Danica carried Max so they could keep up. Donna seemed suddenly in a hurry. *The doors are like the ones in an insane asylum*, Athena thought with suspicion and disgust. They were pale yellow and dingy. At the top of the door was a small horizontal window with a gold checkerboard pattern. "Danica's classroom," Donna announced.

Danica stood at attention as she was introduced to her teacher. Athena hoped Danica felt alright.

Lejla took Max but then passed him to Athena as she entered her classroom and was introduced. The teacher said her name wrong. "Ledge-la?"

"No, it's Lay-la," Lejla said.

"Well, that's different." The teacher smiled and nodded at the class.

Athena never really worried for Lejla, who was always the prettiest girl at school. All the boys had a crush on her and even lots of the girls. When the teacher asked, "Where can Lejla sit?" lots of hands went up. She was always popular.

"All righty, and now just you . . . A-thee-na?" Donna read from the front of the last folder. Mama hadn't spoken a word but was watching intently. Donna knocked quickly two times as she had at the other classrooms and then opened the door. "Mrs. Hamilton? You have a new student."

Athena stepped forward into the room as she had seen her sisters do. Mrs. Hamilton had small, round spectacles and short blonde hair that curled under all the way around. The teacher just nodded to the group that had dropped her off and let the door swing shut. Athena didn't know how she would get home. She didn't know where she lived from here. Panic rose inside her.

"Okay, class. I want everyone's attention," the teacher said.

Fourteen children were sitting at wooden desks spaced two feet apart in three rows. There was a world map on the front wall. The chalkboard was green and about the size of the one in her cousins' basement.

"This is our new student." Mrs. Hamilton glanced down at the folder in her hand and then added, "Why don't you introduce yourself?"

"Hi. My name is Athena Brkovich."

A couple boys let out loud laughter. It was met with a stern glance and stopped quickly.

"Well, thank you, Athena. We don't have many rules in this classroom, but if you follow the ones we do have, we'll all get along. Please raise your hand to speak, only speak if you are asked to, and keep your hands to yourself. Are we clear?"

Athena nodded.

"Great. Please find a seat."

Athena scanned the room. No one put their hands up or waved her over. She suddenly missed her old school very much and took the first empty desk, which was in the middle row.

"Athena, I don't know what you were learning at your other school, but we're doing our phonics unit for an hour. Please come up here and I'll give you the workbooks we're using." As Athena walked forward, Mrs. Hamilton told the children to carry on with their work.

Athena took three phonics books and walked back to her place. When she tried to slide the books into the desk, she found only a small ledge with a pencil on it. Athena leaned around the sides to see if there were openings for the books there. There weren't.

"You lift the top," a girl's voice whispered. Diagonally from her, a sweet face smiled. To demonstrate, the girl lifted the top of the desk as she held her book with her other hand.

Athena whispered back, "Oh!" and the girl giggled. She lifted the top and placed her books inside.

Athena opened the introductory phonics book and completed units one to three. The school clock showed twenty minutes left until eleven o'clock. Athena tapped her pencil on her book.

The girl turned to see what she was doing. "Do you need help?" she asked. "I'm Sarah."

Athena just shook her head. She got up, and Sarah, startled, turned to face the front. Athena walked up to Mrs. Hamilton before she noticed her. She too looked startled. "Is there a problem, Athena?"

"No."

"Well, please sit down and do your work. I can go over it later."

"No. I'm done."

Mrs. Hamilton took the workbooks Athena offered her. She flipped open the first one and hummed. "Well, go sit down, please. You can work ahead quietly."

Athena worked through four more units. There were still ten minutes left. Disappointed, she let her gaze roam around the small room. A Canadian flag stood in the corner, and the cursive alphabet was written around the perimeter. A small blackboard on the side wall said *Class Duties* at the top, with three titles down the side: *Lunch*, *Crafts*, and *Closet*. There were three names beside each. *Evan, John, Karen. Stacy, Kenny, Jimmy. Sarah, Matthew B, Kim.*

At eleven o'clock, Mrs. Hamilton told the children to close their books and hand them in, in single file. The row closest to the windows stood up and marched forward, each placing their books neatly on the corner of her desk. The middle row stood up. Athena followed the procession and made her way back down the aisle clockwise. Then the third row went.

It was time for mathematics. Athena had to walk to the front again to get her new workbooks. As she travelled past one of the boys, he grabbed the back of her dress and threw it up in the air. Athena felt the breeze and spun around quickly, but the laughter came faster. The boy put his face down on the desk. Athena's neck felt hot. She hated this dress! She hated this crummy classroom! She hated these baby books!

Athena took her seat and began to wonder about things. For example, what would she be doing right now at her old school? Reading to Mr. Brennan's class, maybe? She was slumping forward, saddened in her chest and telling herself not to cry, when the foil caught her eye. She looked up and refocused.

"Please turn to page eighteen in your notebooks, children."

Everyone started flipping pages, so Athena did as well, but she took the opportunity to unwrap the gum and pop it into her mouth before anyone noticed. She leaned her head on her hand to help hide the chewing. It tasted so delicious! She balled it up in her mouth, removed it, and placed it on the ledge at the front of the desk where no one could see it. This secret pleasure comforted her greatly.

The students were to complete eight pages of exercises. Athena finished with ease and then walked up the aisle with her book, careful to hold her skirt tightly in the front of her, but Mrs. Hamilton stopped her before she reached her desk.

"Athena, is there a problem?

"I'm done." Athena felt the eyes of the children on her.

"Bring that here, please." Mrs. Hamilton didn't seem to believe her and looked through the pages. "Well, you have to show all your work here. And after you do that, please go to the beginning and do all the work the class has already done."

Athena went back to her desk. She showed her work. She went back to the start of the book and worked diligently on the first seventeen pages, but it was too simple. She looked around, wondering what all the children were doing. There were fifteen minutes left. She picked up the gum. It was sticky so she put it in her mouth and then placed it back on the ledge. Two minutes later, Athena thought she had better perform the lick test again. When she went to put the gum back, though, it stuck to her fingers. She spread her finger and thumb and the gum sagged, so she scooped it with her other hand. Now it was stuck to both hands. Athena held her hands under her desk, desperately trying to pull the gum off, but it was suddenly wrapped around all of her fingers.

"Okay, class. Before lunch I have a handout we'll be looking at after recess. Who wants to pass it around?"

Athena stared down at her desk. All the hands shot straight up.

"What if we let Athena do it, since she's new?"

Athena looked up and shook her head.

"No, thank you, Mrs. Hamilton. Someone else can do it."

But while she had refused politely, Mrs. Hamilton wouldn't hear of it, and to get Athena off to a good start she walked to her with the stack of handouts and said, "Don't be silly. Of course you'll do them today, Athena," and dropped the pile on her desk.

There was only five minutes until lunchtime. Athena's mind raced, and, ever resourceful, she used her chin to slide the stack of papers onto her hands. She balanced them and started up the aisle.

"Take one," she instructed the first person and smiled. "Take one," she said to the next.

The children seemed to accept that Athena was doing it differently. But when she turned down the final row, a loud-mouthed boy slammed his hand down with an exaggerated "Thank you very much!" and sent the papers flying.

Athena burst into tears. It was too much.

"For heaven's sake, Athena, it's fine. Just pick them up."

Athena continued to cry and held up her hands, which were covered in Juicy Fruit and stuck to the underside of the last handout. The classroom erupted with laughter.

"Please go wash your hands and come back for lunch. Children, please!" Mrs. Hamilton had to open the door for Athena and directed her to the bathroom.

Athena stared at her red eyes in the mirror and spoke to her sad face. "So what are you gonna do? Quit school because you got some stupid gum on your hands? Wash it off, kid. It's your own dumb fault for chewing it in class!" When she didn't feel sticky anymore, Athena leaned in close to the mirror and wiped her eyes, "No one likes a crybaby, Theenie," she said, and she went back to class.

Chapter 22

Two whole weeks had gone by. Mama was quiet at dinnertime and snapped at Danica when she asked about figure skating lessons. "I don't know, okay?" She threw the utensils from the dishwasher into the drawer and slammed it shut. "I want everyone in bed early tonight."

No one argued.

Athena saw Mama move noiselessly past her bedroom door when the front door opened. She heard her tata's heavy footsteps up the stairs as her mama pulled out pots and pans to make him something to eat. The keys hitting the new laminate countertop sounded just the same as they had hitting the old nook table.

Words Athena recognized sloshed out of her tata's mouth. "You think I'm made o' money? You don mek any money, but you know how to goddamn spen it!"

Athena lay stiff, staring up at the ceiling, wondering if Danica and Lejla could hear. She looked over at Mitzi. She was sleeping.

"You don't work. I work. I mek the money here."

There it was—her mother's soft, indiscernible murmur. What had she said that lit the fire?

A torrent of rage poured out of Tata. "You stoo-pid id-i-ot! You got yer head up yer ass! You think yer gonna talk like that to *me*?" he shouted menacingly.

Athena slipped out of bed after a while. Tata had taken to slamming drawers as though he wanted to destroy the kitchen. Athena crept down the hallway.

Mama saw her first. "Hey, get back in bed." It was an urgent order.

Tata was standing close to Mama, his face very near hers. He swung around, off balance.

"Stop fighting and go to bed, please," Athena said gently but firmly.

Tata's hand was bigger than Athena's face. That's why she flew so far when it came down unimpeded.

Mama picked her up angrily by the arm, squeezing it and saying, "Get to bed and don't come out here again, ever. Do you hear me?"

There was a giant ringing in her ear, but Athena heard her.

Athena climbed into bed and Mama closed her door and went back to the kitchen. Why was it like this? There was no reason to fight. Mitzi picked up her hand and whispered, "Don't cry, Theenie. It's okay." This made Athena cry harder. Athena felt the blistering sting of the welt on her cheek as, over and over, the shouting rose and receded.

"I will never be like Mama," she vowed to Mitzi, God, and the dark night. "I'll make my own money so no one can talk to me like that."

***

Athena didn't bother telling Mama that there was nothing to do at school. She was easily the smartest kid in the class. It was simple to just get her work done. Mrs. Hamilton loved manners and being eager to please, kind of like Mama did, and if you really overdid it, the other children called this "brown-nosing," which Athena didn't understand or care to.

"Mrs. Hamilton, is there anything extra I can do for you? I could organize the craft closet."

She then spent three days sorting all the construction paper by colour.

Athena was put at a group table at the back of the classroom with the slowest children. She didn't take her seat right away at the small table but instead stood there contemplating going home.

"You're a strong student, Athena. I would appreciate it if you could help Jimmy with his work."

Jimmy was the boy who'd slammed Athena's pile of handouts that first day. His face and nails were never clean. He didn't always have a lunch.

"You gotta help me do the work."

"No, I don't, Jimmy. And don't touch me." Athena hated being associated with him. Sarah was becoming her friend, and she worried that any contact with him could ruin her chance of anyone wanting to play with her again.

"Yes, you do. Mrs. Hamilton just said so."

Perturbed, Athena grabbed the instruction sheet for the project so they could get started as quickly as possible. As she was reading it, Jimmy slowly dragged her pencil case across the table until it fell off the edge and onto the floor beside him.

Athena turned abruptly to him. "Pick that up."

"No, you."

Athena didn't want to argue. She leaned to the side and was reaching down to grab it when Jimmy unzipped his fly and pulled open his pants. She sat bolt upright in her chair. Her hand shot straight up in the air. "I'm telling."

Jimmy pressed himself to the table, and Athena repeated herself.

"Yes, Athena?" her teacher said.

"Jimmy knocked my pencil case on the floor."

"Yes?"

"Well, he should pick it up."

Without hesitation, Mrs. Hamilton replied, "Athena, just pick it up yourself. We'll have no more of that."

Jimmy leaned in and covered his mouth with his hand and said, "Yeah, you just pick it up, Athena."

She raised her hand again.

"Yes, Athena?"

"Mrs. Hamilton, I don't think it's fair that I have to pick up the pencil case when Jimmy knocked it off."

"Oh, for heaven's sake's. Life's not fair. Please just pick it up this time."

Jimmy was gloating.

Athena narrowed her eyes. "I'm not picking it up." Two minutes passed. She couldn't focus. She had no idea what had possessed Jimmy.

"Hey," he said.

Athena continued to stare at her paper intently.

"Hey. Psst," he whispered.

"What?" Athena turned to him.

"I'll show it to you at lunchtime if you promise not to tell anyone."

"You're disgusting!" Athena hissed back.

"Are you sure?" Jimmy was doing up his pants, and as he did, he reached down and picked up Athena's pencil case and laid it on the table. Athena thought about the cooties on it and shuddered. After ten minutes, he leaned toward Athena and said, "If you want to see it, I'll show you behind the big tree."

Athena said nothing. The proposition was titillating, and she could think of nothing else.

She didn't learn anything new in the classroom, but recess was a different matter.

Athena grabbed Sarah's hand and pulled her to the middle of the field. "I have a secret, but you have to promise not to say anything."

Sarah's face lit up and she nodded eagerly.

"We can go right now to the big tree." Athena's heart was pounding.

"Do you really think he'll show us?"

"He had it *out of his pants*!" Athena jumped from one foot to the other, shaking her hands as if trying to get excess water off them. "Do you think we should go?" She was hoping that Sarah would say she wanted to.

"I don't know."

Both girls were smirking. Athena threw out the bait. "He probably would never—not outside. We should go and call his bluff so he'll shut his face about it."

Sarah agreed.

The girls scampered to the tree in a roundabout way, stopping at the monkey bars, balancing on the ledge of the sandbox, and then backing ever so slowly to the tree. They could react if anyone started running over. No one was. At first Jimmy wasn't there, and Athena felt a huge wave of relief; the adrenalin had been rushing through her since she told Sarah. But he must have seen them because they heard a familiar "Psst."

Jimmy was standing on the other side of the ditch. He didn't say anything, just waved them to come over and receded behind the giant trunk. The girls looked at each other and giggled nervously.

"Hurry," Jimmy said, looking over their shoulders. "You have to promise you won't tell anyone."

Athena looked at Sarah and they both agreed, but they could barely contain their nervous laughter. Jimmy pulled down the front of his trousers with one hand and pulled out his penis with the other.

A shock wave went through Athena, and she immediately ran from behind the tree, screaming, *"Jimmy showed us his wiener! Jimmy showed us his wiener!"* Sarah and Athena ran around frantically in circles and shrieked and laughed, until they fell down. They spun around, confirming to the kids who came up to them that they had indeed seen *it*.

"Little Johnny" jokes were all the rage, and the boys changed it to "Little Jimmy." When they played boys catch the girls, the boys chased Sarah more and asked her if she wanted to see their wiener too. But after the time Matthew B. caught her and pulled her down and she freaked out, kicking him, they didn't chase Athena. She felt terrible because she really liked him, and didn't know why she couldn't be cute like the other girls so the boys wouldn't be so rough with her.

That year Athena learned a few more things. There was a small risk of getting pregnant from sitting on a toilet seat, and that was why they made boys' and girls' washrooms. Also, babies came out of your mama's stomach when she puked you out. And if you didn't like boys, you were something called a lesbian.

Athena preferred Sarah to the boys. Sarah had auburn hair and blue eyes. She took gymnastics lessons and could do the splits and a back walkover. Most of the boys were in love with Sarah, and so was Athena. She wanted to be like her because boys were always sharpening her pencil. They picked her first for teams, even though Athena could run faster than her. They sent her notes in class and told her she was pretty.

The boys were different with Athena—they met her head-on. It wasn't that she didn't want to like them; they just made it impossible. They called her a brainiac and "Bark-u-bitch" on the playground. They took offence when she beat them at math games and would push her down to get a spot next to her best friend.

One night, as Danica got ready for bed, Athena was downstairs looking through her sister's things. She had a trinket box on her dresser with things like a random movie ticket stub or a coin. Athena didn't collect things yet and wondered what the items meant. When she asked, Danica screamed, "Get out of my room, you lesbian!"

Athena had heard the word on the playground and knew that it wasn't good. She protested blindly, knowing enough to say, "No, I'm not."

Danica grabbed her and shoved her out the door. "Go upstairs. If you touch my things, I'll kill you." Lejla heard the kerfuffle as she was coming through the toy room. "My room is completely off-limits, Theenie. You better *never* come in here." Danica punched Athena in the arm for good measure. Lejla stepped past them and closed her door as Athena shrank in pain. Danica came close to her face and said, "You are too a lesbian. You like girls. You're going to hell." Stepping back into her room, she slammed the door.

Athena clenched her jaw and her fists. She screamed to vent her frustration.

She went outside. The sun was setting and the field was lit up. Athena walked through the dirt to the trees and cut through the long grass to the field. She stood with her feet shoulder width apart and put her hands on her hips. She had a dilemma. She didn't like boys. She *did* like girls. Athena had wanted to see what Jimmy showed her and it truly excited her, but she preferred to play with Sarah. She didn't want to go to hell. But she could never imagine that God would send her there, not for any reason. She imagined the Earth spinning, flying through space, and thought about how tiny she was. Looking at the wispy clouds that crisscrossed the sky, she took deep, long breaths.

"I'm sorry if you don't love lesbians, God, because Dani says I'm one and I can't think it's not true. But anyone who paints such pretty colours in the sky can't be a mean person, and torturing me for eternity would be awful! And you should be sorry for that and stop it right now." Athena continued to stand. The wind was warm and picked up slightly, rustling the leaves, and the pink deepened until there was purple too. She took this as a sign because purple was her favourite colour. "Thank you, God."

Athena walked back to the house, dragging her feet through the chilly grass to clean the dust off. She went straight upstairs, and, although she tried to squelch the idea that she was in trouble, she couldn't hide from the guilt of knowing the truth and slept fitfully for two nights. During the day, life seemed settled. The school bus ride, the easy, boring lessons until recess and then home again. Athena saw herself fitting in and getting along like everyone else. But when the night came, fear took over. She pictured being shunned and hated. Even God would hate her. She tried to think of liking boys better, but she couldn't.

The third night, Athena writhed in physical pain from the mental torture. She jumped out of bed and ran to the kitchen, where her mama was cleaning and stacking dishes.

"What is it?" Mama's voice was soft, and in the peach glow of the kitchen light, Athena almost fell at her feet.

"Oh my God, Mama! You would still love me, right? Would you still love me?" Athena clamped her hands around her mama's waist and shut her eyes tightly.

"What are you talking about, Athena?" Mama waited for a response.

Athena moved away from her mama, tipped her head up, and looked her straight in the eyes. "I'm a lesbian."

Mama's face contorted. "A lesbian?"

Athena crumpled back down.

"But you're only seven years old."

"But I like girls. I don't like boys."

"Hey!" Mama slapped her hand down on the counter. "I don't like that word, and I don't want to hear you say it again!"

Athena's heart imploded. What was Mama telling her?

"Do you understand me? You are *not* to say that word again. Where did you learn it?"

"Dani told me I'm a lesbian. And I am!" she confessed.

"No, you're not, and enough of that. Your sister doesn't know what she's talking about."

"But—"

"Enough, or I'm going to tell your tata."

Athena froze. From experience, she knew this was no idle threat.

"Now go to bed. I love you." Mama kissed her on the head and marched her out of the kitchen.

Athena prayed very hard to God to make her not a lesbian, or to consider being nice to lesbians if she really was one, just to be safe.

Chapter 23

"I got a call today from Ford's. They're hiring," Mama announced at dinner one night.

Tata put his fork down. "What about the twins?" His voice was quiet.

Athena listened intently. She wasn't sure if this was a good or a bad thing yet.

"I would be on the traffic team controlling parts. It's $36,000 a year plus benefits," Mama said.

Tata let out a long, slow whistle.

"There's a daycare, as they call it, next to the fire station and they take little ones for the whole day, from eight to three thirty, so I could pick them up by four."

"Hold on—let's just slow down a minute." Tata pushed his hand at Mama. "We gotta talk about this."

No one said anything.

"You would need a car." Tata was thinking, and then he picked up his fork, which cued everyone to start eating again.

"I think it would be great if Mama had a car because she'd be able to drive me to my skating lessons," Danica said emphatically.

Tata had missed a couple of lessons. With no bus service, there were no lessons if he didn't come home after work.

"We'd get a good deal on something with the employee discount we get now. We could finish paying everything off," Mama said.

Tata nodded and continued eating.

So Mama went back to work and the twins went to daycare.

New houses were being constructed on their street practically every day. The house next door was almost done. All the families had kids, and the girls liked finding out who was moving in.

Brenda and Bob Benton lived right next door to the Brkoviches. Athena didn't think that anyone could be more different.

They had two little boys. Brenda didn't work, so she made it her business to check in on the Brkovich children.

"Hi, ladies. What's all the noise about?" Brenda said one day.

Danica was chasing Lejla and they were hitting each other with hairbrushes, screaming about who took the other one's shirt. The scuffle had moved onto the front lawn. Athena's sisters stopped. Athena had been watching them go at each other.

"Where's your mother?"

Athena didn't like Mrs. Benton. The woman knew her mama worked but always acted like she'd forgotten.

"She's working, Mrs. Benton," Danica answered. She was out of breath and confused at the interruption.

"And who's watching you?"

"We're old enough to watch ourselves," Lejla retorted.

"*I'm* in charge," Danica said, directing her words at Lejla.

Athena didn't agree with Danica or Lejla being in charge of her. They fought and could hurt her as they'd already done plenty of times. Without anyone there to stop them, life had become a continuous battleground.

"Well, it looks to me like no one's in charge here. Go inside right now, please, and stop this fighting or I'm going to have to speak to your mother."

Danica and Lejla looked at each other and then at Athena. Mama didn't appreciate Mrs. Benton's help or advice. Mama always said it was normal for kids to fight and work out their differences.

Mrs. Benton followed them inside the foyer and saw their school bags. "Let's pick up your things, ladies, and get your homework out and finished. I'm sure there are lots of chores you could get started on for your mother."

"Yes, we will," Danica said picking up her bag. She turned and waited.

Mrs. Benton just stood there. It felt awkward.

"My mama said no one's allowed in the house," Athena said. She didn't like Mrs. Benton coming inside.

"Well, she means your friends and such. I have a key to your house that your mother gave me, girls, in case you get locked out, and she asked me to keep an eye on you. Heaven knows she's got her hands full."

Athena's blood boiled at the way Mrs. Benton talked about her mama. She only had two kids and one car; they had five kids and two cars. Who was going to pay for that? Mama worked so they could have nice things.

"Well, aren't you going to go do your homework?" Mrs. Benton asked Athena.

"I don't have any. I'm going to lock the door behind you when you leave."

Mrs. Benton frowned and sighed and then walked away.

***

Mama got up before sunrise. She made dinner for later that night, and lunches for everyone. If you had notes or permission slips that needed signing, they would be with your lunch on the counter. Danica insisted on a brown paper bag, which she threw away each time. Athena didn't get that—when you had a lunch box, it was so silly to get a new bag out and then throw it away.

"Lunch boxes are for queers," Danica said. It wasn't long before Lejla agreed. Still, Athena held on to hers.

Chapter 24

The summer found Danica and Lejla biking away from Athena as fast as they could.

"She's a baby, Mom," Danica complained. She had taken to not calling her "Mama" anymore, and Lejla followed suit. Athena didn't understand how they could just decide to change their mama's name all of a sudden.

"But I need you girls to stay together and keep an eye on your sister." Mama was getting ready for work. The twins still went to daycare.

"She can't keep up on her bike."

"Then ride slower. And you're not allowed to go past the park, so what does it matter?"

Danica and Lejla looked at each other. Athena knew it would be the same sort of day as always, struggling to keep up to her big sisters, only to catch the tail end of their laughter as they sped away out of sight.

Mama and Tata went to work, and the girls were left to start their summer as they pleased. Athena walked to the pantry and searched for the red box of cake mix. She got a bowl and the electric beater from the drawer.

"You better not make that," Danica told her. "You're not allowed to use the oven."

"I'm not using the oven." Athena got two eggs, milk, and vegetable oil and started to prepare the chocolate cake as she had seen her mama do. She tapped the beater on the side of the bowl. Her mouth was watering. Athena got a spoon.

"Are you just going to eat *that*?" Lejla asked.

Athena nodded.

"You'll get sick," Danica warned.

"Do you want some?"

Both said yes, so Athena doled out the batter into the stackable soup bowls that Mama had bought at a craft fair. They all agreed it was delicious.

"We're going to bike to the big park," Danica said.

"Mama said you have to stay with me," Athena replied.

"Well, you're too little to go on the road."

"You're not supposed to go outside our loop."

"You're not going to say anything about it," Lejla informed Athena.

"Find someone around here to play with," Danica told her, getting her tennis shoes on. "We're going with the Fitzsimmons brothers."

"You're just too small, Theenie," Lejla said, trying to comfort her. "We're going to the store. I'll bring you some candy."

"Go to the park. There will be lots of kids to play with," Danica said.

Athena recalled how she had tried to keep up with her sisters on her bike, but there was no way. In her mind, she could still hear her own desperate plea, *Wait for meee!* Athena's heart was broken as she cried out. She had never felt sorrier for herself. She didn't care to relive the experience.

She said nothing and went to the garage to see her sisters off. As they turned out of the driveway, Lejla looked back at her and circled around. Athena's heart rose for an instant, but Lejla just yelled, "Close the garage door, Theenie, if you go anywhere," and then rode off with Danica. Athena was alone. She pressed the garage door button and watched it come down, contemplating what to do with herself.

Athena walked out the back door in her bare feet to the farmer's field. It was going to be hot. The sky was clear, cloudless, and a perfect blue. There was always a good chance of playing block hide-and-seek after dinner once it was cooler.

For now, she was content with being an orphaned Indian princess with no food or shelter. Survival was key. She picked some plants as she strolled, deciding which magical, medicinal qualities each possessed. She approached the trees. Athena made her way into the thicket after checking to see if anyone had seen her. No one was around.

The spaces under the brambles were just big enough for her to duck under. As she penetrated the undergrowth, the gurgling of water became more obvious. A rivulet ran the length of the end of this field and it burbled over the constant whirring of grey-green grasshoppers, by now quite large and numerous. They could jump as high as Athena was tall.

After locating her felled log, she saw the small clearing she had swept clean yesterday. It was the dirt floor of her house. Right next to her was a miniature waterfall. The area was shady and suitably cool, protecting her from the scorching sun. She hoped that her true love, her Indian brave, would find them a buffalo and hurry home. In the meantime, she would prepare. Today would be a working day.

Athena studied the light patterns as the sun's rays infiltrated her small camp. She found a long stick and stripped the small buds and twigs from it. It had a smooth curve and felt like an ideal fishing rod. After that, she dug up soil from the farmer's field and mixed it with scoops of water from the river, mashing it into clay. She moulded it into three little cups she could also use as bowls, and made two small plates. She left them out in the sun to dry and washed her hands as best she could. Black lines were under her fingernails. In her private enclave, the smell of the earth was pungent.

The bugs weren't bad, so Athena lay back on the ground and studied the treetops. They were almost motionless, but the leaves still danced from the trees breathing in and out. Athena breathed in and out with them, blowing gently and feeling the leaves move each time she exhaled. She was like the wind. She was like God, moving the leaves and bringing the birds to sing for her. She felt very content. But the "wheat" she'd harvested from the long grasses and the purple clover she had picked and sucked the nectar from didn't satisfy her growling belly. Athena decided she would give herself permission to go to her own house for a quick break, and that it wasn't really cheating.

As she walked back, she felt her toes squish into a cement-like mud. She crouched down and inspected this novelty. It could be very useful, although it was too wet to form into cups. Maybe she could use it like plaster.

Athena ran back to the big house to get a real bowl. She was caked with dirt up to her knees. Her hands were also covered. It was a dilemma. She would go quickly. She turned the back door handle, which took two hands since it was slippery with her mud and sweat. She traipsed up the stairs, hopping into the kitchen on her tippy toes to minimize the footprints. She got a mixing bowl and took two large serving spoons as well. When she had just stepped outside, she thought perhaps a towel could serve as a blanket, keeping the ants away from her on the ground. She ran back in and went as directly as possible to the small linen closet and took the first towel she saw. She was having a very successful mission!

About to venture back out, she realized she hadn't fed herself. Athena set her finds down on the picnic table and ran back in. She poured herself a cold glass of milk and drank it while standing in front of the fridge, and then another.

She grabbed two Twinkies from the box on the counter and an orange from the fruit bin.

The day was shaping up handsomely. She spent the afternoon scooping the thick plaster-like mud into the bowl, carrying it to her fortress, and reinforcing the dishes she was making. She made markings with the mud along the path that entered the trees. She used the fallen log as a table and entertained her imaginary tribe, including the chief, who thought her especially notable and esteemed.

Athena ate the Twinkies slowly. She made the mistake of removing the plastic wrap from the first one and then getting dirt in her teeth. She didn't care at all for the grittiness and spat hard to clear it out. She knew not to drink the water from the ditch. She resolved to open the second one as carefully as she could and leave the wrapper on. This worked much better.

Athena lay down on the towel she spread out as her bed. She gathered leaves and after shaking them free of big bugs, she arranged them like a pillow. She watched some ants surround the discarded, dirty Twinkie. It was mesmerizing to watch them use their antennas and lift the giant cake and take it away. Athena thought she was like an ant in lots of ways. She closed her eyes and fell asleep.

It was cooler when she awoke. The street lights weren't on, but surely everyone would be wondering where she was, so she hurried back home. The garage was open and Mama's car was in the driveway. Danica and Lejla's bikes lay flat in the garage amid their other toys. Athena ran in.

Mama appeared at the door to the kitchen, looking dismayed. "You left a big mess with all your dirt! Get outside this instant! Dani, go wash your sister off with the hose."

"Where did you go to, Theenie?" Danica asked.

Athena didn't want to tell her sister. It was her very own place.

"You're in trouble because you brought all kinds of mud into the house." Danica pointed the spray at Athena's legs and had to turn it up to the hard stream to chisel the layers of dried mud off her hands and feet.

Athena wondered if anyone had missed her.

"You're not allowed to just go away for the whole day," Danica said.

"I didn't. You left me, so I was just playing."

"Well, you have to play at the park from now on, Mom said, because there's grass there. She said she's telling Tata." Danica's eyes narrowed and she looked away.

Athena's heart started pounding before the negotiations began.

"Please, please, Mama." She had washed herself completely and even scrubbed under her nails with a small hard brush from under the sink. "Please don't tell Tata. I promise. I promise."

Mama didn't look at her.

Athena felt desperate to reach her. If only she could get her mama to look at her, she would forgive her. "I won't do it again, Mama, I swear." Athena was holding her mother's leg, stroking her, trying to make her understand.

When Tata came in, he put his briefcase down and changed out of his shirt and tie. When he came into the kitchen, he reached for the cigarettes and ashtray on top of the fridge. It was then that Mama informed him. The conversation happened above Athena's head, as though she wasn't there.

Athena clung to her mama's waist. She grabbed for the apron strings but her mama's hands pried her away.

Tata lifted her as though she weighed nothing and carried her to her room. "Is that what you're gonna do? Is that the way you're gonna treat this house?"

It was in between questions full of anger that he brought the belt down on her. She knew better than to try to run away from him. Lejla did that and always got it worse.

When he was done, he said, "We don't work hard so you can ruin things. Now stop that crying. I didn't like doing that, but you have to learn to take care of this house. Stop it."

Athena buried her face in her pillow to stifle the sobs. She wished she knew how to stop them.

Chapter 25

The houses on her street were going up in quick succession. "Who's moving in" and what they were like became the daily topic of conversation. What the parents did for a living and if they had any kids. Athena listened and understood that this was a matter of importance to others. It would have been more impressive to say her tata was a doctor and her mama a nurse, but if this were true, they would be living in one of the mansions on the drive and not in their subdivision. She didn't understand why people thought it mattered, because there was a world beyond the drive in Windsor, Ontario, with bigger mansions where movie stars and rock stars lived. People with bigger lives than theirs. But all the people she knew thought that the circle they were in and their place in it mattered more than anything.

Four doors down was an orange brick bungalow. A single father lived there with two daughters. The eldest was Athena's age. Her name was Joelle and her younger sister was Julie. The Gilchrist girls were odd for the obvious reason that they didn't have a mother. Joelle was also unattractive and quiet.

"Hey, ugly," a boy at the bus stop said to Joelle as she waited.

Athena's heart went out to her, but she did not intervene.

Walking up on her toes, Joelle had a strange gait. Her lips never seemed to close and her eyes drooped down. Her hair, parted down the middle, was thin and greasy. Joelle was introduced in Athena's class. Her clothes weren't new or stylish. She often wore the same brown gabardine pants and a yellow sweater that had pilled with use.

Despite Joelle's efforts to remain out of range, the firing squad closed in as Athena watched.

"Hey, dork!" Boys approached Joelle at the stop, pelting her with rocks.

"Stop it or I'm going to tell the teacher," she retorted, surprisingly vocal.

Tattling was the proof required to convict you of being the dork they said you were. *You could never admit weakness*, Athena thought, *or they would come at you like hyenas*. There was a critical part missing in Joelle; she was too nice.

After stepping off the school bus, four boys followed Joelle. They scooped up pebbles from the ground and tossed them at Joelle's back while taunting her with questions.

"Where's your mom?"

"Did she leave you because you're so ugly?"

"Did she kill herself after she saw you?"

Athena was seized by a sense of compassion and ran up beside Joelle to defend her. "Leave her alone."

"Says who? Hey, the mutt has a friend! It's a dog pack!"

Athena turned back and barked viciously, acting like a rabid dog. The kids jumped back in shock.

"Wow, what the hell is wrong with you?"

"You *are* a dog!"

"Back off or I'll bite you!"

"You're a bona fide freak. A total dog! Woof, woof. Doggie want a bone?" The leader grabbed his crotch as he laughed, and his friends held out their palms. "Gimme five." He slapped their hands in celebration. As he brought his hand up, Athena lunged and sank her teeth into the fleshy part. He yelped and reeled back, trying to separate his hand from Athena's teeth.

Danica and Lejla were walking too far behind to see what was happening but approached quickly as a crowd gathered.

"What's wrong with your sister? She's an actual *dog*! She bit me!" said one of the boys.

Athena just barked and growled, and Joelle walked home without further aggravation.

When they got home, Lejla punched Athena in the arm as hard as she could. "Don't act like that! What's wrong with you? Do you want everyone to think you're a mental case?"

"But I *am* a mental case," admitted Athena, rubbing her arm.

"You don't want anyone to know, though, you idiot."

***

During school, Athena became more and more obsessed with dirty Jimmy. She studied the repulsion that he and Joelle were met with. It intrigued and excited her in a way she had no explanation for. Jimmy picked his nose and ate it in plain sight, making people gag openly. Joelle had dandruff the size of cornflakes in her hair, which made Athena's skin crawl. But apart from these obvious defects, they both clearly rejected the norm that insisted on people trying to belong, and freedom from conforming to this expectation was perhaps what Athena desired most. They were wrong as people.

In Sunday School every week, Athena would cross herself and pray to God to remove the dirty fantasies she had about seeing Jimmy's wiener again. But the thought of it brought such excitement that she could only stop thinking about it temporarily, and she decided that maybe going to church more than once a week would be helpful. When she asked Mama about doing this, she was told absolutely not.

It was a Wednesday after school when Athena ran up beside Joelle and asked if she wanted to play together. Joelle appeared a bit dumbstruck, or just dumb—Athena wasn't sure which and didn't care. She had a plan.

"I'll come to your house," Athena said.

"We're not allowed to have any friends over when my dad's not home. He doesn't get home till after five."

"He won't mind me. We won't make a mess."

Julie was two years younger and not touched like her sister. She squinted at Athena, obviously not trusting her, but she gave Athena the benefit of the doubt, as she had defended Joelle.

"We don't have any snacks or anything," Joelle said.

They entered the house. It looked so different from her own. The walls were all beige and there were no pictures hanging on the walls. It looked empty, as though they had just moved in, but they had been there for almost a year.

"Where's all your stuff?" Athena asked.

"What do you mean?"

"I mean, where's all your house stuff? Don't you guys have any pictures or anything?"

Joelle and Julie just looked at each other and shrugged.

"This is the fourth house we've lived in in four years. We get a new house, and then when we just start getting used to it, we move again. This is as lived-in as it gets," said Joelle.

English, Athena thought. She toured the house. Joelle's bedroom was one of three upstairs and had a bathroom. A big TV room downstairs was visible from the main-floor kitchen. The house wasn't as big or as nice as her house. Athena understood what her tata was trying to protect.

The next day she caught up with Joelle just as she was going into her house, fumbling with the key in the lock.

"Hey, do you want to play?" Athena asked.

Joelle hesitated, uncertain of something, but then agreed.

"I'm going to drop my lunch box at home and I'll be back."

Athena returned with her agenda in mind and put her plan in motion. "No, Julie can't play with us," she insisted. Athena wanted to play in Joelle's room, but with the door closed.

"You're not allowed to have friends over, Joelle. I'm telling if you don't open this," Julie called through the door.

Joelle looked conflicted, but Athena reassured her that everything was okay. Athena ignored her at school and didn't let her know that she didn't want other kids to know they were friends. Danica and Lejla had spelled out the social suicide that being friends with Joelle represented.

The next week, on Thursday, Athena hopped up onto Joelle's porch and rang the doorbell.

Joelle answered. "Yes?"

"Do you want to play?"

"Um . . ." She looked over her shoulder. "Okay, but my dad got mad at me for having you over. My sister told on me."

"Where's Julie now?"

"She's at soccer."

Athena walked in past Joelle. "I'll only stay a bit. Come on, let's go to your room."

The situation was murky to Athena. She knew that what she wanted to do was wrong, but she also sensed that Joelle would play doctor with her if she approached it strictly as a game. "Let's say you're the patient and I'm the doctor," she'd say. That would open things up.

The doctor's name was Jimmy, and he would have the patient lie down and take off their shirt and eventually everything else so they could be examined. "Jimmy" sprinkled talcum powder on the patient and rubbed it in. The patient was asked questions like "Where does it hurt?" or told by the doctor that they knew it didn't feel right but they had no choice but to check. This became a routine every Thursday for six weeks straight, with Joelle learning quickly from Athena how to be Jimmy. Athena would leave brimming with energy, amazed at the electricity in her body. At night, however, the demons would lay hold of her psyche and torture her with visions of eternal damnation.

One Thursday, as Athena lay on Joelle's single bed on the bedspread, the front door opened and her father yelled up to her, "Joelle? Do you have a friend over?"

Athena leaped off the bed and grabbed her T-shirt and pants from the floor and jumped into the closet. By slowing down time with her mind, she was able to wriggle into her clothes in time. She heard the pounding steps of Joelle's father as he crossed the kitchen and came up the stairs. He opened the bedroom door and then the closet door. Athena stood up, fully clothed.

"You have to go now," Joelle explained, her father looking from her to Athena.

Athena didn't particularly like Joelle. She found her stupid and disgusting, just like Jimmy. But she was inexplicably attracted to her depraved game. She was more confused than ever about whether or not she was a lesbian, because even though she fooled around with Joelle, she thought of Jimmy when she did it. Athena knew better than to ask anyone about it.

Athena never went back and Joelle moved before Christmas. Suddenly, the lessons she had been learning about sinners and suffering had more meaning.

***

Athena's shame and guilt fell completely away when Niko was in church. The feeling she had explored with Joelle exploded inside of her when he sat down next to her.

"Hey, Theenie. Long time no see."

Athena's cheeks flushed as the blood coursed through her body. "Yeah. Did you miss me?"

"No, but I know *you* missed me."

"Ha, what's there to miss?"

He grinned because he knew he was cute. He had all the girls' attention. "What's with your hair? Mine's longer than yours," he said, laughing.

"My mama won't let me have long hair."

"That's messed up."

Athena vowed to grow her hair long and never cut it short again. "Well, your teeth are messed up. At least my hair will grow."

Niko had big spaces between his front teeth. He covered his mouth with his hand; she'd hit a sore spot. "My mom says that's how it should be. They'll close when my big teeth grow in. Yours are as big as rabbit teeth."

"I'll need braces," she said.

"Loser." He was still grinning.

"Except you love this loser," she said, and he didn't deny it.

"Niko, where have you been? I was looking for you." His dad came up in a rush.

Niko answered back with bravado, "Relax, Dad."

His father smacked him across the head.

Athena didn't move.

"Don't you talk to me like that," his dad said.

Niko turned from Athena, embarrassed. His eyes were rimmed with tears that didn't spill over. As he left with his dad, Athena desired him all the more.

Chapter 26

Christmas was coming and prosperity was in the air. People were buying cars and the economy was booming, Tata said. It didn't seem to matter in Detroit; all the news channels reported on were daily murders or rapes.

"Will they come here and kill us too?" Athena asked.

"No. There's a border. Americans have guns and we don't. That's why it's safer here," Mama reassured her.

It still made Athena worry. As she watched the six o'clock news, she asked, "Why does the newscaster talk like we do, but the other coloured people in the interview sound so different?"

"It's because they're uneducated. Just listen to them. They're stupid, and then they give 'em guns and it makes them dangerous. They could be nice to your face, but put them in a group and they'll tear you to pieces," Tata said.

Athena took this in. There was only one coloured boy in Athena's school. There had been more at her last school but not as many as in Detroit, even though only a river separated them. It seemed safe to Athena because it wasn't the kind of river you could swim across.

***

The Christmas tree was real and made the house smell like the woods. Athena sat in the family room, helping Mama with all the laundry and watching the lights blink. A brick mantel spanned the length of the family room. Tata built a fire in it all the nights he came home after work.

Even though Mama worked and made money, Tata still came home drunk and yelled in her face that she didn't make as much as he did and she was simply stupid. Ignorant. A moron. She didn't know nothin'. Athena would lie in bed in turmoil, praying for his death or for Mama to leave him and take them far away. "She didn't know nothin'" meant she did know something, Athena always wanted to tell him, but you couldn't tell him anything. She bargained with God on the nights when the keys hit the counter. "If you make my tata die, I'll go to hell in his place." She would cry, wondering if she was even a good enough person to go to heaven in the first place, but she knew that God probably had a soft spot in His heart for children. Jesus loved the little children—red, yellow, black, or white. Athena tried to imagine children actually being these colours, like her crayons. Sometimes nothing made sense.

Mama's job helped to pay the bills but she didn't have any say—not in ways that mattered to Athena. Mama did decide how to spend money on the children, but Danica and Lejla were quickly developing strong opinions about what was and wasn't acceptable as far as what they could be seen wearing.

"They have to be *real* Jordache, Mom!" Danica insisted one day.

Athena found it both amusing and bewildering that anyone would forgo toys at Christmas for boring clothes, and she said so.

"What do you know? Look how you dress—like a welly."

"She makes people on welfare look good," Lejla added.

Athena didn't care at all. She loved her sweatpants and T-shirts. "Jeans pinch you."

"Shut up and go sit over there. I'm doing my nails."

Danica had taken to polishing her nails every other day, it seemed. Because they were always drying, she couldn't help out with things like folding laundry or other chores that had to be done constantly, Athena noticed. Danica was pretty, with shoulder-length black hair that she styled with a curling iron she'd gotten for her birthday. Lejla was always asking to borrow it, but Danica would have a fit if she touched it. Things often came to blows when Lejla snuck it out of her room.

"I hope I get my own for Christmas," Lejla said.

Athena knew that Lejla would get it because Mama always got her everything—to make up for everything else. The curling iron would show Lejla they loved her. Athena couldn't think of anything she really wanted to ask for. Mama always took them shopping the day after one of Tata's angry nights to buy something for them. Athena wanted to confront her mama to tell her that this never worked, but Danica and Lejla always fell for this kind of trick.

Athena's sisters mocked her in the stores: "Aren't you the little martyr? Just get something."

"But if we don't spend any money—"

"Shut up and just get some something like a normal person," one of them would reply.

Athena just couldn't understand the lack of logic and foresight. Even Mama got annoyed with her sometimes if she refused to pick anything out.

"Are you actually Santa Claus, Mama?" Athena asked one day, seeing her carry two extra-large department store bags into the laundry room. Mama had given specific instructions that no one was allowed to go in there.

"Of course she is, you imbecile. There's no such thing as Santa," Danica told her. "For someone so smart, you're really stupid."

When Christmas Day rolled around, there were a hundred presents around and under the tree. The stockings, attached to the mantel, were overflowing. Presents for everyone. Tata got down on his hands and knees and pulled out one present at a time, reading the name of the recipient and gift-giver. *To Mitzi, love Mrs. Claus. To Lejla, love Santa. To Danica, love Rudolph.* Athena waited until her name was called. She didn't rip the paper off too quickly and when she was finished she sat patiently, waiting for another present. Danica and Lejla had made long lists of the things they wanted, and it had been easy for Mama to fulfill their wishes. Athena's wishes were different. Athena wished her mother wouldn't spend any more money so Tata wouldn't yell about things, then feel bad and tell her to spend money to fix it. So when Mama had asked what she wanted, she'd answered, "Nothing."

But now, at Christmas, Athena couldn't understand how her present count was so much less than her sisters'. She opened the gifts in front of her, mustering a show of appreciation so as not to make her mama feel bad, but inside she was hurt and disappointed.

Athena lay in bed wondering whether or not she was a good person, like Jesus. Supposedly, he never sinned, but it seemed to Athena that everything was a sin; being born was supposed to be a sin. Athena didn't accept this, but maybe that was her problem. She was ungrateful. She reasoned that to be the best daughter and sister she could be, she should try harder to be a good person. The next morning she asked if she could fast for Serbian Christmas.

The Orthodox faith required you to fast and go to confession before receiving Communion. The bread was the actual body of Christ. The wine was his blood. Athena wasn't sure if she should believe this, so she asked her church friends if this was true.

"Yes, of course. The bread? It's chewy like meat. And the blood is a bit sticky, but you kind of choke it down. It's Jesus, after all." Katja chuckled at Athena's gullible expression.

"No, not actually, but in theory," Roxana explained.

Kat and Roxy were her Sunday School friends. Their parents went to church, but in a different way from Athena's parents. One, both their parents spoke Serbian, so they understood the fifteen-minute speech the priest gave every week. Two, their families observed all the customs without fail and without help. Athena's family went to her kuma's and she did everything. Mama liked helping with the traditions, but she didn't run things.

Kat was reassuring. "You don't have to say anything when you go up, either. The priest asks you to think of whatever you did wrong and then asks if you're sorry."

"The worst is, you can't eat or drink anything on the morning you go," Roxy added.

"And you can't just go up. You have to have your head covered. Well, girls do." Kat rolled her eyes.

All these rules made Athena's nerves jangle. She didn't want to mess it up.

She followed the orders for a week and her mama did it with her, cooking especially for them. Nothing with meat or milk. Danica and Lejla were going to do it for only three days.

"Why would you do it longer?" they asked in unison.

"I want to."

They shook their heads and looked at each other.

It went pretty well the way Kat and Roxy said it would. Athena felt lighter and relieved, having apologized for her sins.

"Ah, Tilley. Look at dis one. Even she did the fast?" one of the ladies at church said after it was over.

Mama nodded. "They all did. Athena did it with me for a week."

"A whole veek? Tank God she's a good girl, eh?"

Mama beamed with pride.

Athena made note of this in her mind.

"You know, I always hope von o' you girls gonna marry von o' my boys."

Lots of the ladies in the church played matchmaker and talked about who should marry whom. Athena already knew who she would marry.

Chapter 27

The playground was frozen over, and snowball fights were the delight of all, in particular the boys with good throwing arms.

The children built walls from the snowpiles that came from clearing the parking areas. They sculpted them to look like fortresses. Generally, it was safer to stay behind these areas, away from the school. Walking the tarmac was like being a lone gazelle on the African plains.

Athena wasn't sure if it was the cries of "Get Jimmy" that started it. Perhaps he was hoping that a teacher on yard duty would come to his aid, but he was unwisely positioned between the two bunkers, taking snowballs from every angle. With an increasing level of concern, Athena watched the onslaught unfold. He was wearing jeans, had no hat, and didn't own a proper winter coat. His ears were already red when an icy ball exploded onto one of them. Athena winced. The blow only excited his attackers' bloodthirsty hunger and they cried, "Get him! Get him!" They launched all the snowballs in reserve, and at first he crouched, then fell and covered his head and face with his thinly clothed arms and bare hands.

Athena's pity rose as he went down. They were crucifying him. She ran into the fray and stood in front of him, turning and raising her hands. "Stop!" she screamed, "Stop it!" She held up her hands and everyone stopped. "This isn't nice. He didn't do anything. Now stop it!"

Athena felt all-powerful and elated that she was taking a stance for justice and protecting an unfortunate soul. She was about to turn and tell Jimmy it was okay when a voice to her right yelled, "Get her!" It was Jimmy. He had jumped up and run to the other side.

Almost as quickly as the snowballs had stopped at her command, Athena collapsed from the incoming missiles. She sheltered her face and head from the heavy bombs. Luckily, she was wearing her snowmobile suit; the padding afforded some protection.

The bell rang and everyone shouted, "Athena loves Jimmy! Theenie and Jimmy sitting in a tree . . ."

Athena rose like a phoenix from the ashes when she saw Jimmy looking at her. She didn't feel pity. She understood why he had been ostracized and picked on. He was unworthy. She hated him and it soothed her.

Athena lay in bed that night reviewing this betrayal in her mind. How had Jesus felt when Judas turned him in? It probably hurt as much as having a thorny crown pushed onto you. Like her, Jesus didn't cry, but he loved his enemies. This she couldn't understand.

The shouting in the kitchen was increasing in volume and there were loud bangs, that sounded like her brother's cap gun going off, when her tata slammed the cupboard doors. Over and over.

Athena didn't want to feel anything anymore. She imagined her heart and soul extending into space and going on forever into the universe. She pictured herself as a speck of dust, or something even less, on giant planet Earth, spinning so fast yet not being flung off, moving in the blackness of space. Then an enormous coldness, weightless and emotionless, filled her chest. It was her soul staring into an abyss. This was a place she had discovered where she was something else, where her feelings ceased to bother her and thoughts of murdering her tata or Jimmy seemed understandable and even justifiable. Her toes were curled over the edge of this abyss as if she were on a diving board, about to spring. She looked down past her toes into nothing. She could jump, freeing herself, and never feel pain again. She could be the judge and decide what was right and punish those who did wrong. She could make them pay. In this space there was no remorse, no guilt, no shame, no conscience, no crying. Cruelty lived there. This was the space of the Nazis, who believed that they were the ones to decide who lived and who died. Or slave owners who believed they were better than the slaves and could torture and punish those who were weak. Weakness deserved to be punished.

Athena held her breath. She could feel the frozen black abyss in front of her. She was thinking about entering it. If she decided to, it would lead to awful repercussions. She would be alone, but she would stop caring about it. She would hurt others but wouldn't feel hurt. Athena lay there waiting, contemplating.

Mitzi's small hand reached out and landed on her forearm as she noiselessly rolled over. Athena looked down. The glow of the hall light coming through the crack in their bedroom door was enough for her to see in the dark. She lifted her sister's tiny hand and inspected the perfect little fingernail on her baby finger. She could see the teeny lines across the knuckles and feel her soft, angelic palm. She turned her hand over, raised it to her mouth, and kissed it gently. Jumping into that abyss would mean rejecting everyone, even little Mitzi. Athena turned to face her, whose deep breathing soothed her, and she kissed her tiny fingers over and over. Athena wept because she didn't want to be able to stop crying. It meant not feeling anything. Even this deep love for her beautiful little sister. She decided she would never stop loving others, no matter how they hurt her. This was her choice. She would love.

***

There were no sidewalks in their subdivision. Wide V-shaped gutters ran down both sides of the asphalt pavement. As soon as Athena stepped off the bus, she wanted to see how quickly she could get all the way home without cutting through the park. *One, two, three—one, two, three. Right, left, right—left, right, left.* Switching banks of the gutter and listening to the sound of her feet against her breathing gave Athena comfort. She used the technique to transition from school to home in a way she imagined was like time travel or going through a space portal.

"Why do you go running off instead of just walking home normally?" Lejla asked as Athena came up the driveway, breathing heavily from her run.

"What do you mean?"

"I mean, everyone walks home, and even if you run, you run all the way around the park. It's weird. You can't be like that when you're at the big school." In a little less than two years, Athena would change schools again and be with Danica.

"Yeah, you're not going to be allowed to be such a weirdo. You'll have to grow up," Danica added as she walked past them up the stairs to the kitchen.

Athena followed her and slid into the bench seat and said, "I don't want to grow up."

"But you will, and you don't want to be some freaky loser with no friends," Danica said.

Lejla was easily the most popular girl in school. People always had the same reaction—astonishment—when they found out that Athena was her sister.

Lejla seemed to belong to the world of other normal people who had friends and boyfriends. She was allowed to go to sleepovers at friends' places or go to the movies with them. Athena's time was allotted to watching Mitzi or Max or helping with chores.

"I like being weird."

Athena knew how to goad her sisters, or anyone, really. It had to do with playing on their biggest fear, which had to do with impressing their friends. Being embarrassed would be their worst nightmare. This was the only weapon Athena had against them.

"Well, you better not be like this when you're in our school or we're going to tell Mom and Dad," Danica said.

"You mean Mama and Tata? You're too grown up to call them by their names?"

"Their names are Tiljana and Dragan, you idiot."

Athena was pleased with herself. Danica was the easiest to rile. She belonged to her circle of friends but didn't command them the way Lejla did. It was important that Lejla like you. Because Athena would do anything for her, Lejla was usually nice to her.

Athena lifted the hood on her sweatshirt over her head and tucked the fabric behind her ears as she tightened the strings.

Danica, who was making a snack, looked over at her and said, "That's what I'm saying. You're being retarded." And she smacked Athena in the head. Athena pointlessly ducked, laughing.

"If you're going to call me a we-tard, den I will be we-taw-ded." To her sister's chagrin, Athena crumpled her hands up in front of her chest and crossed her eyes.

"Ugh! Grow up!"

"No thank you" came Athena's response.

Chapter 28

The sun had melted the snow, and spring was knocking. The field was greening. When the bell rang, Athena punched the door handle to release her from another nondescript day of school and ran straight for the dandelions.

She dropped down on the grass and stretched her body long. Her sisters weren't around, and she didn't care what anyone thought. She started rolling like a log through the field, feeling the sun hit the back of her neck and then her face. She could smell the earthy freshness. She felt the wind pass over her, and the heat from the ground warmed her whole body, which moved as though it had an internal motor. She came to a stop on her back and, placing her hands over her heart, felt it pounding. Athena closed her eyes. The inside of her eyelids brightened to an orange red. She could see the capillaries, even the individual blood cells moving, coordinating with the beating of her heart. She was alive and unstoppable. Her body was healthy and perfect. She ran her hands from her collarbone to her hips and revelled in her flat strong chest.

Athena didn't want to grow up. Adults were hypocritical liars who weren't the experts they claimed to be. They were careless with the feelings of others, mean and manipulative. Remaining young was wise, and she told her body to stay as it was. "Please, God, don't let me grow boobs," she said.

Athena squinted as she sent her words up so the light stretched into white lines. She pressed her hands into the grass and clover so it was in between her fingers, then closed them and pulled up the plants. She felt at one with every living blade of grass. She was so much smaller than everything in the universe.

When the bell rang again, Athena jumped up. Her vision turned fuzzy and black and she felt dizzy. Steadying herself, she let her eyes adjust to being vertical and waited for the colours to reappear. Then she sprinted to catch up as the backs of all the children disappeared inside. She was covered in yellow splotches of dandelion pollen. Laughing, Athena threw her head back and skipped the rest of the way to the small classroom.

***

"Forty days?" Mama paused to think. "No, I don't think that's a good idea, Theenie."

"Mama, I can do it. I want to."

"You are so weird," Lejla said. She shook her head and her eyes met Danica's. They rolled them in unison.

Athena frowned. "I liked it last time and I want to see if I can do it."

Mama was making grilled cheese. As soon as she stacked the sandwiches on the plate in the middle of the table, they disappeared.

"You can't eat grilled cheese," Danica laughed, taking a big bite.

"Well, I guess there's no reason to stop you. I'm not going to do it for the whole time, though," said Mama.

Lent started, and Athena didn't ingest anything with meat or milk. She worked her very hardest to honour her mother and father, a commandment she struggled with. Athena reflected deeply on her past actions and motives. Although she had confessed, she couldn't bring herself to admit to God, even in her own mind, that she wasn't a completely disgusting pervert who was going to hell and should be ashamed of herself. This time she would admit it and fast the whole time so God would know she wasn't a liar.

"Haven't you cheated even a little?" Kat asked one day.

"I accidentally ate some bread without thinking about it, but I spat it out as soon as I realized."

"That's hard core. Well, I hope you make it. We're going to do a week," Roxy said.

"I'm doing a week too." Kat nodded.

"Did you stay up to watch it last Saturday?"

"I almost always fall asleep, but I need to make it at least to the news desk to see if she does Roseanne Roseannadanna."

"Oh my God, she is hilarious!"

Athena did her impression of Gilda Radner, substituting her own observations of people in church.

"Writing skits for SNL would be the ultimate."

"I don't think my mom would let me," Roxy said.

"I totally want to," Athena said. "But yeah, I'm pretty sure I have to be a doctor if I'm going to take any part in my family's Christmas."

"How would you marry Niko if you moved to NYC?" Kat asked.

"He'd go with me."

***

Athena read a chapter every night from her miniature copy of the New Testament. The pages were thin like crepe paper. When the last week of fasting rolled around, Athena felt good knowing that she didn't have to be ashamed. She would tell God that she thought about one boy in particular and had initiated things with her neighbour.

Athena's mind whirled. "God? What if after I'm done, I still like Niko? What if I still have impure thoughts? Because I know I will. What then? Does it mean it didn't work? Or I'm just not good?"

Athena went to confession with a heavy heart. It was the day before Communion, and because it was Easter, more people than usual were waiting to be seen by the priest. The nave was wide open and everyone waited in single file, like at the end of church, waiting to get bread. Her mama stood with her so Athena didn't feel alone. Her tata never went to confession that Athena knew of. When it was her turn, she stepped up. There was a new priest. His English wasn't very good. In his thick accent he asked if she'd had any impure thoughts.

"Yes," Athena replied.

"Like vat?"

Athena didn't reply because she was thinking of them.

"Please tell me."

Athena's head was bent over, and part of the ornate robe that hung like a vest down the priest's front was lifted over it. She raised her head. "Like some bad thoughts," she whispered, consumed with worry that someone could overhear.

"Porrrr-nographic toughts?"

It took all she had not to burst out laughing. The heavy rolling of the *r* transported her suddenly to the comedy sketch session with Kat and Roxy. She bent her head down. "Hmm," Athena said. "Yes."

The priest launched into a tirade of Serbian prayer that she didn't comprehend.

One more night with nothing to eat. When Sunday morning came, Athena dressed. She stood for the entire Divine Liturgy ceremony, and when the choir sang *amen*, she filed into the line to receive her redemption. When

Athena turned to step back into her place, she floated down, and the old babas commented on how radiant she looked.

She and Mama stopped at the bakery on the way home to pick up dinner rolls, salted half-moons, and chocolate-covered doughnuts. Overcome by a blissful peace, she helped her mama carry everything in. Standing in the kitchen, Athena looked blankly at her mama and said earnestly, "I felt like an angel coming off the altar today."

Mama smiled. "That's nice, Theenie. I'm glad it's done."

"I feel so joyful and rapturous."

Mama nodded as she unloaded the packages from the bakery.

"I love God so much. I know what I want to do, Mama. I want to love God. I want to be a nun." Athena spoke evenly and with complete sincerity.

"A nun?" Mama slammed the bun in her hand down on the counter. Her agreeableness was gone. "You're not going to be a nun!"

"But—"

"No! Not another word. You are definitely *not ever* going to be a nun."

Athena burst into tears, ran into her room and flung herself on the bed.

"A nun? What the hell?" The discussions floated down the hallway. Her tata, Danica, and Lejla had joined Mama.

Athena rolled out of bed again and joined them, unashamed of what she was asking. "Don't you want us to love God?"

"Yes, but in a normal way. Now cut it out," Mama said.

Athena's chin started to tremble.

"You're not goin' to church for a while, kid." Tata looked at Mama. "What are you doing here? See what I gotta take care of?"

Mama nodded in agreement. Danica and Lejla scowled.

"No fair. Why does Theenie get to miss it and we still have to go?" Lejla yelled.

"Because you need more church," Tata retorted.

Athena wondered if she should be ashamed of wanting to be a nun but decided against it. It was better to be weird if that meant she was real. She would rather be ashamed of wanting to be good than be ashamed because she was bad. It gave her a headache and Athena decided to forget it altogether; shame was overrated.

***

There was a soft tap at the door of the classroom.

"Class, may I have your attention? This is Miss Campbell, and she's going to be doing some vision testing. Not on everyone—she'll call some names. If you hear your name called, please go with her and then return to class when you're done, making as a little noise as possible.

"Kevin Rutherford?"

Kevin had thick glasses and sat near the front every year.

"So long, four-eyes," the boys called in the obvious send-off.

Athena sighed, bored. She had taken to reading the encyclopedia at home. Mama had bought a set from the Britannica salesman, who explained in their living room why a leather-bound set would be the highest-quality complete knowledge resource for her family and would last forever. The school had Funk & Wagnalls, and Athena found it curious that the two sets of encyclopedias held different and incomplete information. She was on *G* when the door opened and the fourth or fifth kid wandered back in.

"Athena Brkovich?" Athena's head popped up. She felt as if she had just been sprung from prison.

"Lucky duck," someone said enviously.

"Why did I get called? I don't wear glasses," Athena said as she and Miss Campbell headed down to the nurse's room.

"We got a school report. It says you were kicked in the left eye on the playground last year."

Athena had been learning how to do a Hong Kong phooey. You would hook one leg over the playground bar, which for her involved a lot of manoeuvring because she was short. You balanced on your back foot, and, grasping the bars on the sides, you hurled yourself over the bar, hopefully with enough momentum to make a complete revolution. Dana Merck could go around ten times without stopping. She was legendary.

Athena had just managed to get around. As she attempted it, a couple of boys who were roughhousing swung too close to the bar and someone's foot connected with her cheek. The yard lady insisted that Athena go inside and have the nurse check her eye. Athena inspected the bruise and rather enjoyed the attention. She'd always wanted the romantic look of a black eye, so she grabbed a number two soft pencil and added a little more shading. With pastels, she added purple highlights that faded into yellow and green spots that made it look real. It had been worth the effort, and now it was paying off again.

"We just want to check that you don't have any problems from that accident."

Athena's mind leaped. "And what if I do?"

"Well, you might need glasses or something. If the eye muscles are injured, you might need some exercises."

As it turned out, Athena couldn't read the big *E* on the wall with her left eye. She was legally blind in one eye. Miss Campbell got her assistant and then the school nurse to come and check. The concerned look on Miss Campbell's face satisfied Athena. She was sent back to class with a sealed note that she was instructed to deliver to her parents, which she did.

Promptly, Mama and Tata called her to the kitchen. "Sit down and read this," Mama instructed her.

Little Women was in front of her. Athena started to read.

"Now cover your right eye and read it, Theenie," Tata said.

"I can't," Athena said and looked up at them. Their faces contorted with a degree of agony. Athena found it comforting knowing that they cared that much.

"Whaddaya mean, you can't read it?" Tata's voice was rising.

At this, Athena's instincts kicked in, and she suddenly realized that if she told the truth, things would end badly. "I mean, I can't read it."

Tata ran his hand through his hair and went to the fridge to grab his cigarettes from the top. He lit one and took a long drag.

Mama started to cry, while Tata picked up the phone.

"Can I go now?" Athena asked.

Mama nodded as she blew her nose.

Over the course of the next two months Athena was taken to three eye specialists.

Athena's ear was pressed to the door of the examining room after being sent out on her own. She heard the third doctor confirm what the first two said. "There's nothing wrong with your daughter's eyesight. In fact, in both eyes, she has twenty-twenty vision."

Tata and Mama stood dumbstruck, but the doctor appeared to realize from Tata's stern expression that he'd better prescribe a solution. "Your daughter needs attention. Take this eye patch and place it over her right eye. Sit down every night for a week and have her strengthen her weak eye by reading to you. I guarantee you, she'll be cured, but if not, come see me. Please, whatever you do, do not punish her."

Athena made a full and miraculous recovery in just four days.

Chapter 29

"It's a much better deal if everyone goes in on it," Tata was explaining to Mama. "But then there you go—there's always one wise guy that's holdin' out and thinkin' they're gonna try and gyp you out of paying their fair share."

Mama just nodded as she pinched her homemade pierogies. Athena slid into the kitchen bench to listen as well.

"So it's the green one?" Mama asked. "I don't like the metal. I like that green one with the coating on it."

"Yeah, that's what the price is based on."

"The green what?" Athena asked.

"Fence," Mama said without looking at her.

"For what?" Athena tried to imagine what they could possibly need a fence for.

"For in between the yards," Tata explained.

Athena was perplexed. "Where? Like, in between the houses?"

"Yes. Like we had at our old house."

"No," Athena protested. "No! Why?"

"Well, 'cause it's nice to keep people from just going through everyone's yard."

"But that's the best," Athena cried. "What about hide-and-seek?"

"That's exactly the problem."

"Why is that a problem? You can't just put up fences. It'll cut up all the land. Who are you to block people or animals from walking where they want? You don't own the land."

Tata burst out laughing. "Oh, yes, I do. That's the point, my dear."

"But you can't own the Earth. You can't." Athena blinked, not understanding.

Tata looked back at her with the same puzzled expression. "Theenie, you don't understand. I *do* own the land. It's mine."

"That's impossible. You just tell yourself you do. Someone was here before you. It belongs to everyone. Fences are wrong."

Tata shook his head. "You'll learn, kid." He got up and left the room.

Athena pondered the fences going up. "Mama, you just can't. It's wrong."

"I don't even know what you mean. What don't you get? This is our house. Of course we can put up the fence if we want, and we're going to. So is everyone else."

Athena went to her room. She lay down on her bed, imagining the Earth belonging to all people. Someone just suddenly said, "This is mine. You can't come here or pass through." If fences were wrong, so were borders and countries. She went to her desk. She grabbed a piece of paper and wrote at the top, *Stop the fences! The Earth belongs to everyone. Blocking off the land prevents animals and people from moving freely and destroys the beauty of the world. Do not get a fence. Save our neighbourhood.* She embellished her message with birds, bees, and a big sun.

"I'll be back in a bit."

Athena jumped on her bike and rode to the public library.

"Can I get twenty copies of this, please?" Athena asked the librarian.

The woman looked it over and raised her eyebrows "I guess so. Is this for school or something?"

"No," Athena replied, "I'm trying to save my neighbourhood."

The woman made the copies and handed them to Athena. She put them in her knapsack and rode home, stopping at each house on her street to insert a flyer into the mailbox.

Mr. Gauvin was in his front yard as she plopped her bike down at the end of the driveway.

"What's this, Athena?" He took it from her and started reading it. "Do your mom and dad know you're doing this?" He was smiling.

"They know how I feel."

"Well, they may not appreciate you spreading your ideas. It's not up to you to get involved in other people's business."

"But that's the problem, Mr. Gauvin. It *is* my business. It's everyone's business. No one group has the right to make all these rules to keep others out. It's not fair."

Mr. Gauvin narrowed his eyes to read the paper again. "Quite an unusual take on things."

Athena shrugged. "I guess I should try to stop what I think is a bad thing, right?"

"A fence?" The man cocked his head to the side.

158

"It's not just a fence. It's about freedom."

The fences were installed two weeks later. Mr. Linquist, who lived three doors down, didn't want to pay for the fence, but his neighbours on both sides put theirs up. A couple of months later he just paid someone to fence the back.

Like all the other children, Athena learned how to climb the fences. The chain-link was handy for gaining your footing. Lots of the fences drooped near the poles, affected by the bigger, heavier kids who climbed them. Tata did yell at Athena about the flyer but it didn't warrant the belt. When the fences were installed she felt as if the world had moved further in the wrong direction.

***

"Everyone get in, please. Let's go," Mama said, trying to herd the children into the car to drive to dance group practice at the hall.

Tuesday nights worked best for the instructor. This didn't interfere with Danica's figure skating lessons on Wednesdays and Saturdays and kept them out of trouble, so Mama was all in favour.

Athena was already complaining. "I shouldn't be with the little kids, Mama. I'm nine now. I know all the steps. I'm a better dancer than Lejla or Danica."

"You wish," said Danica.

Athena made a face at her and received a slap to the back of her head.

"Hey, don't start, okay?" Mama yelled.

"She hit me," Athena protested.

"I don't care who started it. I just want everyone to be quiet. And I'm turning that off." Mama flipped the car radio off.

"Hey!" In the front seat, Lejla was busy searching for her station. "The new Journey song was playing, Mom! Turn that back on. It's my favourite song!"

"I don't want any noise right now. I want everyone to see how quiet you can all be."

"I don't want to be quiet," said Lejla quietly.

Danica flicked her hard in the back of the head. Lejla flung herself partially over the front seat and threw two punches, landing one on Danica's shoulder.

"Stop that!" Mama screamed. She was on the expressway and had swerved when Lejla jumped.

Danica kicked the back of her sister's seat.

"Just be quiet, please," Mama said.

"She's kicking the back of my seat," Lejla said.

"No, I'm not."

"Stop it, girls."

"Stop it right now, Dani, or I swear—"

"You swear what? Ooh, like, I'm scared."

"I'm pulling this car over," Mama announced.

Athena giggled at the absurdity of it all and the red-faced fighting of her sisters. "Fools."

Danica launched a punch directly at Athena's leg and gave her a painful charley horse.

"I hate you," Athena hissed at her.

"That's it. I'm telling your father. You heard me."

Max ducked his head behind the back seat and an odd silence filled the car.

Finally, Mama said, "If you don't want to listen, then you girls leave me no choice."

"I didn't do anything, Mama," Athena said.

Danica dug her nails into Athena's leg and, with her face, told her to be quiet. There was still a chance, her expression said. Athena knew to be quiet now.

When dance practice ended, Mama was sitting and laughing with Milka, one of the nicest ladies in the church.

"I'm just fed up with all of these people." Mama gestured to the kids as they approached.

Danica led with "But we love you, Mom," and threw her arms around her, kissing her.

Lejla added, "You're the best mom ever."

Athena didn't need to be prodded; she just hugged her mama from behind.

"Oh, stop, stop." Mama was beaming.

All of the other parents and children filing by took note of the beautiful Brkovich girls and their mom.

"Hey, Mom, can we get McDonald's for dinner? I'm starving," Lejla said.

"Oh, why not?" Mama rolled her eyes, and it was a victory.

"Here, wait, Theenie," Mama said, and she crumpled up the bag her fries had been in, put it in the blue Styrofoam container, and passed it over. "Just throw it out the window."

"Mama, they say we shouldn't litter."

"Well, I'm not going to keep it in the car, honey. They pick it up."

Athena pressed the button on her window to roll it down and squeezed the giant bag of garbage through it. Danica had already told her siblings at dance practice to be as quiet and polite as possible, and Mama was smiling. It had worked. Athena didn't want to press the issue about who exactly "they" were. Shoving a handful of salty fries into her mouth, she just watched the bag of garbage explode on the side of the road.

***

The dream was happening more and more frequently since she had fasted. Athena lay in bed, and, as she closed her eyes, a strange sensation, usually starting in her fingertips, filled and expanded them like air in a balloon. Her fingers would grow rapidly, and the growth would spread to her hand and then her body. Inside, her presence would recede into her centre. The blackness would be so great, she could hardly conceive of it, and eventually she was a speck of dust in the quicksand of space. This was the universe and all of time. She was at the centre of it, and it was inside herself. She was at the centre of her mind and her mind was the universe. How would she ever get out? Athena would always awaken paralyzed, lying straight and stiff as a board on her back, her eyelids snapping open.

"It's the scariest dream, Mama. I keep having it."

"Well, don't." Mama was making poached eggs for everyone.

"That's just it. I don't know how to stop it. I feel it starting and I get sucked into it. Like I'm going to get stuck in my mind and go mad."

"Well, you are a bit crazy," Mama said playfully. She placed the eggs on toast and set them in front of Athena. "Just lighten up, Theenie."

Athena watched her mama glide back to the stove, a beautiful smile on her face. She wanted more than anything to be like her, to be normal. Impersonating her mama, she smiled too.

Chapter 30

The grade four classroom was small, and all the windows were cracked open. Daydreaming of summertime, Athena had her head on her hand, almost ready to doze off. There were only thirty-three more school days. After the teacher finished reading *Tales of a Fourth Grade Nothing* to them, there wasn't anything to look forward to.

Then her friend Deedee walked past her desk and placed a small white envelope upon it with Athena's name printed on it. Athena sat straight up and watched Deedee's back as she continued up the row, delivering another four cards. Children were asking what it was so the teacher instructed them to put the cards away.

At home, Athena finally opened it and read, "Please come to a tenth birthday party for Deedee on Saturday."

"That's nice, Theenie. Do you want to go?" Mama asked.

"Yes." Athena lit up at the prospect.

"Okay, well, call and RSVP. Do you want me to call? You can do it. You know how to use the phone."

Athena picked up the receiver and dialed each number carefully. She heard two small clicks and then ringing.

"Hello?"

"Hi, Deedee. It's Athena."

"Hi."

"I just wanted to call and tell you that I'm coming to your birthday party."

"Okay, cool." There was silence.

"Okay, well, I'll see you at school tomorrow."

"Okay, bye."

Athena hung up, relieved, then said, "The phone is awkward. How are you supposed to talk to people when you can't even see them?"

Mama laughed and shook her head. "I wish I could get your sisters off the phone."

Athena puzzled at what Danica and Lejla were saying as they lay on the ground twirling the phone cord around their fingers. They had just seen the people they were talking to at school, so what was there to say? No matter how hard she tried, Athena couldn't understand the importance of who sat next to whom on the bus, or who wrote what on someone's locker. Who cared? Her sisters, apparently.

This was the only birthday party she'd been invited to. She had seen some invitations get passed out on other occasions but never received one.

"Get her the Rumours album. It has a few good songs on it," Lejla said.

"Who sings that?"

Lejla looked with concern at her sister. "Theenie, you're hopeless, you know? Fleetwood Mac."

Deedee lived in a house on Riverside Drive. Her backyard had grass and an actual sandy beach. They had a dog and a boat. Her mother seemed young, and Deedee had a younger brother and an older sister. Her dad had left them and her parents were divorced. This made Deedee sad. Athena wondered why her own dream of her parents divorcing hadn't come true but knew that there was hope. Deedee's mom and sister helped make a bonfire on the beach and they roasted marshmallows. Deedee's mom brought out the birthday cake she made, and her sister played "Happy Birthday" on her guitar while they all sang.

Deedee got three albums at her party but said, "Oh, I wanted this one," when she opened Athena's gift, even though it was the second copy.

Athena asked Deedee if her dad was mean and she said, "No, he's a great guy. I love my dad," and got choked up.

"Well, I just think now you don't have to worry about anyone hitting you."

"He would never hit me."

Athena didn't believe her, of course; you just weren't supposed to talk about things like that. Two of the other girls who'd been invited, Pam and Sherry, gave Athena dirty looks so she didn't ask about it anymore.

"I'm sorry about your dad," she told Deedee at the end of the party.

"It's okay. I guess I'm just sad because it's my birthday." She seemed tragic and lovely to Athena. She wished she was part of her family.

"Hey, Sherry and me are going to this summer camp, and we think it'd be fun if you came. We're going for two weeks." Deedee ran upstairs and came down with a brochure.

Sherry lived near Athena, one street over. "Yeah, we went last year. There's water sports like kayaking and water skiing. They have horseback riding. There's a hayride. Lots of stuff. And real cottages to stay in, four to a room. Ask your parents."

They were so excited, and although Athena felt special to be considered, she already knew her parents' answer. The camp was $500 for two weeks. Were they crazy? But Athena took the brochure and pretended it would be fine. "Yeah, sure. That would be so cool. I'll ask for sure."

"The deadline is June to sign up, but it gets filled up pretty quick," Deedee said.

When Athena broached the subject later, Mama said, "No, of course not, and don't even bring that up to Tata. That is way too expensive."

"I know, Mama."

Athena didn't want to make her mama feel bad, but the girls at school kept pressing her and she didn't want to make it seem as though she hadn't even tried. Besides, what if by some miraculous turn of events someone thought it best that she go?

***

Athena swore off shoes for the summer. Mostly, no one noticed or said anything. Occasionally, Mama would see her running down the street and shake her head, yelling, "Look out for glass!"

Athena had to carve out a new niche, as the fort she'd built last year had been claimed by three teenagers who were smoking.

"We don't see your name on it" was their answer when Athena told them from a safe distance that it belonged to her. "You gonna make us leave? You and what army?"

Athena suffered the loss but then readied herself for the adventure of finding an even better home for her and her thoughts. Across the street behind the Italian house was a row of trees that separated its backyard from the house behind it. Only the Johnsons had a wooden plank fence surrounding their entire backyard. The other neighbours had never bothered to fence their yards on this side of the street, so Athena could pass from her street through the block.

One day while investigating the shortcut, she noticed that one of the trees had a particularly low horizontal branch that turned upward. The foliage of the maple was thick. Athena checked to see if anyone could see her. She slipped into the curtain of green and she made her way up the tree. It was only about six feet up. She straddled the huge branch and enjoyed her new vantage point.

She could hear children playing at the park. Athena breathed in and out and made herself invisible, as though she were just another leaf. The sun flashed in and out of small gaps as the leaves shook with movement. Birds dropped by. People crossed through the same shortcut and never even detected her. She believed that she felt the tree's life force and was connected to it.

When she told Mama about this, she said, "I think a week with Kuma would be good for you, honey. She has a pool."

"I don't actually think I'm a tree, Mama. I know the difference. Are Dani and Jaja going?"

"No, thank you," Danica replied emphatically and left the living room to head downstairs.

"Please, I'd love it if you spent some time with her. She's your kuma," Mama said.

"She's everyone's kuma," Athena replied.

"Yeah, but you were named after her."

"Christened after her."

"But that makes you special."

"She's so special," Lejla said, laughing as she came up the stairs.

Athena stuck her tongue out at her sister.

"What's the big deal?" Mama asked.

Athena had a fear of going anywhere overnight. "Could I come home if I wanted?"

"Of course, but you won't want to. Not with all of Kuma's delicious cooking."

Athena had her very first meal at Kuma's after being dropped off with a small suitcase.

"Can I have some milk, please?" Athena asked.

"No, sweetie. Dat's no good for your di-gestion. Ven you done all your food, den some, okay?" She smiled sweetly and kissed Athena on the head.

Immediately, Athena regretted coming. How was she supposed to swallow the chicken without something to drink? What was wrong with everyone?

"Tonight, ve gonna watch Johnny Carson and you can stay up vit Kuma."

Athena brooded for a moment and then decided to play Kuma's game. As soon as she ate her food, she would get a glass of milk. It was easiest to tackle one thing at a time. Starting with her least favourite food and ending with her favourite, she cleared the portions one at a time. Then she had a tall glass of cold milk and Kuma's unwavering approval.

Kuma's house wasn't bad at all. All day, Athena sunbathed in a blow-up canoe in the pool, her skin getting darker and darker.

At the end of the week, Mama was slightly horrified by the transformation. "You're like an Indian."

"Yes, I know—you said." Athena was proud of the smooth appearance of her tanned skin. "Kuma made me icy drinks with umbrellas in them."

"Well, she could've put sunscreen on you. You'll have to stay out of the sun for a while."

That was impossible, as the days stretched out longer and longer. You could get around the whole town on your bike and still make it home easily. Athena would bike all the way to Deedee's house, on the way out of town and into the city, to hang out at the beach. One day, Deedee biked to Sherry's and they came over to Athena's, calling from the edge of the driveway. Tata was opening the garage doors when the girls approached him.

"Hi, Mr. Brkovich. Hey, Athena said she asked you about the summer camp. Can she go with us?" Deedee said.

"What? Camp?" He shrugged and pulled the hose to wash the cars. "I don't know nothin' about no camp, girls."

Having overheard the conversation, Athena came out the garage door and nervously grabbed her bike. "Okay, Tata, I'll be home before the lights are on."

Deedee and Sherry stood astride their bikes. "You didn't ask your dad?" Deedee said.

"About what?" Athena's heart started to beat faster. She glanced at her tata. Didn't her friends know not to ask like this? They were so stupid.

"About *camp*?" Sherry said.

"Oh. Yeah, no. I don't want to go."

Deedee and Sherry looked at each other.

"Bye, Tata."

He didn't say anything, just waved as she pedalled off the driveway. She was halfway up the block before she checked back, relieved that her friends had followed her.

Later that night when Athena came home, Tata called her into his office.

"So were you gonna ask me about a camp thing?"

"Nah, Tata. I don't want to go."

"You don't? Are you sure?"

"Yeah, I'm sure." There was a moment of doubt.

"Do you have information on it?"

Athena hesitated. "Yeah."

"Well, get it."

Athena raced up the stairs, arguing with herself over if she should show the flyer to him. She had folded it up and hidden it in her drawer and ran back down with it.

"They have water sports and real horseback riding." Athena imagined what good friends she would become with Deedee and Sherry if she were allowed to go.

When Tata saw the price, he let out a low whistle. "Wow. Five hundred beans, eh?"

"It's for two weeks," Athena said softly.

"Lemme work on it, then. We'll see."

Athena was surprised he would even think of it.

A week later, when he came home later than he should have, he came into her room and sat on the corner of her bed. Athena kept her eyes closed and pretended to sleep. Mama came in, tiptoeing, and whispered, "Hey, Drag, come on out of here."

"Sh," Tata told her. He sat with his head hanging down and his hands folded in his lap. "I gotta say somethin' here. Just go. Go on."

She moved away from the door where Athena couldn't see her anymore.

There was a pause. Then he spoke. "We can't do the camp, Theenie. I'm sorry."

Athena wanted to cry. She'd made her tata feel bad because he couldn't pay for it. She shouldn't have asked and now she didn't dare speak.

"Is too much."

Minutes passed, and Athena thought that her tata had fallen asleep. She opened her eyes enough that they would still look closed and watched him. He was motionless. When she lifted her head just a touch, he suddenly rotated his body and put his hand on her foot. She froze.

"Hey." He wasn't looking at her, just off into space. "Don' ever wish I was dead, okay?" He spoke slowly, slurring his words together in a sad, low tone.

Athena stopped breathing. Did he know that almost every night she prayed for him to die? Guilt and terror overwhelmed her.

"Promise me. Promise me you won' wish I was dead."

Athena nodded imperceptibly, even though he wasn't looking at her.

He patted her foot, caught himself from falling into the corner of the dresser, and stumbled out.

God could see everything in her heart, and she was wicked. Tears streamed down her temples and rolled into her ears. She let them fill up until they were plugged and she could hear her heartbeat as if she were underwater, drowning in her father's sadness.

Chapter 31

Roxy had a pool and invited everyone back to her house one Saturday after a car wash fundraiser in the church parking lot. Everyone was Athena, Danica, Lejla, Kat, Niko, Tommy, and Georgie. Roxy was an only child. Athena felt sorry for her, as she had no one to fend for her. Kat had a way older brother who no one ever saw.

Roxy's parents seemed so strange to Athena. Her father was from the old country. Athena didn't think she would ever marry anyone with an accent. Her dad was always joking with Roxy, kicking her in the bum. Her mom seemed super strict and liked everything neat and organized.

"Your dad seems really nice," Athena said as they floated in the pool.

"He's great. But I sometimes argue with my mom, and he always ends up siding with her."

Athena couldn't imagine him hitting her. But she assumed that was what Roxy meant. You could never tell what anyone was really like.

Roxy's mom brought out hot dogs. They disappeared in one minute. She went back into the house and came out with another plate that disappeared just as quickly.

Kat was tall and shapely, and Roxy had bigger boobs than Danica, but both Danica and Lejla were more developed than Athena. Athena was still like a little kid. She made sure to stay in the water so she wouldn't be noticed that much. Niko was so cute with his dark skin and white-blonde hair, but he definitely gravitated to Roxy. Athena knew in her heart that it didn't matter now, only when they grew up. Still, it bothered her on some level, but she chose to ignore it since she couldn't really do anything about it. It was better to be young and have fun.

***

When Labour Day rolled around, Athena realized she was going to start a new school. What was going to be different was being with her sisters again. Time had changed them subtly on the outside but dramatically on the inside.

"*Do not* come near me. *Do not* sit next to me on the bus." Lejla had seated Athena on the bench in the front hall to explain the lay of the land.

"Ew. Do not sit next to me either," Danica said.

Athena squinted at her sisters. "What if there's nowhere else to sit?"

"This is what I mean," Lejla said to Danica. "What the hell?" She grabbed her bag and stormed out the door.

Athena went to run after her favourite sister, but Danica grabbed her. "No, Athena. That's what we're saying. Just stay away. And don't forget to lock the door."

Athena jogged to catch up to Lejla.

It's true that she wanted to walk with her sisters and even sit with them on the bus, but she wasn't going to give them the satisfaction. Instead, she sat with Sherry, who was glad to see her. She'd grown as well over the summer. Athena sighed.

At the beginning of the school year, the students all filed into a huge gymnasium. Mr. Pikerton made his way to the microphone in the middle of the stage and set down the ground rules and his expectations for the staff and especially the students. These years were preparing them for high school. Athena discovered that she was in the "junior end," which were grades five and six. Lejla was in her end! Athena cheered this small victory. There was something very military about the experience thus far, and it was unsettling. The school was an experiment, a new open-concept building that tried to promote modern educational ideals but still reinforced rules in a primitive way.

A short, old woman you could barely see above the seated children stood at the front with a computer printout and said, "My name is Mrs. Darby. When I say your name, please line up behind me. Mark Anderson. Susan Antonelli. Athena Brkovich."

Athena jumped at hearing her name. She had been focussed on who would be picked for her class.

"Jonathan Cassels. Michael Hebert." She hoped they were very good students. "Niko Jovanovich."

Athena's feet were welded to the floor by the energy that shot through her body. He was there. How had she not noticed him? Niko got up and walked past her without saying anything. Athena didn't look back either. She only saw him at dance practice or church, and not every week. But now they would be going to the same school! Her heart was pounding. She turned to smile at him. He tipped up his head as if to say hi.

It soon became apparent that a lot of girls found Niko quite attractive. Those girls were usually in grade six. It bothered Athena for the first week, but she'd had some practice managing her doubts in the summer. When she thought about marrying him, she realized that dating now was silly. She knew deep down that one day he would choose her.

This school, unlike her last one, took an interest in intelligence testing, and once again Athena was offered the chance to skip grades. Her parents wanted no part of it and made that clear.

Athena noticed Niko trying to hit her in dodge ball or checking to see if she was watching him when they were running cross-country. He looked up when she got to go to the library for personal development work. She became the reigning spelling bee champion and math team captain, beating all the boys. Athena knew that although she wasn't as grown up as the other students, she was the most intelligent and hard-working of them. She also knew she was nothing like Lejla.

Lejla Brkovich was the prettiest girl in her grade, and quite possibly the entire school. She styled her thick blonde hair perfectly. The pink blush on her cheeks accentuated her dimples, and black mascara made her eyes sparkle. She wore braces, but her lips were covered in shiny Kissing Potion gloss.

"Even if I wore all your clothes, Jaja, no one would notice me." Athena said, then begged her sister to explain how to go about making friends and getting noticed.

"Well, I mean, your thing is you're so smart, right?"

Athena nodded.

"Well, maybe just don't be so smart sometimes."

Athena didn't comprehend this. "But you're also one of the smartest in the class, Jaja."

"Yeah, I'm one of the top students, but I don't always have to have the answer for everything."

"But if you know the answer—"

"That's what I mean, Theen." Lejla turned from the mirror where she was removing her makeup to face Athena. "You always have the answer. But people don't always want to be told, you know?"

Athena didn't know. She resigned herself to watching and studying what her sister did a bit more and trying to incorporate what she could.

***

The weather was getting colder, and grey skies were hanging like a low ceiling as Athena's birthday rolled around.

"Ten is the magic age!" Mama kept saying.

Athena didn't understand what that entailed but loved the premise.

To commemorate how special turning ten was, Tata took Athena to a gold shop in Detroit to pick out a chain and a pendant. She chose, as her sisters had, a medium-length chain with her astrological sign. Athena was a Scorpio. The pendant felt heavy on her chest and she liked the feel of it as she slid it back and forth on the chain.

When Athena blew out the candles, she wished to be more like her sisters, pretty and popular. When Mama was tucking her and Mitzi into bed, Athena asked again why ten was the magic age.

"Because you get to do a lot more things now. All the things you were too little to do, like cut the grass, run the washer and dryer and dishwasher, iron the shirts." Mama laughed softly.

"Really?" Athena said, excited to have more responsibility.

"Yes, silly. Now go to sleep. You're so crazy." Mama kissed her on the forehead.

Athena's chore list grew and grew. Mama wrote out what she wanted to get done and by whom. What started out as three columns, one for each girl, eventually became one list with *Athena* at the top.

"Mama, Dani and Jaja don't even have chores. This is so unfair!"

"Honey, look. I can't rely on your sisters. They're not like you. You help me so much and I can count on you. Please, Theenie, be Mama's helper."

Of course, being lauded in the women's circles at church and the hall helped soothe Athena's pain at the unequal distribution of work. It also increased Danica and Lejla's animosity toward her. Athena couldn't win. Deedee and Sherry suggested that Athena ask for an allowance, but Tata shut this down immediately.

"You want me to give you some money every week after giving you a house, a bed, food on your plate, and clothes on your back?"

Under the circumstances, how could Athena ever not be indebted to her parents? She came up with a price list.

"Tata, I'm proposing two dollars per car to have them washed. Two dollars to cut the grass or shovel the driveway. A dollar to vacuum the house or dust everything. As you can see here, I've made a list and I'll give you my bill at the end of the week." Athena was determined.

Her father finally relented. Athena presented her ledger of chores at the end of the week and Tata would give her the money, often eight or ten dollars. Athena liked to have Mitzi count change with her, roll coins, and total her earnings and savings. Soon she had almost eighty dollars, including her birthday money.

Danica had a group of friends—boys and girls—over for a tobogganing party at the hill. It had been planned for weeks. Mama ordered two king-sized pizzas. When they arrived, there was a sudden fuss.

"Athena, how much money do you have?" Mama asked.

She said nothing.

"Athena!" Mama raised her voice.

"Are you going to pay me back?" she asked timidly.

"Yes. Just give it to me. Your father isn't home. Now get it. *Now*. I have to pay for the pizzas."

Athena handed her the money reluctantly. She was too nervous to ask her tata for the money.

After Athena had asked about it every day for a week, Mama snapped at her. "Do not ask me about your money again, Athena. It's *our* money. We gave it to you."

Athena sat silently. She had lost the money. She would have to make so much money so her mama and tata never worried about it again and she could pay them back so they didn't own her. She wanted to be free.

Chapter 32

It was a Wednesday morning, a school day, a day like any other day. Bad things weren't supposed to happen in the morning; it was usually nighttime when something was wrong. But it was before work and school and there was yelling. Athena lifted her head a bit, trying to hear what it was about, but decided not to get involved.

She was putting a pillow over her head when Danica burst into her room, breathless. "Get up, Theenie. Get out here," she said and ran out, leaving the door open.

Athena and Mitzi came out in their nighties. Athena held her sister's little hand and tucked her behind her as they went down the hall. Mama and Tata were standing in the living room. Danica and Lejla and Max were standing facing them. Mama and Tata had their coats on, ready to go to work. Athena was confused.

Mama blurted out, "Do you have it? Did you take it, Athena?"

"Take what?" Athena's heart was racing. Something terrible had started—she could sense it. Everyone was looking at her.

"A watch," Danica said.

"Did you take it, Athena?" Tata's voice was stern and hard. His jaw was clenched.

"No! I don't even know what you're talking about."

"I had a watch in my dresser for Tata for Christmas, and now it's gone." Mama's voice was as hard and as loud as Tata's.

Everyone stood motionless.

"If that watch"—Tata seemed to breathe these words out from behind his teeth—"isn't back . . ."

Athena's body was going numb.

". . . in that dresser . . ."

She stopped breathing.

". . . so help me, God, you're all going to get it."

Mama scanned the girls' faces desperately and then followed Tata down the stairs and out the front door.

Athena's throat was dry and all the blood drained from her face. Dropping Mitzi's hand, she turned to Danica and Lejla.

Danica said, "Okay, so you don't know about a watch?"

"I have no idea what you're talking about!" Athena crumbled at the accusation and dreaded the impending punishment. "What watch?" She started to cry.

Danica and Lejla's faces were pinched.

"Well, I don't know about any stupid watch," Lejla said and started to go downstairs.

"But you do! Because Mom said she showed it to you two days ago! Now where is it?" Danica yelled.

"I don't know, okay?" Lejla ran downstairs, and Danica and Athena followed.

"Well, think, because I definitely don't know," Athena begged her.

"Dani saw it too. But they won't think *she* took it."

"Why would anyone take it?" Athena asked.

"Shut up and go upstairs and get ready for school," Lejla said.

"We can't go to school!" Athena was almost hysterical. "We have to tear the house apart looking for this thing. We have to return it by tonight, or . . ." Athena's knees went weak at the thought and her throat constricted.

"We're going to school," said Danica.

"But we have to find it!" Athena insisted. "Maybe it's in the laundry room. There are so many presents. Maybe Mama threw it out by mistake." But there was no time to search.

On the bus, Athena felt separated from her body. Her mind calculated all of the possible places a watch she had never seen or knew existed could be in the world. She asked God to show her where it was. Other children were speaking about the upcoming break. Only one more week of school. Athena sat stone-faced, staring out the window.

In her classroom, it was agonizing to watch the minute hand on the clocks going around. Athena counted every second, unable to formulate any explanation for the missing watch.

At the first recess, she grabbed Lejla and couldn't contain her anxiety. "Where is it, Jaja? You saw it! Did you take it?"

"No! I did not take it! I swear!" Lejla looked into Athena's eyes.

What would an eleven-year-old girl do with an old man's gold watch? It didn't make sense.

Danica saw her sisters and joined them. "That watch cost five hundred dollars. We have to find it."

"Ohhhh." Athena let out a pitiful moan. The anticipation and sense of helplessness was torturous. There was no way to rectify the situation.

"Calm down." Danica squeezed her arm tightly.

They just stood there in a silent circle of desperation on the playground until the bell rang. This happened again at lunch, and again in the afternoon. Athena didn't remember the bus ride home or her feet carrying her to the house. There was only a pounding of blood in her head when, after a half-hour search of the house, they sat empty-handed in the family room and listened to their parents talking in low tones in the kitchen. Footsteps came down the stairs.

Tata stood in his dress shirt and pants. He had taken his tie off. He held his belt in his hand. Mama stood behind him.

Danica started to cry.

"Danica, go to your room," Tata said.

She was sobbing into her hands, her face and cheeks blotchy as she ran to her room. He followed. The door closed. Her voice was louder than his.

"No, I didn't take it! I don't know! I didn't take it!"

Athena sat stunned with revulsion, her heartbeat so loud that her whole being pulsed like a pounding drum.

That was it. The door opened and then closed again and Danica stayed in her room.

Athena knew what was coming now. It was unstoppable. She wanted the ground to open up and swallow her.

"Lejla, go to your room," Tata said.

Lejla got off the chair and walked quickly past their tata.

Athena knew that her parents thought Lejla had taken it. She was sitting on the couch. Max and Mitzi were sitting beside her. Mama was kneeling on the ground to the right of Athena, her hands on Max and Mitzi's knees. Athena sat frozen, staring at her mama, whose eyes were cast down and never moved.

The latch of the bedroom door closed like a gunshot.

"Did you take the watch?"

"No!"

"Now where is it?" *Crack.*

"I don't know, Dad! I don't know!"

"I said, where"—*crack*—"is it?"

"No, Dad, no!" *Crack.* "No, I don't know. I didn't"—*crack*—"take it. Please believe me! Please!" *Crack.* "Noooo!"

"Where's the watch, Lejla? *Crack*—*crack*—tell me right now."

"I don't know, Dad! I don't!" *Crack.* "I didn't take it." *Crack, crack.* "No! Stop! Please!"

"You're lying! I know you took it." *Crack.* "Tell me the truth." *Crack, crack.*

"No! I don't know"—*crack*—"where it is!" *Crack.* "I don't know, Dad! I didn't take it, I swear! No, stop!" *Crack, crack.* "No! Oh, help me, please! Help me!" *Crack. Crack. Crack.*

There were no more words. Just sounds.

Athena had been staring at her mama, in her mind screaming at her to do something, but unable to speak, unable to move herself. It went on and on, the sound of the belt and Lejla. When the crying got louder, it was because the door had opened.

Tata stood in the doorway, soaked in sweat. "Athena, go to your room."

Mama didn't look at her. Athena felt as if she was walking to her death, already dead. She moved, not quickly, past her father. She heard Lejla's moaning from her room. She had sat paralyzed with fear, listening to her sister being beaten mercilessly, and had done nothing, but now she realized that her legs *would* climb the stairs. When she got to her room, she sat on the edge of the bed. She waited. Tata appeared and closed the door.

"Athena, did you take the watch?" Tata asked. His lips formed one line and he was huffing crazily, sweating from the savage beating he had given Lejla.

Athena fell on her knees in front of him, crying, "No! No, Tata! I didn't even know there was a—"

Crack. The belt came down on her back.

"No! Please, Tata!"

Crack. It fell on her legs as he dragged her up onto the bed.

"Where is it?"

"I don't know." *Crack.* "I didn't take it!" *Crack.*

She wished her tata would beat her as badly as he had Lejla. She deserved it—she had done nothing to help her sister. Her poor, beautiful Lejla. Athena believed her that she hadn't taken the watch. Even with all of his force, Tata hadn't found the answer he wanted and that had infuriated him more. He continued to beat Athena, but the punishment was short-lived and weak compared to Lejla's. He was spent from beating her sister. Athena cried and slid onto the floor while he hit her, asking futile and meaningless questions. She hated her tata and herself, and nothing mattered anymore.

Athena was the only person to enter Lejla's room that night. She snuck downstairs and opened the door.

"Get out," Lejla said, whimpering.

Athena brought a glass of water and a cold washcloth and set it by her.

"Get out of here now." Lejla was wounded.

Athena went in the bathroom upstairs, turned on the light, and locked the door. The welts on her legs were red and hot. She glared at her weak self in the mirror. She pulled her hair and slapped her own face, scratching her cheeks and scalp until she drew blood.

"You did nothing. You did nothing," she growled at her reflection. Lejla's screams bit into her as though she was being eaten alive by a wild beast. She clawed at herself without shedding a tear. She couldn't feel the pain from the belt anymore, but the pain in her sister's voice had branded her soul.

***

On Thursday morning, Mama told Lejla to stand on a chair she had brought into the kitchen. "Get up here."

Athena was sitting at the bench. No one else was there, just Mama and Lejla.

"Take those pants off. I want to see your legs."

Sitting through the monstrousness had been sickening enough, but Athena gagged at the sight of Lejla's body. The welts cut the skin all down the backs and fronts of her legs. There was dried blood everywhere, and it had pooled where Tata's nails had punctured her skin as he'd held her down. The welts ran up her lower back too.

Athena gauged her mother's face, which was both grim and flustered. She was shaking as she tried to absorb the severity of the injuries.

Mama retrieved the antibiotic cream from the bathroom. "Get washcloths and a basin of warm water, quick," she instructed Athena.

Athena felt some relief knowing that Mama loved Lejla after all. She hadn't asked to see Athena's legs.

"You're not going to school today or tomorrow. We'll see how it looks next week, but it's probably better if you stay home and rest." Mama gently cleaned Lejla's legs, applied the ointment to the cuts, and then helped her back into her sweatpants. She walked Lejla downstairs and tucked her in.

When Mama passed Athena, she said, "Keep an eye on your sister. I'm worried about her."

Athena was a vigilant guard.

When night came, terror seized Athena. For the next week, she sat every night in the hallway outside her parents' bedroom door. She was convinced that robbers had taken the watch and was consumed with the idea they would come again and she would have to relive the nightmare. Athena reprimanded herself for her own inadequacies. For her, sleep was undeserved.

***

Christmas represented falseness on such an epic scale that if Athena hadn't witnessed it herself, she couldn't have taken anyone's word for it that, after completely extinguishing someone's joy, you could then demand that they show up for guests with a smile and be entertaining, because, after all, that's life. Later, Athena stood in church, the incense streaming out of the golden chalice, the candle glow illuminating tears she only imagined were there, and asked God to show her why, to help her understand.

Over the break, Mama took the girls to see *Ice Castles*, a figure skating movie about a blind girl. When they were leaving the theatre, Mama said, "Hey, at least we can all see."

There was a puzzled pause, and then laughter bubbled up and out of them as the futility hit them. Of course there was always someone worse off, and Athena, unable to cry, laughed until she cried, and she realized that this was the answer. Sadness and joy were actually side by side on a long spectrum of emotion, and pain fuelled laughter and laughter alleviated pain. The adult world was ridiculous, full of injustice and hypocrisy. The antidote to the anxiety it caused was laughter. Mama's irreverence carved out Athena's path. She would not grow up. She would deliver the gift of laughter to soothe people's suffering. She would become a true student of comedy and write sketches for *Saturday Night Live*.

Athena felt removed from her parents. The days of "Mama" and "Tata" were gone, and she could understand how her sisters had already moved past this point. Athena didn't want to be mature, though. She *did* want to get out from under her parents, who she saw differently now.

It was a month before she heard her tata call his father-in-law "Pops." She realized that this was her chance. "I'm going to call you that," she announced.

"What?"

"Pops." Her father made a face as though it wasn't totally okay with him.

This pleased Athena. Her mother was more difficult to find a name for. *Chilly Willy* was a cartoon that came on after school about a penguin. Athena sang the theme song and inserted "Chilly Tilley." That would become her new nickname. Chilly. The informality suited Athena's purposes.

***

There was an aftershock to the earthquake. It came near the end of January. Since Christmas, Athena's father had come home regularly from work so the house could resume some semblance of normalcy. One night when he didn't, Tilley stood in the kitchen and lit a cigarette.

"You don't smoke, Chilly," Athena said.

"Sometimes everyone needs a little break, okay? Why don't you go downstairs now before it's bedtime?"

Everyone was in the family room watching TV when the front door opened. The heavy footsteps alerted them to Dragan's presence. Athena sat up. Lejla curled up in the chair. Tilley went to intercept him.

"I want to know who it was!" he shouted as he marched down the stairs. "I got a phone call today from chil-dren's ser-vices. Does anybody know anything about that?" He looked at Lejla. "You phoned chil-dren's ser-vices?" he asked mockingly.

Lejla was quiet and shrank before him.

"Get to your room!" he shouted.

The voice in Athena's mind couldn't be contained. *No!* Lejla walked to her room quickly and tried to shut the door. He went to grab her but Athena jumped on him from behind, as did Danica. Mitzi and Max ran underneath him.

"Mom, don't let him!"

Athena's voice shook her mother out of her silence. Tilley faced Dragan. "Hey, you're not doing *anything* right now. You go upstairs." She stood her ground and they all faced him.

"Well, who called them?" Dragan asked.

"Probably Brenda," Athena shouted. "The whole neighbourhood could hear Jaja screaming."

There was suddenly silence, for a bigger secret had just been divulged. No one was allowed to talk about anything, but it didn't mean people didn't know.

Tilley gave Athena a stern look. "That's enough. We're done." She shooed Dragan out of the room and steered him upstairs.

It seemed that everyone pitied their father in his shame, but his situation was his own doing. It was wrong, but it wasn't only him that mattered. Why did she feel as though no one could stand to hear the truth? Athena lay awake in bed and struggled with the idea that none of them mattered as much as a five hundred dollar watch. Her father had put a price on their flesh and blood and she was owned like a slave. She belonged to her father. Even her mother did. He would have to die for her to be free, but why? Athena deduced that his power was in his money. She would become the person who made the money and she would hold the power. She would have so much that it would protect her and the people she loved. It would stop all the fighting. She would become a millionaire, and then everyone could finally be free and happy.

Chapter 33

Back at school, Athena asked Sherry, "How many people do you think live in Windsor?" Athena was hanging upside down on the monkey bars, holding her T-shirt.

"I don't know. Maybe a hundred thousand."

"So if every person gave me ten dollars, I would have a million."

"Why would every person give you ten dollars?"

"'Cause I'd ask them."

"But that's begging. You can't do that. No one's going to just give you ten dollars."

Athena had been focused for months on how to get her hands on some money. Since she had been doing almost all the chores, she had increased her prices. Danica and Lejla would help with the dishes when their mom insisted they do something, but if she was too tired she would default to asking Athena.

"What about asking one million people for one dollar?" Athena tried to work out the logistics. "So if you got ten dollars a day, that would be a hundred thousand days, with three hundred and sixty-five days a year. No! That would take way too long."

"You have to have a job where you make lots of money. Like a doctor or a lawyer. All the rich kids have parents who do stuff like that. Our parents have regular jobs—that's why they don't make as much."

Athena knew that becoming a doctor was always an option, but it seemed so distant. Instead, she tried collecting pledges for a fake fundraiser. She was surprised by how many people gave her a five-dollar bill simply because she had a clipboard with a piece of paper upon which she had written *Shoot-a-thon*. After twenty-five dollars or so she would stop. Athena would spend two dollars at least on candy at the store; it would be difficult to save all the money she'd collected. She would move out eventually and would have to spend more of it. Getting money was harder than it seemed at first. Keeping it was impossible.

***

It was a simple decision to be happy once she left the house. Athena decided it was no use being sad and afraid all the time. She believed deeply in her unique abilities and had already made some significant choices.

"I'm just not going to grow up." Athena's sweatshirt hood was over her head, its strings pulled as tightly as possible. She was resting her chin on the back of the green bus seat.

Sherry was sitting sideways in front of her. "You can't just decide that."

"Yes, you can. I instruct my body to stay little."

Acting silly in class was one thing, but getting all the juniors to notice her was quite another. It was springtime and the field was considered off-limits. A small lake covered most of it due to the high water levels and melted snow. Athena wore her knee-high boots. At lunch, she walked calmly out toward the water.

"Young lady!" she heard just as she started to wade in. "Young lady, the field is off-limits."

Athena paid no attention. She walked to the middle of the lake and then turned to face the school, the playground, and all the children.

The yard duty volunteer plodded steadily along and stopped at the edge of the water. "Come out of there at once!" she yelled.

Athena simply didn't reply. It made no sense that this should be off-limits. She was wearing tall boots. She wiggled her feet to help sink her into the thick muck.

"What do you think you're doing?"

Athena shrugged and put her hands in the air, palms up.

Noticing the commotion and the gathering crowd, more and more children wandered over.

"Get back, you kids!"

"What's your name again?" Athena asked.

"Mrs. Fields."

Athena gave an exaggerated nod and the children erupted in laughter. "Of course it is," Athena said, giggling.

Mrs. Fields's face was beet red. "I'm reporting you to the principal, young lady! Come out at once!"

With a big grin, Athena shook her head.

"I'll go in when the bell rings. I'm not hurting anyone."

This was met with raucous approval and applause.

Athena had sank herself into the mud so much that the water level was within an inch of the top of her boots. She leaned to the right.

"Whoa," said the children in unison. Laughter followed.

Athena leaned as far as she could to the left.

The voices were louder. *"Whoa!"* Cheers and laughter again.

It was like a magic act. Athena could go in any direction, and probably because she was so short, she could make herself almost horizontal without budging her boots or falling out of them. Mrs. Fields was shaking her fist as she yelled at Athena, who was completely unperturbed. This was what children relished most Athena thought: a disdain for authority.

When the bell rang, Athena wiggled her foot and lifted one boot out, then the other, with a huge sucking noise. Mrs. Fields marched her straight to the office, holding her by the sleeve as if she were trying to escape. Athena was so delighted by the success of her escapade and so confident she wouldn't be blamed that she had little fear of the principal. Her hunch proved to be right. Having top marks and a reasonable excuse for your actions deflected responsibility from you in many situations, especially if you remained pleasant and respectful. Of course, Mrs. Fields was fuming, but this only fed Athena's deep conviction that adults whose main purpose was to control and punish children should themselves suffer.

***

A time frame passed. The dimensions of the frame felt different for everyone. For Athena, it was an eon. For her sisters, it was likely a decade. And for her parents, it might have been weeks. By the calendar, it was almost one year.

In all that time, Athena didn't grow taller. Danica and Lejla sprouted in height and their figures developed. Athena rejoiced, knowing her time would never come and she would remain a stout five-foot-one flat-chested, pot-bellied kid.

She worked diligently on accents and impersonations, walking backward, pratfalls, and sketch writing. She researched what made certain comedians more successful than others. Men were funnier. Not because women weren't funny, but because you had to be completely self-effacing or else comedy was uncomfortable. To her delight, Pops found her antics entertaining. She was always first in her class, so there was no need for concern. Tilley, on the other hand, found her childish behaviour unbecoming.

"Exactly!" Athena would say to that, and she'd jab her index finger into the air as if exclaiming, "Eureka!"

Tilley would shake her head and then crack a smile. "You're crazy, you know that?"

"Yes, indubitably. I do know that, and I have all of you to thank for it."

Athena's life, for the most part, was a repetitive cycle of church, home, and school that involved work, performing, and surviving. Time moved slowly, and she wondered how she could reconcile supporting herself if she refused to grow up.

***

"*Mom!* You've got to do something about her! She acts like a retard! It's completely embarrassing!" Danica cried.

Tilley frowned at Athena, who crossed her eyes and stuck out her tongue and then answered, "I dunno wha' she mean."

"Ugh! Mom!"

"You're the one who's embarrassing, talking all stupid to David Elliott on the bus. Ew."

Danica's face went red.

"What's this?" Tilley asked.

"Oh, nothing," Dani said to her mother and then mouthed, *You are so dead* behind her back at Athena.

Athena made a gesture as if tightening a noose around her neck. "I'm tho thcared." She futzed around in her seat.

"Mom! Do something!" Danica yelled and stormed out.

"Why do you have to be this way?" Putting down her spatula, Tilley looked at Athena for a moment. "I mean like *this*," she said, pointing at her. "Why do you have to be like this? Why can't you act normal?"

"Philosophers have debated normal for centuries, Chilly. Who's to say I'm not normal?"

"Just stop it, okay, Theenie? Please, my head needs a rest."

Athena left the kitchen and went downstairs. She pulled out a Journey album and used the headphones. She felt as if Steve Perry was singing just to her.

When Danica walked by, she kicked Athena in the side and said, "Stop being stupid," then walked into her room.

"Couldn't be stupid if I tried." Athena smiled at the closed door.

***

Athena's dad called the three girls into the living room. "Danica, Lejla, Athena, come in here. We want to talk to you."

Athena's heart rate escalated, and she tried to read her mom's expression.

"Your mother has something to say to you." He stood behind Tilley, who glanced at him.

"Yes, well, we know you girls are starting to grow up, and we want you to be smart. You know you're not allowed to have boyfriends right now, but when high school comes, things are going to change. We want you, obviously, to marry someone Serbian, but we realize that may not happen. It would be best if he were white. We would even tolerate someone Chinese or brown." Here she took a breath. "But under no circumstances will we tolerate anyone black in this house, not even as a friend."

There was silence. Danica, Lejla, and Athena sat still.

"Do you understand? You will not be a part of this family any longer. You will not be our daughter."

Stillness.

"Are we clear?"

The girls nodded.

It was impossible for Athena to know how her sisters felt about this decree. For her, there was only relief. Nothing had been taken. No one had done any wrong. No one was getting the belt. Athena tried to think if there were any black boys at school but couldn't think of one. So what would the odds be? Well, none. This would be a simple rule to follow.

The twins' summer birthday party rolled around. Max and Mitzi were each allowed to invite four friends. Tilley had the girls plan an obstacle course in the backyard. There were door prizes. The cake was a double slab, half chocolate and half vanilla. There was even a piñata. As the children showed up, the hosts were expected to greet their guests, show them around, and offer them something to drink.

Athena wondered what the scene looked like to Reggie, when he stepped out of the car, if it looked as if everyone were frozen. He was black! Athena searched for her mother's face, eager to see her reaction. Max ran down the driveway, waved at Reggie's mom, took a present, and threw his arms around him. Athena watched this with her mouth open. Tilley had disappeared inside.

"What's going to happen now?" Athena whispered to Lejla.

"Nothing. Shut up."

Tilley and Dragan came out. "Well, who's your friend, Max?" Dragan asked.

"Dad, this is Reggie."

Reggie smiled. His teeth looked so white. Athena had never seen anyone black up close in real life, only on the network news.

"Hi," Dragan said.

"C'mon and see my *Star Wars* collection," Max said, and he and Reggie and three other boys ran inside, leaving stunned faces in their wake.

"We're not going to say anything," Tilley said.

Athena could see the troubled look on her father's face. *He should have told all of us, not just the girls*, thought Athena.

Chapter 34

Danica had graduated from grade eight. This left only Athena and Lejla. Athena felt slightly liberated. Lejla still threatened Athena, telling her not to come near her, but never told on her for any of the weird stuff she did. Having your sister as the most popular girl in school had both advantages and disadvantages. Though she was unlike Lejla, being her sister afforded her the protection she needed to be whoever she wanted.

Starting grade seven, Athena decided she was going to try to be nicer. She had always been helpful to her teachers, but she was thinking more along the lines of befriending the other weirdos who couldn't just snap themselves out of it. Her first friend project was obvious.

Frederica Ficas was fat. Not the chubby fat that's normal for kids, but the saddlebags fat of an adult. She'd managed somehow to get through the lower grades, but Athena had witnessed the cruel way that people, especially boys, treated her. Athena often wondered why she didn't change her name; it would have been so easy.

Frederica lumbered into class, ignoring the jeers and taunts that followed her. She found a seat in the new classroom. The desks were like tables and each sat two people. They were modular and could be rearranged according to the activity.

"This is the senior end now, and we expect you to start acting more mature." Mrs. Paulson said.

The teacher was ancient. She looked up at the ceiling when she addressed a student and pointed in a completely different direction from where they were seated. Though Athena wasn't going to grow up physically, this challenge would be good for her.

Halfway through the morning, Mrs. Paulson asked for everyone's attention. "Class, we have a new student who is joining us from Chatham. Her name is Fiona Finn."

Another FF? It was a sign from God.

Standing before the class was a skeleton of a girl, like an anatomical model in a biology lab that was just bones with skin over it. Fiona's T-shirt hung from her shoulders as if from a hanger. Fiona and Frederica were at opposite ends of the continuum of the body weight universe.

Chad Pemberton coughed and said, "Skinny" into his hand.

"I am not going to tolerate any of that business, young man. Now get out in the hall."

Everyone looked at Chad, who just ran his hand through his feathered hair. He didn't care. Everyone knew he was rich.

Mrs. Paulson walked toward him. "I will not have any of your attitude, Chad."

He leaned against the wall partitioning Athena's class from the second of three grade seven sections. Niko wasn't in her class.

"Okay, Fiona, find a seat."

Fiona, of course, sat next to Frederica. They didn't speak to each other all day. *If life were to design moments so exquisitely ironic as this all the time,* thought Athena.

She was enrolled in the senior enrichment program and could go to the library after she completed her in-class assignments. This left her plenty of time to plan how she would improve the lives of these two unfortunate souls. Though Athena knew she wasn't as pretty as her sisters, thinking about what Frederica and Fiona had to face daily made her appreciate and love her own body. As she looked at herself in the mirror that night, she showered love on her medium frame, well-proportioned limbs, and acceptable face. She was also very proud of her ability to show kindness. Tomorrow she would start, but she would tell no one.

Frederica lived in Athena's neighbourhood and took the bus. Athena had never spoken to her before. She couldn't remember if one of her sisters had explicitly told her not to or if she simply understood that you don't associate with someone who draws so much ridicule. *Frederica Ficas.* That name—it was easier to make fun of than hers, which was very easy.

Athena watched her walking through the park. It looked like such an effort. She felt repulsed but reminded herself that this was exactly why she had to help her.

"Hey, Frederica! Freddy! Wait!" Athena jogged to catch up to her.

Frederica didn't look at her or even turn around. "What do you want?"

"Just thought I'd say hi."

"Hi." Frederica stopped and faced her.

She was a lot bigger close up, a head taller than Athena, and didn't have a trace of friendliness in her voice. Athena suddenly felt a bit scared. Then Frederica turned and started walking.

"Do you want to sit together on the bus?" Athena asked.

"Look"—Frederica stopped again—"I don't know if you're going to get all strange like you do on the bus, but I don't need it, okay? Thanks, anyway."

Athena had to think for a moment. "No. I don't want to make fun of you. I just wanted to sit with you."

"Why?"

"I dunno. I thought since this was a new year, we could be friends."

Frederica frowned.

"Okay, well, think about it." She smiled and, seeing Sherry, waved and ran to meet her.

"What were you talking to Fat Freddy about?"

"Don't call her that."

Sherry flinched. "Wow, is she your new best friend now?"

"No, I just thought maybe she could use a friend. It must be hard to be her."

"It must be *fat* to be her."

Athena laughed, despite her noble intentions. She felt repelled by how big Freddy was but was determined to help her.

It was easier with Fiona.

"Everyone, find a partner for this maps unit. You're going to draw and colour in a map of Canada," Mrs. Paulson said one day in class.

Athena jumped and put her hand on Fiona's arm. It was bony. "Wanna be my partner?"

Fiona hesitated.

"I'm smart, don't worry." Athena laughed.

On the playground, Deedee and Sherry were interested in why Athena would want to make friends with the "F crowd"—the freaks.

"They're people, too. They have feelings. Imagine if you were them," Athena replied.

Freddy was sitting by herself against the school's wall near the entrance, and Fiona was walking all alone along the boundary of the junior end, her hands in her pockets.

"It's hard to get to know them. It's like they don't trust the idea of having normal friends," Athena explained. She was more excited than ever to see her project succeed.

Athena started to sit with Freddy. She completed the maps project with Fiona. She convinced Deedee and Sherry to let both girls have lunch with them. They saved them seats at the assemblies.

Athena felt smug knowing that Freddy and Fiona were having a better life because of her. She really was like an angel. The cohesiveness of the classroom had improved, as Athena took to destroying anyone who picked on either of them. No one wanted to take on Lejla's sister and risk being an outcast, so everyone followed along. Athena felt proud and powerful.

Chapter 35

"It was too good a deal to pass up," Dragan said, standing in the driveway as everyone ran around and explored the new car. The station wagon was gone.

"Is that a good idea right now? "Tilley asked.

"We got the money."

Athena was standing next to her father, listening.

He explained, "Don't buy things on credit, Theenie. Interest rates are through the roof right now and guys aren't even buying our cars. They're buying the Jap models because they're makin' 'em better and cheaper than we are. It's the damn unions that're killin' us, protecting people who don't show up to work."

Athena nodded. Everyone knew that Chrysler cars were junk.

"And now we're on the verge of goin' under. But am I worried?" He paused dramatically, raising his eyebrows. "No. Because I'm smarter than the average bear. This house is paid for. This car is paid for. When you want somethin', you save up the money and then you buy it." He mimed the motions of counting out the bills. "You understand?"

Athena nodded. Her dad worked hard, and although he said he wasn't worried, he had missed dinners more often lately, yelling about bankruptcy and that they could all be out on the streets. It worried Athena. Tilley had explained how much stress he was under because his boss was an idiot who didn't like him and deliberately held him back.

"Whatever you do, Theenie, you work for yourself. You hear me?" he said.

She was their great hope.

He placed his hand on her shoulder. "You don't wanna take orders from nobody."

Athena thought, *Which means you do want to take orders from somebody.* Maybe it was this kind of thinking that always got everything confused.

"Athena! Make sure these white walls are clean, kid."

Athena gave her dad a thumbs-up.

***

As the holidays approached, decorations went up even earlier than normal at the mall. Athena hated Christmas. The anxiety it triggered was immense. She didn't want her mother to buy anything, as it could go missing. And even if it didn't, buying things wasn't the purpose of the holiday. It was Jesus's birthday. A time for love and peace on Earth. Athena liked to believe that her generation would be the one to teach their elders, to show them that life wasn't about money and greed. They would save the planet. But children had no rights and their opinions had no weight.

On Christmas Day, the phone rang and Athena ran to get it. "Oh, hey, Deda. Merry Christmas."

With a strange look, Tilley took the receiver from Athena. Before she put it to her ear, she grabbed Athena's arm and stopped her from running out.

Athena would recollect this moment many times, how Tilley knew that her own mother had died. Athena struggled through the holidays, but for reasons other than people thought. She thought of her own mother dying and instantly cried. She saw her mother crying so hard and she could understand why, but Athena wasn't sad at all that her baba had died. Was she a robot? People in the church who saw her crying told her, "You poor thing. You loved your baba. She was a good woman." But Athena felt no sense of loss. She only felt sad that her mom was sad, and at the prospect of losing her one day.

After the last visitation, Tilley went to bed early and their dad came to check on them. "You're going to stay home tomorrow with the twins, Athena. Mama thinks the funeral will be too much for you."

Athena didn't quite understand why but asked, "Is it okay if we open our presents tomorrow?"

Her dad sighed and shook his head. "You better not. You better wait."

After he left, Athena felt guilty about her lack of feeling and her selfishness. Who would it hurt if she opened her presents? She wondered if other people felt sad when their grandmothers died. *Christmas brings bad feelings*, she thought before falling asleep.

***

In downtown Windsor, a lot of businesses had wooden boards over their windows. They didn't drive around much anymore, but since it was spring, Dragan wanted to take the car out for a Sunday drive.

"Iacocca's got some new ideas and I think he's gonna lead us outta this, but I can't be taking any stock options. I said no, I need the cash. I gotta feed my family."

Tilley nodded. "You're doing the right thing. I'm still going to be good because they aren't laying off. The seniority they gave me when they called me back saved my job."

Dragan nodded slowly.

It was nice to see her parents in agreement over something.

The Brkovichs all got out of the car and walked down to the guardrail along the riverfront. A Russian tanker was going through, and they waved to the sailors on board, who waved back. It was a sunny day. The peace fountain spouted water. She watched the murky black water slap against the rusted, corrugated metal embankment.

"You never go swimming in the Detroit River." Inevitably, their father's speech about this came every time they went to the park. "It's deep and the currents are really strong. They'll pull you straight down. "

"People drown every year," Tilley added.

"There's always some cuckoo who thinks he's gonna to be the first one to cross," her father said with a guffaw.

Athena looked over at Detroit. It seemed so close but it was in a different country. The river was probably what kept all the black people over there. She pictured slaves trying to swim across to freedom and drowning. Athena choked and couldn't breathe. She broke away and went running with Max and Mitzi in the park.

"Keep an eye on the twins, Theenie," Tilley yelled.

Athena was holding their hands and admiring the fountain when, from the corner of her eye, she thought she saw a small girl fall into the river. It was about five feet down from the paved walk and the railings to the water. There weren't proper waves, just a continuous wake from the ships and currents that caused the water to slap against the sheer drop. Athena looked at the people along the railing. An older woman in a kerchief was reaching toward the water blathering incoherently. She didn't speak English. No one moved.

"That girl just fell in," Max said.

And there she was. A glimpse of pink surfaced in the dark waters and disappeared again. Without hesitation or thinking, Athena dropped the twins' hands, took a deep breath, ducked between the bars, and dove straight for her.

The water was cold, and Athena cracked her eyes open once but saw nothing. She was diving forward with her hands outstretched and, as luck would have it, knocked into the child's arm. She grabbed it and, kicking with all her might, dragged her to the surface. She struggled to tread water and lift the child up.

"Help!" Athena shouted.

Many hands were outstretched, but none reached her. She kicked from the metal wall as she was pushed into it. A man lay down and hung off the edge while people held his feet. He reached down and grabbed the toddler first. Athena felt one of her shoes come off. Her pants were slowing her legs down. Athena kicked back again and tried to jump partially off the wall. The man grabbed her wrist and the people dragged him back and lifted her out of the water. A crowd surrounded the old woman who wrapped up the child and ran away with her.

"Are you okay, kid?" the man asked Athena, shaking his arms of the water. "You can't go in there, you know?"

Athena lay on her back, panting and feeling a rocking sensation even though she was on solid ground.

"What happened?" Tilley raced to her and Athena sat up quickly. "Did you go in the water?"

Before she could answer, her father hit her on the back of the head. "What are you, stupid?"

Everyone was staring.

"There was a little girl. She fell in."

But there was no little girl in sight.

"Where's your shoe?" Tilley asked, looking her over from head to toe, "You're dripping. You can't get in the car like that."

Her parents threw up their hands.

"If you ever pull a stunt like that again, I swear to God, Athena . . ." Her dad marched ahead of them.

Tilley just shook her head at her. There was no point trying to explain.

Her sisters surrounded her, holding their jackets like a curtain so she could peel off her wet clothes by the car. Tilley wrung them out and Athena wrapped herself, shivering, in the two jackets.

"You could've died, Athena. And then what would we do?" her mom said.

Athena wondered about the answer to that question all the way home. *A lot of housework*, she thought.

Chapter 36

"Will the following students please report to the principal's office immediately: Shannon Brady and Lejla Brkovich." The announcement was repeated.

Athena's adrenalin shot to her fingertips as everyone in class looked at her. Mr. Pikerton was mean. He gave the strap. He was a self-proclaimed disciplinarian. That meant he was someone who didn't believe that children had any rights.

Someone passed her a piece of paper. *I heard Lejla got caught smoking in the bathroom.* Athena's stomach dropped. She crumpled the note and stared straight ahead as Mrs. Paulson droned on. Shannon Brady was in Athena's grade and she got up from her classroom just down the hall and walked by. About forty minutes later, she returned to her class. Her hands were clasped together. Her eyes were puffy and red. Athena would have to wait to see Lejla at lunchtime.

Lejla looked a bit better than Shannon, but Athena demanded to see her hands. There were two welts, one on each. Athena wanted to kill Mr. Beakerton, as he'd been dubbed because of his big nose.

"Did you do it?" Athena hoped against hope that Lejla was innocent.

"Shut up, Theenie, okay?" Lejla was just trying to ignore her.

"Jaja!"

"Don't call me that. I told you." Lejla pinched her arm and dug her fingernails in.

Athena cried out, "Stop it!"

"Then *you* stop it. Yeah, I smoked. So what?"

"So what? Is Beakerton going to call home?"

"Let him."

Athena almost fainted at the thought of what was coming: her father holding a cigarette, pointing it at them, saying, "Don't ever let me catch you doing this."

"Oh my God, oh my God." Athena danced back and forth from the intense anxiety.

"Theenie, I swear to God, get the hell away from me."

Other people wanted Lejla's time and attention. She was the rebel of her generation, the beautiful and the beaten. She broke the rules and did so unapologetically. Athena only felt fear and couldn't understand how her sister didn't. That was what made them so different.

That night was unlike any other. Instead of sending Lejla to her room to receive punishment, her father decided to humiliate her in front of the family, calling her all the usual names and throwing cigarettes at her while everyone had to sit and listen.

"You're a loser. And you'll never be anything but a loser."

Athena wondered how this could be remotely effective when Lejla was anything but. She was the most popular girl at school, with both boys and girls. Surprisingly, there was no belt, just slaps on the head to emphasize Dragan's point. Athena felt as if this was a victory won and disaster avoided.

She snuck down to see Lejla. Knocking softly on the door, she heard, "Go away." But she opened it anyway. Lejla was crying into her pillow.

"What's the matter?" Athena asked.

Lejla looked up incredulously. "I'm a loser, is what."

Athena was taken aback. "Obviously not. Just because he says so? You can't believe that." Athena thought Lejla was being delusional. "He has issues. *He's* the loser."

"Well, it takes one to know one."

"Are you just saying this to feel sorry for yourself?"

"Sorry for myself? Sorry for myself?" Lejla was getting worked up.

"Yes, that's what I said." Athena didn't understand.

"Yeah, that's it, Theenie. I feel sorry for myself. Poor Lejla who gets told she's a loser and no good. Who gets the shit kicked out of her all the time. Who never does anything right. Maybe I do feel sorry for me."

Athena felt unmoved. "You're the most popular girl at school. Everyone wants to be like you. No, they want to *be* you. You're fearless and smart. How can you believe otherwise?" Smoking in the bathroom and getting the strap secured Lejla's legendary status at school. Athena watched other kids change the way they spoke and acted when she was around. She watched Lejla do it as well.

***

The "F Project," as Athena had dubbed it for "friends" and the obvious alliteration of "Freddy" and "Fiona," weighed on Athena. Although she managed to get people talking to the girls, they themselves were shaky and weak inside. Athena wanted them to be confident and happy, like she was. She doubled down on her efforts to compliment them whenever she could, defend them when needed, and encourage them to raise themselves up and accept who they were. After all, they couldn't help being built the way they were. Over time, Athena even caught herself laughing at one of Freddy's jokes or being impressed with Fiona's answers in class. They had their moments.

The school year was winding down, and Fiona announced to the girls while getting ready for gym class that she would be moving again. It was difficult for Athena to explain why she felt as she did at this news. Perhaps it was because Fiona didn't tell her first and thought that everyone would care she was moving at all. Perhaps it was because all the girls, even the mean ones, pretended they were sad she was leaving and surrounded her to give her hugs. It could have been for these reasons or none at all, but Athena's heart hardened into a cold steel trap that Fiona was about to step into.

When Fiona finally circled around to Athena, it was as though Athena didn't recognize her. "What's the matter with you?" Fiona asked.

"Quite the attitude now. Pfft."

"What's your problem, Athena?"

Everyone's eyes turned toward them and the dressing room grew silent.

"I've got no problem, Stick. You're leaving." Athena smiled coldly, staring straight at her.

"They're right. You *are* a bitch."

Athena wanted to gut her alive. What happened next was a grade school crucifixion. Athena undid Fiona Finn with a cruelty that brought every girl in the room to her defence, then silenced them for fear Athena would shine her sinister spotlight of truth on them next.

"Do you really think these people like you? You're as phony as they are. They laugh behind your anorexic back. They were never your friends."

"I hate you. You're the meanest person I've ever met."

As it spiralled, Athena realized what she was doing. But she was powerless to stop it. One of the girls ran and got Miss Wilson, the gym teacher. She took Fiona and Athena to the guidance office. For Athena, it was the only place worse than the principal's office. She had no time for a person who wanted you to talk about your problems and make you explain your feelings like a weakling. As if they could ever help anyone. Athena sat stone-faced, admitting freely to saying all the cruel things she had to Fiona, who was sobbing uncontrollably. Athena hated her.

"What is wrong with you, Athena?" Mrs. Stevenson was horrified and dumbfounded.

"Nothing. Nothing's *wrong* with me, Mrs. Stevenson." Athena stared in her eyes, wishing everyone, including herself, would die.

Mrs. Stevenson's mouth hung open. Her cheeks flushed red and she stammered, "That's, well, that's enough, then. Athena, you can go." The guidance counsellor was scared of her.

Athena was so livid, she wanted to spit on the ground. Her friend had betrayed her and acted so false to everyone. Fiona had never even cared about her. She'd just used her to try to be friends with all the other girls. Well, let her be. Athena decided that life alone was less harsh, but there was still the issue of Frederica.

Freddy didn't say anything to Athena in the change room. She also didn't say anything to Athena on the bus. Athena was self-destructing; it was as if a bomb had detonated. The first shock wave had gone out and blasted a hole in Athena's ideas about being a good and kind person. Athena glared at Frederica, holding her in contempt. She felt as if the girl embodied everything that was wrong with society.

When Athena stepped off the bus, she ran her usual three steps right and left all the way home. Sitting at the kitchen table, she looked at her mom with a critical eye for the first time as she cooked dinner. Her arms were flabby in the back. The bridge of her nose was red and indented from where her glasses with the thick lenses sat. She had a small spare tire around her waist that her apron strings were sucked into and hidden. Athena felt repugnant. This startled her and she shook herself as if she'd been falling into a dark place she knew already.

"I hate Fiona Finn," Athena said.

"No, you don't, Theenie." Tilley stirred the dish in her saucepan without looking up.

"Yes, I do. I hate her and I hate Frederica Ficas."

"No, you don't, sweetie."

Athena wanted to say, "And I hate you too," but she was suddenly overcome with grief at the thought, as if her mom had died.

"I hate them. You don't know how I feel."

"Maybe you don't like them, but you don't hate them. I never want you to use that word. It's a bad word." At this her mother turned and faced her. "To hate someone, you have to use your energy. You can use your energy for good or evil. Hating someone doesn't just destroy the person you hate—it eventually destroys you too, so you must never hate."

Athena listened intently. Her hate had already destroyed her. None of the girls in her class even liked her anymore. Probably Deedee and Sherry wouldn't even want to be her friends, and she'd scared Mrs. Stevenson, arguably one of the nicest teachers in school.

"Well, I definitely don't like them at all."

"Why not?"

"Because they're disgusting losers."

"Maybe they think *you're* a disgusting loser."

"I'm sure they do." This was more than a possibility; it was a probability. "I did a really mean thing today, Mom."

Tilley kept stirring and said, "Well, think about what you did and why. If you think you've been mean, you can always apologize."

"I don't think they'll accept it."

"That doesn't matter. What matters is what you think of you. Now go on outside until dinnertime. It's nice out."

Athena wandered outside across the street and went to her tree. She climbed up and sat on the limb, obscured from view by the thick green leaves. It was cool. What she felt toward her mother marked the lowest point of her day. She wanted her mother to love her and be proud of her, to hug her and tell her everything would be okay. Athena felt afraid of how unstoppable her feelings were. She truly didn't want to be mean, but she felt so little remorse about what she'd done. Athena sat in the tree until the lights came on.

***

"Who would like to take art lessons?"

Lejla liked to sketch on a big drawing pad with charcoal pencils. Athena wasn't allowed to touch them. Lejla was in, and Athena was thrilled that she could attend something with her sister.

When they walked into the art studio, Athena's heart sang. Framed paintings hung on all the walls. There were wooden easels off to the sides, smocks full of paint hanging on hooks, and old windows throwing slanted sunbeams on quaint garden statues and pottery. It smelled like turpentine.

The teacher's name was Lorraine. She had thinning black hair, parted in the middle, that fell to the sides; you could make out the receding hairline underneath.

Lorraine gave Athena and Lejla stools and then walked them through the contents of their kits. She moved an easel in front of each of them, and the girls slipped the smocks over their clothes as Lorraine arranged some fruit in a bowl over a plaid tablecloth on the centre console.

"This is going to be our first study. We'll probably work on it for four or five weeks, depending on how you ladies catch on."

"I want to paint people," Lejla said.

Athena wished she wouldn't say anything. She was just enjoying the paint and the brushes.

"You will eventually," Lorraine said, laughing, "but we're going to build up to that. Here, we want to work on shading and depth, so it's easiest with what's called a still life." Lorraine gave a tutorial for a few minutes and then gave pointers as the girls progressed.

After the third class, Athena could see her painting taking shape and recognized the form she was trying to depict. The class sped by and she didn't want to leave.

As they were finishing packing up, Lorraine said to Tilley, "They're both good, but this one has real talent."

"Really?"

"Yes. She's special."

Athena's back was to them and Lejla was already walking out ahead of her. Athena wondered who she was talking about.

That night, Tilley came in as they were getting ready for bed. Athena pulled her nightgown over her head and saw her mother picking up the art box on her desk.

"What are you doing?" Athena asked.

"You're not doing art anymore."

Athena stood like a stone. "But why?" She could barely push the words past her lips. "I love it."

"Yes, and apparently you're quite good at it. But you're good at lots of things. Your sister needs something to be good at. So you're done with art."

Athena struggled for a mere minute. The memory of her sister suffering, her screams, drowned out Athena's internal protests. Her eyes started to well up, her tears betraying her pain.

"Just climb into bed, okay? I'm not going to discuss it. You'll be fine."

Athena nodded and climbed into bed.

Tilley flipped the light switch and the room went dark. Athena lay on her back and let her eyes adjust. Dark, grainy images came from out of the blackness. The hall light shone through the crack of the door. She spoke through the ceiling, the roof, and past the night sky and stars straight to God, whispering, "Yes. I'll be fine."

***

As rapidly as the economy had declined, talk of nuclear war, espionage, and fallout shelters took precedence. Athena felt as if her generation would be the one to save the planet from waste in landfills, corporate greed, and now nuclear war.

"Pops, listen to me. If they're going to drop a bomb somewhere, it's going to be Detroit. It's a major manufacturing city. We need to move or build a lead-lined shelter."

"Hey, can you zip it, please? I just got in the door and I wanna relax, alright?"

Athena's frustration mounted, as she was unable to bring the importance of self-preservation to the forefront of the dinner conversation.

"I tell you, the interest rates are gonna kill us, and they just keep raisin' taxes. Used to be you paid your house off in your lifetime and you were good, but these days the banks wanna own ya."

Athena knew her dad was speaking the truth. It was hard for poor people to lift themselves up. She was lucky that both her parents worked. Just the other week, some guy had jumped off the Ambassador Bridge because he went broke.

Athena wondered how much money a life was worth, exactly, or if it differed person to person. She thought of herself as valuable.

Athena took over the concrete storage area under the stairs and stockpiled it with what the newspaper deemed useful items: a transistor radio, blankets and pillows, canned goods, batteries, candles, a first aid kit, and a stash of candy.

When she'd set it up to her liking, she sat inside with Max and Mitzi and explained that if they heard a bomb alarm, they should report there immediately. "Look, it's a real thing. We'll be annihilated. The world will be over if they start a nuclear war."

"They dropped bombs in Japan and the world didn't end," Danica answered. "Mom isn't going to like you bringing food down here."

"It's totally dirty in there," Lejla said in her best Valley Girl accent.

"You sound stupid when you talk like that," Athena replied, going up the stairs with white dust all over her feet.

"You're making a mess. Gross!" Lejla exclaimed.

Athena rolled her eyes. "I'm going to clean it up, *obviously*," she said, yelling this last word. Athena returned from the garage with a bucket and mop.

"Nobody wants to, like, go in your stupid closet," Danica said, then joined Lejla in the family room to watch their favourite soap opera.

"You both sound so lame and fake." Athena stepped in front of the television to enlighten her sisters. "Neither of you is from California, so why, like, do you think, like, anyone is going to, like, believe that you, like, talk like that?" She flipped her hair, which had grown almost to her shoulders since she'd made a stand against the onslaught of her mom's scissors.

"Get out of the way, you brat!" Danica tried to look around her.

Athena knew that neither of them would get off the couch. She knew better than to extend her unwelcome behaviour beyond the one taunt. Athena loved the daytime love stories too, but couldn't tolerate something always happening to prevent the lovers from getting together. It was just too hard to take.

Chapter 37

"The award for highest academic average goes to Lejla Brkovich."

Athena watched from her seat in the senior band as her sister walked across the stage to receive her award. It was the third one that night. She was the valedictorian and gave a glorious speech, making everyone laugh.

"Of course, I couldn't be prouder. Brilliant and beautiful." Dragan shook congratulatory hands extended toward him.

Athena gave Lejla a hug. She smelled of smoke. She wanted to stand next to her for the picture, but her mom pulled Lejla to the side as the parents were leaving. There was a dance afterward. Athena looked suspiciously at her sister. Why couldn't she just do the right things?

"Why does Theenie have to stay?" Lejla had made her point many times that week that Athena wouldn't fit in. But the dance was for the seniors, and that meant Athena.

"Please stop it. She's your sister," Tilley said.

"Yeah, I'm your sister," Athena said loudly.

"You too. Stop being a moron."

"She can't. She's embarrassing, Mom," Lejla said.

"I'll talk to her."

Lejla marched off to be with her friends.

"Listen, don't embarrass your sister. But keep an eye on her, all right?"

Athena nodded. It was tricky watching Lejla, trying to prevent her from doing something that would get her in trouble and then worrying about lying to her parents. "I won't embarrass her." This was lie number one.

When the dance started, Athena nourished the smallest hope that Niko would want to dance with her. As she looked at the girls, all grown up with their hair and makeup done, she knew that no boy would ever be interested in her. She determined that the wide-open gym floor, which would be for dancing if anyone got over their awkwardness, was an invitation to do cartwheels from one wall to the other. On occasion, Athena would yell, "Coming through!"

and take a push or a punch. Inciting this anger delighted her, and she laughed heartily at injecting an otherwise fake-filled night with fun.

Lejla grabbed her by the arm and yanked her to the side. "Stop it, Theen. Just stop it."

Athena would stop for Lejla, but not just because she was hurting her arm.

The only lights that were on were the stage lights. "Lovin', Touchin', Squeezin'" was on, and Lejla turned down the first two guys and then said yes to Zack. He smoked and did drugs, and Athena didn't like that. She circled the perimeter of the gym walls on the cinder blocks, pretending she was scaling a window ledge forty stories off the ground. Niko was dancing with Christine LeBoeuf. She was graduating and had the biggest boobs in the school. Even the teachers made jokes with the boys about Christine's boobs. Lejla and Zack were kissing.

Athena snapped back to reality when she heard "Hey, are you gonna jump?"

Charlie Proctor was in her grade but not her class. He was a richie and a stoner, but everyone liked him.

"Yeah, I was thinking about it."

"How high up are we?" Next to Athena, Charlie pressed himself against the wall.

She laughed. "Too high to jump and make it."

"Well, I really hope you don't jump."

"Oh? Is that so?" Athena smiled freely and laughed.

"You have a pretty smile."

Athena felt suddenly conspicuous and icky. She withdrew her energy. Tilley had constantly told them that boys have no self-control, and if you give them the slightest idea you'll do anything with them, they won't be able to stop themselves and then whatever happens will be your fault. That was the only conversation about sex Athena had had with her mother.

"Okay. You're making me want to jump now." Charlie laughed. "Come on, let's dance."

Athena wanted to very badly but didn't want to lead him on. "Listen, you're nice, but I'm not allowed to have a boyfriend."

"Wow. You have it all figured out, Athena." He was still laughing. "Don't worry. I just like you as a friend."

Of course, Athena thought, suddenly crestfallen that he wasn't madly in with love for her. She followed him to the dance floor.

"Sorry my hands are sweaty. I'm afraid of heights." Charlie laughed again.

He had sweet brown eyes and a little upturned nose. His hair was longer and tipped blonde. The song ended.

"That was nice, Athena. You have a good summer."

"Yeah, you too."

For the rest of the night, Athena wondered what would happen if she married Charlie instead of Niko. Niko had danced with almost all the girls in grade eight and made out with two of them. It didn't matter to Athena. Charlie was like the safety net underneath the window ledge.

"I saw you dancing with Charlie," Lejla teased her.

Athena blushed.

"Stop!" she said, but then added, "He's nice. We're just friends."

Athena felt reassured that someone eventually would like her, even if she weren't pretty enough for Niko.

After the dance, Lejla emptied out her locker. There weren't many people left.

"Mom said she'd be here by ten o'clock," Athena reminded her.

"I'm going with Shannon to her house to sleep over. There's going to be a pool party. *You're* not coming."

This stung. Shannon was in her grade. Athena started to think of a protest but pictured everyone in swimsuits and her flat front being front and centre.

"Here, take my stuff," said Lejla.

"Come on, Lej, my mom's here now. Hey, Athena." Shannon smiled at her.

She waved to Lejla, who was already gone out the front door to the circle. Lots of cars were lined up. Athena went outside.

Please don't let me be the last one, Athena prayed. Relief flooded through her when her mom pulled into the parking lot. She didn't wait for her to drive all the way up; instead, she burst into a run to meet her, the air filled with the fishy smell of June bugs and the street lights making the summer night sky look purple. Athena felt a lightness as she thought about how proud she was of her sister, and how pleased she was that Charlie had asked her to dance.

***

Danica's voice interrupted Athena's conversation with her dolls. "Come out of your bunker, weirdo. Mom wants to talk to you about camp."

Athena made a careful inspection of the safe house, pulled the chain on the lightbulb near the entrance, and crawled out.

"Camp? Am I going to camp?" Athena was delighted to finally earn a week away with real cottages, canoes, and horseback riding. She would need to find out which weeks Sherry and Deedee were going.

"Yes. I'm signing you and the twins up for two weeks," Tilley said.

Athena tried to comprehend how this would work. "Wait, I don't—"

"You leave this Saturday morning. The bus is going at six from the church, so we have to get packing. Here's the list."

"Mom, what? What camp?"

"Serbian camp."

"It's *church* camp." Danica's eyes widened as she mocked her.

"Are they going?" Athena motioned to Danica and Lejla.

"No!" Lejla said dramatically, as if it were even an option.

"Then why do I have to go?"

"Because I want someone there with the twins. Besides, you'll love it." Tilley added this last part with an unconvincing lilt in her voice.

"You have to go to church three times a day," Danica said, laughing.

"It's only twice," Tilley added, and then they all laughed.

Athena was hurt. "Well, I don't want to go."

"Too bad, kid. You're going." And that was that.

Athena sulked and cried hard into her pillow, cursing her family for their dismissive control over her. She was appeased by Mitzi's excitement.

"Kat and Roxy are going too," Tilley informed Athena two days later.

"Why didn't you say so?"

Saturday came quickly. The sky was getting lighter as they loaded their suitcases, kissed and hugged everyone, and drove to the church.

"Athena is in charge, and you will listen to her," Tilley instructed the twins. She looked at Athena. "If anything happens to them, you'll be responsible."

"*Theen!*" Kat was hanging around the top step and waved her over.

Athena bolted, but then stopped and hugged her mom. "Thanks, Mom."

"Be good. Remember your manners."

Athena winked and ran onto the bus.

***

Mosquitoes were starting to come out, so everyone got sprayed from head to toe with repellent. The girls changed into their skirts and everyone marched up the hill and across the road. It was peaceful at night, and the church felt cool compared to the damp heat of the evening. There were no ornate stained glass windows, just panels of amber leaded glass that filtered the lavender blue of the evening sun from the oranges and reds. Athena enjoyed watching the colours change as they followed along in the prayer book, singing responses. Church had an immediate effect on Athena. Her heart rate slowed and she felt calm.

After three days, she realized that she didn't have to worry if her dad was going to come home drunk and start a fight. She just had to wake up for the morning bell, after she'd stayed up all night with six girls from the States. They'd all lain across two beds, sharing stories about boys at camp, boys in life, and life in general. Athena listened and learned.

Bobby-Rose had definitely kissed the most boys. "I just love kissing, y'all. I don't care if I'm a-goin' to hell. It's worth it. Y'all need to lighten up. It's not like I'm havin' intercourse."

No one had done that before. The boys seemed small and so silly compared to the girls they were trying to impress, but Bobby-Rose had kissed them all by the end of the first week, sneaking out of the cabin to meet them. Athena wondered how she even stayed awake to do that.

One day, Father John led the older group of campers to a willow tree near the far side of the lake. They had all hiked around and sat on the grass.

"I know times are changing. Things aren't the same as when I was young, and I want to talk openly with you about something that's important to God. And that's abstinence," Father John said.

When he spoke, Athena didn't feel self-conscious. He was married, like most Serbian priests, so he didn't seem creepy. She could tell he was kind and honest from the way he spoke. She had a great respect for him and so didn't take his words lightly.

Athena raised her hand. "What happens if you do have sex before you're married? Will God forgive you?"

Father John looked thoughtful. Trying to find the right words, he covered his mouth with his hand and tugged his beard a couple of times. "God will always forgive a repentant heart, Athena. But when we know the difference between right and wrong and we choose to walk God's path, this pleases Him more than anything."

Athena made up her mind right then and there: she would definitely wait until she was married to have sex.

Later, the girls discussed this. "Y'all are crazy. I won't be able to wait!" Bobby-Rose laughed as she hung down from the top bunk.

"Bobby-Rose, you're goin' to hell," Kat told her.

"God'll forgive me!" She laughed again.

On Thursday of the second week, Roxy ran into the older girls' cabin and tapped Athena on the shoulder. "Mitzi's crying."

Athena jumped out of bed and rushed to see her sister. "What's the matter?" she asked softly.

Her little sister burst into sobs. "I miss . . . *home*." She struggled to get the words out and breathe.

"It's all right. I'm here." She crawled into bed next to her and hugged and kissed her. "Today we're going to the amusement park. We're going to go on rides and play games."

"But . . . I . . . want . . . Mommy." She cried even harder into Athena's chest.

"We'll be home in three days. Let's have a good day today. Let's not wish away our fun. It'll be Saturday soon, and by then you'll think camp is so fun, you'll wish you could stay longer."

"No, I won't!" Mitzi insisted.

Athena chuckled softly. "Okay, maybe you won't." She pinched Mitzi's small knuckles. Her hand was so tiny. "Can I have some knuckle skin?"

"You made it, Mitz!"

Her little face shone in the moonlit sky. Thousands of stars twinkled overhead.

"Look at all those stars. Let's make a wish!" Athena said.

Mitzi shut her eyes tightly.

As Athena watched her, she felt a deep love for her and wanted her wish to be fulfilled. She looked back up and saw a light streak across the sky. "I think I just saw a shooting star!"

"You did!"

"Let's lie down for a minute here, Mitz. I want to watch for more."

They lay down in the soft, clover-filled grass. Crickets chirped and frogs croaked in the stillness.

"There's one! Is that one?" Mitzi pointed excitedly.

"Yes, I think it is," Athena said, smiling.

One after another, at least ten stars dove down to Earth, drawing a thin white line before disappearing. Athena felt the entire Earth's mass underneath them, supporting them, and the vast sky covering them like a blanket, the universe cradling it all in its arms.

"Mitzi?"

"Yeah?"

"I love you."

"I love you, too, Theenie."

"Tomorrow we go home. Let's go to sleep now so it comes fast!"

Mitzi smiled and jumped up. Athena followed her into the cabin, not knowing exactly why she felt so sad.

Chapter 38

Although it was Athena's last year in grade school, this was overshadowed by Lejla's high school debut. Every day a new conversation arose regarding her meteoric appearance on the scene.

"I heard Lejla is dating Chris Grant. Is that true?" Sherry asked Athena.

"Who's Chris Grant?"

"A senior, the president of the student council, the most popular guy?"

"How do you even know this?" Athena squinted at Sherry.

"People talk. How do *you* not know? She's *your* sister."

Athena just shook her head. She had heard Lejla speak on the phone with her friends of boys she liked, but only if her dad wasn't home and her mom wasn't within earshot.

"You're not smoking, are you?" Athena later asked Lejla.

"No," Lejla shot back.

But Athena could smell the smoke on her as she walked past her, despite the heavy dose of perfume. "Don't do that, Jaja. Dad'll kill you."

"He's not going to catch me, and you wouldn't dare tell him."

"Of course not." But Athena worried for her sister's life.

***

"Get your dad for dinner, please, and ring the bell," Tilley said.

Athena stood at the top of the stairs. She shook the china bell, the tinkling summoning everyone. Athena was required to tell her dad in person. At the bottom of the stairs, Athena opened the sliding door to the toy room where his desk sat and coughed, waving the thick blue smoke cloud away from her face.

Athena chopped the words out. "Dad. Dinner." She ran upstairs.

Tonight was lasagna, so everyone was there early.

"Are you going to go out for any teams or clubs?" Tilley asked the high schoolers.

"No one does teams, Mom," Lejla said.

"No one does teams? Sure they do," their dad said. "Maybe if you weren't so busy wasting your time doing your hair and your stupid makeup, you'd be interested—"

"It *isn't* stupid."

This is not what you should do, thought Athena. *This is not what you should do.*

"Are you talkin' back? Don't get smart with me, young lady!"

"Okay, okay, let's not start." Tilley put a salad on the table.

Everyone sat very still.

Dragan pushed his glasses back up onto his nose and lifted his fork, then slammed his hand back down on the table. "Goddammit! This is *my* house! And you don't speak to me like that!"

"Like what?" Lejla muttered. Her voice wasn't even as loud as striking a match, but it had the same effect.

"You little—" He rose and lunged at her across the table.

Athena reflexively darted away, and Lejla dodged to the side to avoid his hand. She blocked him and struck back, yelling, "Don't hit me!"

Athena inhaled sharply. What on earth was this? No one talked back. You couldn't even look back. Fighting back was unheard of.

He lifted the table out of the way to get to her. Tilley shoved Max and Mitzi out into the dining room, telling them to take their plates, as Dragan hauled Lejla out of the kitchen.

But this is different, Athena thought.

Lejla dug her heels in and punched and scratched at his hands to keep them off her, shouting, "Don't touch me!"

Her dad was as much in shock as she was. He wasn't drunk. He got a few slaps in and held on to her, but as soon as he released his grip she ran past him and down the stairs, yelling, "I'm leaving! I'm not staying here."

"You better not leave!" he shouted.

But the front door was wide open and the screen door hadn't shut before Lejla was off the driveway and out of sight.

The first time was for almost a week. When Lejla was gone, Dragan drank almost every day and it was difficult for everyone, especially Athena. No one said a word about her. When she came home, no one talked about it.

"Don't mention your sister. It will upset your father," Tilley told them.

There was always some reason now for a fight. Dragan would interrogate Lejla. "Have you been smoking? Have you been drinking? Are you high on drugs? Where have you been?"

It would be easy to blame Lejla for acting out in all these ways, except Athena knew what her sister's life had been like.

"Why would you steal liquor out of the cabinet, Jaja? Holy shit, you're going to get yourself killed," Athena would say.

"I hope so."

"Don't say that!"

This was the theme repeated week in and week out.

***

Athena doubled her efforts to make a barrier between school and home so that when she stepped over the line, she would forget her sad home life and feel well and happy. She was working on a character, Barbara, she was especially fond of. She had taken one of her father's cigarettes to hold and talked like an old Jewish lady from New York, expounding on everything she saw.

Mrs. Zezel was a stay-at-home mom who had volunteered to teach the library class. Athena thought the course was pointless, and one day in class she went into character as Barbara.

"So whaddaya gonna do when they invent a totally se-pa-rate course and call it li-bary? You gonna go and pretend that the Doo-ey decimal system ain't just a matta o' knowin' the alphabet and countin' from one to ten? How the hell is this even a course? It's pathetic. Pa-the-tic."

Charlie, who had grown to have a fond appreciation for Barbara's rhetoric, laughed.

"It's a class for morons. That's what alla youse are—mo-rons."

"Is there something you want to share with the class, Athena?" Mrs. Zezel said.

Athena smirked and shook her head.

"Well, then, perhaps you should pay attention."

"No, thanks," Athena mumbled, lowering her head.

"I beg your pardon?"

It could've been that Charlie was watching, or that there was a shakiness in Mrs. Zezel's voice, but whatever it was, something triggered Athena.

"I said no, thanks." Athena lifted her head and spoke plainly, looking straight into the woman's light eyes.

"How rude." Mrs. Zezel's nose wrinkled up and she looked around at the students' faces. They were all sitting on the library floor like kids in grade one.

"It's not rude—it's just the truth."

"I'm sorry . . . and what exactly is that?" stammered Mrs. Zezel.

"The truth is, this course is stupid and unnecessary."

The woman's mouth fell open and her face flushed crimson, spreading into her neck. "I beg your pardon, young lady," she said with effort.

"No need. It's not your fault. You want to make something that's important to you—that matters to *you*—important to us. But it doesn't matter to me or probably anyone else here. We all know how to use the library. This is the most boring thing I've ever listened to, and that's because you're just a housewife who wanted something to do. You're as stupid and unnecessary as this course."

Everyone's mouths hung open.

Athena had made her statement calmly because she believed it was true, and when Mrs. Zezel burst into tears, she knew she was right. People hated hearing the truth, and Athena wished she could have taken it back.

When she was getting up to go to the office, Charlie said, "That was cold, dude."

Athena didn't want to be cold. It just happened.

***

Charlie and Shannon Brady were friends. They had gone to the same grade school before. They both lived on the drive; everyone who lived there was rich.

Charlie fought alongside Athena when she played army on rainy days. She would fall to the ground with pretend grenades, calling for backup on hand-held pretend walkie-talkies. None of the other girls played this game; it was childish and strange, they told her. But plenty of boys gravitated to Athena's make-believe antics. She came up with different scenarios, immersing herself in the jungle or desert, making the hour-long recess fly by.

James, Karl, and Shaun were three losers who were always good to be on the squad. "That was fun," they'd often say. Athena noticed that the boys were pretty kind to one another, and Charlie didn't go after the guys who weren't cool the way the girls went after the uncool girls.

"Men cause all the wars, but they seem nicer to one another than girls," Athena mentioned to Charlie as they were strolling around the playground.

"Guys are not nice," Charlie observed. "They'll kill you if you cry or show any weakness. You have to be tough. Like kill or be killed. For sure."

"Girls are mean." Athena laughed when Charlie's eyebrows lifted and he looked as if he hadn't just heard her say that. She hesitated. "I know, but it's not like I go out of my way to be mean."

Charlie stared into her eyes and pressed his face closer.

"Well, why are you my friend, then, if I'm so mean?" Athena asked, cocking her head.

"Because you're funny and smart."

Athena felt her neck getting hot. "And you're dumb." Laughing, she shoved Charlie and ran past him. She turned and waved him to come with her since he was hanging back.

Reluctantly, he jogged after her. "You are weird." He smiled.

"Why, thank you, shuga," Athena said as her character Madge, using a Southern belle drawl. "Whateva adventures are we gonna get up to today?" She skipped toward the monkey bars with Charlie in tow.

Later, in math class, Athena took a note from Kathy, who sat next to her.

"It's from Shannon," Kathy whispered.

Athena opened it behind her textbook, which she stood up to block the teacher's view. One question was written on it: *Do you like Charlie?* And then two boxes with *yes* beside one and *no* beside the other. Without thinking anything other than *That's simple*, Athena ticked the yes box, folded the paper up, and handed it back.

When the class moved from math to music, Shannon caught up to Athena and grabbed her sleeve. "You know, Charlie likes you too."

"Yeah." She already knew this.

Shannon's smile made her look as if she just bitten into a lemon. Athena was confused and looked at her face intently. "What do you mean, he likes me?"

"Like *likes* you."

Athena felt sick. There wasn't anyone, boy or a girl, she liked more in the whole school than Charlie. He was so funny and sweet. They were best friends. "Now what?"

"Now he's going to ask you out."

"What?" Athena shouted in protest.

Shannon laughed.

"No!" Athena was revolted.

Shannon was a grown-up in Athena's eyes. She wore a C-cup bra and had a boyfriend in high school.

"I don't want to do anything like hold hands. Or kiss!" Athena was panicking.

Shannon grabbed her hand and pulled her into the girls' washroom. She checked the stalls. No one was in them. "You don't have to do any of those things."

"Then why would we go out?"

"Because he likes you."

"Right. And I like him."

"Exactly."

"So we're friends. Going out is different, though. It'll make it awkward." Athena wondered what Niko would think of it. She didn't want him to think she wasn't his.

"No, it won't. I promise."

"Please tell him not to." Athena pushed past Shannon and ran to catch up to her classmates.

Nearly two weeks later, when Athena was grabbing her things from her locker between classes, she turned abruptly into Charlie. "Hey," she said.

"Hey, can I talk to you?"

"Sure. What is it?"

Charlie shuffled his feet and blushed, and Athena suddenly hated him. "Would you go out with me?"

"You? No!" Athena didn't filter her words; they just flew out into his hurt face. "We're just friends. Gross me out." She wasn't lying. Feeling uncomfortable was what grossed her out; it just came across as if she meant *him*.

They stood by the lockers. Charlie's eyes watered and he rubbed them with his finger and thumb and then looked squarely at Athena. "You are . . . a . . . bitch."

Her very best friend, the one person she looked forward to seeing every day, the one person who actually made her feel special, had condemned her. She couldn't get away from it; it was who she was.

***

The eighth graders were planning the year-end celebration. Ten people sat around Athena's table. As luck would have it, Shannon was next to her. Her relief was palpable. Athena pushed her insecurity down. The boys outnumbered the girls and started talking about blow jobs the second the teachers were out of hearing range.

"I'm just saying you could suck it, Shannon. I think you'd like it," Adam said. He already shaved his face. If he didn't, he'd have a full beard.

"You're a pig, Adam. Suck your own dick."

"I've tried. I'm not flexible enough."

Laughter erupted. Athena nervously went along. Adam changed the subject to the discharge he got every time Miss Freeman bent over in her low-cut tops.

"Just shut up, Adam. Let's do our work." Shannon was in charge.

"Yeah," Athena said in a small voice.

"What did you say, punk?"

"Nothing," Athena answered.

"Yeah, you did. You're a little bitch, Athena. I'll bet you don't even know what a dick looks like, do you?"

Athena stared hard, steeling herself to the eyes riveted on her. There was no proper way to answer this question, but she replied calmly, "I've taken health class."

Adam looked away and came back with "I'll bet you don't know what discharge means. You're a little kid. You don't belong in grade eight. You should be in grade four."

"Yes, I do," Athena bluffed.

"Yeah? What is it?"

"It's gross. I don't want to say."

"You won't because you don't know."

Athena paused and then leaned toward Shannon and, shielding her mouth with her hand, whispered as quietly as she could into her ear, "I don't know what it is."

Shannon looked at him and said, "She knows."

Gratitude flooded Athena's body. She reflected that some moments shake the foundation of generalizations, like "Girls are mean," and that those generalizations, whether they're about yourself or others, must be re-examined. These epiphanies were part of growing up. Athena understood.

***

It was perhaps naive of Athena to think that by her good grades alone she would be elected valedictorian at the end of the year. Since becoming a senior, she had made three teachers cry and been in the principal's office no fewer than twenty times. She rarely spoke plain English in school and had to be told repeatedly to remove her hood so she could see the board or hear the question being asked. Still, it was an egregious oversight.

The situation with Charlie had lightened up. He was going out with Stella now. Shannon and Athena sat at the back of the bus that took them to a different school because theirs didn't have the facilities. Boys had woodworking and girls got cooking lessons. Charlie had his ghetto blaster and carried it on his shoulder. His favourite was an AC/DC song, and when it came on he would stand up and play the air guitar. He looked consumed with happiness, and Athena liked to see that.

It was the last shop class. Athena felt a tap on her left shoulder from the aisle. She turned to see Dwight, the only boy in class shorter than her, standing there.

"Athena, all the boys wanted to get together and make you something special to remember us by." He was holding it between his hands.

Athena's heart fluttered.

He extended a block of wood. "Every single guy in our class signed it."

Maybe it was because of all the help she gave them in class or because of the fun way she goofed around. She knew she wasn't exactly like the other girls, and maybe they saw that too, that she was special. The signatures of all the boys completely filled the back of the block. Athena tried to think of how she could thank them graciously without making the other girls jealous.

Dwight handed her the block, spinning it around, and said, "We even engraved your name."

A metal plate near the bottom had *Athena* scratched dully into it. Above it, burned into the wood in huge capital letters was *SUPERBITCH*.

All of the blood drained from Athena's face and went to her heart.

Shannon leaned into her, squeezed her leg slightly, and said, "*Do not* cry."

Cheering and laughter rumbled from the back to the front as Dwight turned and raised his fist in victory. He high-fived every boy on his way back to his seat.

Shannon repeated herself firmly. "Athena, don't give them the satisfaction. Do not cry."

Athena didn't. She stood and held the plaque. "How sweet. You guys got the spelling right. Too bad you couldn't come up with the two dollars to get an actual engraver, but it's cheap and tacky, so it's perfect—it will always remind me of all of you." She slid back down into her seat and put the plaque beside her. It was as if it were burning her leg.

"Good job." Shannon looked impressed.

It took all of Athena's focus to keep the shooting pain in her heart from pushing past the back of her throat and erupting into a sob. She would save that for when she was alone in her room.

Chapter 39

The preparations for graduation were extensive. What was the big deal? They were moving on to the next year. Why was this particular year so important? What significance did it hold? Athena felt a million miles away from anyone in her class.

Shannon had been a beautiful person to sit next to; she worked well on projects and was fun and loyal, but there was no reason for them to remain friends. With Shannon being the most physically mature and Athena the most immature person in the class, they made an odd pair. Only convenience would make Shannon want to continue their friendship.

"You're one of the best friends I've ever had. I'm really going to miss you, Theenie."

Athena took Shannon's kindness as simply another exception to her assumptions about people with money.

Athena spent a considerable amount of time looking for the perfect graduation dress. She finally found a high necked, long-sleeved white dress at a boutique downtown.

Lejla helped with her hair and makeup. Her braces had straightened her teeth quite dramatically over the past year. She looked at herself in the mirror. "I'm actually kind of pretty," she said. She'd never thought it was true until that moment.

As all the girls gathered in groups, crying and hugging and promising to keep in touch over the summer, or saying lies like "I'll never forget you," Athena watched them in wonder. None of those emotions touched her. She wasn't going to miss them, since most of them were going to her high school anyway. Pretending this year meant more than any other didn't make sense to her; it wasn't as if she had suddenly become someone else. Girls who she knew spoke badly of one another were saying, "I love you so much." All that acting was so much effort and so ridiculous. Athena couldn't help wanting to laugh at all of it, but she made sure to laugh *with* everyone. She remembered her manners. She refrained from telling everyone how silly they all were being and for once let herself enjoy the show. She just told everyone she was happy—and she was. She wanted to remember this night, and she wanted them to remember her like this.

At the dance, Athena stepped up and asked Charlie. He hesitated, then agreed. "You look really pretty, Athena." She danced with every boy there.

Athena had packed an overnight bag for Shannon's pool party. Her backyard was lit up just enough to keep it mysterious. In the darkness, Athena felt secure in her bathing suit. She still hadn't begun to develop like the other girls but she didn't care.

Athena turned and saw Shannon laughing and was struck by a strange nostalgia. She got choked up, as she admired the girl who had stood up for her and would soon no longer be around. *This is what it feels like to miss someone,* Athena thought. The moment slowed and almost stopped; Athena committed it to memory.

The moonlight caught the water droplets dripping off everyone in their perfect youth, in their newness. It was magical. Athena observed all of this and herself in the same small moment, somehow outside of their reality. The water splashing, people in the midst of a game . . . she was a part of it. She longed to be the person who was watched and to abandon this awareness. It didn't seem possible, so she simply allowed the images to float into her consciousness so she could capture them.

***

Although Athena had become Shannon's friend in school, she reverted to Sherry, who was close by for the summer. Frederica had been in hiding, as usual. She hadn't come to the pool party and no one spoke about her or cared much. Athena had stopped speaking to her and felt it best to just leave it at that. Sherry's parents had bought a cottage, though, and she would be staying there for six solid weeks.

With Sherry gone, Athena wondered how she would find things to do for the summer.

Preparing to leave for work, Tilley pushed open Athena's bedroom door. "Athena, you're in charge of the twins, and I put the list on the fridge. Thank you. You're the best."

Athena only processed the information when her mom was halfway down the stairs. She bolted out of bed. "Mom! Wait, wait! What list?"

"On the fridge."

Athena ran to the kitchen. On the fridge was a Post-it Note filled with her mother's handwriting. At the top was *Athena* and underneath was every conceivable chore.

"Mom!" Athena yelled, running out onto the driveway in her bare feet. She slammed the hood of her mother's car as she was backing out.

Tilley stopped abruptly and put the window down. "Athena, I'm going to be late. What is it?"

"Mom, this isn't fair."

"I'm not discussing it."

"Dani and Jaja don't do a thing!" Athena stomped.

"Stop that right now. You will do as you're told. Besides, you know your sisters won't help me. You're the only one who does."

Athena struggled under the guilt and pressure, but she was no match for it. Her need for her mother's approval outweighed everything. Her occasional outbursts were simply to draw more attention to the fact that she would do as she was asked.

"I love you, Theenie. You're my favourite."

Athena watched her mom back out of the driveway. Chores were one thing, but the twins too? Athena blew out a heavy sigh.

The grass needed cutting, and she decided she would do it first thing, as it was already over eighty degrees outside. The mower had a detachable bag. It was heavy, though, and the sweat ran in a small river down the middle of her back as she struggled to empty the grass into black trash bags that were practically melting in the sun.

She was pouring herself a tall glass of orange juice when her siblings started waking up.

"Why are you all sweaty?" Danica asked her, pushing her away from the open fridge, where Athena was cooling herself down.

"I did the grass. It's boiling outside."

Danica grabbed the milk and shut the door. "Oh, Mom left you a list."

Athena said nothing. She slid into the bench and watched Danica get the cereal out.

"You could do something too, you know," Athena told her.

"Oh, I did—my nails." She held up her long red manicured nails.

Chapter 40

"You do not talk to me. You do not approach me. We are not related. Do you understand?"

Athena nodded warily to Lejla.

Danica had already left for the bus. It was the first day of high school. Athena watched Lejla leave and run ahead to catch up to Danica.

"Don't forget to lock the door!" Athena yelled to the twins, but there was no answer.

Seeing Sherry at the bus stop was a relief. The crowd seemed so much bigger and taller than she remembered. Athena had grown only about an inch taller over the summer, and she looked so much younger compared to her cohort.

"See you're still a midget, Brk," said one of the boys in her year.

Athena noted all the new jeans. She was wearing sweatpants. Danica and Lejla had insisted she wear a polo shirt so she wouldn't be a "complete embarrassment."

"Are you nervous?" Athena asked Sherry.

"Kind of excited more than nervous." Sherry was smiling and looking over Athena's head at the other people assembling.

"Do you want to sit with me on the bus?"

"Um . . . sure."

Athena felt as if Sherry had taken stock of her other options before settling for her. It would be this kind of year.

"How do we know where to go?" Athena asked Sherry once they found their seats.

"We go to the gym, and then you find your name on a list. That will tell you where your homeroom is, and then you get your schedule there."

Why had her sisters failed to tell her this? And why hadn't she asked until now? But she knew the answer: she didn't live in the future. Things just crept up.

Athena followed Sherry to the gym, and then Sherry was gone. There must have been five hundred people, mostly standing in circles. Chart paper was taped around the walls with letters of the alphabet from *A* to *Z*. A lot of people were in line for *B*. Danica and Lejla were nearing the front already. Athena knew better than to cut in line with them, so she stood at the back. She carried an empty milk bag with her lunch in it and a purse Lejla had given her to hold her pencil case. Athena registered the weight of the strap on her shoulder and felt awkward with her hands full. She shuffled forward.

Athena scanned the list. *Bowman, Bradford, Brennan, Brkovich, Athena.* Right underneath that was *Brkovich, Danica* and then *Brkovich, Lejla.* How would no one know she was their sister? Athena traced a line from her name across the page. It said *AP*. Athena tried again. Same line, *AP*. She looked at her sisters' names. *Brkovich, Danica, 223. Brkovich, Lejla, 124.* Athena looked around; suddenly the gym looked quite empty. She scanned quickly for a teacher and saw none. Her heart started to pound.

"Okay, Athena, stay calm," she whispered. "Excuse me?" She turned to the boy behind her, who was stepping around her to look for his name. It was on a different sheet. Once he located it, he turned to leave. "Excuse me," Athena said.

"Can't help you, frosh," he said and walked out abruptly. Apparently, that was how everyone felt.

Athena thought she might try to find AP. As she wandered through the hall, she started to panic. Other people rushed past her with purpose.

Twice she attempted to ask someone where she should go, but a shrill bell rang and everyone scattered into classrooms she wasn't a part of. She stood in the empty hallway.

Lejla stepped out of her room and, seeing Athena, ran over and yanked her by the arm toward the lockers. "What the hell are you doing?" She glanced around to see who might be watching.

"No one would help me," Athena said.

"Shut up. Where's your class?"

"I don't know," Athena said, as though this were obvious. "It just said AP."

"Oh my God. That's art portable. It's outside. Go. Go." Lejla shoved her down the hall and started to go back to her classroom.

"Lejla!" Athena pleaded, her hands outstretched with her milk bag and purse.

Lejla gave her a horrified once-over.

"Help me. Where is it?"

Lejla just pointed down the hall, said, "It's outside," and disappeared.

Athena rushed down the long hallway, looking for an exit. She saw the entrance where the bus had let them off and went outside. It was raining. She held the milk bag over her head as she clung to the brick wall, searching for the portable. There it was! She ran to the door and opened it to find twenty very mature-looking people, waiting for the teacher.

"Is this the art portable?" she asked.

The students only laughed.

Athena stepped out and, looking just past the portable, discovered four more. The third one was the art portable. She was dripping wet and her feet squished in her shoes. She poked her head into the classroom.

The art teacher, aggravated, stopped speaking instantly and said, "I'm Mrs. Jackson. You must be Athena Br-br—"

"Brkovich." Athena was happy to tell anyone so they could connect her to her sisters, but it didn't appease her teacher.

"There's one seat left here." It was at the very front, right where she was standing.

Mrs. Jackson spied Athena dripping and explained to the class as she shifted the art supplies from Athena's place, "I expect everyone to be on time, and of course we're going to have to deal with the weather. Don't bring it in here. Leave your wet boots and clothes in the hallway."

Athena stopped shimmying up the centre aisle, which was blocked with gym bags and knapsacks, as lockers hadn't been assigned yet.

"Do you want me to go out?" Athena was mostly mouthing the words.

"No" came the rigid response.

Athena struggled onto the stool and put her bag and purse on the bench.

"As I was saying, these pencils are art pencils. They're expensive. Do not drop them, as the leads will break and they will be useless."

Athena thought it wise to make room on the table. The milk bag caught the box and sent it flying, and the pencils spilled across the floor. Mrs. Jackson slapped her forehead and stared with disdain at Athena, who was dripping water onto the bench. The teacher turned the empty box over in her hand.

***

Athena tried to find one familiar face in each class but failed to do so. Her lunch was in sixth period. Athena spotted Sherry and made a beeline for her immediately, as if she were an orange life preserver in the middle of the ocean.

"Oh my God, am I happy to see you!" Athena exclaimed.

Sherry was carrying a cafeteria tray. She looked at Athena's milk bag and sighed. "What happened to you?"

As Athena started to pour out her drama, Sherry interrupted her. She spotted two girls she had just met in her math class. She walked over and sat next to them. Athena followed. The girls stopped speaking, questioning with their eyes why Athena had taken it upon herself to join them.

"And you *are*?" the blonde girl with freckles said, drawing out the last word.

"Oh, hi. I'm Athena." She looked at them and smiled.

They said nothing.

Athena climbed over the picnic table bench but didn't sit down. "And you *are*?" she said in her best imitation of the girl.

Athena passed the test.

The girl giggled and said, "I'm Annette. This is Carrie. We went to Puce."

"We went to grade school together," Sherry explained.

Athena clung to her life preserver for a whole forty minutes. After reviewing their schedules, Athena discovered that she would see Annette in her history class.

"I'm in your art class too. I was near the back, so you didn't see me, but everyone saw you." She laughed.

Athena laughed too. At first it felt hollow, but she knew that if she didn't surrender to the nonsense, high school would swallow her up.

She wondered about the people who weren't fortunate enough to find a place here. Whether a person could fit in was dictated by the whims of fashion and popular opinion. She was aware that looking and acting a certain way mattered to her peer group, but she wasn't even mildly interested in pretending to be like them. If she was in her own imaginary world, as Danica and Lejla were always telling her, she couldn't discern the difference between it and reality. Just because everyone said something, didn't make it so. Athena was trying to support her argument that everything in the adult world was just an illusion.

She even brought this argument into history class.

"Athena, please." Her teacher blew out his breath with an audible sigh. "We don't have time for this. We're going to operate under the assumption that the government is valid, alright?"

***

"Mom, you've got to tell her to stop," said Lejla.

Danica and Lejla were standing on either side of their mother. Athena sat eating a bowl of Cap'n Crunch, enjoying their comments.

"She's embarrassing. And she's just trying to humiliate us. She walks around the school like a welfare case. Look what she's wearing. She won't even take a shower," said Danica.

"At lunch yesterday, she crawled under six tables to pick up a nickel," Lejla said.

At this, everyone looked at Athena to hear what she had to say about it.

"So? Sherry bet me five dollars I wouldn't do it." Athena smiled at the recollection of collecting her prize.

"Everyone—*everyone*—was looking at her. She's a freaking loser. I can't take it." Danica stormed out.

Athena paused, her mouth hanging half open, milk pouring out.

"Argh! I hate you!" cried Lejla.

"I love you," sang Athena cheerfully.

"Ah, c'mon, Theenie. That's enough," Tilley said.

Athena never argued anymore. She just shook her head in disbelief. "I think I must have been adopted. I don't even see baby pictures of me around here."

Tilley laughed. "You're insane. You were the third baby in three years. We were busy as hell. Hey"—she tugged on Athena's arm as she was putting her bowl in the sink—"your sisters love you, you know."

Athena searched her mom's eyes. "Sure, Mom. I'm sure they love me to death."

***

Danica had turned sixteen in the summer. There was a lavish surprise party with almost seventy people in attendance at the house. She also got her license. Now Danica could drive her sisters places after school or on the weekend.

As they were on their way to dance practice at the hall, Athena's sisters started to talk about Lejla and David, Danica's love interest. Athena sat in the back, watching the heated discussion turn into a battle.

"I'm telling you to back off," said Danica.

"I can't help it if he likes me."

"Oh my God. I hate you so much."

Then Athena poured lighter fluid onto the spark. "What would David think of either of you if he heard this conversation?"

"Shut up, Athena!" Lejla cried.

From the front seat, Lejla turned and swung her fist, catching Athena in the arm. She jumped back. Athena started kicking the back of Lejla's seat.

"Don't!"

Athena continued to anyway.

"I swear to God I'll murder you if you don't stop."

Athena flicked her fingers at the back of Lejla's head. Lejla launched herself over the seat and grabbed a fistful of Athena's hair. She dragged her head down and punched her. Fighting her off, Athena dug her nails into her hand and arm.

Danica swerved and hit Lejla in the side. "Stop it! Stop it! Dammit, I'm driving!"

No one cared.

"You're both crazy!" Danica screamed. "I can't wait to move out. I'm getting as far away from here as I can."

Athena snapped back to reality. It had never occurred to her that things could change—that Danica or any of them would ever really leave. Even Lejla always came back. At first it made her sad, but then she was thrilled to realize that not only would things change for Danica, but also for her. Lejla punched Danica back and the car swerved again, and they fought all the way to the hall. When they walked in, they looked and acted like everyone else. *No one really knows them*, Athena thought. She also knew that others could just be putting on an act too. You could invent how you wanted to be if you had the chance. Athena's heart spoke to her: she wanted to be loved and live in peace.

***

"Hey, how's it going?" At dance practice, Niko leaned in and kissed Athena's cheek.

They didn't go to the same school now. He went to a city high school. When he kissed her, it made her knees weak. It didn't feel like that with anyone else.

"It's goin'," Athena answered. "How's high school?"

"I love it. I'm playing football, so that's been awesome."

The thing hanging in the air was anticipation; the yoke of pretending that because they were young, they didn't know they were in love. They hadn't followed the pattern. To validate being together, you had to go through all the stages for all the right reasons and have all the appropriate reactions. It would be a long wait before she could grow up and compete with the type of girls Niko dated, but she knew that once she was ready, they would be together.

"Nice sweatpants," he said, chuckling, and shoved her gently.

"You know you want me." She teased.

"Can't resist." They locked eyes, challenging each other to look away, comfortable in knowing that their time would come.

The dance instructor pressed play and a scratchy recording filled the room with accordion music. "Okay, every-vone—les go! We ain't got all night."

Niko grabbed Athena's hand and led her to the circle. They both smiled, happy to be there.

Chapter 41

"Listen, your father has been under a lot of stress at work."

Tilley and the three oldest girls were sitting around the dining room table. Dragan had left early that morning to go golfing at the small public course on the drive. A big private club was beyond it, but the Brkovichs didn't have that kind of money.

"His boss doesn't like him." She looked around to make sure that everyone understood it wasn't his fault. "That's why it's been difficult. But he's your father."

No one spoke.

The night before had been loud. Lejla had started getting high at school, pouring shots from the liquor cabinet into a thermos, smoking, and skipping classes. Last night she'd stolen the car and gone for a joyride with Krista, who lived two doors down, but the car ended up on someone's front lawn. Tilley took the phone call, as it came before Dragan got home. Tilley screamed at Lejla for an hour.

"Imagine if they knew *all* the things she did," Athena whispered to Danica.

"Theenie, if you ever breathe a word about her to Mom or Dad . . ."

"I would never." Athena's eyes flashed with a vehemence she usually reserved for outsiders. Both girls knew it would be the end of Lejla if they ever told on her.

"Why did she steal the car, though? Doesn't she get it?" Athena's anxiety was real. It was simpler if you followed the rules. Granted, the rules changed and sometimes you were punished for no reason, but the only hope of keeping the peace was to follow them.

"I don't know. Don't you start being stupid too, though. I can't take it. Now get out and shut my door," Danica replied.

That conversation had taken place during Tilley's tirade. She'd slapped Lejla pretty hard in the face. It wouldn't have hurt as much if Dragan had done it. No, Athena wasn't afraid of her mom hurting Lejla, but she was shocked at how belligerent her sister was to Tilley. She almost hit her back, and Tilley actually seemed scared of her. But Tilley threatened to tell Dragan, and this was enough to stop Lejla.

"Your dad gave me some money and we're going to go shopping. He wants you all to go get something," Tilley said.

Athena was surprised to see Danica and Lejla smile. She, however, couldn't be bought. "But all you fight about is money."

"Oh, stop!" Lejla groaned at Athena.

"Yeah, just be normal for once and get some new clothes, Theenie. You totally need it," Danica said.

Athena was too tired to present the same argument she always did, again. As they rode into the city, Athena let the wind hit her face. She imagined the air dissolving her so that when they got to the mall, she would no longer exist.

***

Athena spent four hours every other night lying awake, hovering between exhaustion and terror. The mood in the house was gloomier than usual. Athena slept on the bus; she got a new gym bag for her books and used it as a pillow. She worried desperately about Lejla, whose behaviour was getting more reckless.

She saw her sister in the hallway between classes. She was acting strange and laughing loudly. Athena gravitated toward her.

"*Hey*, Theenie." She smiled and put her hand on Athena's shoulder.

Athena's stomach dropped. Something was wrong. Lejla's eyes were glassy and bloodshot. Her pupils were huge and she was talking in a spaced-out way.

"Are you sick?" Athena asked anxiously.

Lejla looked at the girl next to her and they erupted with laughter. "Go to class, brainiac," Lejla said and hugged her.

"Something's not right. You're acting nice. That's weird."

"I'm fine." Lejla pressed her face close to Athena's.

"You're drunk," Athena said.

"No," said the girl, "she's high."

"Do you want your brain to be fried like an egg?" She was going into a panic.

"It's okay. My brain is fine."

Athena didn't like to see her sister high. She didn't want her brain to be destroyed. She didn't want her to get in trouble. She didn't want to have so much anxiety.

A man stood in one of the classroom doorways. "Girls, shouldn't you all be somewhere now?" He looked at his wristwatch. "Is everything okay here?" he asked Athena.

She wiped her face quickly and nodded.

When she turned back, Lejla and the girl had gone. They'd exited through the door leading to the smoking area.

Lejla didn't come home on the bus that day.

***

It had been five days now. Every day at school, Athena looked for Lejla. She didn't ask anyone if they'd seen her, not wanting to draw attention to the fact that if she was skipping out, she would get in bigger trouble when she returned. It was Friday. Her best chance of seeing Lejla again was at school. She sat brooding about it at lunch.

As she rode the bus, Athena had a strong intuition that something unavoidable was going to happen. Walking home, she felt gusts of wind lifting her hair. She loved wild winds.

In the living room, Athena watched the wall clock with the plain numbered face. The small wooden door with the window exposed a brass pendulum. It was five o'clock. *Bong, bong, bong, bong, bong.* The mechanism clicked and turned, advancing the minute hand. Her father wasn't home yet.

When the front door opened, the clock hadn't struck seven. It was as if everyone had been waiting.

Tilley jumped from her seat. "Okay, shut that off. I want everyone to go to bed."

"It's too early for bed," Max complained. "I'm not tired."

"Well, go read a book," she said, stepping lightly up the stairs. Danica was already in her room.

"Let's go. Go." Athena ordered the twins to move with urgency but tried not to scare them. They needed to get upstairs and past their dad.

"C'mere, gimme a hug," he said to them.

Dragan sat on the wooden bench, his head hanging low. He swiped at his dress shoe, trying to undo the short black laces. He rested his elbow on his knee and waved to them. Athena tried to steer the twins ahead—he wouldn't remember—but they went to him.

He scooped them up. "So how're we doin'?" He slurred his words heavily.

Tilley stood at the bottom of the stairs. Athena could feel her mother's agitation. "That's enough." Tilley tugged at the twins to get down from his lap. Max was happy to see his dad despite his condition.

Athena tried to help. "Come on, let's go upstairs, guys," she said softly, stepping forward.

"Hey!" Dragan's tone suddenly changed. "Was . . . was I talkin' to you?"

The twins jumped off his lap, and Tilley directed them and followed behind. Athena stood on the landing.

Her father stood up unsteadily, pointing his finger at her. "Answer me!"

Athena bounced back from the unexpected jump in volume. She shook her head. He raised his hand as if to hit her, and she flinched. Then she stood up straight, watching in disgust as her father wobbled back and forth.

"I'm not Lejla," she said defiantly, lifting her chin. She looked him in his face.

His hand moved hard and fast, striking her, and she almost fell to her knees. As she touched her face, she wondered if this was how Lejla felt.

"I haven't done anything," Athena said as she stood back up.

The second time her father struck, it was with the back of his hand.

"Are you talkin' back to me?" His school ring had caught her cheekbone and cut her.

Athena contemplated her answer as she watched the blood drip onto the foyer floor. She knew she would have to be careful not to get it on the rug. Dragan slumped back down onto the bench, the alcohol rendering him silent after his efforts. He had passed out and was snoring loudly when Athena returned with a washcloth to wipe the floor. She had placed a Band-Aid over the small cut, which was starting to swell already.

Her mother stood on the third step, her tongue between her teeth. "Go to bed. Come on."

Athena didn't feel sorry for herself. She thought of Lejla, of all the times Dragan had sought her out to do just this sort of thing. She wondered about men and their ability to hurt others, to take their aggression out on another person, not recognizing that the person has the same feelings and rights they do. But they're not given the same rights. Athena felt owned by her parents. They could do what they wanted and no one cared. She understood why Lejla left. She also believed that being treated this way was her punishment for not helping Lejla, for not fighting against their father.

When she climbed into bed, Mitzi was crying into her pillow.

"I'm okay, Mitz. Don't cry."

"I don't like fighting."

"No, me neither." There was a pause as Athena thought of how to turn things around. "Do you want to play Trivial Pursuit?"

Mitzi wiped her eyes.

"We'll do it quietly under the covers."

She smiled.

Athena got a flashlight from her desk drawer and pulled the blue box out from under the bed. They played until they were too tired to read the cards anymore.

Athena was awakened by shouting in the kitchen. She was wondering what time it was just as the clock chimed: *bong, bong*. She rolled over, but her cheek reminded her why she wasn't on her side and she slumped back. Athena knew she was stronger than her mother. She prayed that Lejla never came home. Athena couldn't run away. She needed to protect Mitzi and Max; she couldn't just leave now.

Chapter 42

"Hey, listen to this."

Athena was standing in front of a cafeteria table filled with seniors, their expectant faces inquisitive as they stared.

"Do Mrs. Borden," a boy said.

In her best Mrs. Borden, Athena said, "And to what do I owe the pleasure of your company, young man?"

The table exploded with laughter. "That's hilarious!"

"Mr. Jeffries!" someone shouted out.

"Kid. Listen to me, kid. You're goin' nowhere."

Laughter spilled out of their mouths.

"Oh my God! She sounds just like him!"

"Mr. Cooley."

"You don't got a hope in hell," Athena said.

Down at the end of the table, she heard "Who is this kid?"

"She's a little Brk. Lejla's sister."

"Very nice."

"That's incredible."

The kids smiled and nodded approvingly. Athena's mimicry and fearless performances were earning her a reputation. Entertaining. Outrageous. Hilarious.

She listened intently to not only what people said but also how they said it. She spoke in other voices more often than her own. These voices circled inside her head like a tape being replayed, helping her gather the subtle nuances of speech and convey the flavour of the person she was imitating. Athena loved hearing laughter. Making people laugh authentically was a hard thing to do. They sometimes faked laughter to hide their insecurities, to pretend something didn't bother them, to mask fear. In its purest form, laughter was medicine. It cleaned the air. Laughter transmuted tension into ease. She felt as if she had the power of an alchemist when she made someone laugh, and the laughter of others buoyed her up.

***

Outside the hall, Athena was sitting on a picnic table with Kat and Roxy. The *kolo* music was playing loudly. It was a bit chilly and overcast. They were sipping Cokes out of plastic cups. The men and boys had started a pickup soccer game in the field.

The girls continued trying to avoid being asked to do dishes or clean up.

"Do you have any tickets left?" Athena checked her pockets. She wanted another pop.

"Here's one." Roxy ripped one off her strip.

Athena swung the wooden door open. The salty, warm air was thick with smoke and the smell of Serbian whiskey enveloped her as she squeezed her way up to the counter. Niko and Tommy were working behind the bar. Athena felt a sharp pang of jealousy but quickly let it go. It would be fun to help out back there, but the girls never got to.

Niko saw her and smiled. "Hey, Theenie, what can I get you?"

"Um . . . " Athena pretended to think so she could keep his attention a second more. He had grown a lot over the last year. His hair was longer. His eyes were still as piercing as always. "I'll have a Diet Coke, no ice."

"DC no ice, coming up." He moved quickly to get the drink.

"Niko! *Daj mi jedno pivo!*" Tommy said.

Niko grabbed a cup from under the bar and pulled the tap, tipping the cup to cut the foam of the beer down. He glanced at her and winked.

"Niko!" Maria and Violeta, two girls a year younger than Athena, had manoeuvred their way next to her. Although they were younger, they looked like women. They rested their breasts on top of the bar and tapped their tickets impatiently.

Niko held up a finger.

"No, we can't wait," they said, giggling.

"You're going to *have* to wait," he said, leaning toward them and smiling mischievously.

They twittered with delight.

Athena rolled her eyes.

"Hang on, miss." Niko lifted his index finger.

"Can't do it," Athena said firmly, and ducked out.

She was almost out of the door when Niko grabbed her arm. "Hey, whoa, whoa! What's your issue?"

"I don't have an issue." Athena smiled, staring deep into his eyes.

"I think you do."

"So?"

"So I think you should admit when you have an issue."

"And I would if I did." Athena lit up inside. There was something so exhilarating about engaging Niko in this banter.

"Well, I think we should at least talk about it."

"You should talk about it with your fan club." Athena nodded toward Maria and Violeta, who were watching them.

Niko scoffed and laughed. "Them? *Please.* Listen, I gotta get back there, but here's your pop, you hard-head."

"Oh, thank you. You shouldn't have." Athena laughed through her sarcasm.

Niko winked at her again and hopped back toward the bar. All of the girls wanted him. Well, except maybe Kat.

She pushed the door open and climbed up onto the picnic table, her feet on the bench. "Yeah, I definitely would marry Niko," she said to Kat and Roxy.

***

The phone rang. Lejla's feet pounded as she ran up the stairs. "I'll get it!" Racing footsteps came from the living room. Danica and Lejla crashed into each other, and Danica slid on her stockings across the kitchen floor. Lejla blocked her sister with her body and reached the receiver first. She swung her fist at Danica as she brought the receiver to her mouth.

"Who is it? Who is it?" Danica said.

"Brkovich residence. This is Lejla."

Even though she had been away for almost two weeks, she still got the most phone calls. *Lejla has such a fake voice on the phone*, Athena thought. She was sitting at the kitchen table and could have easily reached the phone but had no desire to. She didn't like it; she would much rather speak to someone in person.

"Who is it?" Danica still insisted on knowing who the caller was.

Lejla covered the mouthpiece with her hand and said in disbelief, "It's for Theenie," then extended the phone to her.

"Who is it?" Athena scrunched up her face, wondering who would call her.

"I think it's Niko," Lejla said in a teasing tone.

Athena shook her head while she silently melted at the thought.

"Take it!" Lejla extended the receiver and knocked her on the head with it. "Take it. Here." She shoved it at Athena again.

Lejla and Danica stood there listening.

"Hello?" Athena spoke naturally, not wanting to sound like Lejla at all costs.

Her sisters watched her, waiting. Athena was listening as she slid off the bench. Lejla tried to lean in toward the receiver. Athena shoved her away. Danica motioned with her hand to indicate she should speed it up.

"When is it?" Athena asked, her throat dry. "And, yeah. I guess. I mean, sure."

Her sisters pressed in on her. She pushed through them and walked as far down the hall as the spiralling cord would go, twisting her finger around it, then turned back.

"Okay, that sounds good. Thanks. Yeah, bye." Athena hung up.

"What did he want?" both sisters said in unison.

Boys weren't allowed to call the Brkovich girls, but everyone knew that didn't really apply to Athena, and Niko was Serbian, which made it acceptable.

"He asked me to go with him to his spring dance," Athena said. Her elation was subdued, as it was weighted down with disbelief.

When the day of the semi-formal arrived, Athena felt uncomfortable and anxious, like she had to go pee the whole day. She really liked Niko, but everyone knowing it made her feel conspicuous.

"Settle down," Lejla told her. "You don't have to kiss him if you don't want to. But why wouldn't you?"

Athena couldn't overcome the idea that it didn't make sense for Niko to like her. On the one hand, they had a deep, lifelong connection, but on the other hand, every girl liked him and she was still just like a kid compared to them.

"He probably doesn't like you—not like that, anyway, Theen. I mean, you're, you know, like, little," Lejla said.

This small fact hurt and reached Athena just in time to prevent further suffering. Niko's invitation was probably just a joke.

The cafeteria tables were set up along the outside walls, clearing the middle for the dance floor. It was quite dark. The lights from the dee-jay's sound booth were lit up. After three or four fast songs, two slow songs in a row were played. Couples came together, in preparation for making out. Athena felt self-conscious and marched away to sit down.

Niko followed, looking a bit put out. "Is everything okay?"

"Yeah. Why wouldn't it be?"

"I don't know. Because it seems like you don't wanna dance with me."

Athena shrugged. "I have to go to the bathroom."

The bright fluorescent bulbs in the hallway made her squint and shield her eyes with her hand. Niko's high school was huge compared to hers. The cafeteria was bigger than their gym. The girls' bathroom was right across the hallway. Five or six girls stood at the mirror, the green glow of the paint on the walls made everyone's complexions look as if they'd eaten something bad.

Athena sat on the toilet, debating with herself. It wouldn't hurt to dance with Niko. She did it all the time in the dance group. She was being stupid. Counterpoint: if she danced with him, he would feel that she had no boobs. It would be embarrassing. She checked herself in the mirror but didn't stop long, as two bigger girls had stopped talking and were looking her up and down. She quickly headed to where Niko was sitting.

"This is the last dance—they just said," he told her.

Athena looked back at the two girls coming out of the bathroom.

"Well, then, we better dance, right?" Athena grabbed his hand.

He smiled and jumped off the bench he'd been straddling. He was the most handsome boy there. Niko led her to a spot in the middle of the dance floor. Athena could barely walk, her knees felt so weak. When he spun around and placed his hands on her hips, she placed her arms around his neck to help hold herself up. The song started softly, and soon they were pressed closer together by the couples arriving on the dance floor.

"This is nice," Niko said.

She looked up into his face, smiling. Their closeness was intoxicating; the romance of it filled her senses and left her defenceless. She didn't want the song to end. The last note lingered on and on. Niko kept his hands around her and leaned his head against hers. He smelled so good.

When she got home that night, she told Lejla, "We just slow danced once."

"And then what?" With a big grin, Lejla flopped onto her back.

"And then nothing. His dad picked us up and I came home." Athena couldn't stop smiling. "I could totally marry him," she said dreamily. "Good night, Jaja."

"Good night, Theen. You looked pretty tonight."

Athena smiled and headed up the stairs, filled with love and desire. Niko would wait for her.

***

Life was on track as far as Athena was concerned. She took little notice of what her sisters or friends did, but rather how they did everything. She wanted nothing to do with being like them. While studying their mannerisms, she observed all levels of falseness. It was as though everyone was pretending, and no one, including the person doing the pretending, could see it. The whole world seemed to Athena like *The Emperor's New Clothes*. And the masquerade of growing up was so blinding that people couldn't see the disguises that sat plainly on their faces. Her silliness allowed them to laugh, lifting their masks for a moment to allow them to breathe.

Athena didn't grow because she didn't want to grow. As the months passed, she watched everyone at school changing, their voices and their bodies. She wanted no part of it. Adults, across the board, pretended way more than kids.

"Do Mrs. Stilson." Lejla said. She was in the kitchen spreading peanut butter on her toast. Athena obliged and Lejla stopped to watch. "That is so crazy good. How do you do that?" She licked her fingers.

"Some people are easier than others. Some have big gestures, unusual voices, or patterns that define them easily. Most people impersonate others to an extent. They're hard to do because they aren't authentic."

"Maybe you could act like you're in high school," Danica said, walking in to grab her lunch.

"I don't know. It's pretty cool actually," Lejla said, winking at Athena.

"Really?" Athena flushed with the approval.

"Yes, but I still don't want to hang out with you. No offence." She said it with a nonchalance that baffled Athena.

But the start of grade ten seemed promising. With laughter, she deflected all the put-downs and comments about her immaturity. She truly didn't care what anyone thought of her. Most of the people she went to school with she'd known since second grade, and they couldn't change that much. They wanted to be different, but she knew who they were. She would remind them if they forgot. Walking her sisters' path gave her clout, and a cloak of protection from which to forge her own path. Athena had known all along she was different, but finally everyone knew who she was and was starting to accept her and even celebrate her.

***

"Write down the names of all the friends you think she would want there. Wait—start with all the family."

Athena had a pen and paper. Lejla's surprise sixteenth birthday party plans were underway. Danica was listing off the names of everyone she could think of.

"There's going to be, like, a hundred people," she told her mother.

Surprising her would be almost impossible, since Danica had been given a huge surprise party the year before. Athena was happy to contribute all of her energy to making it a smashing success.

"She's really into music, so we should probably get a dee-jay."

"I think finger foods, shrimp cocktails, chips and dip, then pizzas should be good."

"Dad will pick up all the balloons."

The party was going to be on Lejla's actual birthday, a Wednesday. Last year, Danica's birthday had fallen on a Saturday, so it worked out perfectly. Lejla would be thinking the party would be on the weekend.

"We'll have it on her exact birthday, just like Danica's," Tilley exclaimed.

Athena liked the idea. She checked the calendar hanging in the broom closet. It had a small version of 1984 at the back of it. Her own sixteenth would fall on a Friday.

Danica and Athena wrote and handed out invitations to people at school. They stamped and mailed others if they didn't hand them out at church. Lejla's friend Tammy had been engaged to occupy her with a small gathering of friends at the local hangout. Athena had told Tammy at least ten times not to get high. The girl's mother would bring the small group to the party at their house.

All the guests parked two blocks away so it wouldn't look as if anything was going on. Athena waited with excitement as the people piled into the house and headed downstairs. After about a half an hour, the upstairs was also packed.

Athena watched her parents; they seemed happy. At least her mom was relaxed because her dad had come home. Athena had her reservations about Tammy, but right on time, the car pulled up in the driveway.

"They're here! They're here!" people whispered.

All the weeks of planning, and now everything was coming together. When Lejla walked in, there was a huge "Surprise!" The house was hot with all the people, and Athena opened the windows as ordered. She cleared plates and glasses all night. She smiled with delight as, safe under everyone's eyes, Lejla was showered with attention and opened present after present and thanked each person individually. Music and laughter filled the house. Athena refilled chip bowls and cut up more cheese for the crackers, which seemed to disappear as soon as they were set out.

The crowning moment of the night came when Lejla was handed the gift, wrapped carefully in a small box, from her parents. Lejla opened it and showed everyone the earrings. They were flowers formed of six blue sapphires. Lejla took her small hoops out and put the new earrings on. Her friends followed her to her room where she could look at herself in the mirror. Everyone was very impressed and knew how much Mr. and Mrs. Brkovich loved their daughter.

Athena helped find the guests' jackets; she had placed them on her parents' bed when they came in. Lejla didn't have to help clean up because it was her birthday. Athena brought cups upstairs while Tilley packed up leftovers into containers.

"That was a really great party, Mom," Athena said. She knew that her mother wanted to hear it said.

"You think so? I think everyone had a good time."

"They had a *great* time."

"The pizza was a little later than I wanted."

"But there was so much food, no one noticed."

"Oh, that's good," Tilley said as she rinsed plates off and placed them in the dishwasher. "Next time will be your turn."

Athena just smiled. The party was beautiful and the earrings so special, but Athena couldn't help thinking that the evening could never make up for all the other times that weren't like this one. Birthdays were only once a year.

Chapter 43

Athena sat in her homeroom history class. Mr. Hillier was droning on about the Senate, facing the chalkboard and drawing the structure of the Canadian government. Athena was so tired, she felt nauseous. She crossed her arms over her binder and put her head down.

There was a light tap on her shoulder. "Athena Brkovich."

She lifted her head, her eyelids heavy, a pool of drool connecting her cheek and her forearm. Her teacher was standing over her. Mr. Hillier was a kindly man, overweight but gentle. He never raised his voice; the soft tone worked like a lullaby on Athena.

"You are the rudest person I have ever taught."

Athena blinked, trying to understand.

"You fall asleep in my class every day." He said this in the same tone but even softer, so as not to draw attention.

Athena pushed herself upright and swiped her arm across her face. "I'm sorry, Mr. Hillier. I can't help it."

He frowned.

"I, uh . . ." Athena struggled to answer. "I don't get much sleep at home these days." She spoke with the same gentle tone Mr. Hillier used as she stared into his eyes.

He watched her for a moment. She was one of the best students in his class. "Okay, Athena. If you need to rest, just close your eyes."

This was one of the kindest things a teacher had ever said to her. She laid her head back down until the bell rang.

It was a Tuesday in October, and it seemed ordinary enough. But important events fall on days that start out like every other day but end differently. Only when you think back on them do they take on significance. Athena believed that every day mattered, because any day could be the day that changed your life.

"Will Danica, Lejla, and Athena Brkovich please report to the office immediately? Danica, Lejla, and Athena Brkovich?" came the announcement over the PA system.

Athena felt everyone's eyes on her.

Mr. Hillier looked at her and nodded. "You can go, Athena." He spoke calmly but looked strange.

She couldn't put her finger on it. Why would they call all three of them to the office at the same time? Her heart began to pound. When she turned down the main hallway to the front office, she saw her sisters and her mother standing at the desk. Tilley had been crying. Athena felt a surge of energy rush through her. Their father must have died! She held her breath as she approached.

"Athena." It was Mr. Reaume, the principal. "Your mom is here to collect you and your sisters. You're changing schools today, so you'll have to clean out your locker completely." He turned to Tilley. "It was truly a pleasure having your daughters as pupils here, Mrs. Brkovich."

Athena couldn't process his words. "Why? What's happening?"

Tilley blew her nose. Athena looked at her sisters.

"Go get your things," Danica said calmly.

Athena just stood there.

"We already got our things. Go get yours now." She emphasized the urgency. "We have to *go*."

"Why, though? I don't understand."

"I'll explain in the car," Tilley said.

"Athena, please listen to your mother," Mr. Reaume added.

Athena turned and left everyone standing there. She felt so confused. When she opened her locker, she realized that she didn't know where anyone was right now. All of her friends were scattered all over. Where was she going? Why was she leaving? Even if she ran to find them, she wouldn't be able to explain what had happened.

Athena started to cry.

Mr. Pepper, her geography teacher, saw her and stopped. He was an awkward man people made fun of. Athena could do a perfect impersonation of him, but she respected him for being unique. "Are you okay, Athena?"

She stopped and stared at him, tears streaming down her face. She didn't answer at first. She didn't know how. "I have to leave here," she said bitterly.

Mr. Pepper stood silent, and Athena went back to her locker. She stopped unpacking when he spoke. "You're one of the nicest students I've ever had. Whatever's happening, you're smart and you'll get through it."

Athena wanted to scream and cry about the unfairness of it all, about the fear and uncertainty she felt all the time. But when she considered this small act of kindness, her heart was pained and she could only acknowledge him with a simple "Thank you, Mr. Pepper."

He stood for only a moment longer and then continued on his way. His words resonated with her. Whatever happened, she would be okay.

***

As Athena walked to the parking lot, she braced herself, imagining her life now that her father was dead. There would be no more drinking, no more fighting. It would all be okay, a relief. When they got in the car, Danica and Lejla did the talking.

Danica started. She was sitting in the front seat and turned to explain things. "So, Theenie, Mom is leaving Dad and we're moving to Windsor. We're going to go to Montcalm."

Lejla joined in. "It's going to be fine. We know people there. We're going to live at Deda's."

"So you both knew about this?" Athena shrieked.

Her selfish, self-absorbed sisters knew that they were going to change schools, that they were going to move, and she didn't?

Danica and Lejla looked at each other and nodded in an obvious way.

"So you got to say goodbye to your friends?"

They nodded again.

Tilley said, "You see, you're too sensitive, Theenie. We didn't want you being upset like this."

"I'm upset you *didn't* tell me!" Athena's rage bubbled up and she tried to clamp down on it. "I'm not leaving. You can't just tell me like this and take me away."

"It's done," Danica explained. "Dad's an alcoholic and we can't live there anymore."

"When did you decide this?" Athena demanded of her mother.

"We convinced her it's best. We've been talking to her for months about it," Danica said.

"I wasn't talking to you!" Athena leaned forward and screamed, feeling the blood rush to her face.

"Yeah, she's too sensitive," Danica said to their mom.

"I'm sensitive," Athena cried, "because no one thought about how it would feel not to know. You don't know how it feels because you only care about yourselves. I don't want to change schools."

Tilley just kept driving, staring ahead.

"We didn't tell you because we didn't want you to be upset," Lejla said softly.

Athena rolled down the window and laid her head beside it, letting the cold air sting her wet cheeks. She was trying to process moving to her grandfather's tiny house and transferring to an inner-city high school. How would she explain to her friends that she'd just disappeared? She watched the fields passing and disappearing behind her. She would never be able to explain it so that it made sense, any more than she could pick out a plant on the side of the road as they passed and then turn around and find it again. It was lost forever.

"One day I'll have a place, a family, and I will matter," Athena said, her voice filled with anguish. Her words were sucked out of the window.

No one said anything.

***

In one single afternoon, it was possible to pack their things and change their whole lives.

"Don't take everything, just enough clothes, girls," Tilley instructed.

Athena moved slowly up the stairs, trying to take the house in. With her fingers she traced the green velvet wallpaper, the pompoms at the bottom of her window blind, the purple pattern on the bathroom tile, her father's old oak desk. She could sense her mother's high anxiety and her sisters' excitement. It was as if they were making a prison break. It would have been easier if he had died.

Tilley kept looking over her shoulder. "Get moving, Theenie. We're going to the school after we drop your stuff off."

Athena stared into space, worried about her father and his reaction when he found out they were gone. He would be so sad. Athena went to her room and shoved some T-shirts and sweats into her gym bag. She took the music box she'd received when she was ten years old that played "Raindrops Keep Falling on My Head." She took her toothbrush from the holder in the bathroom. She dropped her bag on the bench in the foyer and went downstairs and sat at her father's desk. Athena wanted to leave him something to let him know she loved him.

She got the tape recorder and an empty cassette from the box by the stereo. She pressed record and spoke. "Tata, I'm sorry. I don't want you to be sad. . . . I'm so sorry. . . . I love you." She hit the pause button. Her voice was choked with emotion. It didn't seem like enough to express how she was feeling. She went to the stereo and lifted the lid on the record player. She pulled out a tambura record her father played often and dropped the needle on the song that spoke to her in that moment. A slow, melancholy melody poured out of the strings. A man's voice started singing, "Don't look so sad, I know it's over." Athena pressed record and taped the song, then left a note for her father on his desk. She felt a deep sorrow in her chest, but Danica and Lejla acted as if they were packing for camp.

"Don't act like that, Theenie," Danica said. "This will be better. We can't stay here like this. You'll see."

Athena didn't expect her sister to know what she felt like.

***

"So you'll know Kat," said Tilley.

"Kat's a year behind me."

"And Niko. He goes here. Tommy and Georgie too, and all their cousins. We know lots of people."

Athena didn't want to see anyone she knew. As they walked down the bright white halls, the sound of her mother's shoes echoed off the metal lockers. Athena thought of running away.

They arrived at the guidance counsellor's office and sat down. "Did you skip a grade, Athena?" He looked from Athena to her mother and back.

"No, she didn't. She's just small for her age."

"So you're fourteen? Going to be fifteen soon." He checked the papers in front of him and looked back at Athena. "Let's pick an elective to complete your schedule."

The guidance counsellor was speaking patiently to her, but she was being difficult. Lejla and Danica had already chosen their curriculums prior to arriving. Athena simply stared at him.

He appeared to be losing patience with her cold despondency. "What about data processing?"

"What about it?" Athena said snidely.

"Athena." Her mother gave her a nudge in the back.

Athena spoke again with heavy sarcasm. "Oh, I'm sorry. Data processing? Of course, yes, of course, how lovely." She pressed her hands together against her cheek and closed her eyes to indicate sleeping, then folded her hands under her chin. She batted her eyes and slumped back into her chair.

"Yes. Data processing will be fine," her mother said to the counsellor, who wore a look of relief and, with a nod, acknowledged how tough it must be to be Athena's mother.

"Welcome to Montcalm. We're very pleased you're here, Athena. I've included a mandatory guidance appointment on Friday mornings, just so we can check in and see how you're doing." He placed a business card on top of the schedule.

Athena picked it up. It said, *Athena Brockovich has an appointment with Mr. Dunlop, Friday, October 14, 9:00 a.m.*

"You have the wrong person, Mr. Dumb-lop," Athena said dully and flicked the business card at him, hitting him in the chest. She stood up and walked out, Tilley's disappointment gnawing at her back.

"Once you get some friends, you'll fit right in," Tilley said as they walked through the parking lot. Ten-foot chain-link fences with barbed wire surrounded them. The seams of the building and the fence were crammed with cigarette butts, gum wrappers, and pop cans.

In the car, Danica said, "You might want to update your wardrobe, Theenie."

Tilley shot her a look.

"What, Mom?" Throwing her hands up, Danica said, "I'm just saying, she doesn't look old enough to be in high school. Why make it worse for herself? She could wash her greasy hair too. It wouldn't kill her."

"Oh, shut up already," Lejla said.

Danica stopped talking.

Athena didn't care what her sisters thought. She didn't need friends, and she was not going to go to school here. As they rode back home to pick up the twins and conclude affairs with their father, she closed her eyes and thought of not being anything.

***

All five of the children were seated upstairs in the formal living room. Dragan was seated on one of the green velvet armchairs, his head lowered into his hands.

Tilley stood in the midst of them all and announced, "We're going to go around the circle now, and each of you will tell your father how his actions have hurt you. This is your chance." She looked at Dragan. "And *you're* going to sit here and listen."

Danica started. At first she was vague. "I don't like things right now. It hasn't been good for a while." But then her words flowed like water running downhill. She talked about how he said things, that he was mean, that he was no good. Lejla went next. She didn't hold back. It was no surprise to any of them. It was true, all of it. He hurt her. He called her names. He picked on her. He was a bully. With each truth, Athena watched her father crumple over, as if a piece of him had been extracted, and he sank farther into the chair. Athena listened to her sisters. They were angry and sounded mean. They weren't crying. They didn't care. Athena hated her mother for leaving. And she hated her sisters for trying to destroy their father.

"Okay, Athena. It's your turn."

Athena fixed her gaze on her father. She focused on his chest, on his heart, wondering if it was hurting as badly as her own.

"Athena!" her mother yelled.

Athena said nothing. She didn't move and didn't acknowledge anyone or anything.

"Athena! Stop being such a martyr!" Danica spat the words at her.

"Say something! You're such a little loser!" Lejla added.

"You will tell your father right now what you're thinking!" Tilley's voice was shrill and sharp.

Athena knew without looking what her mother's face was doing. She sat like a statue, wondering how she could possibly fulfill such a request.

Tilley continued, "You each get five minutes to say how you feel, and this is your only chance. You're not going to get another one."

Athena didn't need chances. She didn't want the five-minute opportunity. She didn't want to be a part of this family or this ugly crucifixion while they hammered nails into their father's hands and feet. Mentally, Athena floated away. Most of them had their arms crossed. Mitzi was leaning her head on her hand. Her father was bent over, broken. Her mother was agitated, like a bull that has been beaten and prodded and finally released. Athena was still, quiet. She didn't want any of the anger. She wanted peace. She didn't want any of the hate. She wanted forgiveness. She did not move. She did not speak.

"And what were you thinking, making your dad that tape? What were you trying to do? Make him kill himself?" Tilley said.

"You're being stupid," Danica said.

"She's an idiot," Lejla added.

"Fine, be that way. You're ridiculous. Even the twins are going to speak to their father, and you can't even muster a sentence. Shame on you."

Athena didn't listen to anything her younger brother and sister said. It was twisted with tears and sadness, and she was closing off the source of that, slowly turning some inner valve to stop the flow of emotion.

She didn't speak on the ride to their grandfather's house. She listened as Danica and Lejla consoled their mother as she cried, grieving and fearing the consequences of her actions. They cheered her on with supportive words.

There were only two bedrooms at Deda's house. Tilley and Mitzi would sleep together in the double bed. Danica and Lejla were in the second room with two twin beds. Athena and Max would each take a couch. Athena lay down on the hard clear plastic it was wrapped in. There was only a thin white blanket with three blue stripes. Athena stayed in her clothes, shivering. The sound of her teeth chattering filled her ears. Apparently, her body had something to say, even if she didn't. No one cared that she was cold.

Chapter 44

"You can't go like that." Lejla was looking at Athena. "Make her change, Mom."

With satisfaction, Athena stared back at her sisters' vicious looks.

"Are you not going to speak now?" Tilley slammed the spatula down on the counter. She was making eggs and toast for breakfast.

Athena just blinked.

"I don't know what to do with her." Exasperated, Tilley looked at her watch. "I'm taking the twins to school. You girls are walking. Don't be late."

Athena watched her younger brother and sister. She wondered if they knew what was happening or if they were scared. With encouraging words, Danica and Lejla hugged and kissed them. Smiling and nervous, they followed their mom out the door.

"You look like a freak," Lejla said.

"Wash your hair, at least," Danica added.

Athena took a deep breath. It was so easy to irritate her sisters.

"Be like that. We don't know you, and don't come near us," Lejla said.

They were picking up their Nike backpacks, their hair and makeup done. They wore Ralph Lauren polo shirts with the collars flipped up. Lejla put her Walkman headphones on and checked the tape before walking out the door with Danica.

Could she go the whole day without speaking? She decided that if no one talked to her, she wouldn't speak to anyone. Maybe no one would ever speak to her again. She reached into her gym bag and pulled out her Rubik's Cube. She slung the strap around her tiny body, and stepped out onto the porch.

She used to visit here as a child. Her deda was moved to an old folks' home on the waterfront. "He's happy there. He has his friends and he meets them for coffee downtown and they go play the horses." This was Tilley's standard update to anyone who asked. Athena hadn't seen him in a long while. It was cold and the rose bushes were bare.

Athena started walking the six blocks to school. When she arrived, she put the solved puzzle in her bag and turned up the sidewalk to the front entrance of her new reality.

"Is it 'bring your little sister to school' day?" a boy joked to his friends as they approached Athena and passed her, laughing.

She found her homeroom. She wandered in as students were sliding onto desk chairs, spinning around to talk to their neighbours, taking no notice of her. Athena walked to the teacher and handed her a slip of paper.

"A-thee-na," the woman said. "Interesting." She looked directly at Athena. "I am Miss Warner, and this is marketing. Grab a desk—we're getting started in a minute."

Miss Warner had tight blonde curls and wore a golf shirt. Briskly, she checked her oversized watch. Her movements were terse and exact. Athena would have no trouble impersonating her.

She glanced across the room, which was filling up from the back to the front. There was no reason to even try. She stood at the front, waiting until only the desk right in front of her in the corner remained. She slid in and listened to the lesson, not opening any books, not speaking to anyone. No one asked her a question. Athena moved to her next class, and then the next. Seventy-minute lectures, and the subject matter may as well have been on mute—none of it mattered to her at all. She watched her teachers carefully, assembling their mannerisms and vocal idiosyncrasies. It was more out of habit than desire.

At lunchtime, Athena wandered down to the cafeteria. She got in line and bought a strawberry shortcake ice cream bar. When she started to climb over the bench at one of the long army mess-style tables, she heard, "Not here, punk."

"No way."

"I don't think so."

"Someone's sitting there."

The comments were always followed by laughter. She went outside. A small gathering was at the smoking area doors. Athena started to make her way through.

"Hey, kid, you lost?"

She turned to look.

"The grade school is that way." A girl pointed across the parking lot and brought her hand down to connect with the outstretched hand of another smirking student.

Athena said nothing.

As she pulled her combination lock open on the green locker door, she realized that without even trying, she hadn't spoken. It wasn't necessary to speak, because no one wanted to speak with her. They spoke at her or around her, even to her. But no one was interested in what she had to say. Athena decided that until someone was interested, she would remain mute. This gave her a simple goal and made a game of the loneliness she felt. She was sad as she recalled the feeling of belonging even though she was different, of being accepted. That had been removed. She didn't feel like making anyone laugh, including herself. She caught a glimpse of Lejla talking excitedly with three girls who were surrounding her; they were heading out to smoke. To avoid being seen, Athena went the other way, then walked home alone.

***

"How did it go? Your first week?"

Athena was sitting at the small dining room table where she'd sat as a child for Sunday dinners. She shrugged.

"How come you're so quiet?" Tilley looked concerned and stopped stirring what was on the stove, then wiped her hand across the front of her apron. "Theenie, I'm worried about you."

"I'm alright," Athena lied.

In truth, barely anyone had spoken to her the entire first week. Not that she was invisible. Day after day went by, and she would receive the occasional shove or mean comment to let her know what someone thought of her.

Tilley paused, meeting her eyes. "That's my girl. I know it's hard, but we make the best of it, right?"

"Yes, Mom. It's okay."

At bedtime, Athena rose and walked to the living room, which was now her bedroom. "Can I take the plastic off the couch?" She didn't look at her mother. She just stared at the couch, which was so old but looked brand new, wondering what the purpose was of saving things from being used.

"Um, it's better if it stays on there." Tilley was standing at the entry, looking at the couch. Neither one of them could go against their mother's wishes.

Athena watched her brother, who was breathing deeply as he slept, his arm hanging off the front of the couch, his legs stretched out. She was glad he fit. Athena had been given the other couch because she was small enough to lie flat on it. Moonlight filled the front room. Athena played with her eyes, squinting them almost shut so the light would stretch and dance, then opening them wide so the room would go black and white, as if she had entered a page in a magazine. She lay there listening to the couch creak until she finally fell asleep.

***

The girls' change room was like a concrete prison block. Athena faced the wall. She brought a different T-shirt for gym. She already wore sweatpants. As she pulled her sweatshirt over her head, her T-shirt lifted up. Suddenly, she felt someone gripping her arm and dragging her toward the middle of the room. Athena breathed in sharply. The hands picked her up so one foot barely touched the floor and the other dangled in the air. Her sweatshirt was caught over her face, her chest and back exposed.

"Look at this! Hey, everyone, look at this piece-o'-shit boy here."

Athena struggled to free herself. She tugged her sweatshirt with her free hand but the girl's hands pulled mightily in the other direction.

"Ha ha ha! It's a ten-year-old boy. Flat as a pancake. Look at his ribs!"

Athena twisted to release herself, but the hands were too strong and held her arm and her sweatshirt together.

"This is a girls' change room. Should I kick the shit outta this boy for being here?"

Athena started to breathe hard. She couldn't see.

"Hey, leave 'er alone," someone said.

"What's that?"

Athena felt herself being moved toward the defender.

"I said, leave 'er alone."

The hands let her go. Athena stood up quickly and pulled her sweatshirt down. In the long mirror that spanned the far wall, she caught a glimpse of her face. It was beet red. Athena felt a flash of disgust. She should have known better. She was smarter than this.

Athena pushed on the door to leave.

"She's goin' to the boys' change room," someone said.

The person who had defended her had already blended back into the crowd. A kind person, but not someone who wanted to be associated with her. She would just wear her clothes to gym from now on. She hadn't yet spoken a word, and it was day ten.

***

The teacher walked up and down the rows of the classroom, handing back the tests from the first week. "Athena, good job."

Athena looked at the mark in the top right corner: 78 percent. She saw 96 percent on the paper of the girl in front of her. Her body was flooded with loss and shame. She turned the paper over.

The girl in front of her spun around. "Hi."

Athena turned and looked over her shoulder, then back at the girl. She nodded and managed a half-smile but remained silent.

"I'm Paula." The girl waited patiently, her face calm and friendly.

"I know," answered Athena.

It had taken two weeks. *Two whole weeks.*

"How do you know?"

"Everyone knows you. I'm Athena."

"I know." Paula smiled.

Athena didn't reply.

"Hey, I was wondering, do you understand any of this new math?"

"We were working on something else at my last school." Athena kept her paper down.

"Well, I could really use someone to help me, you know . . . help study and understand it."

Athena processed Paula's untruth.

"Do you want to come to my house for lunch today? I make a mean omelette."

Athena calculated the likelihood that this could end poorly, but her heart didn't allow for mistrust on any deep level. Instead, it melted into deep gratitude on the walk over as they chatted.

Paula's mom and dad were divorced, and she lived with her mom, her brother, and their two Siamese cats.

"So you see, the key is to move the eggs around in the pan." Paula demonstrated how to push the eggs from the edge to the middle, allowing the runny part to settle. "This makes it fluffy. Then I like to tear up the cheese." She peeled the plastic wrapper off the cheese slice. She folded it, flipped it, and slid it onto a plate. "Voilà."

Athena smiled. "Very professional."

Paula laughed.

Athena liked her. "I know you don't need help in math," she confessed.

Paula tipped her head to one side.

"I saw your test mark," Athena added.

"I just thought you might be hungry," Paula said sheepishly.

Athena looked down at herself. "Do you think I'm malnourished?" She burst into a peel of laughter.

Paula laughed too. "You mean you're not?"

Athena laughed harder.

"You just look so small, I thought—"

Athena cut her off. "I know I'm small. I just haven't started growing yet."

"That must be kinda hard."

"No. I always thought it was kinda good," Athena told her.

Paula shrugged. "Look for me at lunchtime. You can sit with us. I'll introduce you to everyone."

Athena's heart swelled. Maybe it was time to start growing.

When she got home, Tilley asked, "How was school today?" as Athena opened her math book at the table.

"Great," Athena said. "Someone spoke to me today. Her name is Paula. I thought I was going to go the whole year without speaking, but it only took fifteen days."

Later, Athena lay awake, running her hands up and down her chest. She was tormented. She had exercised too much power to stop herself from growing and now worried that she was destined to stay eternally undeveloped. "Please, God. Please, please, let me grow some boobs." She didn't feel anything happening. A wave of anxiety swept over her. She repeated her prayer and advised God that she wanted to reverse her earlier request and hoped it wasn't too late.

Chapter 45

It was almost a month before Athena ran into Niko. She heard him before she saw him. He was loudly giving his opinion to a couple of guys. Three girls with skin-tight jeans, teased hair, and thick black mascara were hovering nearby. Athena had heard some people say that Niko was an asshole. She watched him argue with the bigger guy. They were exchanging swear words in second languages.

Niko saw her. He slapped the guy's arm and jogged over to her. "Hey. How are you?"

They didn't kiss each other on the cheek at school.

"I'm okay."

"Are you coming to the football game tonight? I'm playing."

"That's great, but I don't think I'm going."

"Come out. It'll be fun. Everyone goes," he said as the bell rang.

He walked backward, then tucked his books under one arm and straightened the other. He pivoted as if making a football move and bounced against the lockers. Niko looked back at her, winked and then disappeared around the corner.

Athena used the payphone near the cafeteria door to call her mom at work. "Is it alright if I go to the football game?"

Athena was relieved that she said yes. There was no third degree. She realized it was because her father was no longer there to ruin everything. Her mom seemed happier lately.

***

Paula was pouring an ounce from every bottle in the liquor cabinet into a thermos. "It tastes like shit, but it will give you a buzz." She twisted the white cap and popped the plastic top that doubled as a cup over it.

"I could have got you girls some beer."

"No thanks, Mom. This is good."

Athena was frozen with fascination.

"Your mom is so cool," Athena told Paula as they left for the school.

"She likes to party with us sometimes. As long as we don't drive drunk, she's okay if we drink or smoke up." Paula was already sixteen.

Athena felt a strange sadness for Paula. Her own mother would never allow any of those things, which comforted her. The friends sipped the terrible-tasting mix out of the thermos. Athena felt a bit sick after the second shot and decided to pass after that.

Athena had never seen a football game in person. She tried to follow what was happening. It was easy to pick Niko out because of his hair. Their team won. As she stood in the bleachers watching Niko in the huddle afterward, he raised his head and scanned the stands. His gaze finally landed on her, and he smiled. Athena felt a rush of energy from her head to her toes. She bounded down to rejoin Paula, who was standing in a small crowd; she had met a few of them before.

For the first time in her life, Athena wanted to fit in. She wished she had boobs, jeans, makeup, the right sweater, and the perfect purse. She told herself that acting silly would make them not like her, and right now, belonging was the only thing that mattered. Although she was pleased Paula was becoming her friend, Athena grieved for the child inside that she was rejecting. It was as if she'd put her hands around her throat and squeezed, choking the life out of her unique voice, not wanting to spoil their opinion of her. She was a traitor. She was being like her sisters. But they had friends. Athena wanted friends so badly and she needed to become the version of herself she thought they wanted. Her cold side emerged internally. She had to grow up and stop being a child but killing herself was killing her.

***

Athena rolled over on the couch and jumped up in pain. Her chest felt bruised and there was a small bump. She ran her hand over it and gasped, then sat up, pulling her T-shirt forward. She raced to the bathroom and locked the door. Yes! She caught a glimpse. Her left breast was bluish and sore. The right breast was starting, but not as much. God had heard her! She wouldn't remain small.

Later that day, Danica said to Tilley, "We need to go shopping."

"Yeah, I need some new clothes," Lejla added.

Athena noticed her mom's concerned look, but at the moment she didn't care. She wanted a few new things as well.

"Okay. I think we can go downtown. You can each get something."

"What does that mean? I need some new shoes and jeans," said Danica.

"Well, it's not like I have all the money in the world now."

"Well, we need stuff, so I guess you'll have to get money from Dad," Lejla said. Tilley bit her lip.

At the department store, Athena walked out of the change room, the cotton polo shirt exposing the bumps on her otherwise smooth torso.

"You're disgusting," Danica said.

Athena blushed and pulled the shirt away from her chest. She slipped desperately into the change room. She could hear through the curtain.

"You can give her one of your old training bras, Dani."

"Ugh. I don't have any training bras. Why are we even having this discussion?"

When Athena came out of the change room again, Danica spoke to her without looking at her. "Come with me." Athena followed her to a different section. "I don't know why I have to do this. You're completely embarrassing."

Athena didn't understand until her sister shoved her into a change room and threw a boxed beginner's bra at her. Athena's whole body blushed. She turned the box over to read about the bra.

"Hurry up, for God's sake," Danica yelled through the curtain.

Athena worried that she might come in. She stepped out. "It's good," she said to Danica, who said nothing and walked far ahead of her.

The saleslady hopped around pairing tops and bottoms for endless mix-and-match looks to build a better wardrobe. After adding up in her head the cost of the big piles of clothes and realizing what that would mean to her mother, Athena lost her appetite for shopping.

"Put the things you want here," Tilley said, unable to say no.

Athena told her, "I don't want anything more," and slid the box toward the saleslady.

"You have to get something else."

"But I don't need anything."

With a disapproving look, the saleslady carried the clothes Athena had tried on from her change room. She obviously thought that Athena had wasted her time. Tilley was holding court, posing like a director in the play, and Athena and her sisters had to follow the script.

"Of course she doesn't need anything, the little martyr," Lejla said, partially to the saleslady behind the counter, who took the stack of items from her hands.

The sick look on her mother's face intensified at the sight of it.

"You don't need anything either," Athena said to Lejla.

Danica came out with more than Lejla.

"Oh, what's the martyr saying now?" Danica asked.

Athena stood there wondering why her mother couldn't just tell the truth. She couldn't afford all these designer clothes. She couldn't afford regular clothes. She couldn't afford second-hand clothes. Tilley bit her lip and stared past the counter full of items, her chin tipped up. Athena knew the truth but couldn't point it out at the risk of crushing her mother.

The saleslady's hand was on the big pile Danica had placed on the counter. "So can I start ringing these in?"

Athena said, "I'll be waiting at the elevator," and walked away.

Athena held the small parcel in her hands and rolled her shoulders in, rounding her back to hide her sprouting chest. After taking a long, slow, deep breath, she gradually blew it out.

She could hear her sisters berating their mother for not knowing who Calvin Klein was, for driving her gross little car, and for the ancient glasses she wore.

When they reached the street level, Tilley erupted. "I've never been so embarrassed in all my life!" Her face was red, her lips tight. She threw the bags of unnecessary clothes into the trunk and slammed it down. "You girls are the rudest, more spoiled rotten—"

"Calm down, Mom," Danica said.

"Calm down? *Calm down?*"

"Yes. You're going crazy for nothing."

Athena felt sorry for her mother.

"All three of you are rude."

"All three?" Athena had just gotten in the car and jumped off her seat. "All three?" She was louder than any of them, all trying to make their points heard.

"Yes, all three of you are. How dare you speak to me like that in front of that saleslady!"

Athena laughed incredulously, recklessly. But no one was listening. No one ever listened to anyone else.

***

Athena stared at her reflection in the bathroom, confirming that the smallest beige bra sagged around the mismatched walnuts that were supposed to be breasts. Disappointed, she threw a T-shirt and a sweatshirt on. As she stepped out of the bathroom into the small hallway, Lejla punched her hard, her fist landing squarely on her ripening breast. Athena yelped and almost buckled to her knees, gasping at the shock of the sharp pain.

"Hurts, don't it?" Lejla stepped past her to the kitchen and joined the discussion between Danica and her mom.

"We can't stay here. I don't have a room. I can't stay with *her*." Danica pointed at Lejla as she walked in.

Athena was holding her left breast bud as she slipped into one of the four chairs around the table.

"I mean, we're poor here, Mom. We have to go back."

Athena jumped up. "You can't, Mom! You can't go back. Don't listen to them." Although they didn't have fancy things, they all slept soundly. "No one yells at us here. We're free here. You can't go back!"

"Shut up, Theenie. You're being stupid." Danica barely looked at her.

"No, *you're* stupid," Athena said. "You're all stupid and *you're* the ones who wanted to leave. Are you forgetting why? Are you forgetting what our dad is like? Don't you care about that? And now you want to go back because you don't have your own room? Who cares? Mom, don't listen to them. I'll help you. Don't go back."

She was talking to the familiar wall of three faces, all looking off into the distance, all thinking without actually understanding the bigger picture. Tilley continued to stir the pea soup on the stove. The old cupboards held thick ceramic bowls with a green stripe around the outside. They were unfashionable and disgraceful, but Athena didn't care. She had moved forward. She couldn't go back to her old ways. She'd made the junior basketball team under Paula's tutelage. Although she was small, she was strong and athletic. She was becoming accepted. She had to grow up now. And she wanted to grow up without the fear.

Lejla fired verbal shots at her mother. "This house sucks. It smells bad and I hate it here." "Yeah. I'm not staying here." Danica spoke often of her friends. "I want to go back."

"What about you?" Tilley asked Lejla.

"I don't know. I think I'll stay at Montcalm. I can drive in. Athena can go wherever she wants to."

"She'd go with you," Tilley told her.

Athena's hand was still pressed against her chest. Lejla looked at her and she shrank. Her life wasn't her own, and the one she was living made no sense to her.

"Mom, we've only been here six weeks," Athena said. "Give it a chance. It'll get better. We can all get jobs."

"Ugh." Danica walked past her, and Lejla followed. They went to their room and closed the door.

"Mom," Athena said gently.

Tilley was leaning against the counter. One arm was across her stomach, and her other arm supported her bowed head. She covered her face with her hand.

"I'm tired, Athena. Please set the table."

Athena's mind raced for the words to convince her mother, but the sense of futility was as thick as the pea soup. Still, she was going to try, for all their sakes.

Chapter 46

"I think we might be moving back, but I'm going to finish the year here." Athena was debriefing Paula; her boyfriend, Anthony Mazza; and his best friend, Duncan.

Getting together with them was becoming more and more common, as she and Duncan wanted to see their friends. At lunchtime, they played euchre, which Athena had picked up quickly. After school she went to practice, watching the boys in the gym.

Paula and Anthony were a class favourite. Everyone knew how much he loved her. He sent her romantic notes, which Athena read at Paula's house. People asked Athena if she liked Duncan. Paula told her that he liked her, and she gushed about how fun it would be if they were both couples.

They all played basketball. Anthony was the point guard. He was Italian. His hair was glossy black with big curls that covered his neck. He had very defined muscles.

"I like his abs," Paula said to Athena as they sat on the stage in the gym watching the boys practise. They were playing shirts and skins. Anthony wasn't wearing a shirt.

"Do you like his big dick?" Carol asked, laughing. She had gone to school with Paula since kindergarten.

Paula laughed and smirked mischievously. "It doesn't hurt."

"Or maybe it does," added Athena.

They all laughed.

As Athena was putting on her runners, she tried to nonchalantly check out the bulge in Anthony's shorts. It was very definitely present, and the hem was tight around his muscular legs.

"He has a beautiful body," Paula said, confirming what everyone else was thinking.

Athena felt envious. She looked at Paula and suddenly felt like a terrible friend. Girls weren't supposed to like their best friend's boyfriend.

"And he's a great kisser."

Athena sank back, wondering what it would be like to kiss Anthony. If she could do it, then she would have a reference for a great kisser. Guilt spread through her in a second wave. She jumped off the stage.

***

"The boys are coming by," Paula said. "We're going to watch a movie. My mom's going out and my brother's going to my dad's." Athena was going to sleep over.

Paula was spelling out the situation, but Athena was still surprised when Duncan sat on the couch and patted it, motioning to Athena to come sit by him. She did. When he put his arm around her, she finally understood and froze. Anthony and Paula were making out on the other couch, lit up by the blue-grey light of the TV. Athena allowed Duncan to pull her closer and turn her face to his. His lips felt thin as they devoured hers. She didn't like it. His tongue darted into her mouth. She opened her eyes and saw Anthony kissing Paula, and she was jealous. She shut her eyes but felt revulsion at the whole set-up, the assumptions that had been made. What was she going to do? Make out with him? And what if he tried to feel her non-existent boobs? What would he say to everyone?

No. No. No kept repeating in Athena's head until she said it out loud. She pressed her hands to Duncan's chest, and got up and went to the bathroom. She quickly locked the door and turned on the tap, scooping water into her mouth and spitting it out. She rubbed her teeth with her finger, like a toothbrush. When she walked back out, a lamp was on and everyone was sitting up.

Paula jumped up and grabbed her hand. "Come into the kitchen and help me make some popcorn." She giggled and Athena followed suit.

"What's happening?" Paula whispered as she pulled out a bowl and a Jiffy Pop tray.

"Nothing," Athena said, shaking her head. "No, thank you."

Paula laughed but looked disappointed.

Athena felt regret but couldn't help it. Kissing Duncan was revolting. She wanted to kiss Anthony, but she didn't tell Paula. For the next awkward half hour, she just went along with things until the boys left.

Later that night, Athena carefully lifted the thin blanket and quietly swung her feet down. She looked at her friend in the bed. Paula was breathing steadily, asleep. Athena didn't turn on the light in the bathroom until she had silently closed the door.

She stared at herself in the mirror. "You are a terrible friend," she whispered sternly. "She's the only person who's even been nice to you, but you want to be with her boyfriend?" Disgusted, she shook her head slowly. "Look at you." Athena turned sideways. She had grown about four inches recently but was straight up and down and skinny. "Who'd want this, anyway? Except Duncan." Athena stared hard into her slightly bloodshot eyes. "You'd be lucky if any boy noticed you, let alone wanted you."

Upon absorbing this information, she let herself go back to bed.

Chapter 47

As the choir bus pulled into Windsor, Athena's back was aching. She moved slowly and got her things. She was getting dropped off by Roxy.

"You make sure you tell your mama, Theenie."

"Yes, I will," Athena replied. "Thank you for taking me."

Roxy's mother didn't look pleased that Athena had become so intoxicated at the festival on her watch.

It was late, and Athena walked up the steps to the small grey bungalow and in through the unlocked front door. The kitchen light was on. No one was around. Max was asleep on the couch.

"Hello?" Athena called.

Tilley came out in her housecoat, her finger to her lips. "It's late. Get to bed."

"Good to see you, Mom."

Tilley hugged her and took her bag and placed it on the kitchen table. "Did everything go okay?"

"I got drunk and threw up on Saturday night. But other than that, it was fine."

Tilley stood up taller for a second, as if forming a thought, but then it passed.

"Well, then, get to bed now quick." She disappeared back down the hall.

Athena unzipped her bag to get her toothbrush out. She went to the bathroom. When she wiped herself, a dark brown smudge filled the toilet paper. It looked like diarrhea, but she had only peed. Athena stared at it. Had she destroyed part of her liver by drinking too much? There was a puzzling stain on her underwear; she hadn't felt herself go.

Athena brushed her teeth and looked at herself in the mirror. "You shouldn't drink that much if it's going to make you shit your pants." She shook her head, smirking.

***

"There's school today, so you better get moving," Tilley said.

266

Athena's back was throbbing. "I think the bus ride did something to my back. It's killing me."

"You're going to school, and I don't want to hear another word about it." Tilley kissed Mitzi and Max on their heads.

Athena was walking to school when she felt something between her legs. It was an uncomfortable sensation. She walked more quickly and entered the first girls' bathroom she could find. After dropping her bag in the stall, she pulled down her pants and gasped when she saw the blood-soaked underwear. This must be her period.

The blood had smeared a film all over her inner thighs. Athena pulled some toilet paper from the roll and wiped herself. She spat into the dry, flimsy paper, hoping that the moisture would help remove the stickiness. She was late for class.

Athena knocked lightly on Lejla's homeroom door. When Lejla saw her, she didn't ask the teacher if she could go; she just got up and walked over to her.

Lejla grabbed her arm, squeezing it, pushing her out of sight of the classroom. "What do you want?" she demanded.

Athena's shame rose to her face and made her blush, but she had no alternative. "I got my period," she said, barely audible.

"Oh my God." Lejla turned to go.

Athena grabbed her in desperation. "I don't know what to do, Jaja."

Lejla clamped her hand over Athena's mouth. "Shut the hell up," she ordered.

Athena choked her embarrassment down and shut her tears off, having perfected this trick. She became numb, walking rapidly behind her sister, who was speeding down the hallway. They didn't speak.

Lejla grabbed two tampons from the top shelf of her locker and slammed the door. "Here." She shoved them into Athena's hand and pushed past her back toward her classroom.

Athena looked at the cylindrical paper-covered tubes. "Wait, Jaja!"

Lejla stopped and turned. "What?"

"I don't know . . ." Athena struggled, revealing her complete ignorance.

"Well, what do you have now?"

"Toilet paper."

"Shut up. You just put it in." Her contempt was loud and clear. Lejla turned and left.

Athena trudged back to the bathroom. The wads of toilet paper had dried and were pulling as she peeled them off. Athena placed one tampon in her bag and carefully tore the wrapping off the other. She stared at the cardboard roll with a string hanging out of one end. Athena was unsure. She took a deep breath.

She felt between her legs for the opening. There was a fresh blob of blood. The cardboard got sticky and her fingernails looked as though she had been crushing tomatoes all day. She was fumbling with the tampon, moving it to find a spot without resistance, when she dropped it into the toilet. Her heart fell at the possibility of dropping the second one.

A lump formed in her throat when, after spitting on her fingers, she tried to clean her hands so she could get the second tampon out of the wrapper.

Athena gave herself a pep talk. "Okay, look. You can do this. Just take a deep breath and press it all the way in. Girls can do cartwheels on the beach in white pants. This will work."

Athena's gaze was fixed on the junction between the stall and the granite pebble floor. She listened to her own breathing and willed the tampon to glide easily into her body. When it did, she smiled triumphantly. She padded her underwear with more toilet paper and pulled up her clothes.

She winced as she moved to the sink and saw herself in the mirror. "This is awful. I guess that's why periods suck."

***

In math class, Athena sat side saddle on the hard wooden chair, allowing her bum to hang off one side and crossing one leg over the other. The tampon sat like a painful post in her vagina.

"Are you feeling all right?" Paula asked. "You don't look that good."

Athena was sweating by lunchtime. But the embarrassment of just getting her period now kept her from asking her friend for any advice. She had to leave.

"I have to check out. I don't feel well." she told the receptionist, who looked at Athena and just signed the slip for her.

"I'll have to call your mom," the receptionist said.

Athena nodded. She stopped in the bathroom to remove the tampon and topped up the padding for the walk home. The relief was instant.

Athena wondered how it was that she had a mom and two older sisters but had never been told how to handle her first period before. She locked the bathroom door and opened the cupboard under the sink. Rummaging behind the towels, Athena pulled out her mother's pads. Seeing the thickness of the pad, Athena almost gagged. It was giant. She hastily stuffed everything back into the box and pulled out the next box, a yellow one with much thinner pads. Athena read the instructions: *Peel strip and apply.* The glue pulled on her pubic hair when she moved certain ways, but the pad was way more comfortable than a tampon.

The phone rang and she picked it up.

"Hey, what are you doing home?" her mom said.

"I'm okay." Pausing, Athena didn't want her mother to ask her if she got her period so she told her.

"And? Are you good?"

"Yes," Athena responded, too embarrassed to tell the truth.

"It's not a reason to miss school."

"I know." Athena didn't want to say that it was because it was the first time.

Athena hung up. She was tired and her back hurt. She looked out the window. The leaves were turning colour. Winter was on its way.

She went directly to Lejla's room when her sister arrived home.

"Can I ask you something, Jaja?"

Lejla didn't answer; she just stared at Athena.

"I don't know what I'm doing."

Lejla grimaced at her.

"The pads are tearing my hair out. I don't know how anyone—"

Lejla burst out laughing. "What the hell? If you weren't a genius, I'd swear you were special ed, Theen." Her laughter continued. "You stick them to your *underwear*, moron."

This came as a surprise and a relief to Athena.

"But pads are for losers. They're disgusting. Use tampons."

"I couldn't. They hurt too much."

Lejla stopped laughing and just looked uncomfortable again. "Well, I don't know about that."

"It's the cardboard part, I think."

"What the fuck is wrong with you?"

Athena stared at her sister's gaping mouth. Her palms were open as if she welcomed a response. There was silence. Finally, she said, "That's the applicator, you idiot. You don't leave it in."

"Well, how does it—?"

"Look at the instructions. This conversation is over." As Lejla went back to reading *Cosmo*, she chuckled and shook her head. "Holy hell, you're stupid."

Athena exhaled. The humiliation was a small price to pay for this important information. She was hopeful that her days wouldn't be spent being tortured.

Chapter 48

Some boys were playing half-court pickup basketball while Athena sat alone, writing an English essay due later that day. She listened to the boys' discussions. They centred on getting "head," which she didn't understand, and girls' boobs, which she didn't have.

The ball bounced off someone's foot and came clattering up the stands near her. Athena glanced at it but didn't try to retrieve it.

"Hey, brainiac! Do my homework while you're at it," one said.

"Do this," suggested another, grabbing himself.

Athena said nothing and went back to writing.

"Hey, sorry about them."

Athena looked up. A lanky, dark-haired boy about six feet tall grabbed the ball and smiled kindly at her.

He stopped, placing the ball on his hip. "Whatcha writin'?" His teeth were a little crooked, but in a cute way.

"Just an English essay."

"Come on, Nate! Nate!" the boys called.

Athena smiled, and he kept smiling at her as he looked over his shoulder. He passed the ball to his waiting cohort. "You'll have to read it to me sometime."

"Sure." Athena felt all of her words fall away under his gaze.

"Ooh, Nate likes the little girl."

"Shut up," he replied, laughing. Smiling, he looked one more time at her and then went back to shooting.

***

Expressionless, Athena listened to Paula.

"No, no. Not Nate Kirton. He's had the same girlfriend for three years and they are, like, totally married. Rianne Jakolew."

Her eyes opened wide and she sat up. "Rianne? That loud-mouthed, crass girl in our science class?"

Paula nodded emphatically.

"The one who held me up in the change room?"

Paula nodded. "They even have sex at each other's houses. Like, their parents know about it, I think."

Athena sighed. She could never compete with that. And how could a sweet, cute guy like Nate go out with a rotten bully like Rianne?

Nate, Anthony, and Duncan were all friends. They played on the basketball team together, and life revolved around which game, which school, and which play. Athena was part of the audience but she sat in the front row now, next to Paula.

A dance was happening at the Polish hall on the weekend. Everyone was going. Athena went to Paula's after school on Friday to stay over. Her mom had moved to a new apartment on the east side of town.

"Pick your poison," Paula's mom, Sandra, held up a six-pack of beer in one hand and a baggie of weed in the other. "I've got rolling paper in the drawer."

Paula took the pot from her mother's outstretched hand.

Sandra was short with orange-tinged bushy hair and big glasses that practically covered her face. "I'm going out tonight. Might meet up with Mr. Right. You never know, so don't wait up. I left money here for a cab home if you're not sober enough to drive. I know I won't be."

Paula and Athena sat quietly. Athena's eyes flitted to her friend when her mother went upstairs to get ready.

Putting the twenty dollars in her purse, Paula explained, "She'd never let me drive drunk. She doesn't care about the money."

Athena wasn't sure why she always felt sorry for Paula.

The plan was to drive to the bash, get high in the car, and then be sober by the time they were leaving so they could keep the twenty dollars.

Athena pulled the turquoise knit dress with a paisley pattern over her head and wiggled it down over her skinny frame. It was Lejla's but she didn't wear it anymore. She had small breasts now, although she frowned because the right one looked smaller. She stuffed three Kleenexes into that side of her bra and inspected herself in the mirror. Tonight she had Paula's hot rollers in. After removing them, she flipped her head down and brushed out her silky brown curls. As she tossed her head back, a giant brunette halo fell over her shoulders.

"Wow, you look hot!" Paula said. Athena wasn't sure about hot but she did agree that she looked acceptable for once.

When they pulled into the parking lot, Paula found a spot near the back. It was dark. There was no lineup yet.

"We don't want to be stuck in line. Usually, if we're in by nine we'll be okay," Paula said.

"Did the boys say they were coming?" Athena asked again.

"Yes. Stop worrying. They'll be here."

Paula reached across Athena and snapped open the glovebox. A pink lace garter hung on the rear-view mirror. She tore a piece of white paper from a small book. The joint looked like a candy. Athena thought of Mojos or Rockets. She wasn't certain she wanted to smoke it.

"I'm good. My mom taught me well," Paula said.

Again Athena felt a pang of sympathy. She couldn't imagine her own mother showing her how to roll a joint or giving her a choice of drugs or alcohol.

"I'm not sure how to smoke this," Athena admitted.

"I'll light it. It's easy. This stuff isn't too harsh. It can make you cough, though." The paper crackled orange and red as Paula sucked on one end. She offered some advice. "You have to breathe in and hold it." She was doing this as she explained, her voice climbing higher.

She passed it between her thumb and index finger to Athena, who took it the same way. The whole car smelled like sour cabbage cooking. Athena placed the wet, twisted end between her lips and slowly sucked on it, feeling thick smoke tickle her throat. She tried to hold it but just started coughing.

"You'll get the hang of it," Paula said.

"What will it feel like?"

"You'll feel laid-back. Like everything's funny."

Athena looked at the man taking her ticket. He was yelling over the music, a Prince song. "If you have a coat, you have to use the coat check."

"No, I don't have a coat." Athena started giggling. She didn't know where she had been for the last ten minutes.

The hall was dark inside and the music was good. "I'm going to request a song," Athena told Paula.

She danced back through the crowd. Suddenly, the boys were there. Athena wasn't sure if she'd spoken to them already. It worried her when she realized it, but then she drifted away again. Duncan was moving her to the dance floor, his hand on her waist, when she saw Nate. She pushed Duncan's hand away and walked straight toward him.

"Hey, Nate."

"Hey, Athena. You look *really* nice."

"Is Rianne here?" With a bold smile, Athena put her hands on his chest, and he shook his head. "Then let's dance!"

She grabbed his hand and marched him toward the dance floor, pressing through the small space crowded with couples. Their bodies came together as Athena wrapped her hands around his neck.

"I had to stand in line," he said.

"There's a line?"

"Yeah. It's cold outside. But you feel warm." Athena smiled. She did feel warm. She closed her eyes and laid her head on Nate's chest.

"It might be too warm in here now," Nate said. "Do you want to go outside for some air?"

Athena nodded wordlessly. Hand stamps were needed for re-entry, and she watched those being applied to her wrist. Athena had no awareness of the time in between these moments. Where had she been and what had she said?

They could hear and feel the bass of the music outside. The moon was high and stark white, but there were no stars. White fog came out of their mouths as Nate held Athena's hand and led her to the side of the brown brick building. He pulled her around the corner and leaned against the wall.

"Look—it's like we're smoking." A long trail of breath left Athena's lips. She could feel the cold and her teeth chattered suddenly.

"You're so pretty, Athena. Are your lips cold?" Nate asked.

Athena pulled her lower lip under her teeth and felt it with her tongue. She nodded. He tipped her chin up and kissed her gently and carefully. He took her bottom lip into his mouth and sucked it softly. Athena moaned. His hands touched her face, ran through her hair, then down her waist and hips. They were travelling up her ribcage. Athena pulled back and her hands flew down to grab Nate's. It had been so rapturous, but she had Kleenex in her bra.

Nate looked surprised. "Don't you like it? You're a great kisser."

"No, I love it. But . . ." Athena paused and struggled to find a better reason than her inadequate breasts. "You have a girlfriend."

Nate looked away and then back down at her. "Let's just be here right now."

"We *are* here right now."

He laughed. "I know I'm not going to win an argument with the smartest girl in school." He laughed again and lifted his back off the wall. "Come on, let's go back in."

Athena's heart sank and she ached to kiss Nate more, but now she was really here—not floating in and out of time but in the cold moment of seeing Nate's back ahead of her as he strode quickly back up the driveway. She had to gallop to keep pace. The lineup had disintegrated into a large circle of people all trying to explain why they had to find their friends inside. She could see Nate, taller than everyone, nod and wave to the bouncer and just step inside, but the opportunity to follow closed and she was swallowed up in the crowd. Athena squirmed past people, explaining as politely as she could that she had a stamp.

She worked her way up to the bouncer and showed him her wrist, but he grabbed her arm as she tried to re-enter. "We're at capacity."

Her shame rose at the rejection. Athena was shocked but determined. "I've already been in. My friends are in there."

"Sorry, it's full." He looked her over. He was older.

Athena felt deflated and her throat constricted. Her sweat started to freeze as the temperature fell. "I have to go in."

"Look, kid. It's a no. You can wait here like everyone else."

Athena stood waiting, watching people coming out, and still no one was allowed to go in. People kept coming up to the bouncer. Some spoke Polish to him and he let them in. He simply stared out over Athena as if she weren't there. She had nowhere to go. Her toes felt numb on the frozen concrete, and she shuffled from side to side to stay warm. Athena didn't have a watch, but it must have been late, as the hopefuls were peeling away, discussing where else they could go. The bouncer moved inside and Athena finally followed since no one was there to stop her.

The lights went on. She scanned the hall; clear plastic beer cups littered the tables surrounding the abandoned dance floor. She couldn't see anyone she knew. Paula was gone. The boys were gone. No one had waited for her. Athena felt a penetrating loneliness.

"Dance is over, kid. You gotta clear out."

"I have to check the bathroom," she replied.

Athena went to the girls' washroom. Toilet paper floated in the puddles on the floor from wet shoes, and spilled drinks. She opened one of the stall doors. The toilet had overflowed. A girl stepped out of the next stall and glanced at her before leaving quickly. Athena entered that stall and peed nervously, wondering what to do. She hadn't brought a purse or any money. Paula must be waiting in her car! She wouldn't just leave her! Athena hadn't finished wiping herself before she yanked up her tights and pulled down her dress.

She sprinted for the front door, certain that her friend would be waiting. She ran around to the parking lot. The back door of the hall was propped open. Two guys were carrying equipment to a white van. There were no other cars. Athena took two steps back to conceal herself against the building. The guys were laughing and talking. She held her breath.

"Think, think, think," Athena stuttered in a demanding whisper, jabbing her finger into her temple.

It was after midnight. She had no money. She had no way home. No one knew where she was and no one cared. There was nothing else to do but walk. She would stay on the main streets, under street lights. The dark night loomed over her. Athena walked quickly, listening to the crunching of dirt under her synthetic soles. Her baby toes were bleeding from the pointed shoes, not made for her wide feet.

"Don't cry. What good will it do? Do you want to freeze to death outside? Oh, that would look great. Where are your friends? What friends?"

A bitterness surged into the back of her throat as she pictured everyone leaving without her, no one remembering she was even there.

The buses stopped running after midnight. During the first thirty minutes or so, a couple of cars went by. Athena thought of hitchhiking, but her fear of being abducted, tortured, and killed overcame her.

"Okay, let's jog this block." Athena approached a cross street and looked ahead at the next stoplight. It didn't seem far, but her feet were throbbing. "On your toes, now. Nimble and quick. One, two, three. One, two, three." She ran as lightly and quickly as she could.

Moving faster only made the night air cut through her dress. She could feel the pattern of the knit, and Athena pictured the loops of yarn with their infinite voids allowing the cold air to sneak through.

"They're all stupid. That's it." A British voice filled her head and scolded her so-called friends. But then she defended them. "They must have looked for me. They were probably worried." Her excuses comforted her.

Another hour or so passed. Athena's cheeks were burning with the cold. She finally reached the road where her friend's apartment was. She could see the building in the distance. Athena was exhausted.

She raised her gaze to the sky, dark like blackish-blue oil pastels. "Where are all the stars? Have you all fallen from the sky because I'm alone? Don't be sad for me. It's okay, I'm good. Look at me go—even though I'm frozen to the core and my lips are blue. They kissed Nate Clark tonight and I looked beautiful. Even though my boobs aren't grown, they will be soon. Maybe you're not here because I got high? Are you angry with me? Don't be. I don't like it. I lost time. My time here." Athena muttered as she walked the final mile and a half.

Fear kept Athena's conversation going. "Who needs friends, anyway? You have a family who loves you and friends at church who would take you in if you had nowhere to go. You're not alone. God is always with you." Athena heard herself and wondered if she was lying. She wasn't. She believed this. But the feeling that God had let her down filled her up. "You could do a little better, you know. Send a ride along. Send some real friends."

It took three attempts before Paula picked up the phone and opened the front door. Paula had propped the front door open with the bolt lock and gone back to bed before Athena got to the apartment. The cool water felt burning hot on her hands as she tried to thaw them in the bathroom. She had mild frostbite. A comforter and pillow sat on the couch, and it felt warm as Athena wrapped the blanket around herself and dropped down. She didn't need anyone. Life had prepared her for this. Paula and the others weren't her real circle of friends. She didn't matter, but she didn't care. Athena's eyelids closed before her head hit the pillow. As though she was still high, time jumped to the morning, sleep escaping her notice.

***

"What happened to you?" Paula asked, as though it was Athena who needed to do the explaining.

"What do you mean?" Athena's mouth dropped open. "You left and I looked for you."

"The guys wanted to go for pancakes."

"I was at the front door."

"Oh. We left out the back." Paula hummed as she opened a package of bacon.

Athena said nothing.

"So why did you leave?" Paula asked.

"Nate kissed me."

Paula slammed down the spatula. "What? Oh my God, tell me!"

Chapter 49

Nate didn't break up with Rianne. Instead Rianne knocked at the door of Athena's classroom.

"Excuse me, Mr. Hayden? May I speak to Athena Brko-bitch, please?"

There was a smattering of laughter. What madness. As if Athena herself could get out of class to speak to someone on a whim!

Mr. Hayden motioned with a "Be my guest" gesture. "Yes, of course. Athena?"

Athena frowned. She stood up hesitantly, aware that she had no allies in the room and a foe to face just outside the door. Athena joined her in the hallway.

The look on Rianne's face was one of smug condescension. "Let's go for a walk."

"No, let's not."

"I'm not making a suggestion. I could beat the shit out of you in broad daylight, but I'd rather be reasonable."

Rianne was poor. She had a bad haircut and pockmarked cheeks. "Nate is mine. I don't think you know this."

"People don't belong to other people."

"You're not listening to me. Nate is mine and I'm his. We're together, and whoever comes between that is going to get hurt or killed."

Rianne wasn't looking at her, and Athena wondered if she knew they'd kissed.

As if on cue, Rianne said, "I know about your little kiss. Nate tells me everything. You're a home-wrecking bitch, one of those girls who can't get her own guy and goes for another girl's. Back off or I'll take you down." At this declaration, she stopped and faced Athena as casually as though they'd been discussing homework. "Are we clear?"

Rianne had large pendulous breasts that swung around when she moved. Athena always wondered if she wore a bra. She pictured Nate and Rianne having sex. Athena felt sorry for her. Nate was the love of her life, but it wasn't going to work out. Rianne wasn't smart enough to lift herself out of these circumstances. She wasn't pleasant to look at or talk to. If high school was to be her crowning moment, it was sad. Athena briefly thought about explaining reality to Rianne but wanted to go back to class.

"Yes, I'm clear."

Rianne seemed to take this as a win. "You should be humiliated for thinking you could get Nate. Look at you."

Rianne went further, even though it wasn't necessary. Athena allowed her to. She didn't believe anything Rianne said. Rianne was a kid acting like an adult.

"We've all known each other for years. We've gone to school together since kindergarten. You're some rich bitch who thinks she can come in here and change it all up. Well, I'm here to knock you down if you try."

Athena wondered why Rianne thought she was rich, why she had to listen to this person at all. Suddenly, Athena hated Rianne and her ugly face.

"People don't belong to other people, Rianne."

Rianne wagged her finger in Athena's face and looked at her with squinty eyes. Her pasty thin lips parted and she spat, "You're dead. You're *so* dead."

Athena calmly looked at Rianne's finger, planning to bend it back and break it if she touched her. She looked up at the much larger girl and saw the flicker of fear in her eyes. Athena walked away, disgusted by her own pleasure in the moment.

"I'm gonna kick your ass after school. You asked for it."

The words hit Athena in the back as she turned down the corridor to her classroom. When she sat back down, fear caught up to her.

***

The student parking lot was adjacent to the smoking area. Metalheads, stoners, and Lejla— these were the people who hung out there. It looked like a small penitentiary. Six overcrowded picnic tables sat in the small space. Black leather jackets or red plaid shirts were acceptable attire, as were angora sweaters.

When the bell rang and Athena left Mr. Dubeau's physics class, she felt her classmates' attention on her. Most of them didn't move in the circles Rianne did, but they knew someone who did. As she went to her locker, she could feel the murmurs as though they'd tapped her on the shoulder.

It seemed unreal until two rough girls, Melanie and Trish, pointed at her in the crowded hallway. "Hey, bitch! You're dead! Rianne is gonna kick this little bitch's ass!" Melanie shouted.

Athena disliked swearing. She felt superior to them, knowing that, being rude and simple, they wouldn't amount to much in life. But fear welled up inside of her. She said nothing. Everyone else did enough talking for her.

As Athena moved toward the parking lot, she recalled a student who had been kicked and punched in the stomach until she had a miscarriage, having gotten pregnant by someone else's boyfriend. Athena was sitting on the stands near the football field and saw some students drag the girl by her hair out of her car. They slammed her face into the curb. Athena had been filled with horror for weeks at the sight of it. She determined that she would fight if she had to, but she didn't want to lose any of her teeth.

People were gathering as she walked, traipsing alongside her, and they kept reiterating the word "fight." There was always a schoolteacher at the exit where the cars were. Athena turned toward that exit, but Melanie and Trish suddenly appeared.

"Oh no you don't," Trish said.

"Trying to get away?" Melanie added.

"Don't think so."

"Rianne's waiting for you."

One on either side of her, they practically lifted Athena off the ground and carried her to the side door. This led to a small empty lot beside the school, just around the corner from the parking lot, out of sight from everyone except the hundred or so people who had already assembled, thirsty for blood.

Athena was dumped into the middle of the arena.

"So you showed up?" Rianne said.

Athena didn't reply. She had a gym bag slung across her body and a small purse over it. Rianne wasn't carrying anything, her hands and arms flailing as she gestured to the crowd.

"Aren't you gonna put your stuff down?" Rianne asked.

Athena remained motionless. It occurred to her that Rianne and most of these kids probably didn't have great home lives. Their parents probably hit them, as she was hit, and they were angry and sad.

"Whatsa matter? Cat got yer tongue?" Rianne pressed her face in close to Athena's.

Athena didn't look at her. She didn't want to fight Rianne, but she wasn't going to run and she didn't have to be like her either. She didn't have to follow these rules; they were wrong. In that exact moment, she released her fear. Athena watched Rianne and the entire scene as if it didn't involve her.

"Fight! Fight! Fight!" The familiar playground chant broke out.

Rianne laughed outrageously and walked around the small circle that surrounded them, encouraging the crowd to raise the volume. Like a vulture, she landed in front of Athena.

"What do you think you're doing?" a voice shouted.

Rianne looked over. It was Lejla. Almost instantly, everyone quieted.

Rianne stammered, "I'm gonna kick this loser's ass, Lejla."

Lejla stepped between Athena and Rianne. Now shorter than Athena, she was an inch from her tormenter's face. "That loser is my sister."

Rianne's face turned pale. "Uh . . . I didn't know . . . Honest, Lejla. How could anyone think you two are related? Look, sorry, it won't happen again."

"You're damn right it won't happen again."

And with that, Lejla grabbed Athena and marched out of the circle, the people parting like the Red Sea to let them pass. Lejla didn't look at Athena and walked stormily ahead of her, straight to the car. Neither of them said anything.

When they arrived at their baba and deda's house, Athena quietly said, "Thanks, Jaja."

"Jesus, Theenie! Why do you have to do this shit?" Lejla hit the steering wheel with her palm.

Athena watched her sister, full of admiration, like a real-life superhero. She had studied Lejla her whole life but could never imitate her coolness. She was so grateful for her.

"You saved me."

Lejla stopped as she was about to get out of the car and stared at Athena. When she spoke, her voice was thick with remorse. "And now everyone knows you're my sister."

Athena felt the car door slam and realized it would have hurt less to face Rianne alone.

Chapter 50

The end of the school year came quickly for Athena. Between basketball, homework, listening to her sisters badger Tilley about the intolerable living conditions, sleeping through a major growth spurt, and trying to understand how to fit in, Athena was exhausted.

There was a school assembly. It was imperative to have someone to sit with. Athena found Paula. She had recently broken up with Anthony. She showed Athena the long love letter he'd written her. Why did no boys write her letters? Her body had developed more curves; she had small hips, perky breasts, long legs, and broad shoulders. She was almost five foot seven. So many people were talking while the principal spoke that Athena didn't hear her name when it was called.

"Oh my God! You just got the highest average award!" Paula said.

Athena got up, hesitantly at first, and then quickly stepped down around people to shouts of "Keener!" and "Brainer!" She couldn't remember the last time she was recognized for being intelligent. Mr. Henrik, the principal, handed her a plaque with her name engraved on it. "Congratulations, Athena, for the highest average in grade ten."

Mrs. Bondy, her homeroom teacher that semester for English, gave her a hearty thumbs-up. Athena was filled with an embarrassed pride.

"My best friend is the smartest person in school. That's why she's friends with me," Paula said, laughing.

***

Athena bounded up the four concrete steps, grabbing the iron railing to haul herself up even faster. Seeing her mom's car on the street, she flew through the front door.

"Mom! Mom! Look! I won an—" Athena stopped short.

Her father stood in the kitchen, leaning against one counter while her mother, her arms crossed, leaned on the other. Danica and Lejla sat at the table, looking smug and happy. Nothing good could be happening.

"Sit down, Athena. We have some news we want to share," Tilley said.

Before Athena sat down, Danica explained, "We're moving back home. We don't have any space or money here."

Athena turned and watched her mother bow her head. When Tilley looked up, Athena was looking pleadingly at her.

"Your dad realizes that drinking isn't good, and he's going to try his best from now on."

"I want to go back to my old school," Danica added. "I'll get to graduate with my friends."

"But you and I get to keep going to Montcalm. I'm going to get the car to drive in," Lejla said. "Or you can change back—whatever you want."

Nothing was ever how Athena wanted. There was an awkward silence.

"Athena won the highest average award," Lejla announced.

"Hey, that's great, peanut," her dad said.

"When you love someone, you give them a chance and forgive them." Tilley put her hand on Dragan's shoulder. "Right, Drag?"

Her father looked sheepish, as though he would start crying, and tipped his head to one side. Danica and Lejla were beaming. Athena was confused.

After they all moved back, Baba and Deda's house got sold immediately.

***

It was one month later, almost to the day, when they noticed that Dragan hadn't come home. It was five o'clock. *Bong. Bong. Bong. Bong. Bong.*

Athena glared at her sisters. She wanted to scream. She glanced at Tilley. "Why, Mom? You knew this would happen!"

"Please, Athena. Stop." Tilley put down the paring knife she was using to peel apples for the apple crisp and smoothed her apron. "Go play outside."

Incredulous, Athena scoffed.

"Go find Mitzi and Max and keep them outside until dinner. Do as I ask, please."

She couldn't disobey her mother or press too hard on her for fear she would break. Athena ran to the garage. The door was open. She pulled her three speed from the pile of bikes and ran it down the driveway, then hopped on it and pedalled as hard and fast as she could.

"One day I won't look back. I'll leave and never come back here. I don't need any of you."

***

"Didja really think?"

Each sick, drunken word fell loudly and slowly out of her father's mouth, travelled down the hall, and hit her ears before assaulting her heart.

"Didja? Huh? You? You're a stupid idjet. You're a dummy."

Athena was lying in bed, wondering where she got her intelligence from. What if she were really adopted? That made more sense. Maybe her birth family would come find her and say, "We made a huge mistake, and we missed you so. We knew you would be amazing." But no one came. Everything was almost exactly as it used to be.

It only took a couple months before Dragan hurled a small orange portable TV at Lejla. She was in the corner of her bedroom, huddled in the fetal position. It only took one more day for Lejla to leave. She moved into a Jewish girl's house just in time for the start of the school year. Knowing that their dad would be out on the weekends, Lejla sometimes came home then to get some clothes, food, and money.

Athena now had to get rides into school with her dad because the buses didn't run out there. Getting home every day was almost impossible. Without her grandparents' house, Athena didn't really have anywhere to go. The fighting and drinking had escalated so quickly and become more violent than before that she couldn't process it. She was in the line of fire but she couldn't contemplate leaving. Athena focused instead on fitting in.

Lejla was wrapping the cord of her curling iron around it when Athena tapped on her door. "C'mon in."

Athena sat on the bed and watched her sister as she looked in the mirror. She missed her. "Jaja, how do I get boys to like me?"

"Well, look at you. Your body is ridiculous. Boys are going to like you, no problem."

"But they don't."

"Stop being so smart." Lejla turned. The advice wasn't new.

"But I *am* smart."

"Yes. Stop it. Boys don't like it when you're smarter than them."

"But you're smart."

"Yeah, but they don't know it. I act dumb and let them fix stuff and help me. Act like you don't know anything, and boys will flock to you to save you. Use your brain to play the game, Theenie."

Athena never understood but she was going to try. It was all she had. She watched Lejla shove the curling iron in her bag and walk out.

***

Niko still dated all of the hottest girls in school, but no one for very long, so Athena didn't pay much mind. What she *did* mind was that she had no experience compared to him. She would have to get some.

Paula and Anthony hadn't got back together over the summer. Athena knew that Anthony was a very private person and wouldn't gossip about her, because he didn't about Paula. She wanted to fool around with boys but didn't want anyone to know. Paula had said that Anthony was a great kisser and had a big penis. Athena would pretend to him that she liked him.

The boys' basketball team had just won their game. She followed Anthony down the hallway to his locker, where he loaded his books and things in.

"That was an awesome game you played," Athena said enthusiastically. "You can really jump."

"What are you doing down here by yourself? Where's Paula?"

She took a deep breath. "I wanted to come and congratulate you myself." She pushed the locker door back and moved in to kiss him on the mouth.

"Whoa. What are you doing?"

Athena blushed intensely.

"Hey, I'm sorry. I didn't know you liked me."

"Well, I do," Athena lied.

"Let's try it again." He moved her against the lockers and kissed her gently, expertly.

She could feel his hardness through his gym shorts pressing on her leg. Athena panicked. "Wow, okay. That was, you know . . . Wow. Good game."

He laughed and grabbed his penis through his shorts. "You really have an effect on me."

Athena giggled, backing down the hall. "Yeah, I guess I do. Wow. Okay." Feeling a throbbing between her legs, she turned and scurried back to the gym, her heart filled with a curious guilt and her head wondering why she'd kissed him if she didn't really like him.

These encounters became a habit. Anthony and Athena didn't date—not where anyone knew of them. Athena thought it suited Anthony because he probably still really liked Paula, and it suited her because she was horny.

No one was waiting to pick Athena up after her practices. She sat in the gym doing her chemistry homework in the bleachers and watching the boys practise after the girls had already finished.

She waited at their meeting spot, the stairwell just beyond his locker. Athena sat on the third stair up, her gym bag at her feet. She heard the locker door and stood up to peek down the hallway. Anthony and Duncan were there. She watched them talking and laughing. They started to walk away and she felt a pain in her stomach. Then they stopped and Anthony waved Duncan away. The two boys high-fived, and Anthony headed back toward her. Athena became very excited.

"I'm so glad you didn't forget," she said.

"How could I forget?"

Anthony closed the stairwell door quietly and their mouths met the instant they faced each other. The stairs were metal so you could easily hear someone coming up or down.

Athena let Anthony put his hands wherever he wanted. He slid his fingers under her sweatpants and rubbed her over her panties, then said, "You're soaking wet." She explored Anthony, trying to learn as much as she could without seeming too inexperienced. She knew that Niko had been doing this with girls ever since she could remember. She didn't want to be completely green. Athena placed her hand down Anthony's sweatpants and grabbed his erection. She studied the shape and size of his penis. There was a mushroom top with a small hole she could probe. The shaft was very soft and smooth and pretty big around. She didn't have anything to compare it to. Below his penis were two sacks of skin that were extremely sensitive, and Anthony didn't really like it when she touched him there.

They were kissing and heavy petting when Anthony stopped and looked at her. He pulled back and studied her face.

"What?" she said.

"I don't know. I just . . ."

"What's wrong? What is it?"

"Well, I mean, we've been doing this for a while, and I really like you."

Athena smiled.

"And I hope you like me."

She nodded.

"I mean, I'm really starting to like you, but there's something about you."

At this, Athena's smile faded. She pulled her top down. "I don't understand. What are you saying?"

"I mean this." Anthony motioned to the stairwell. "Like, why aren't we going out?"

"I thought you just wanted to have some fun."

"I do. It's just," he said, searching for the right words, "there's something cold about you. I can't put my finger on it, but I'm worried because I'm starting to get super attached to you, and I feel like you could just say you don't like me in an instant."

He wasn't far off—there was something wrong with her. She couldn't tell him that she wanted enough experience so she could be with Niko but didn't want Niko to think she had dated anyone else because she wanted to be his.

"I really like you, Athena."

A shudder of disgust went down Athena's spine. The thought of becoming close to a boy other than Niko repelled her, and Anthony's analysis of her, though accurate, only led to his fears being confirmed.

"Well, I guess we're done here."

Anthony looked shocked. "What do you . . . ?" His voice trailed off as she stood up.

Athena felt she had collected enough experience for the time being.

"I mean, you're right. I am cold." Athena bent down and grabbed her gym bag. She straightened her sweatpants and tucked the front of her T-shirt in.

Anthony sat dumbfounded. His cheeks flushed and his eyes grew wet.

Her disgust grew so fast that even she was surprised at how remote she sounded. "Don't get all mushy on me. This was supposed to just be fun. It was good while it lasted, eh?" Athena had never told Paula and now she wouldn't have to either. She went to leave, pushing open the door. She had to walk back to the pay phones to call her mom for a ride. "Are you coming?" She held the door and waited.

Anthony just shook his head. "I knew you could be like this," he muttered.

"Like what?" Athena asked. "Cold?"

"Cold-hearted."

There was a familiar feel to this conversation, but she wouldn't thaw. Hard as icy steel, she pushed down any discomfort as far as she could. When the door banged shut and Anthony left to walk home, Athena reached into her pocket to get a quarter and dialed their number. It was busy. She hung up. It took nine tries before someone picked up.

"Persistence pays off," Athena told her faint reflection in the glass.

The night janitor, Mr. Fergus, came around the corner with his pushcart. "Oh, you're still here, Athena?"

"I am, Mr. Fergus. My ride's coming."

She knew all the custodial staff from having to move from where she was sitting, studying, or sleeping in the hallways before or after school as they cleaned up.

"Okay, you have a good night."

"You too."

See, I'm not cold, Athena thought. *I'm kind.* She had no remorse for hurting Anthony's feelings. She couldn't muster any empathy. She didn't want him liking her. Telling him it was over was the kind thing to do.

Chapter 51

Athena had been counting down the days on the 1984 calendar that was taped to the inside of the broom closet. Their father's drinking happened regularly, and the ugly truth that their mother was being punished for having left was spilling out. Athena held on for the bright moment that would be her sweet sixteenth. It fell on a Friday; she couldn't believe how perfectly everything would work out.

The morning of her birthday, Athena was excited at the prospect of getting her driver's license. Lejla had moved back home in October and drove them both to school. She had given her the keys to the car and let her drive it around the block at lunchtime to learn.

Athena sprang out of bed and checked her face in the mirror. "Ah, Mitzi! It's a great day! My skin looks good—no major zits!" With a huge smile, she clapped her hands together.

Mitzi rolled over and pulled the covers over her face.

Athena hummed as she got dressed, wondering who would be there. The party would be indoors, as the November cold had surrounded them. She walked to the kitchen in her thin nightgown and shivered as she slid onto the faux leather bench.

"Good morning, Mom," Athena sang, smiling.

"Oh, good morning." Tilley was writing Mitzi and Max's names on their lunch bags with a red china marker. She didn't look up.

"Today's going to be an amazing day!"

"Is it?" her mom asked with a smile.

Athena smiled wider. Everyone always pretended they had no idea about surprise parties.

"You know it's the best day in the world!"

Athena slid out of the bench and walked to her mom, her forearms crossed over her chest to hide her breasts. Tilley stopped what she was doing and hugged Athena, who purred and leaned in.

"I have to get ready for work."

"All work and no play, Mom," Athena chided her, then giggled.

Tilley giggled back, and Athena was pleased that her mother was doing such a good job with the production. It would be a splendid affair. She picked up the china marker on the counter and pulled the white string, cutting through the layers of paper around the greasy red centre.

"So what time should I be home today, Mom?"

"Um, the usual."

Athena waited for more instructions.

Tilley looked up from her purse, which she was organizing on the counter. "Don't be late, okay, sweetie?"

Athena beamed at her. "You're so pretty, Mom."

Tilley chuckled. "*You're* the pretty one. Now go get ready."

Lejla drove them to school. Athena's plan was to borrow the car and go to the licence bureau at lunch.

"Duh. You can't drive yourself to the place. You don't have a licence and I'm not driving you."

"Please drive me. I want to get it today."

Lejla looked conflicted. "I have things to do."

Athena knew what she was alluding to and just smirked.

"It'll be quick."

"Okay."

Athena walked excitedly toward her locker. She turned the corner and saw the pink and yellow streamers taped to the door of her locker. Today was the start of a new beginning—she could feel it.

"Surprise!" Paula said, laughing while Athena pulled her books out of her locker. "I didn't want to tape my card to your locker in case someone took it."

Athena nodded. "You could've given it to me tonight," she said, fishing.

"I wanted to give it to you first."

Athena was delighted.

By lunchtime, Lejla had changed her mind. "Listen, you take the car, alright? You can drive there, get your permit. Then you can get yourself home. I have plans tonight."

"Of course you do." Athena beamed at her sister.

She wondered how many people Lejla had told at school. She pictured her sister asking her friends to the party. Of course they would all want to come if she were organizing it. It was going to be amazing.

Athena got in the car. Nothing felt the same. Today she was going to be able to drive herself and not have to ask anyone else. She turned the key in the ignition and soon arrived.

"Well, look at you. You're not wasting any time." The woman behind the counter spread the application out.

Athena had carried it with her all week after Paula had got it for her. Athena had forged her mother's signature, as Tilley wouldn't have wanted her to go during school.

"I want to get my licence today as well," Athena informed the woman.

"Well, you can't do the driver's test the same day you get your temporary permit."

"I've been practising, so I think I'm ready."

The woman frowned.

"You have to book an appointment, and you can only do that once you pass the test."

Athena took the instructions and the paperwork from the woman and slid into the one-piece wooden desk and chair. There was one other person in the whole place.

The written test cost fifteen dollars. The driver's test would be twenty. She couldn't afford to fail it. Athena ticked off the boxes and then handed it in. It only took a moment.

The woman lined up the answer sheet with her test and marked it. "Well, you passed. Happy birthday."

"My family will be surprised. They all pretended not to remember my birthday because they're actually throwing me a surprise party."

"Oh, like the movie."

"I loved that movie," Athena said.

"Yes. Maybe you'll get a guy like that, with a sports car and all."

Athena laughed, thinking of Niko. She wondered if he would give her a special birthday kiss.

"So can I get my licence?"

The woman hesitated.

"Well, you need your own car."

"I have a car." Athena held up her keys.

Again the woman frowned.

It doesn't matter now, Athena thought. *I have my temporary, so I'm allowed to drive.*

"Yes. We can do the test at two."

Athena had never skipped class. Her stomach dropped, but she thought how much sense it made to do everything together. The gentleman behind the counter would be the examiner.

When she finished the driving test, thinking she'd aced it, he read down the list of infractions. "You rolled through the stop sign. You didn't shoulder check when you changed lanes. You were speeding at times, and you used one hand to turn the wheel on most of your turns." She drove exactly how her father and Lejla did. "Your total is seventy-four. You need seventy-six to pass." Athena had never failed a test.

"Oh, please, sir. It's my birthday today. My actual sixteenth birthday. I'm going to be taking driver's ed in January. I just couldn't sign up for it until then."

The man was thinking; she could tell he was on the fence.

She added, "It cost twenty dollars. My dad will kill me if he has to pay for it again."

At this, the examiner made two strokes with his pen and sent Athena back inside to have her photo taken. They assembled her stickers and the licence. The woman and the examiner hugged her and congratulated her, wishing her a wonderful birthday.

"It already is."

The day danced along. Athena caught up to her classmates.

"Where have you been?" they asked.

"Getting my licence!" Athena shrieked, jumping up and down.

They cheered.

"What's everyone doing tonight?" Drawling, Athena extended each word.

"Nothing" was the universal response.

She closed her locker and saw Lejla heading quickly toward her. "Hey, I'm not going straight home, so you can just drive yourself," her sister said.

"Why? Do you have big plans?" Athena grinned knowingly.

"Yes, I do," Lejla answered, smiling.

"What are they?"

"I'm not telling you."

Athena nodded, not wanting to say anything.

She got in the car, unsure of the best way to go home, as she had never actually driven on the expressway. The main road took much longer than she thought. How would she have time to get ready?

As she pulled into the driveway, the house looked still and dark. It was getting darker earlier and the grey sky cast a pall on everything, even though it was only three thirty. It had taken a while to get home. The street was emptier than usual. Everyone must have hidden their cars on another block.

Athena's heart was pounding as she went to the front door. It was locked. She fumbled with the key chain until she found the house key. She turned it slowly. It was eerily quiet. There was no one home.

"Hellooo?" Athena called out.

She stood for a moment in the foyer before she ran downstairs and landed at the bottom of the steps with a loud thud to startle the waiting crowd. She walked through the empty family room. A sharp jab of pain went through her chest.

"Well, obviously no one would be here. It's only three thirty! I have to get ready." She laughed at how worried she was that no one was around.

Athena decided to have a shower downstairs in Danica and Lejla's bathroom because they had all kinds of bath and shower extras. Athena shaved her legs and underarms. The door finally opened and Mitzi and Max came in together. Athena flew out of the bathroom and stopped at the top of the stairs, expecting something. She couldn't hear their conversation, but it was something about school.

Athena sat in front of her mirrored dresser, putting hot rollers in her hair. She laid outfits on her bed, deciding which would look best. She tried on three different tops. She might ask Lejla to help her if she didn't look quite right.

Ten minutes later the door opened again. Athena flew down the stairs. Her mother was setting her purse down on the bench.

"*So,*" Athena sang as she alighted on the top step and swung from the railing, "what's for dinner?"

Celebration dinners were giant affairs. She had helped put so many together with her mom that she knew how the long fold-out tables in the garage would be arranged, decorated, and filled with all the good crystal and china.

"I just walked in the door, Athena. Can I at least put my purse down?" Her tired mother sat down on the bench and unbuckled her dress shoes.

A cold sensation ran down Athena's back from the top of her head to the base of her spine. She gripped the railing and a sickening wave of fear lapped over her. She swayed from the impact. Then another wave hit her. Her throat closed as she watched her mother hang up her coat, then tidy up Mitzi and Max's shoes by the back door. Athena headed to her room.

An hour had passed when the front door opened again and heavy footsteps ran up the stairs to the kitchen. She heard Lejla's voice and then her mother's. Their words didn't come through, but there was activity. Crying? Or moaning? She couldn't be sure. Then footsteps down the stairs and the front door slammed. Athena lay motionless on her back with her hands crossed over her chest to try to weigh down the pain in her heart. Tears streamed out of her eyes.

It was completely dark outside now. Lejla tapped on the door and opened it. "Hey, Theenie," she whispered. She stood in the doorway, a black silhouette. The hall light reached into the far corner of the room. "Hey, happy birthday." She tiptoed to the side of the bed and sat down, placing her hand on Athena's leg. "Come to the kitchen. Come on." Lejla took Athena's hand and lifted it. There was no resistance in her. While Lejla held on to her hand, Athena followed her down the hallway to the kitchen.

A small cake in plastic packaging sat on the table. A bag from the drugstore was next to it. Lejla led Athena to the bench. She sat down. Mitzi and Max were seated but silent, looking between their red-eyed mother and sister.

Lejla took the lead. "It's Theenie's sixteenth birthday, guys. Come on. Let's get some candles on this cake."

She ran to the junk drawer and rummaged through it, finding an old package. There were three candles and she sunk them into the icing. She grabbed the lighter on the top of the fridge and expertly flicked it and lit one candle, then the next.

"Happy birthday to you . . ." Lejla motioned to Mitzi and Max to join her in the song, which they did. Tilley tried, but her voice was shaking too much to be effective.

"Open your present," Lejla said.

Athena looked at her, not understanding. Lejla pushed the drugstore bag toward her. Athena looked inside. She reached in and retrieved two eyeshadow trios, a tube of mascara, and some lip gloss.

"Thank you. I'm not hungry. May I go to my room?" Athena said to her mother, who burst out crying.

It was seven o'clock when the front door opened again. She heard the keys crash into the key holder. The door to her room flew open. It was Lejla. She grabbed Athena's hand.

"Come on, we're going out to the movies. It's your birthday. We're not staying here," she said as they crossed the distance to the front door. Lejla grabbed Athena's runners and slid them on her feet as she sat expressionless on the bench.

"Where d'ya think you're goin'?"

Their dad was dressed in his work clothes, his tie pulled loose at the neck. He was struggling to remove a heavy houndstooth coat as he tried unsuccessfully to balance himself. His arm kept getting stuck when he bounced from the wall to the door.

"It's Thee-nie's birth-day, Dad. Her six-teenth birth-day." Lejla said this loudly, enunciating every syllable as though she were speaking to a ninety-year-old foreigner.

"Ooh. Hap-py birth-day!" His arms went up and he threw them around Athena and fell into her, almost taking them both down.

Athena stood motionless, propped back up by Lejla.

"We're going to the movies. We're going to take your car," Lejla said.

Their father had just procured a new Fifth Avenue sedan. Dragan grabbed the keys from the small bowl where he had thrown them. The bowl sat on a shelf attached to a wall mirror that hung to the right of the front door. Athena liked it because you could check how you looked right before you left the house.

"You wanna take my car?" He dangled the keys in front of Athena's face.

She didn't move or respond at all.

"Hey!" he shouted. "Whatsa matta with you?"

"It's her birthday, Dad."

"I don't care whose birt-day it is. I assed you a queshun. You wanna take my . . ."

"I don't care about your car," Athena blurted out.

The mirror shook but didn't fall off the wall when her head flew into it from the slap. Dizzy, she righted herself and saw his finger pointing in her face.

"You can take the bus!" He accentuated every word, tossing the keys onto the shelf, then stumbled back.

Lejla grabbed the keys and dragged Athena quickly past him and out the door. "He's too drunk to notice."

"I don't want to go to the movies," Athena said.

Lejla kept driving toward the Cineplex. It was an old bowling alley that had been converted recently. She didn't say anything but kept looking at Athena.

"I don't want to do anything."

Lejla drove to the movie parking lot and left Athena while she went across the street to the plaza. She arrived back in twenty minutes with two brown bags. Athena was sitting exactly as she had left her. From one bag she brought two cartons of lemonade and from the other a twenty-six-ounce bottle of vodka. Lejla emptied half of the lemonade and added the vodka slowly.

"Here, drink this. You'll feel better."

They were parked at the end of the lot. There were a lot of cars, but no one noticed them.

"I don't want to feel anything."

Lejla let out a heavy sigh.

"It's not like the movies, Jaja. None of you remembered. Not one of you." Athena gasped with the pain of the words. "I'm invisible. No one sees me. I'm just here. I know I've never felt like I belonged, but it's like now I *know* I don't. It hurts so much." Athena pressed her hand to her chest, kneading the incessant heartache.

"I'm sorry, Theen. Cheers to your sixteenth birthday."

The two girls sat and drank.

"Don't drink all that and drive," Athena reminded Lejla.

"Don't worry. You need most of this tonight. You're so smart, funny, and pretty. You're so talented."

"I don't need you to tell me any of that. It doesn't matter because no one notices. Forget the party or a present. How about just remembering? No. What do I get? A slap in the face." Athena felt the hard red welt on her left eyebrow and the sting on her right cheek. She brushed her salty tears across it.

The early movie let out and people piled into the nine o'clock movie. Athena thought how simple it all was for them. She was drunk and slurring. A tall street lamp cast a pyramid of light across the street, capturing the front end of their dad's new car.

"I think about death all the time, like, every day. I think about what it will be like, the last breath you take. Is this one it? Or this one? But then there's always another one, and another one. Pretty soon you think there will *always* be another one. But that's a trick of the mind. We have to remember death and honour it. It's the way out of here. It's a relief. I wish I were dead."

Lejla didn't say anything. She just put her hand on Athena's and held it.

***

Athena moved around in a depressed haze. She lay on her bed every evening with her arms crossed over her chest.

There was a tap at the door. It was her parents. "Hey, we want to say sorry for forgetting your birthday," her mom said.

Athena nodded.

"We got you this."

Her mom sat down on her bed. Athena opened the card. It was a flowery one that opened twice, and it talked about what an amazing daughter the recipient was. Tilley had signed for both herself and Dragan. They gave her a small box. Athena opened it to reveal a large diamond and opal ring.

She snapped the ring box shut and held it out to her mother. "It's beautiful, but I really don't want anything to remind me of this birthday."

Tilley started to cry. "But I want you to have it."

"I don't want it."

"Is that how you're gonna be? A little ungrateful brat makin' your mother cry?" Dragan said.

Athena stared through the window into the distance. Beyond the chiffon curtains, the backyard trees, and the soy fields was an entire world.

"Hey! Answer me."

Athena didn't move. She wanted her mother and father to be upset. It didn't matter anymore what they did.

Later, Danica told her, "You're a complete fool. I saw that ring. You should've kept it. What were you thinking?"

"I was thinking that one day I'll have a family of my own, and they'll see me and love me."

"Pfft." Danica shrugged. "You're so weird." It wasn't like the movie at all.

Chapter 52

The nights of lying awake and listening to the bullying and arguing became much more frequent. She was the one her father looked for now if he wanted to pick on someone. Danica talked non-stop about leaving for Toronto. Lejla didn't live there most of the time. Everyone had become accustomed to her showing up at random times.

Athena walked into the laundry room to find Lejla crying to Mitzi and Max. "Don't forget me. Don't forget that I love you," she told them.

Athena felt angry. "Stop doing that."

"Don't tell me what to do."

"They don't need to listen to that too. They're just little. Maybe if people were normal around here—"

Lejla struck her in the arm. Athena saw red. She grabbed Lejla by the hair and pulled it as hard as she could. Lejla attacked, but Athena had grown much bigger than her and was filled with rage, which exploded out of her.

"Don't! Ever! Hit! Me! Again!" Athena beat Lejla down while Mitzi was crying.

Max reappeared with a steak knife. "I'm going to kill you, Theenie, if you don't stop!"

Athena felt betrayed. They didn't understand. Lejla didn't deserve all their love—she did.

"Put that away," she scolded her brother.

Lejla pushed past her to leave.

"Yeah, leave. Act like you know what goes on around here. Well, I'm actually *here*. I'm the only one who is. If you touch me again, I'll kill you, I swear." Athena was shaking.

Lejla had left, and she went to the bathroom. She was shocked. Where had so much hatred come from? It had fuelled her in a blind rage. She hadn't meant to hit Lejla. Now her sister would probably never want to talk to her again. Looking at her face in the mirror, she felt despondent.

"Well, that's what you get for caring. You get hurt. You don't need anyone here. She shouldn't hit you."

The pit inside Athena's stomach grew steadily, anxiously gnawing at her insides while she debated whether or not she had done the right thing. She should never hit Lejla because she got hit the most. But then what about *her*? Did that mean she didn't matter? But why didn't she matter? Obviously, she didn't. Mitzi and Max were angry with her. Didn't they see Lejla hit her all the time? Didn't they see that their father hit her too? But she didn't matter. If she didn't change herself, nothing would get any better.

***

"Good night, girls." Their mother stood in the doorway looking at Athena and Mitzi lying in the queen-sized bed. Her now blonde hair was illuminated by the little light in the hallway, which gave her a golden halo.

"You're so pretty, Mom," Athena said.

Her mom walked in and leaned over to kiss them both. "No, I'm not," Tilley said with a teasing smile.

Athena always marvelled at how happy her mother could seem amid the fighting. No one got picked on more than her.

"You are so."

"You are the prettiest," said Mitzi.

Tilley chuckled her soft, melodic laugh.

"I love you, Mom," Athena said.

"I love you too."

"Leave the little light on," Athena instructed, as she did every night.

"I know, Theenie." Her mother left the hallway light on and closed the bedroom door only partially.

"I'm going to try and be like Mom. She's always happy. Trying to find the best in everything," Athena said.

"Yes, that's a good way to be," Mitzi said, sleepily rolling away from Athena.

Athena watched her little body breathing. She laid her hand on her shoulder and leaned over and kissed her head. "I love you, Mitzi."

"I love you, too, Theenie."

Athena lay down on her back and felt the anguish of those words. She needed to hear them more than anything. As much as she wanted to shut herself off from everyone, she determined that if she were a better person, a happier person, then people around her would be happier too. *I'll start tomorrow*, Athena thought.

***

Tommy pulled into the driveway, and the bumper of his vintage Mustang came within an inch of the car already parked there. The three girls in the back seat shrieked and giggled.

"You're such a terrible driver!" Athena shouted.

"I am an *amazing* driver!"

"He's the best!" Niko turned around, grinning at her. "What are you talking about? He didn't hit it, did he?"

They all laughed and got out into the frosty night air. This was the third house, and they had two more.

"I ate way too much at the last house," Roxy said. "I didn't know there would be so much food."

"Yeah, they fed us way too much," Kat added, patting her stomach and letting out a burp.

The choir was carolling. Roxy was now the directress, the youngest one ever. Roxy and Niko were also seeing each other. Athena didn't understand how he could date other girls when there was such an undeniable electricity between them, but then people pretended lots of things, so it made some sense to her.

Niko was trying to scoop some snow. "It's not packing," he said, then threw it anyway at Athena and Kat. It dispersed like powder in the air.

"It's cool how it glitters," Athena said with delight, watching the snow flutter.

Niko looked back, smiling, and then turned to walk in with Roxy.

This house was very similar to every house they'd been to. Low ceilings and small rooms. A pile of wet shoes had mounted in the cramped entryway. Four people were seated in the formal front living room—it was pretty much at capacity—and the thirty or so carollers searched for a place to squeeze into. The house smelled of whiskey, meat, and good baking. Three icons hung on the walls. A wooden cross sat on the small mantel, and a real fire blazed inside the hearth. A white donation envelope was on the table.

First the choir had to sing some carols. Athena loved to watch the faces of their hosts. People either relaxed and drifted away to another place, another time, or simply stayed in the moment. Some of the carols were in Serbian and some were in English. Athena loved both. She thought the choir sounded better than it did in church. Perhaps the hot whiskey passed around in shot glasses made everyone sing better or listen better. It would be insulting not to eat and drink, so Athena did her best, taking a glass from each tray. After they were done, it took another fifteen minutes to get everyone back out to the cars and confirm the next location.

"Climb in!" Athena pulled back the seat and admired the pony interior. She loved this car. Tommy's dad had gotten it for him and had it restored.

She felt a push on her back and when she turned, Niko was climbing in next to her. Kat had gone to her other side. Athena was in the middle. She felt an instant thrill when Niko's leg pressed against hers. Why had he climbed in the back with her? Wasn't he going out with Roxy? Maybe she was making too much of it. Roxy happily climbed into the front seat and reviewed how the night was going with a giddy excitement that was contagious.

As the Mustang turned down an icy side street, fishtailing, Roxy grabbed the dashboard. Tommy pounded the steering wheel, hand over hand, pretending to lose and regain control, making the car swerve whenever he could. Niko's hand landed on Athena's leg, his palm covering her inner thigh. Athena's body responded but she didn't; she wasn't supposed to. There were rules about this sort of thing, and she could pretend with the best of them that he had no effect on her. But in the face of her charade, Niko looked her deep in the eyes just as a street lamp flooded the car with light. Athena stared at him, and they smiled at each other.

"What?" Without taking his eyes off her, he held up both hands, and laughed.

***

"New Year's Eve is going to be at Niko and Tommy's. They're having a huge party. I'm not going to be able to go. I have my big family thing at my aunt's," Roxy explained to her and Kat.

Athena took this as a sign from the universe.

There was a real bar in the basement of the Jovanovich house. It had a brass rail, and tall, leather-backed stools that swivelled. During the party, the lights were low and Kat and Athena made a beeline for Niko's room, lying on his unmade bed. Kat didn't like him the way Roxy and Athena did.

"I think I'm going to marry him," Athena said.

"I feel sorry for you, then. You don't want to marry him. He's a player. He's with every girl around. Besides, he's dating Roxy."

"Yeah, but I don't think that will last."

"They're pretty hot and heavy."

Athena always pictured losing her virginity to Niko, but this information made her contemplate otherwise. She wanted to know what she was doing before sleeping with him.

"I didn't think anyone would be in here," Niko said, scooping up his Calvin Klein underwear and Levi's. "Can you please get out of my bed?"

The girls flirted, refusing to go.

"Wouldn't you like both of us?" Kat laughed. Niko rolled his eyes and shook his head.

There had to be over a hundred people as it got close to midnight. The ball dropped and the countdown started. "Ten, nine, eight . . ."

Kat and Athena hugged and kissed each other and, wading through the crowd, did the same with everyone around them.

When Athena ran into Niko, he grabbed her hand and pulled her toward the kitchen. "I gotta get outta here. Come with me."

Athena was buzzing. The house was hot and she was sweating. There were so many shoes in the entrance she couldn't see hers, and there was water everywhere.

"Careful. Throw these on." Niko tossed her a pair of his shoes and she slipped her feet into them. He held her hand and led her out the side door towards the driveway. It was freezing and Athena's teeth started chattering.

Niko unlocked the car parked there. "Hurry, get in. I'll turn on the heat." Athena jumped into the front seat. It was a long velvet bench. It wasn't as cold as leather. He ran back in and came out with a big sweatshirt. "Put this on."

"It heats up fast," Niko said, rubbing his hands together. "I just had to get out of there. Too much noise."

Athena just smiled.

"Turn on the radio."

There was a drum roll and the radio announcer said, "And next up, The Police, 'Every Breath You Take.'"

"I love this song," she said, facing Niko.

"Me too," he whispered.

The entire song played while they listened to it, staring into each other's eyes, their faces coming closer together. By the end they were only about an inch apart.

"Did you listen to the words?" Niko whispered. Athena watched his lips moving as he spoke.

"I always listen to the words," Athena answered.

Athena remembered her friend. "So are you and Roxy pretty serious?"

"Yeah. . . . No. I mean, I don't know. She's nice, but I don't think we're going to last long."

Pulling apart was like separating two magnets.

"Bad timing." Athena raised her eyebrows a bit. "We should go back in the house."

Niko didn't say anything as Athena opened her door. Wearing his shoes and sweatshirt, she felt like she belonged to him. A familiar longing opened up in her heart. She wanted to be his girlfriend but she wasn't, and she didn't know why.

Chapter 53

Athena spent the long school days in January trying to find something to do or somewhere to go. Lejla had moved out for good, and even though her mother implored Athena to find her and take some food to her, she didn't want to, so she didn't. Her homeroom teacher stopped asking her why she couldn't get to class on time.

After school, she was no one's responsibility. She had over two hours to kill before the boys' basketball game. Athena felt exhausted. She always finished her homework in class, so she wouldn't have books to carry. She could go ride the bus around; but she was always worried about getting lost. She wanted to fall asleep. Athena decided she would walk to Kat's.

She turned the corner onto her street and saw the familiar red wooden fence, a tiny landmark that differentiated the brick bungalow from all the other houses. She counted as she walked, her hands shoved deep into the satin-lined pockets of what used to be Dani's dark blue suede jacket, fashionable but completely impractical for a Canadian winter. She climbed the steps and rang the doorbell. She waited and rang the bell again.

Kat's dad opened the door. He scared Athena. He worked nights and she'd probably woken him up. "Katja no home." His thick eyebrows knitted tightly together. Athena couldn't understand how Kat wasn't afraid of him. He repeated, "Katja no home," in a thick, blunt accent and started to retreat.

Athena was so tired that she stuck her foot out to stop the door from closing. Athena stammered, "I know. Is it okay if I go lie down in her room?"

He opened the door, eyeing her quietly as she stepped quickly inside.

"I'm sorry. I know you're sleeping. I won't make any noise." Athena walked down the hallway to her friend's empty room, lay down on her bed, and almost instantly fell asleep.

When she woke, the moonlight was casting shadows through the small horizontal blinds. Kat was at work. Athena got up, refreshed and grateful. She tiptoed out of the bedroom and went to the bathroom. There was a fancy ceramic soap dish and a shaggy rose bathmat that felt plush under her feet. The light was deep amber and made her skin glow in the mirror. Athena's face had matured more.

As she slipped on her shoes, she heard a growl from the front of the house. Kat's dad was sitting in the dimly lit kitchen. Athena jumped.

"Thank you for letting me come in," she said, throwing her jacket on and zipping it up.

"You come," uttered the deep voice. "*Evo. Here,*" he added, holding out a twenty-dollar bill.

"Oh, no, you don't need to."

"*Evo!*"

Athena jumped and took the bill. He sounded so gruff, but he was being so nice. Athena still didn't trust it. "Thank you so much."

"You come. Anytime you need." He slammed the table hard with his hand, and the knife and fork on his empty dinner plate rattled slightly.

"Thank you so much," Athena said again, then hugged him.

He smiled and his eyes crinkled up. They were kind. Athena sighed with relief as she bounded down the stairs. *Good to have ones like him on my side*, she told herself before setting off with a light jog toward the school. "One, two, three. One, two, three," she whispered softly as she went, holding the rolled-up twenty-dollar bill in her pocket.

***

This became Athena's new routine. At first, Kat seemed surprised and then annoyed to find Athena asleep in her bed. Then she accepted it and embraced it, having always wanted a sister.

One lunch hour, Athena saw Kat leaving the school grounds. She normally hung out with her friends. Athena ran and caught up to her. "Where are you going?"

"To my aunt's, my Teta Nadia's. She lives right here." She pointed to the block of houses between the school and the main road. "She has me over for tea. She'd love it if you came."

Nadia Marinkovich seemed like a fairy to Athena. She wore a flowered kaftan and had an angelic voice that rose and fell as, in her excitement, she emphasized certain words. Nadia's dark chocolate eyes were big and wide. Her hair was long and pinned back on the sides. She had a beautiful face and a soft, feminine smile that she shared freely.

"So lovely to have you, Athena." She floated toward Athena and spread her arms to welcome her into the cozy front room. The kitchen was just steps from the front door. The small couch and loveseat took up the whole living room. Teta Nadia brought out English bone china for tea, as well as lemon biscuits. She had a proper teapot filled with hot water and tea bags with strings on them. It was very fancy, even if the surroundings weren't.

"Sit down. Sit down, please. Is that all there is to your jacket, Athena? You'll downright freeze if you don't dress for this cold! Ah, slaves to fashion, we girls are."

The girls sat to take tea and listen to Teta Nadia espouse some divine wisdom.

"You don't need a man in this world to help you. If you could do it on your own, 'twould be a lot better. Fewer headaches, for certain."

Athena studied the lilt of her English accent as she spoke.

"And fewer backaches." She giggled. "I'm bein' a bit cheeky."

Athena liked her very much.

"I've got three lads. I'm hoping you'll marry one of them."

Athena nodded and smiled. They were Serbian, but they were also poor.

"Come back anytime, gals," Teta Nadia told them both. Athena knew she would.

***

Anthony and Paula were going out again. They'd gotten back together after the Christmas dance. He was always writing her long love letters. Athena was listening to her read one.

"You are just the sweetest, nicest, prettiest girl I've ever met, and I'm the luckiest guy in the world."

Athena wasn't jealous—she was curious. Paula was very sweet, but she didn't seem to do anything extra special to make Anthony think she was the sweetest. And here she was sharing all his private letters, which read, "And whatever you do, please, please don't share this with anyone else." So what was so sweet about her? And she wasn't the prettiest girl either. She wasn't ugly, but she went on about how big her bum was and about the hump on her nose. She was pretty but not the prettiest. What was it that made Anthony think so?

"I wish someone thought those things about me," Athena said.

"Tons of guys probably like you but are too intimidated to talk to you."

"I don't even know what that means anymore. I can't stop thinking about Nate. I can't believe he's still with Rianne." Athena sighed.

She was putting on lip gloss in Paula's makeup mirror. She stood up and looked at herself in the full-length mirror in the corner of Paula's room.

"You're lucky. Look how skinny you are. I'd kill to look like you."

"I heard my mom tell her friend I haven't filled out yet. I don't want to fill out too much."

"You won't. You're naturally skinny."

Athena turned sideways and ran her hand across her perfectly flat stomach. Girls were always trying to lose five pounds for the next event. She didn't have to worry like that, but she always pretended she did.

"Maybe if I lost five pounds."

"What? Where? You'd have no boobs."

"Then maybe not." Athena laughed, sticking out her chest.

"You're crazy pretty and crazy smart. You could get any guy you wanted."

"That's just it. I can't. I've tried. I don't know what's wrong with me."

"Nothing. There's something wrong with *them* if they don't like you. And if they don't, none of us stands a chance."

From under the bed, Paula pulled out the shoebox with the stack of letters Anthony had written her and added the latest. She was one of the most popular girls in school. Athena didn't understand what made her so universally likeable, but she was thankful for her friendship. She looked in the mirror and then back to her friend. She decided she would try to be more like Paula.

***

The summer Athena was sixteen was shaping up to be magical. Niko and Tommy both had cars. Roxy had a pool and Athena could walk to her house. Kat went to England and came back with instructions from her cousin Marija about how to make yourself orgasm.

"I've tried it. It works."

"She just told you? How did that even come up?" Thinking about it, Athena blushed.

"I don't know. We were chatting one night, and she asked if I'd ever had one, and I was like, no, so she told me if you rub the top just right you can get yourself off." She said it in a thick English accent. The girls laughed their heads off.

Masturbation became Athena's new side project. She never did it in bed because of Mitzi, so it became her thing in the bathroom. She challenged herself to finish as quickly as possible because someone else always needed the bathroom and she didn't want to be found out. Athena was successful after only her second attempt. It took some concentration and she had to block out all images of real people. She didn't know why, but when she pictured anyone— Niko, Nate, Anthony, or Rick Springfield—things would fizzle. It had to be a faceless man. She pictured some sort of controlling or denigrating act and, *poof!*—ecstasy. Athena became adept at including it as part of her bathroom routine, and no matter where she was, she could fit in an orgasm. It was tricky in public washrooms where the doors had gaps and prying eyes might discover her activities. Usually, she would hold off if someone else was in the washroom, but not always. There was a thrill in getting away with it.

"It says lots of women have never orgasmed," Roxy said. She was reading from *Cosmo* around her pool.

"I find that hard to believe," said Athena. "You can do it yourself, so a person can figure out how."

"I don't think it's hard to believe. People don't have good imaginations," said Kat as she got herself up. She cannonballed into the deep end.

Kat and Athena had developed a routine. First stop was the corner store. They would pool their money: five dollars for gas, three dollars for smokes, and one dollar for candy.

"I got Du Maurier Light. They aren't that harsh," said Kat on one of their trips.

Athena dumped a fistful of gummy bears on the counter.

"Let's cruise the main drag downtown a couple of times and then just drive around," Kat said.

"Sounds like a good idea to me."

Athena had to be aware how much gas she had so she would be able to get home. She was working at the grocery store as a packer.

It was a measure of good manners to offer money for gas if people drove you around. It was a measure of status if you didn't need to take anyone's money for gas and still drove them around.

"Remember when we first tried smoking?" Kat asked.

"Oh, my God, you told me to inhale slowly, and I sucked that huge ball of smoke into my lungs and almost died," said Athena.

"Then my mom came home and we sprayed furniture polish all over to hide the smell in the kitchen, and it made the floor deathly slippery."

"She almost broke her neck bringing in the groceries!"

Athena took a long drag on the cigarette and blew it out and sang with DeBarge. When they got out of the car, she and Kat moved from side to side, dancing and singing. Athena felt happy.

"Here, take these. I don't want to be a smoker and I can't have my mom find them." She tossed the package to Kat.

Chapter 54

"So are you going to sneak out?" Kat asked Athena excitedly.

"I don't know. Everyone's kissed him. That's kind of gross."

"But he's the cutest guy here. He wants to meet you at two in the morning by the lakehouse. And everyone says he's an amazing kisser."

Athena was having anxiety about breaking the rules, but this was the last night and she'd be too old to be a camper next year. It was kismet.

"Yes! Yes, I'll meet him!" Athena tittered. Her hands shook and she clutched her stomach.

Kat squealed and ran off to tell Goran, who would tell Damir.

A silver cast covered all the trees, and the lake lay perfectly still, reflecting the moon in its glass-like surface. It was warm. Athena's heart was racing as she ran on her tiptoes down to the lakehouse. For a moment she wondered what she would say if he wasn't there, but she spotted him instantly. He smiled and reached out for her hand. Damir was all the girls' favourite. He had a handsome, kind face and he was funny.

"Hey." Athena mustered a word. Nerves filled her as they walked along the path that wrapped around the water. "There are so many stars here," she said.

"Yeah, it's so pretty. Like you."

Athena blushed. She hoped he wouldn't compliment her too much and try too hard, making it awkward.

"I saw a bunch of shooting stars last night," Athena said to distract him.

"What did you wish for?"

"If I tell you, it won't come true."

"You believe that?"

"Well, yeah. A wish is like something secret in your heart that you hope for more than anything. You can't just share that or it wouldn't be the same."

"I know what I'd wish for."

Oh, geez, thought Athena.

Damir stopped her and tipped her chin up gently. He stood almost six feet tall. Athena pictured what it would have been like for him doing this with Bobby-Rose, who couldn't be more than five foot one. His hands were steady and his mouth smelled like peppermint and his teeth were pretty. He pressed his lips on hers in just the right way. Not too hard, not too soft. Athena studied what he did while he kissed her and then she did it back to him.

He pulled away from her. "Wow. You're a great kisser."

Athena smiled and bit her lip, feeling the exquisite sensations in them. "We could be the only people left on Earth," she said. She blushed again when she realized that would mean they would have to have sex to repopulate the world.

"It feels like it, doesn't it?"

They had continued walking all the way around the lake and were on the far side. It was off-limits.

"I've never been here," Athena said, looking back at the low, white camp buildings. "It seems so far away."

"Jovan brought me and Goran here. The counsellors come here to hang out and smoke and stuff." Jovan was one of the boys' counsellors.

Athena stiffened and looked around.

"Relax." Damir laughed. "They're not coming now." He patted the space next to where he sat on top of a picnic table. His feet were on the bench. The wood was smooth but felt damp with dew. Damir wiped his arm across the seat.

"You're different from the other girls."

Athena smiled. "What do you mean?"

"I mean you're not into all the things they are, like makeup and clothes and stuff."

"Oh? I guess not." Athena laughed, looking down at her stained hoodie from the amusement park.

"I mean that in a good way. You're smart."

Athena wanted to cringe.

"I like that."

"You do?"

"Yeah, it's sexy."

Athena watched his mouth form more words but started kissing him before he could say anything else. She let him kiss her neck, which flooded her body with tingles, but she stopped him when he tried to go up her shirt. She didn't want him to be disappointed. Bobby-Rose may have been short, but she had really big boobs.

When the sky started changing to periwinkle blue, Athena and Damir held hands and walked back. Then he wrapped his arms around her and she breathed in his pleasant smell, which mingled with the lake, the night air, and a hint of campfire.

"I had a really nice time with you. You're so beautiful."

Athena felt this was genuine and her smile broadened. "You're beautiful too."

He laughed. "What? I don't think anyone's called me beautiful before."

"Well, you are," Athena insisted.

***

In the morning, Athena rushed to put her things on the bus. She was both anxious to get home and overcome with dread at the possibility of seeing Damir.

"I feel crazy, Kat."

"Calm down. It was just for fun."

"I don't know. It's like he got too close to me or something. I feel icky. I just want to go."

"You're so weird. You just kissed, right?"

"Yeah."

"Then what are you talking about?"

"Yeah, you're right. I don't know." Athena really didn't know.

She let out a huge sigh of relief when the bus door closed and the vehicle pulled away; everyone gathered around and waved them off. She could see Damir near the back, waving to them and smiling. To avoid him, she'd practically hidden on the bus, not going to breakfast or saying goodbye to anyone else.

"I thought you said you liked it!" Kat said with exasperation.

"I did. I'm just grossed out by feelings right now. I just want to go home."

"Me too. I can't wait to fall into my own bed."

"Me too!"

Athena plumped up her pillow against the window and fell hard asleep into it, happily dreaming of a beautiful scene and a faceless boy kissing her.

***

The bus pulled into the church parking lot in the early afternoon. Parents were there to pick up their children from camp. Athena saw their mom. She glanced over at Mitzi, who was waving frantically at their mother from her seat near the front.

The bus driver hopped down and opened the side that hid all of the sleeping bags and suitcases. Athena's duffle bag appeared as a couple of gentlemen steadily unloaded the cargo. She lugged it to where her mother stood. Tilley was smiling. Athena hugged her and felt only a weak pat on her back in return.

"Mom? What's up?"

"Listen carefully to me, Athena."

Athena froze as her attention centred on her mother's face. She barely even perceived the other campers flying around her. Something was wrong.

Her mother spoke softly, "You are not coming with me right now."

"Why not?" Athena tried to connect with her mother's eyes but couldn't.

Her mother gripped her arm tightly and continued in an unwavering, expressionless voice, "Just listen. You're going to be moving in with the Lalichs. Our house is gone. I packed up your things, but we couldn't take everything. This is what I thought you'd want to keep." She pointed to a legal storage box next to her feet, but Athena wasn't sure where it came from. "Now you will not make a scene."

Athena was trying to absorb the information. She wasn't going home with her mother.

"What about Mitzi?"

"She and Max are coming with me."

The pain in Athena's chest made her expel her breath. Her throat was closing so hard, she didn't think she would be able to take another breath in. Her mother averted her eyes to look for Mitzi. Athena sensed she had very little time.

"Mom, please."

"Do not cry here, Athena. *Do not.*"

Athena felt a crazy desperation. She took a huge breath in. She would have to speak normally to keep her mother's attention.

"Where are you guys living?"

"We're going to Kuma's house."

"Mom, I can go with you."

"There's no room for you, Athena. It's done—the arrangements have been made."

"Mom, please." Huge tears welled up in her eyes. "I'll sleep on the floor." The sound of her own sad voice—the begging, the rejection, the humiliation—broke Athena's heart.

"No. Now pull yourself together. Your clothes are already there."

"What happened to our house? I don't understand."

"The house was seized and had to be sold. Your father was arrested for embezzlement. Now do as I tell you, please." Tilley stared hard at Athena.

"No, Mom. Wait!" Athena's voice rose sharply. "I can just go to Kat's."

"Don't embarrass me. I've made arrangements already. Stop it right now, and do as you're told."

Athena stared at her mother, who was not looking at her as she said, "I love you."

Tilley turned to get Mitzi, her face breaking into a false smile, and hugged her. Athena saw her kuma sitting in the front seat of her mother's car where she herself should have been sitting. Mitzi was talking excitedly and smiling. *Yes*, thought Athena, *make sure Mitzi's okay. Don't cry in case she sees you. It would scare her.*

Mrs. Olga Lalich, a lovely woman from the church, was suddenly standing next to Athena. She had a thick accent but was smart and funny.

"C'mon, Ateena. Let me help you, sveetie."

Athena moved in a fog. Her mind felt numb. She climbed into the strange car and heard the trunk close. Then another trunk and another. She thought about everyone going home—except her.

"Eez gonna be okay, Teenie." Teta Olga was looking at her in the rear-view mirror.

Athena had climbed into the back seat. She didn't belong in this car. She didn't know where she was going. What day was it anyway? The legal box on the seat next to her read *Athena*. It represented her entire childhood. Things didn't matter. People didn't matter.

"It doesn't matter." Athena sat motionless as the car pulled out of the parking lot and turned in the opposite direction from home.

Chapter 55

"Go on. Eat someting, Ateena."

"She won't eat, Ma. She doesn't eat." Andrew Lalich talked to his mother as though Athena wasn't there.

His older sister Vanessa had gone to university, and Athena was staying in her room. Andrew and his younger sister Lily were still at home. Lily was shy and quirky, and Athena liked her very much. Teta Olga ran her household. Her husband, Vlado, didn't speak English at all. He worked on the line at one of the car factories, so he didn't have to. He just had to know what buttons to push a thousand times a day. He was always soft-spoken and smiled kindly at Athena.

Athena didn't have an appetite. She felt incredibly uncomfortable imposing on this family that had taken her in. No one was giving them money to feed her.

"I can give you something for groceries," Athena said.

"Don't be silly, Teenie. You a part of my family now. You don't hafta pay for anyting."

The Lalichs lived in a beautiful area called Walkerville. It was filled with historical two-storey brick homes that surrounded a giant gated park enveloping Willistead Manor, a Tudor castle open as a museum and cafe.

"Lemme guess? You're not hungry?" Andrew teased Athena again about how little she ate.

Athena thanked Teta Olga for dinner and rose to clear the plates and help clean the kitchen.

"You see? Teenie's got manners and helps me. You just sitting down like you don't live here and give no help for your mother. You can stay, Ateena. You my favourite."

Athena smiled weakly. With heavy legs, she walked up the stairs to "her" bedroom. The stairs had a carved wooden railing and a wool runner that looked very posh. The bedroom door was solid wood with a crystal knob, and a lovely chandelier hung low in the bedroom. The bed had a white iron frame with brass accents and was covered by a lavender quilt and shams. Athena didn't dare touch or rearrange anything. Her suitcase remained on the floor with her clothes in it. Olga had cleaned out the three drawers in the mirrored dresser for her, but

Athena didn't want to put her things away; she wanted to be ready to leave quickly should her mother come to pick her up. She hadn't heard from her yet.

School started the next day. Athena sighed. She hadn't called Kat or Paula and told them anything. She wasn't sure she could explain it anyway. She heard the phone ring downstairs.

"Teenie! Telephone! Your mama!" called Olga.

Athena ran down the stairs. Her heart pounded and a tidal wave of emotions built in her chest. "Mom!" She grabbed the phone, anxious to hear her mother's voice. "Are you picking me up?" she blurted out.

The cool response was "No, Athena. I'm not. Stop that, okay? You're all right."

Athena wanted to scream and cry, but she had already disappointed her mother and she didn't want her to hang up, so she said nothing.

"Are you there?"

"Yes, Mom. I'm here."

"Okay, so you're starting school tomorrow. I'm working and have a lot to sort out here with Mitzi and Max—"

"I can help you with that!"

Tilley let out an exasperated sigh. "I don't need this. I need to figure out what's right at the moment, okay, Athena? Please. You have to be strong and look after yourself right now. I know you can do that for me."

"Yes," Athena said. Covering her mouth and extending the cord of the phone as far as it would go, she moved as far from the living room as she could so the Lalichs couldn't hear her say, "But I miss you, Mom." She could barely get the words out; they choked her, and hot tears fell down and hit her fingers as she clutched the receiver tightly to her mouth.

"I miss you too. I love you. Don't worry, okay? Everything's going to be alright. You do well at school this year."

"This *year*?" Athena balked at the notion that her mother was trying to say that she would be here all year.

"Athena, please." There was a long pause. "Things aren't going to get sorted out quickly. Do your best so I don't have to worry about you too, okay?"

Athena's nerves were jangling and the brave face she'd tried to put on had melted. She sobbed into the phone, "Okay, Mom."

"I gotta go now. I love you."

Before Athena could say, "I love you too," her mother had hung up on her. She turned to hang up the phone and saw Andrew standing just beyond the kitchen door.

"What? I wasn't listening. I just came to get some milk in my own house."

Athena ran upstairs. She could hear Teta Olga scolding him for being mean to her. Why would she do that? Now he really wouldn't like her. Athena turned the doorknob noiselessly and eased the wooden door closed. She tiptoed to the bed and climbed in, contemplating how insignificant she was, like a speck of dust in the universe, inconsequential. Then the universe became engulfed in her mind and swallowed her up, telling her that all of the love in the universe was what she deserved. She heard her tears hit the pillow and tasted the saltiness of being lonely. Her chest ached. She crossed herself and prayed.

Athena awoke. She got up out of bed and looked out the window. She stared at the gas-lit street lamp. The light was almost orange. She squinted and the light stretched into a golden needle through her tears. She thought of when people died and they saw a light. Athena imagined the light would be more like this one, golden candlelight, not stark fluorescence.

"It's going to be okay." Athena whispered toward the darkness of the street. Athena crawled back into the strange bed. She rolled herself up into a very small ball, hugging herself, and fell into a deep sleep.

Chapter 56

September in Canada knows herself better than anyone. It was already cool, and Athena had only a thin Oxford shirt for the first day of school. She walked three blocks to the bus stop after going all the way around Willistead Manor, since the gates were only open on the weekend.

When Athena stepped past the fire station on the corner, she saw the bus coming and jogged to the stop. She would have to remember to be a bit early. After dropping her thirty-five cents into the coin holder and asking for a transfer, she took the first seat. The bus drivers no longer dispensed change. Athena would have to change buses to get to Montcalm. Outside it was still dusky, but by the time she got off at her transfer point, it was much brighter. The 1C that pulled up ten minutes later was already full of people. She had to stand. She then walked the four blocks to the school on her own.

She felt exhausted by the time she found her name on the gym wall, stood in line for her timetable, and located her newly assigned locker. As Athena dumped her backpack into her locker, she realized she didn't have a combination lock. She felt like crying.

"Theenie!" Athena turned to see Anthony and Duncan, both smiling, calling out in unison behind her.

"How've you been? Looking good!" Anthony said.

"What's your homeroom?" Athena asked.

"Business. We got put together. I feel sorry for Mr. McIntyre." They high-fived and laughed.

"I forgot my lock."

"They sell them at the office for two dollars," Anthony said as he and Duncan walked ahead of her.

"Hey, have you seen Paula yet?" Athena called.

Anthony turned, walking backward. "Nope, and I probably won't."

Duncan was behind his friend, drawing his finger across his throat to signal that she should cut the conversation.

Athena nodded and smiled. She pulled her things out of her locker and headed to the office. She would be late for homeroom.

When she arrived at class, the teacher said, "Oh, there you are Miss Brkovich, notoriously late, just like your classmates said you'd be. You will not be allowed in my class without an admit slip—"

Athena held one out. "I had to get a lock. Sorry."

"As I was saying, without an admit slip, and if you're going to continue acting with such an obvious sense of entitlement, you will not find yourself getting a very good mark here. Are we clear?"

Athena slid into the first bench, where she sat alone. Once the class started, she peeked around to see who was there, pretending to look back at the clock. Three rows behind her was Niko. Athena's heart jumped and she spun back around. As the class ended, Athena became nervous, not knowing what to say to him about her dad, the Lalichs, her life. She suddenly felt embarrassed, and when the bell rang, she slipped out of the door without even turning around.

Halfway down the hall, she heard Niko calling her. "Athena! Hey, Athena!"

She stopped. He was pushing past all the students spilling out into the hallway from all directions. She couldn't help but smile.

"Hey! How are you?" he asked.

"I'm good."

"I heard about—"

"Yeah. We don't have to talk about that now, you know?"

"Okay." He paused, looking into her face with tenderness in his eyes. "Yeah, I didn't mean to bring it up. Sorry."

There was an awkward silence as Athena wondered why anyone like Niko would want someone like her.

"I'm going to need help with all those equations. Figured I'd get the smartest girl in school on my team early," he finally said.

"Sure. Yeah. Anytime." Athena started to walk away. *Try to be positive,* she thought.

"We got our first game tomorrow. Don't miss it!"

"I wouldn't for the world!" Athena sang over her shoulder.

***

It was at the football game that Athena saw Lejla. She wasn't sure whether or not to go over to her. Paula had brought a thermos of hot chocolate and Baileys that her mom made them. As the alcohol set in, it convinced Athena to at least check on her. As she approached the stands where Lejla was, she felt worried. Her sister looked high, her eyes red and half closed. She also looked very skinny.

"Lejla," Athena said, walking straight up to her amid five or six people she didn't know.

As Lejla turned, blowing smoke out of the side of her mouth, she struck Athena as irresistibly tragic. A sadness pervaded her, and no amount of makeup or fancy clothes could cover it. When the glaring floodlights lit Lejla's face as she stepped forward from the shadow cast by the towering metal bleachers, Athena gasped. A large bruise marred her sister's right cheek.

"What happened to your face?" Athena blurted out.

"Ah, that's nothing."

Lejla looked around, wavering slightly. She took a long drag of her cigarette and inhaled through her nose. Lejla was one of those smokers that Athena considered authentic. Her dad was another. Some people didn't look cool smoking, but Lejla made it look like an art form.

"Who did that?" Athena's stomach twisted as she imagined her sister being hit by someone other than her father.

"James. But he said sorry."

"No, Jaja. You don't let anyone hit you. Ever!"

Lejla laughed. "So what do you want?" she asked loudly.

This got the attention of her friends. They moved closer, turning at the call of their leader.

"Nothing. I just wanted to see you. To make sure you're okay."

Lejla laughed again. "Yeah, sure. I'm great."

"I love you, Jaja."

She tossed the cigarette on the ground. "Is that it?"

Athena barely nodded .

"Then go fuck yourself, kid."

She turned and laughed at her putdown with some stranger. Athena felt as if she had slapped her in the face.

Athena ran quickly to the school and headed to the bathroom just outside the cafeteria. It was all too much. Lejla didn't want her. No one did. She looked at herself in the mirror. "Go fuck yourself, kid," she repeated. She gripped her head with both hands and pulled her hair as hard as she could. "Stop that crying." She spat the words out and felt the tidal waters of emotion receding, revealing the rocky, hard shoreline of composure.

Athena marched back to Paula. "Any more hot chocolate?"

"A bit. Mariela also has this."

Their basketball teammate, a stocky girl, pulled a flask from inside her cowboy boot. "It's whiskey."

Athena didn't like rye whiskey, but she didn't like lots of things, and that didn't stop any of them from going down, just like that rye was about to.

"Easy!" Mariela grabbed at the flask. "Save some for the fish."

"Sorry." Athena shuddered from the medicinal burn that went down her throat, and removed the awareness of how empty she felt. "Let's go, Marauders!" she screamed, her hands cupped around her mouth like a megaphone. "Let's go, *green*!" Athena told herself to do what everyone else was doing. It seemed to work.

***

The girls' basketball season was short compared to the boys'. There were glaring disparities between the teams, despite the girls having won the city championship the previous year. Unlike the girls' team, the boys' team was scheduled for four out-of-town tournaments and would receive new uniforms with warm-up suits.

"No one's going to give us anything," Mariela said gruffly. "We're the ones winning and people pack the gym to see us. What the hell?"

Paula and Mariela were co-captains. Athena was always very careful to sit quietly and do as the other girls did. She watched what they brought to a game, how they dressed, how they wore their socks, their attitude. She mimicked them and felt like a fraud. Athena spun around on her heels as she thought about it.

"You're a odd one, aren't you?" said Carol.

Athena just shrugged. Even with her impersonation skills, she couldn't quite pass for a normal girl.

As they were doing their foul-shooting drills, the boys filed in. There was only one night when the boys didn't get the after-school spot; four nights out of five the girls had to come back for six o'clock. For Athena that meant hanging around because there was no time to get to the Lalichs' and back. She didn't tell anyone where she lived.

"So what's the scoop with you and Anthony?" Athena asked Paula one day as they practised.

She saw Anthony and he waved at her and smiled. Athena remembered kissing him and was thinking about rekindling their friendship.

"I broke up with him. He was a bit too possessive, you know. I just want things to be easy and free right now. I don't want to be tied down."

Athena felt a stabbing jealousy. How could some people have so much stability, only to just throw it away? She longed for someone so reliable in her life.

"Hey, cutie," Anthony said to Paula as he retrieved a shot she had missed that rolled long toward him.

"Hey," said Paula, not really looking at him.

"Hey, Anthony," Athena said, smiling.

He smiled and nodded, his gaze lingering on her but with a hesitancy she could feel. She would have to be the one to approach him. After all, Paula didn't want him.

Their meetings started like their last "relationship." No one really knew about them. Athena had gotten taller since last year and they were almost exactly the same height, or maybe Anthony was half an inch taller.

"I'm afraid you're going to do what you did last year," Anthony said. "You're really special, but if you're going to be my girlfriend, I need to know that you mean it and you're going to be honest with me."

"I promise." With every intention to follow through, Athena smiled.

Anthony had, over the summer, worked hard at the plastics factory where his mom worked and earned enough to buy his own car. He didn't drive her home. They just drove to the parks along the river.

One night they climbed into the back seat. Athena's hand slid down over Anthony's jeans and she felt his hard penis. She helped him unbutton his pants and touched it all over without looking at it, trying to get a picture in her mind of what it looked like. Athena felt Anthony's hand on her head as he guided her down. His penis was very smooth. Athena was licking it along the sides and all around the head, not sure how to blow on it, when her hand ran into something sticky.

"Ugh. What's this?"

She pushed herself up. Her hair was pulled back in a ponytail and her bra was undone, dangling inside her shirt. Her first thought was that she had drooled on his stomach.

"What?" he said.

"What is this? It's all wet."

Anthony reached into the front seat and grabbed a Kleenex out of a box. "What the hell, Theenie?"

"What?"

"You're a piece of work, you know that?"

Athena had no idea what was happening. Anthony zipped up his pants and climbed into the front seat.

"I don't know what you're talking about."

"As if you don't know," he said, almost yelling at her.

She winced. Her neck grew hot and the heat spread into her cheeks. She crawled back into the front seat as he started the car and was backing up.

"Wait, please." Athena was trying to get her bra done up. "I need to put my seat belt on."

"As if you don't know what just happened. Please!"

Athena sat quietly, desperately trying to put it together.

"You want me to believe you're that innocent when clearly you're not."

Athena's cheeks burned with indignation. She wasn't sure what was worse, not knowing what had just happened or Anthony believing she was the type of girl who obviously knew all about it.

***

"It's gross and gooey like egg whites," Kat said. She and Roxy were helping her to connect the dots.

"*Oh!*" Athena laughed, perplexed as to why she hadn't understood. "I just didn't know so much *stuff* came out."

Her friends gave her a quick tutorial about blow jobs as well, and a healthy debate ensued about spitting versus swallowing.

"Guys want you to swallow it. They love that and they'll think it's sexy," Kat explained. Athena nodded as she took notes in her mind.

***

"Have you had sex before?" Athena asked Anthony as they lay in the back seat.

She was trying to clear her throat. Athena had just swallowed what had shot out and liked the powerful feeling it gave her.

"Yes, at a tournament, but the girl was older than me and I was really nervous." Athena was relieved she wouldn't be his first.

Athena thought Anthony was sweet, even though once they had agreed they were seeing each other, he felt the need to meet her between every class.

"What were you saying to that boy?" he asked.

"Who?"

"The guy you were talking to."

"Ethan? He's my lab partner. I was just going over the answers for our experiment."

"Couldn't you have partnered with another girl?"

Athena laughed, thinking it was ridiculous. "No one likes me. You're worried for nothing."

"You're my girl."

"Yes, I am."

Athena felt wanted and revelled in Anthony's possessiveness. When he wanted to know exactly what was said in a conversation, she would dutifully report it word for word. He would also issue instructions.

"Put your hair up."

"I like it down. I curled it today."

"Put it up. Too many guys are going to look at you when it's down. I don't like it."

Athena would find a hair tie, knowing that she belonged to someone who saw her and only her.

Their appetite for getting naked in the back of the car increased. No one ever wondered or knew where she was. She told Teta Olga that she was at basketball or school, and there was no one to say any different.

"So no one knows you're here?" Anthony asked, concern in his voice.

Athena didn't want him to feel sorry for her. It made her sad when people did that. "There are a lot of people in way worse predicaments."

"Your dad is going to jail and your family has no house."

"Both temporary situations, if you think about it."

Anthony then did. "You're actually really normal for what you've been through, and that's what scares me. What's under there? Can you just turn off all your emotions? I'm really attached to you."

"No, I won't leave you. I promise."

Athena loved having Anthony's attention, even if it wasn't always in the way she wanted. You had to take the good with the bad.

***

"We're going out tonight, just the girls." Kat was standing at Athena's locker. "I haven't seen you in forever. You have to come."

"Let me ask Anthony if I can go."

"Ask? What are you talking about?"

"He said he'd like to know if I have plans, that's all—to run it by him."

"That's crazy," she said huffily. "Whatever. It's only your teenage years. Why not waste them acting like you're married?"

Athena didn't respond. She was trying to be the best girlfriend she could be—she'd promised.

"I just don't think he's the guy for you."

Something deep inside Athena agreed, but she pushed it away.

***

Paula and Athena were in the same math class and sat next to each other. Everyone knew Athena and Anthony were dating now. More and more Athena noticed that Paula held court with her other friends with her back to her and then worked on her assignments. She remembered how Paula had reached out to her first.

"Hey, Paula, what are you doing this weekend?" Athena asked.

Paula hesitated, and Athena felt as though she overstepped by asking.

"Um, there's a house party. It's a bunch of Riverside people. You wouldn't know them."

"Oh . . . sounds fun. . . . Have a good time."

On their way out of class, Paula was arm and arm with Josie Fanucci. There was a bottleneck at the door, and Athena bumped Josie by accident.

Josie turned and said, "Hey, watch where you're goin'."

Athena simply replied, "Sorry."

But Josie turned back. "Thought you were trying to steal your friend back, like you stole her boyfriend." Fed by peals of laughter and coaxing, Josie went on. "Oh, that's right—lying and cheating run in the family. Her dad's going to prison."

The traffic cleared at the door as the volume of the cheers rose. Paula never looked back at Athena. *What have I done?* Athena wondered.

"Well, why did you have to say anything?" Anthony was very anxious and animated.

"But that's what I'm telling you—I *didn't* say anything. She was just being mean."

"That's why I don't want you going out with any of these people. They don't act the way they should and they don't treat you properly."

"But it wasn't Kat. It was Josie and Paula." He didn't respond.

Anthony didn't have to tell her. She knew what his expectations were. Athena didn't go to the girls' night out with Kat. Anthony went to hang out with his friends, and she went to sleep early.

***

Kissing and petting, they lay undressed in the back seat of his car. He was pressed in between her legs, eager to enter her. Athena was struggling with whether to do it or not. On the one hand, she wanted to be a virgin for Niko, but then he had slept with tons of girls. Also, having sex for the first time was supposed to not be that fun. And then there was the thought of being damned to hell.

"Let's do it," Athena whispered in Anthony's ear.

He pushed back, straightening his arms, his glossy black curls dampened by their exertions. "Really?"

They looked at each other. But when Athena reached down, his penis was like a deflated tire.

"What's wrong?" she said.

"Nothing's wrong." His voice was rising. "I'm just a little nervous now. You're making me nervous."

"I'm sorry. I didn't mean—"

"Forget it, okay? Just forget it." Anthony grabbed his wallet and looked frantically for the condom he kept there, but he couldn't find it fast enough.

"You just put so much pressure on me. You can't just spring that on me, you know."

"I'm sorry."

Athena made herself very small. She let a minute pass. She still wanted to do it and was wondering if he would come around.

Anthony put his hand through his hair. "You're just so pretty. If we do this, you're my girl. Mine."

"That's all I want to be."

"And no one else's! Ever!"

"No one's. Just yours. All yours." Athena giggled, loving the words and his desire for her. But a nagging voice told her she was lying. It felt like a game to her, a pretend game.

Anthony found the condom and, quite forcefully, took Athena's virginity.

"Oh my goodness, you're so tight. That was amazing."

Athena climbed into the front seat. Knowing that God had seen what she'd just done and she was going to hell, she felt like throwing up.

"We need to stop at McDonald's," she said.

Athena ran in and was assaulted by the harsh light. She didn't order anything, just went straight to the bathroom. What they had done hurt, and when she peed it stung like rubbing alcohol on a paper cut. She yelped and wiped herself carefully. She could feel the swollen lips of her vagina through the thin paper squares. There was bright red blood on her underwear.

She returned to the car and said, "I think you did it wrong. I'm still a virgin."

Anthony's mouth fell open in surprise and he laughed. "No, you're not."

"Yes, I am," Athena said emphatically, frightened that her choice may have condemned her for eternity. "It hurt and I was bleeding, so I'm pretty sure you did it wrong."

Speechless, Anthony shook his head and laughed.

Athena didn't care. She was not going to allow this to be the way she lost her virginity. It wasn't romantic at all.

At the Lalichs', she scrambled under the bed for the shoebox that held the few trinkets her mother had kept for her. There was a small ceramic statuette, ticket stubs from when her mom took them to see *Annie* at the Fox Theatre, a bookmark of Snoopy wearing thick reading glasses, and a key chain of dulled resin housing a real four-leaf clover. Underneath these was a compact version of the New Testament with a red cover. Athena stayed on her knees and crossed herself, then opened the book to a random page and started reading. The words had little meaning for her. She read about ten verses out loud and then clasped her hands together. "Dear God, please forgive me. Restore my virginity and I promise, I promise that I will never, ever, ever do that again."

***

It had been three weeks since Athena sat on the McDonald's toilet. She counted on her fingers twice to be sure. She'd had sex nineteen more times since then. She'd given up on getting out of bed to ask God forgiveness.

Athena lay in the strange bedroom, wondering where her mother was. She wondered where her brother and sisters were. She wondered if they wondered about her. She didn't wonder about her father. The local newspaper ran a few articles on the story: Local man arrested and charged with fraud and tax evasion. The topic came up quite a bit at school. Athena could tell that it aggravated Anthony, but not in the way she thought it should. It wasn't her fault that her father did those things. She couldn't change it and she wasn't like him, so she didn't see why people thought she would carry so much shame over it. She barely gave it any thought.

A more pressing situation had arisen, her imminent descent to damnation. Athena tried to figure out God's plan. She wrote her name in the air and said, "If God doesn't want us to have sex, then why does He make us want to? To put temptation in front of us so we must resist it. If we fail, we'll be punished. Forever? Yes, forever and ever. But God is kind and God is good. He wouldn't want us to suffer in hell for doing something as natural as following our instincts. But if you're going to do it, you should be married, right? Says who? God? No, men. Men say you should be married, because if you aren't you'll be punished. Yep. That sounds like men to me."

Athena smiled as an idea popped into her head. "What do you think, God? I think I'll marry Anthony one day. Just not now. If I promise you I'll marry him, would it be okay to have sex?"

Athena felt that God would be pleased with her offer. After all, she really wanted to marry Niko, but he had other girlfriends all the time, and she should be happy to have someone love her at all.

Athena awoke in the middle of the night with a scream.

"Vat is it? Teenie?" Teta Olga came into the room. She went straight for Athena, who was sitting up in bed, hugging herself. Teta Olga threw her arms around her. "Eez okay, eez gonna be okay. You get some bad dreams, huh?"

Athena had dreamed she was getting married to Niko, but when she lifted her veil and turned to him, it was Anthony.

"Vat did you dream?"

"Nothing, Teta Olga. Thanks. I'm sorry for waking you up."

Athena felt comforted but then bitterly missed her own mother.

"Vas just a bad dream, sveetie."

"It all seems so real," Athena said into the sleeve of Olga's bathrobe.

Chapter 57

The fall dance was held in late November.

"I don't want to go, and I don't want you to go," Anthony said.

"But I love to dance. Everyone's going. Even Duncan said he was going," Athena replied.

"Dances are stupid. Everyone just gets drunk."

"A couple of drinks don't kill you."

"I don't like it."

Athena didn't care. She listened to Anthony to please him and prove that she was the type of girl he wanted to be with. The sex was great and transported Athena to a different place, one where she didn't have to think about being alone. But the emotional part of the relationship was empty, just as he'd feared. Her heart wasn't in it, but she didn't admit this to anyone. She wanted to go dancing. She'd earned it.

Athena went to Kat's after school. She was going out with her girlfriends to the dance, so they got ready together.

"Grab your hair with a brush and then hairspray it"—Kat demonstrated—"then blow-dry it." Her hair on the sides was stiff, rising up and away from her face before cascading down.

Athena was busy backcombing and then employed the technique, effectively producing large swooping sides.

"Very Flock of Seagulls," Kat said, admiring her work. "I miss you, Theenie."

"Me too."

"You hardly ever come over anymore. You're always with Anthony."

Athena was quiet but then said, "I love him, Kat." She said it because she was supposed to.

Kat didn't say anything.

"He wants to marry me."

"Of course he does. Look at you. But you don't have to marry the first guy you sleep with."

"That's not it. He's sweet. He buys me jewellery and sends me roses."

"And he tells you what to do."

Athena didn't understand. How would it ever be any different? Men just told you what to do. "He means well." In defending him, she felt she had proven her love.

"Well, you're missing out on all the fun."

"Not tonight!" Athena beamed, looking at her friend.

The girls hugged.

"My parents never come down here. We can do what we want," Kat explained, unscrewing the cap from a twenty-sixer of vodka she'd pulled from a hole in the fake wood panelling. She poured it straight into two plastic cups. "Better we don't mix. We'll just have to go to the bathroom more."

The shot burned Athena's throat. She blew out the alcohol fumes. "Let's do a couple more to get buzzed and then walk over," she suggested, and Kat agreed.

"Oh, I love this song." Athena sang to "I Would Die 4 U," gesturing as if pointing a gun to her head and then pointing at Kat. "I'm going to dance."

Athena left Kat, who had already found her big circle of friends, and entered the propped-open double doors. Athena's head was buzzing and she was sweating a bit when she saw Niko's blonde hair near the back. She danced her way over to him and bumped his knee from behind.

"Hey!" He turned and then laughed, surprising her by throwing his arms around her in a big bear hug. "Look at you!" He held her away from him and eyed her up and down.

Athena's body was in full bloom. She'd hit five foot eight. The cropped white cotton shirt showed off her perfectly flat stomach, and the tight navy sailor pants and deck shoes screamed preppy chic. Her lips were glistening with strawberry gloss.

"You're lookin' hot, Theen!" he yelled above the music.

Athena felt herself light up and her body arched into Niko's hand, which rested on the small of her back.

"Come on, let's get out of here!" he said.

"What?" Athena didn't think she'd heard him right.

"Come with me. I got some stuff in the car."

Athena hesitated. What if Anthony found out?

Niko had read her mind. "We're friends, right? Like since forever. Nothing can change that."

Athena nodded and let him lead the way. They left past the smoking area. Her ears rang as the school doors clicked closed behind them.

"Quick, quick. Oh, my God, it's freezing," she said.

"Well, where's your jacket?"

"I knew it would be hot inside, so I didn't wear one."

He smirked at her.

"I didn't know I'd be going out again so soon."

They jogged the half block and jumped into his car. He turned it on and cranked up the heat.

"It's blowing cold air," Athena laughed, feeling sexy and high.

"There's something under here." Niko rummaged under the passenger seat and pulled out a bottle of vodka.

"Perfect," said Athena. "That's what I'm having."

Niko took a long swig and then passed it to Athena. She took one and passed it back.

"You seem different, Theen. I mean, you look amazing, but, like, I don't know . . ."

Athena bowed her head. She was still smiling, happy to be there, but she didn't want Niko to know she had slept with Anthony.

Niko adjusted the radio until he found some good music. "This reminds me of *New Year's Eve*." They said the last three words together. Niko took another drink and offered it to Athena, but she shook her head.

"No, I'm feeling it."

"Just one more."

Athena didn't want to disappoint, so she took another shot.

"You look so beautiful, Theen." Niko put his hand on her thigh.

Electricity shot through her body. She licked her lips and her mouth watered at the sight of him so close, gazing at her. "We did this on New Year's too. Just stared into each other's eyes." She was entranced by his eyes locked on her. "But I really wanted to do this."

Niko put his other hand to her face and reached gently behind her neck, pulling Athena into his kiss. From the second their lips touched, a powerful attraction travelled through every part of her body. It was the most natural, perfect kiss she could ever imagine and it propelled her into immediate ecstasy. His right hand was on her waist. Their tongues touched, hesitated and then moved together, knowing exactly where to go, as if in a choreographed dance. Athena poured her passion into his mouth and he drank deeply of it.

The kiss ended and Niko sat back. "Wow," he looked searchingly into her eyes.

"Wow." She was panting, breathless.

Niko cocked his head toward the back seat. Athena realized what this would mean. If she went there, she would have sex with Niko. There was nothing in the world she wanted to do more. But if she did, she would break her promise to Anthony and to God. She would be a terrible girlfriend, and all of his friends would hate her for it. It was too soon for her and Niko because there was no way he would give up all the other girls for her. Not now. Maybe if they got married one day, but definitely not now. Niko's lips had created a bliss from which she might never recover, and she didn't think she could survive being let down by him; it would ruin everything. Plus, she didn't want him to see that her boobs were probably still growing. It was a bad idea. She made her decision in a billionth of a second. Athena pushed Niko's hand away.

He looked incredulous. "But this . . ." He motioned between them.

Athena nodded. "I know," she whispered.

He smiled. Their faces were almost touching. His warm breath hit hers.

"Athena."

She wanted Niko for the rest of her life, but this wasn't the time. It was too soon. "We can't."

"That kiss . . ." Niko caressed her face, staring into her eyes.

Her body was flooded with an almost paralyzing ecstasy at his touch. "I know," she said again. She placed her hands over his and pulled them down.

They walked hand in hand back to school. When the greenish glare of the hall lights hit their faces, they took in the messy scene. The floor was being mopped up where a drunken girl had thrown up. There was a swirl of activity near the cafeteria doors, as the dance was ending and some of the students were looking frantically for a last-minute partner so they wouldn't leave feeling as alone as they'd come.

It was here that Anthony stood, his head turning back and forth as he searched. He was looking for her. Athena had forgotten about him. Revulsion shot through her at the sight of him. But this was her boyfriend. She had slept with him. She was going to marry him.

Anthony saw Athena with Niko and lost his mind. "Where have you been?" he said in disgust.

"What the hell is your problem?" Niko answered.

Athena was amazed. She hadn't anticipated that Niko would get involved.

"Shut up! I'm not talking to you!"

"You are now."

"I'm talking to my girlfriend." Anthony raised his voice further and stared into Niko's grim face. Both had their fists clenched.

"Stop this right now," Athena ordered, but they didn't listen.

"I want to know where she was." Anthony turned toward her. "Were you with *him*?"

Athena nodded, not wanting to say anything, as he was becoming furious.

"You're drunk!" he shouted, grabbing her arm and pulling her away from Niko.

"Take your hands off her."

"Who the hell do you think you are?"

"I'm her friend. We've known each other our whole lives. Who the hell are you?" said Niko.

Anthony turned back to Athena.

"Please calm down," she said softly, slurring her words. The extra shots of vodka were taking hold. And the warm air after being outside had hit her. She felt hot.

Nearby, people were assembling, sniffing blood.

"I'll kick your ass if you did anything," said Anthony.

"I'd like to see you try," Niko replied.

"You better not have done—"

"We kissed," Athena said. She couldn't keep it back any longer. It didn't matter because she didn't want to be with Anthony. She wanted to be with Niko.

"You *what*?" Anthony's hands flew up and he pulled the sides of his hair. "What? You kissed?"

Athena wasn't enjoying this attention. "It was nothing."

Anthony's mouth was agape and so was Niko's. They both looked at her with hurt eyes, then back at each other with hatred. She wanted all of it to go away.

"What a bitch! Whore! She cheated on Anthony!" someone said. The match had lit the gunpowder and the news flared up through the dancing throng.

Athena wanted to go dance off her buzz and find Kat. She hadn't seen her all night.

"It was nothing?" Anthony asked.

"Tell him, Theenie," Niko insisted. Athena assumed he knew what the truth was since he was there. She was sure of it.

"No. It was nothing. Now calm down," Athena replied.

Niko batted his hand down in frustration and walked away, then pushed the bar on the exit door with both hands, sending it crashing open. He was swallowed up into the darkness, and the click of the door closing left Athena with Anthony.

He grabbed her arm and led her away. "I've got to get my stuff from my locker."

Athena simply followed. She didn't care anymore.

"I can't believe you. I knew you would do this. I *knew* it."

"I'm sorry."

"You're drunk. Look at yourself. Is this how you act? Is this who you are? I don't even know if I want you as a girlfriend."

Athena's mind was fuzzy but she paused, wondering what he was saying. So he wasn't going to break up with her? Or was he? Athena believed that if he broke up with her, it wouldn't be her fault and God would understand.

"I hate that guy." Anthony slammed the locker door. "You kissed Niko?" He punched it and shook his hand fiercely from the pain. "I love you, Athena, and this is what you do?" His eyes implored her for a reply.

This wasn't who she was. She followed the rules and she was a good girl. She couldn't let him think otherwise.

"I'm sorry. I'm truly sorry. I didn't mean to." Her words spilled out to help remove the pain she had caused Anthony. He was her boyfriend and she'd broken all the rules. But she loved Niko and he'd walked out. She started to cry.

"I'm driving you home."

"I'm going to stay at Kat's tonight."

"No, you're not. I'm taking you home so I know where you are." He stopped in the hallway and faced her. "No one could love you like I do. No one ever will."

Athena felt nauseous.

As she slid the key into the red front door of the Lalichs' house, Athena felt removed from her hand, and from her body and her life. She didn't recognize anything, herself included. She wanted to be a good person. She didn't want to hurt anyone. She didn't want anyone to think badly of her. She wanted to be loved. Anthony loved her. It was obvious, and she was lucky someone did. Without him, who did she have? No one. Athena quickly brushed her teeth and fell into bed. She wondered why she didn't feel as bad as she should have. She'd broken all her promises. She'd hurt everyone. But when Athena touched her lips, a wave of remembrance flooded her being. Thinking of Niko's kiss, she could only smile.

***

It had been ten weeks since the school dance and the kiss. Anthony had already paid for the semiformal tickets and wasn't going to have Niko get the best of him, so he had told Athena right away that they were going. She had worked very hard to get back into Anthony's good graces.

Athena was wearing a crushed velvet dress with a peacock feather design. Anthony had insisted she wear ballerina flats because she was almost a half inch taller than him now. She'd pulled her hair back and kept it low on the nape of her neck so as not to add any height.

Athena looked at the chicken on her plate. It was dry. She had fasted for two weeks and gone to confession over Christmas, trying to atone for her sins and was still bargaining with God, asking that if she was good, He should reward her with the happiness she deserved.

It didn't take long for word to spread to Athena that Lejla had arrived. Athena could see her from across the ballroom, standing in the middle of a circle of people. As she watched Lejla, she became aware that someone was watching her. Niko approached the circle, his eyes on Athena. He looked so handsome wearing a sports jacket of a lighter blue than his pants and a crisp white collared shirt. When he extended his hand to Lejla to dance, he broke his gaze from Athena. He pulled her sister out of the crowd.

"What are you looking at?" Anthony's low snarl sounded in her ear, accompanied by the thud of his fork on the table.

"My sister's here." Athena rotated her body toward Anthony, careful not to undo all the progress she had made in proving she was trustworthy.

"She's no good, so don't even bother."

Athena felt a burst of rage from her stomach to her throat, but it passed quickly. Shame washed over her, not because her sister was no good but because Athena didn't defend her.

"Come on, let's dance," Athena said. She didn't want to waste the occasion and was trying to make the most of things. She headed to the dance floor. "I love this one. The video was amazing." But the song was ending when Anthony arrived on the dance floor.

A slow guitar intro signalled it was time to find your person. People who had come solo quickly cleared away to the side, annoyed with the slowdown. There would be a lot of slow songs since it was a couples' event.

Athena placed her hands on Anthony's shoulders, slouching slightly. She looked up and saw Niko across the dance floor, mirroring Athena's position, her sister's back to her. He leaned down and Lejla spoke into his ear. He smiled and nodded, all the while staring at Athena, then took Lejla's hand and led her off the dance floor.

Athena didn't have a buzz but very much wanted to get one. Since the last dance she'd been extra careful not to party too much so she could win Anthony back. She looked at the purple wrist corsage Anthony had given her. He really was thoughtful, and Athena told herself she was lucky to have him. He wasn't wrong that all the drinking and drugs were bad. Avoiding them kept her out of a lot of trouble. And if she wanted to get the same amount of sex she had with him, she'd have to sleep with lots of guys and for sure would be known as a slut. So in lots of ways, he helped her reputation. He was popular with his friends and others because he was kind, and he was smart enough. He worked as a bank teller. She needed someone with ambition. She was going to be a somebody one day. Athena kept her big plans on the inside and worked on making herself smaller on the outside.

Lejla had left. Anthony overheard and five minutes later suggested that they leave too. "I want you all to myself," he said.

Athena felt instantly repulsed and then chastised herself again. Clearly, she wasn't the prettiest girl and she was fortunate to have a boyfriend who wanted her.

Later, Athena lay between the white hotel sheets, having expended enough energy to want to close her eyes. Anthony was softly snoring next to her. She'd had to run into the drugstore to buy condoms because he didn't have any. He didn't want to be seen buying them. The oily wrapper lay on the glass covering the bedside table. Athena stared at it in disgust until her eyelids became too heavy to hold open.

Chapter 58

"How do you have time for homework?" Kat asked Athena as she lay on Kat's bed. It had been almost three months since her kiss with Niko.

Athena had developed a routine. "I focus extra hard in class to get as much work done there as I can. I do most of the rest on the bus or I sleep. I make practices by hanging out at school or here or at your Teta Nadia's house. It's not bad." Few people even knew she lived outside of the school district, and the new place would be as far from the school as she was now.

"How long until your new house is done?" It was as though Kat had read her mind.

"It'll be soon. I have to have these meetings with the builder since my mom has taken second shifts at a coffee place. It's super annoying. You can't imagine how many things you have to pick out."

"It sounds like fun."

"Actually, it would be if there was time. Besides it's not like I really have a choice. Most of the time I just ask the lady what the cheapest option is. Then I try to pick the most neutral colour so it won't look stupid in a year, you know?"

"That's good." Kat stared up at the ceiling. "I can't even get my math homework started. I just don't want to. But if you said, 'Let's make a mixtape,' I'd be all over that."

Athena listened, but her mind was far away. She had barely spoken to her mother since the summer, and this weekend was going to be the first time she would be with her and the twins. Tilley had called to tell her that they would be moving into a small house in a new subdivision. It was being built, but money was going to be very tight and she would need Athena's help to make it work. Athena felt nervous.

Schoolwork, sports, sex at the motel off the expressway, and long weekend shifts at the grocery store kept her occupied. She realized that she was wasting too many hours on the bus. It took so much longer to stand there waiting than to take a car; with a car you just went. The bus stopped a hundred times. All of this was very unproductive.

Athena used her time on the bus to strategize how to make herself wealthy. She contemplated business schemes. If there were no age limits for agents, she could get into real estate. She could invest in stocks and do trading. She imagined buying low and selling high and getting paid. She could also be a stripper or a *dancer*, as they liked to be called now. This made her heart sink, because of all her ideas it was the most feasible. Several girls at school danced at the club only a few blocks from there. The clubs downtown were notoriously lucrative. Athena pictured herself being businesslike and perfecting lap dances to earn big tips as she tried not to absorb how demeaning it would be. It made her cry. She didn't want to do it, but she could if she had to.

"I just need to make some money. It doesn't matter how cheap that new house is, we can't afford it." Athena rolled off Kat's bed and collected her things to go to work.

***

The sun was shining. The sky was such a bright blue that Athena squinted as she carried the legal box down the front steps. Teta Olga was already in the car, along with the suitcase Athena had brought with her from camp. She was going to drop her off and then head to work. Athena moved quickly. She didn't want to make her late. No one else was up yet, as it was a Saturday.

"We gonna miss you, ya know?" said Teta Olga.

Athena chuckled.

"I'm serious. You such a big help around da house."

"I'm going to miss you too, Teta Olga," Athena lied. She wanted desperately to move back in with her mother, Mitzi, and Max. It was all she had been able to think about all week.

Mrs. Lalich drove the sedan to the east end of the city and turned down a narrow two-lane road and followed it to the end. The expressway ran busily behind a noise wall that followed the curve to the left. One block in, the nondescript brown brick house waited.

Athena's heart started pounding and her eyes filled with tears. She tried to calm herself, but her voice was shaking. "There it is!"

Teta Olga gave Athena's hand a squeeze.

Athena jumped out as soon as they pulled into the driveway. "Is anyone home? Oh, yeah, we don't have a car. And I have a key if no one's here." Athena patted her jeans pocket.

"I vould come in but I hafta go to work."

"I know. You go. Don't be late."

"I love you, Teenie."

"I love you too, Teta Olga. Thank you so much for what you did. It was very kind." Athena stared at the woman in the car, whose eyes were welling up. "I'll be okay."

"Your dad . . ." Teta Olga stopped.

"He's going to be away, I guess, for a bit. He's not in jail anymore, which is good. I'm not really sure where he is, but it's not my worry. I'm working to help so it'll be alright," Athena reassured her.

"If you need anything . . ." Mrs. Lalich checked her rear-view mirror and started to slowly reverse the car.

"I'll call you. Thank you." Athena waved at her impatiently. She wanted everyone to go away and leave her alone. She wanted to run inside.

Teta Olga backed out, turned, and sped away. Athena was suddenly alone. She looked around. Athena felt ceremonial as she took the concrete step onto the front porch and opened the screen door. It pulled back noisily and rested against her back. The door was locked and no one answered the doorbell. She fumbled for the key in her pocket.

Athena stepped into the front hall. The beige linoleum was shiny and clean and the neutral carpet looked pretty in the small connected living and dining rooms. The green velvet loveseat and chairs were arranged in the front room. Athena felt a wave of nostalgia for her old home. She brushed the top of the pillow on the loveseat with her hand. The dining table was set up with the old hutch and chairs. It looked dark against the modern-coloured walls. She walked the short distance around to the kitchen. The newness of everything made Athena very happy.

"Hello?" she called out.

There was no answer.

The small kitchen table with the cane-backed chairs from Deda's house sat against the railing, from which she had a view of the unfinished basement. Six stairs up led to the bathroom and three bedrooms. Mattresses were on the floors of two rooms and boxes were stacked in corners. Athena ran downstairs. Great—the other small bathroom was done. She ran back upstairs and noticed the small sticky note next to the phone. *Gone to get groceries and things we need. Be back by noon* was written neatly in her mother's handwriting. Athena glanced at the clock. She must have just missed them.

Athena pulled the fridge door open. There was nothing in it except some taped ice cube trays and plastic separators for the drawers. She swung the door shut and sat down at the table.

Her heart was racing. "Don't panic. They'll be home. They're coming home," she said out loud to calm herself. "Go put your things in your room."

Athena went upstairs but she wasn't sure where she would be. In one room, she saw an alarm clock on the floor next to a mattress and comforter. She crawled onto the bed. She lifted the covers and pulled them around her face, the smell of her mother wafted up and surrounded her. Athena curled up into the smallest ball she could and fell asleep.

***

Since moving back in with her mother, Athena spoke cautiously to her. Tilley's nerves seemed frazzled. Their father had been found guilty of tax evasion and would start a sentence in a halfway house after his rehab program. "There's Al-Anon for family members," Tilley said.

Athena didn't want to go. She had to work most nights anyway. The idea that any of them would openly discuss private matters with strangers seemed foreign.

At least from here Athena could get everywhere by bus. They didn't have a car yet, but her mom was working on it. She also picked up another job, her third, at a defence lawyers' firm doing reception and typing. No one was really home much. Danica was back in Windsor now. She had transferred home to study nursing because she missed her boyfriend too much and lived on campus. That suited Athena fine. No one knew where Lejla was. Mitzi and Max had a new school within walking distance, as were Athena's two jobs. The second was at a children's clothing and furniture store. She tried to work back-to-back shifts when she could.

Athena came in one Thursday night from the grocery store to find Tilley with her head in her hands, crying. She was seated at the kitchen table.

"What's the matter, Mom?" Athena asked gently. She always felt scared if her mother cried.

"I don't know what to do. I just don't know what to do."

Athena looked at the letter from the government. They owed over a quarter of a million dollars, plus the interest, which was compounding daily.

"They took all the money I had in the bank. They took it all." She sobbed softly. "It was only four hundred and thirty-eight dollars."

Silently, Athena sat down across from her mother. She took a long, deep breath and thought of all the ways she could fix this.

"Look, tomorrow you have to ask the lawyer on your case what to do, okay, Mom? Mom. Listen. It's important. You can sign your paycheques over to me and I'll cash them at the grocery store. We can't let them take any more money. We don't have any to begin with."

"This is due." Tilley produced a hydro bill for $122.

"Okay, Mom. I got it. I'll pay that, okay? I'll pay as much as I can. It'll be okay."

Tilley just held her head. Tears splashed onto the table.

Athena got up and put the kettle under the tap and placed it on the stove. She did the math in her mind to figure out how many hours she would need to work to pay for hydro or the phone every month. She glanced upstairs to her brother's and sister's rooms, where they were sleeping. She couldn't let them down.

After setting her teacup down, Athena pulled her books out and spread her calculus and physics homework out. She had tests tomorrow. This year's and next year's marks really counted, so she had to study. When she was done, her mom was already upstairs, asleep. Athena went downstairs to where her room was. They'd managed to find a cheap carpet remnant. The mattress was on the floor. There were no blinds yet; they couldn't afford them. She lay down in her bed. The moon was framed by the window. Its silvery-blue light made the room look cold and stark. Athena tucked herself in. She imagined that she'd won the lottery. She pictured getting the big cheque and paying off everything for her family. She knew she would get the money somehow.

Chapter 59

Athena closed her books and slid them into her gym bag. She turned the light off in the cubicle she'd been studying in. It was easier to leave her textbooks in her locker than carry them home. She walked down the empty school hallways to her locker near the front entrance. She was about to head out the front door but thought she might swing through the gym just to see if anyone was in there. There wasn't—Athena was alone. She went to the side door. It wasn't dark outside yet. When she pushed the door open, she saw Lejla sitting on a curb, crying. Athena jumped and sat down next to her.

"Lejla! What's wrong?" She put her hand on her shoulder.

"It's hopeless. My life is over."

Athena's stomach knotted up. She always worried Lejla would kill herself. "Don't say that. It can't be that bad."

"This *is* that bad."

"What is it?" Athena said tenderly.

Lejla sobbed into her hands, lifted her tear-streaked face to Athena's, and said softly, "I'm pregnant."

Athena sat quietly while that news sank in.

"What about an abortion?" Athena asked, almost afraid to make the suggestion.

Lejla wailed, "I just came back from the States today. It's too late. They won't even do it there."

"How did you get there?"

"Niko drove me."

Athena froze to the concrete she was sitting on. "What do you mean? Why did Niko drive you?"

"Because it's his," Lejla said, wiping her puffy red eyes and nose with her sleeve.

Every breath Athena took dug deeper than the one before, ripping out her insides. "Niko? . . . You slept with Niko?"

Lejla nodded.

A boiling hatred came up from the core of Athena's being. "How could you?" She started crying.

Lejla stopped crying and looked at her. "*I'm* the one with the problem! It's not your problem! I need you to tell Mom. I can't come home. I don't know what to do."

Athena's mind jumped to the possibility that this must be a misunderstanding, but it wasn't. She couldn't understand what was happening. She watched her sister, trying in vain to be detached. She was going to have to face the situation, but she wanted to kill her. Athena walked inside and pulled a quarter out of her coin purse. At the payphone by the exit, she dialed her mom's work number.

"Hey, Mom."

"Hi. What is it? I'm at work."

"I have to tell you something." Athena only paused a second. "Lejla is pregnant."

There was no answer.

Athena breathed into the receiver, nauseated and devastated, unaware of what her mother felt.

"Where is she? Are you sure?"

"She's in the parking lot at school. She tried to go to the States for an abortion, but she's too far along. She says it's Niko's."

Silence.

"I gotta go, Mom." Athena hung up the phone. It was official. She leaned her head on the phone. She listened to the sound of someone sobbing uncontrollably before she realized it was her.

Athena didn't remember how she got back home.

She wasn't tired even though she hadn't slept all night. She wasn't hungry. She was still in pain. Athena dressed carefully. She sat on her bed, staring into the mirrored sliding closet doors. Athena didn't recognize the person looking back at her. There were no tears, only a deep anguish. It was obvious that she and Niko could never be together; Athena had too much pride. They could never have a baby together without it feeling like second place, the runner-up to Lejla's child. If it had been any other girl, it would have been forgivable. But Lejla? The closeness disturbed her. Athena applied her mascara carefully. She understood Lejla and forgave her for all of her infractions and poor choices, but this was final. Now they were even. Lejla could have had anyone.

She had to catch the bus for school. She paused. "I'm not as pretty as Lejla, but I'm still pretty." She looked up at the heavens, and it felt as if the universe was swallowing her alive. *"Why?"* She let the ragged word escape from the bottom of her throat. When she resumed looking at herself in the mirror, she answered her own question. "Because God is punishing you. You made promises you never intended to keep, so He's preventing you from having what your heart truly desires." Athena nodded.

The bus ride was interminable. With every stop, Athena was jolted. Numbly, she walked by herself into the bustling school hall.

"Hey, heard your sister's knocked up," a passing boy said.

Laughing, raucous voices responded with answers she tried to ignore.

Athena pulled her books from her locker and went into her homeroom class. Niko was sitting where he'd been when they started the semester, three seats back from her. Athena jotted down everything the teacher talked about and doodled lines and shapes all around the page to busy her mind, which kept trying to see a way where it all worked out. But she couldn't. It didn't mean she didn't love Niko; she just couldn't ever be with him. It was the saddest thing when people who should be together weren't.

The bell rang. Books slammed shut. People had conversations Athena would never know about or care about. Without looking back, she got up to leave.

Niko ran forward and grabbed her arm. "Athena." He faced her, his back to the periodic table that hung on the side wall, while some people lingered to overhear their exchange.

Athena looked down at his hand on her arm. She recalled his hand on her waist, and involuntarily she reeled with agonizing desire. Nothing again would ever feel like their kiss. Athena looked at Niko and stared into his eyes. He searched her face. His look was pleading and desperate.

"How could you?" Athena whispered the question.

Niko's mouth fell open.

She looked at his hand on her arm and continued, "You ruined everything."

His expression reflected her pain and he covered his face with his hands, then ran them through his hair. Athena walked out before he opened his eyes.

The rumours surfaced like sea monsters looking to swallow Athena up. She sat stone-faced in her classes, listening to people bark at her about her family, her jailbird father, and her tramp of a sister. The ugliness of cruelty transformed them. She wasn't affected in the way they had hoped. Athena wasn't attached to her family in the normal way, and this spared her from suffering for their mistakes. What her father and sister did was their business, or at least this was what she told herself. She was impatient and more concerned about the world holding her back because she was too young and had no money. She needed to escape.

Chapter 60

Athena sat by the phone, afraid to go out in case she missed the call. When it finally came, she answered.

"This is Amelia calling from Ford Motor Company. How are you today?"

Athena was about to burst. They asked if she could come in.

Athena was assigned to the engine plant by Albert Road, for the summer. She needed two bus transfers to get there. The hand-me-down steel-toed shoes were a bit tight. The bus let her off right in front of the plant, but on the first day, Athena rode it one more stop and got off just past Fred's Variety.

Her old house was still sitting there, pretty and pink. She paused. A woman came out of Fred and Freida's house, but it wasn't Freida. Athena didn't bother to talk to her. Athena went into Fred's Variety. It seemed so much smaller than she remembered. The glass cases were still there, but half the candy had been replaced by cigarettes, lighters, and all kinds of cheap toys from China. Fred was still there.

"Hi." Athena smiled at him as he unpacked a box.

He didn't say anything, but he never had said much. He still had thick brown hair and a big bushy moustache—that hadn't changed—but both were frosted grey.

"My name is Athena Brkovich. I used to live across the street." Athena smiled.

"Yes, I remember your mom and dad and all you kids. How many were there?"

"Five."

"Yeah. Your dad got into a bit of trouble, didn't he?"

Athena's voice didn't waver. People always liked to talk about it. "Yes, he did."

Fred stopped unpacking the box. He stepped to the register and rang in a bottle of Coke and a bag of chips for a man in dark navy-blue coveralls.

"I see you got rid of the big cooler with the bottle opener," Athena said.

"Yeah, that. We got to keep up with the times. Now it's over there on the wall." He pointed. "Do you need anything?"

"Yes. I'll have two Mojos, five berries, and two ribbon licorices, please."

Fred expertly snapped open a small brown candy bag and filled the order.

The smell surrounding the plant was thick as varnish. It was dark as you approached the entrance, like a black hole. Inside, the low ceiling made Athena feel as if she had to duck to avoid hitting her head. She held a map of the plant in her hand. She had to report to the HR office, which sat like a fish tank in the middle of the floor. Three other students were standing around the entrance, waiting to take refuge in the light, when a man in a white shirt and brown tie jogged over, jangling a huge ball of keys.

"Welcome to Ford's. Please take a seat. We have to review safety precautions first," the man said.

Athena came away with the understanding that not losing your fingers or a hand was the real trick.

"Now you will be assigned to your foreman."

Three men were suddenly standing inside the door.

The first foreman looked pleasant enough. "Hi, I'm Mike Carrier. I'm looking for Rob Sheffield."

The young boy who'd been chewing his gum too loudly stood up and they exited, shaking hands.

The second foreman was young and looked almost like a student himself. Athena sat up straighter. "I need Kari McIntosh and Wayne Needham to come with me."

The other two students stood up and exited, leaving Athena alone with the third foreman. He waved his paper at her to follow and turned, then left closely on the heels of the other group. Athena had to run to catch him. He'd been talking.

"I'm sorry. Excuse me?" Athena asked, a bit out of breath.

She was surprised that, being so overweight, he could move that fast. His big beer belly hung over his pants. Athena couldn't catch his words, as they were filtered through his huge moustache. The whole hairy thing moved when he talked, or rather shouted, now that they were outside the quiet of the HR room.

The foreman stopped abruptly and turned.

Athena bumped into his stomach and bounced back. "Sorry," she said.

"Look, I don't like students—I don't think they belong here. And I'll tell you right now, this ain't no place for a girl. So the fact that I got you is a hoot." He waved the paper in her face as if dismissing her.

His attitude didn't surprise Athena or hurt her. She was going to make Richard—the name on his shirt pocket—appreciate what a good worker she was.

They marched deeper into the plant until they came to a more open area. Stacks of bins and boxes lined the walls.

Richard turned to her abruptly. "Listen, kid."

"Athena."

He rolled his eyes. *"Listen, kid,"* he said with sarcasm, "I'm puttin' you here at the front end. You're gonna load these engine blocks on the line. You have to lift them and lower them. If you so much as scratch one, you're outta here. Understand?"

Athena nodded, still uncertain what her job was.

Richard started flying around a track that looked like a ladder lying on its side. It was waist high. The horizontal slats were actually round metal rollers that spun on a big conveyor. Two old men wandered over.

"Vat's he got you doin'?" one said.

"I'm loading the blocks. But I'm not sure how. He hasn't shown me."

"Oy vey!" The man brought his hand to his head. He spoke a different language from his co-worker.

When Richard came back from flipping switches and barking orders into the walkie-talkie hidden on his belt under his enormous stomach, the two old men approached him. They spoke softly, so Athena couldn't hear, but she did hear Richard.

"If she doesn't like it, she can quit, and if she can't do it, she's fired."

Nothing could make Athena quit.

"Za pulley iz broke." He pointed to an overhead hoist with a giant hook. "If you gonna mek it like iz job, no gud."

Richard turned to Athena while the two men watched. "So your job is to pick up a block." Richard struggled to fit his arms around his belly and the block, his face instantly flushing beet red. "And you place it carefully on these rails"—he exhaled forcefully—"so that the notch here, it lines up." Gasping and huffing, he practically dropped it down. "This stamp has to be face forward or the whole engine will be assembled backward and won't fit the cars." Beads of sweat dripped from his forehead. He pulled a handkerchief out of his back pocket and wiped his face. "This line will hold five hundred engine blocks, so if it goes on wrong, you lose a day's production—two million bucks. You get a ten-minute break every ninety minutes, and thirty for lunch at noon. When the

bell sounds, you have to be back at your station. The line don't wait for no one."
He pointed at her.

"Where's the washroom?" Athena asked. She already had to go.

"You got a map. No breaks till break time, kid. This ain't grade school."
Richard turned back toward the line. "This button here stops the entire thing."
He pointed to the giant red button that read stop in capital letters. "You don't
press it unless you're dyin'. Understand?"

Athena nodded. The two older men shuffled forward again. Athena knew
they were pleading her case.

She spied the electric hoist sitting dormant to the side, wondering why it
wasn't being used. She walked over to the blocks, six to a skid, and tried to lift
one. It didn't budge. One of the older men ran to help her, but Richard stopped
him. "Ivan! If you so much as touch one of those blocks . . ." he said, and Ivan
stopped, looking at Athena apologetically.

Athena shook her head and smiled at Ivan, appreciating that he would have
helped her.

"Dey be eighty pounds," Ivan told Richard, pointing to the blocks. "She be
a hundred."

Richard shrugged with exaggerated glee.

"I've got it," Athena said.

She bent her knees. Her father had taught her to get her back into something
and make sure she found a good grip. She lifted the block and carried it *one,
two, three, four* steps to the line and tried to lower it. The edges were sharp and
with some metal barbs. Her baby finger got pinched between the rail and the
block. She gasped and lifted it quickly. She shook her hand as her eyes watered
from the pinch.

"I'll give it till break," Richard said, looking at his watch. He walked away.

Ivan shook his head and spoke to his friend.

Athena watched the engine block creep forward and the next opportunity open
up. She crouched down and lifted—*one, two, three, four*—and lowered. Careful.
Careful. She didn't pinch her fingers. Five hundred blocks. Stamp facing forward.

"Dey no right to do dis," Ivan told her as Athena started on the fourth block.

She had already divided five hundred blocks by eight hours and then by the
number of skids. She would have to do about ten skids an hour, which seemed
like too much. Athena saw the skids stacked up, three to a stack. So she would

have to do three and a bit stacks an hour. Athena smiled as she worked out these details. She wore the mandatory orange earplugs, so she could hear herself humming or counting her steps back and forth to the skid. How many there were depended on the distance to the block.

"Here, here." Athena heard something but was so focused on not pinching her fingers, she didn't turn around. She felt a tap. It was Ivan's friend. "I'm Janko. Dat's Ivan. Put dis on."

He held out the navy-blue coveralls Athena always saw the men wearing as they spilled out of the plant. She looked down. Her shirt and jeans were already smeared with oil and had small tears from the metal. Ivan brought a pair of work gloves. They were a men's large and conformed to the shape of someone else's hands, but they made the blocks less sharp, though it was difficult not to catch the extra fabric of the glove.

"Thank you," she said.

"Looks good on you." Janko said, and he and Ivan laughed.

Athena smiled and winked back. She was happy to have them around. She wasn't sure what their job was; it seemed that they spent a great deal of time just watching her load the blocks.

Athena felt impatience charge up her spine. She wanted to be done, but then she counted the stacks remaining. She had done three stacks when what sounded like a school bell rang out for about ten solid seconds. Athena threw the gloves off and picked up the map on the table. She noticed how stiff her hands felt. Her arms were shaking as she tried to locate the bathroom. While she was peeing, the bell rang again. It couldn't have been ten minutes! She panicked and wiped before she was totally done, then pulled up her coveralls and raced out. Running in steel-toed shoes was difficult, especially on the slippery stones. Imagining how happy Richard would be to fire her, she could hardly see through her tears. Ivan was loading a block for her.

"Oh my goodness. Thank you, Ivan. I'm so sorry!" Athena winced as she scrambled to get the damp, crusty gloves on.

"Relax, iz okay. Dis not a real job. Richard no like students. Iz not good."

"It's fine. I can do it."

"Vat's your name?"

"Athena." She bent over to start again. Ivan had to help with the first one. "It's harder when you stop."

Ivan tilted his head to one side and lifted his shoulder. "You good voorker, Ateena."
Athena smiled, but she had to pay attention to the line now.

When the lunch bell rang, Athena realized she had to be quick. Her baby toes were burning where the steel toe band had made blisters. There was a lineup in the cafeteria for the two registers. It was moving, but Athena didn't want to sit down for fear she would be late. She walked slowly back to her work area. A picnic table sat near the back corner. Ivan and Janko were over there, as were two other gentlemen.

"Ateena, come sit down." Ivan waved her over and moved, shooing everyone aside. "Dis iz da girl." He nodded.

The two men she didn't know raised their eyebrows and nodded, impressed.

"Vat you doin' in school?" Janko asked before taking a bite of his sandwich. Athena's attention was caught momentarily by the contrast between his blackened fingers, each with a line of dirt and oil under the fingernail, and the soft white bread.

"I'm not exactly sure. Maybe a doctor or a dentist."

"Yeah. So you smart, huh, for dat?"

Athena just nodded and took a bite of her sandwich, noting that the condition of her hands and nails had already deteriorated.

"Good for you. You don't vanna end up here."

Athena had never conceived of that. Their father had always impressed on his children that they would attend university and could be whatever they wanted. Athena didn't want to agree with Janko because all of these men worked here. Yet it was unfortunate.

"I been here for-ty years," Janko said.

"Now you get to just siddown and watch the goddamn line," one of the other men said loudly.

Janko laughed. His gums showed, and the white sandwich bread was caught in his teeth.

"Ve be union," Ivan explained to Athena, "so dey can't touch us. Ve got jobs ve no like, but mekin fifty an hour. Can never leave dat, right?"

"Iz trap ven you young. Money not everyting."

"No, but it is something," Athena replied.

All the men nodded.

"Yeah, she smart one," said Ivan.

Chapter 61

Athena didn't have time when her mom asked her to find her sister and to bring her home.

"I had a premonition, and now I have a bad feeling. You have to find her and tell her to come home and live here with us."

Athena couldn't describe her inner struggle to her mother. She was certain Tilley wouldn't have cared anyway. "How am I supposed to find her?"

"Ask around. I'm worried."

Athena wondered if her mother thought Lejla would commit suicide, but neither spoke it aloud. It was possible. Maybe it would be for the best. "If she wanted to come home, she would."

"If anything happened to her, I wouldn't be able to live with myself. Please do this for me, Athena."

Athena saw the deep lines of worry on Tilley's forehead. She acquiesced and started asking around.

***

"Why are you even doing this?" Anthony demanded. He was begrudgingly driving Athena to the downtown restaurant where Lejla apparently worked.

"Look, I'm helping my mom, all right? Wouldn't you help your mom if she asked you?"

"My mom wouldn't be asking me to do anything like this."

Always aware of the shame people threw on her like a blanket, Athena knew it was true. Anthony's mom was sweet and kind. His parents lived together and had built a beautiful home filled with love, laughter, and respect. Athena had grown to admire his family, and this soothed the pain of losing Niko. Anthony's brother and sister were fine, upstanding human beings. But Athena didn't see why, because of this, her sister and mother shouldn't matter at all.

The restaurant downtown was dark with black interior walls. The staff was getting ready for the Friday-night crowd. Athena wondered which job Lejla held. Maybe she was a bartender. When she asked, the man at the bar told her, "Lejla's in the kitchen, just through that swinging door."

Anthony was with her, and she didn't have to tell him to wait. Athena swung the black door open to reveal a commercial galley kitchen. Lejla stood with her back to Athena. In her tight sweater, she looked surprisingly skinny. Athena had anticipated she'd appear much fatter. Her sleeves were rolled up as she bent over a giant industrial sink and, with bright red hands, placed two more glasses onto a rack. Lejla was a dishwasher! Athena was offended. Their father was so proud of their abilities, inherited or otherwise. It was fine for people who couldn't do other things, but certainly not her sister, even though she had dropped out of high school.

Lejla turned and saw her standing there. "What do you want?" she said sharply.

"Mom wants you to come home."

Lejla went on washing glasses and said nothing.

"You can't stay here doing this."

"Don't tell me what I can and can't do, okay? I'll do whatever I damn well please."

Lejla didn't look pregnant. Maybe she wasn't.

"Are you pregnant?"

"Yes!" Lejla spun herself to face Athena.

"You don't need to yell at me," Athena said, her voice steady.

She imagined that if she yelled at her sister and then Lejla killed herself, she wouldn't be able to live with it, since it was what she wished for deep down.

"You can't do this on your own. Dad's gone." Athena paused. "The house is nice and peaceful. We all get along." *Which is why you shouldn't be allowed to come back*, Athena thought. She could feel a bitter taste in her mouth, like heartburn. She wanted to spit in Lejla's face. She didn't deserve to come home.

Lejla stood at the sink, her head down and eyes closed. "I'd have to get my stuff. I'm staying at a friend's apartment."

"You can't smoke or do drugs there." Athena worried about Lejla's influence on Mitzi and Max.

"Duh. I'm pregnant."

Athena had heard from lots of people that Lejla got drunk and high regularly and smoked like a chimney.

"Yeah, duh," Athena replied. "Anthony's here, so he can take us to get your things and then drive us."

Lejla hesitated.

"Come on, he's not going to want to wait much longer."

"Give me a minute." Lejla untied her apron hurriedly and went to talk to a man at the other end of the kitchen. "Okay, let's go," she said, as though it had been her idea all along.

Athena cringed.

The apartment was in a very rundown part of town. With each passing block, more and more of the contents that should have been inside the buildings had accumulated outside. Hers was a four-storey walk-up. Lejla was on the third floor. Athena imagined this was like the tenements in Detroit, filled with crackheads and rapists. Her heart pounded.

Anthony didn't want to leave his car. "Hurry the hell up, please," he said, trying to make light of his fears.

Lejla gave a knock and then used a house key to open the door. No one was there. As Lejla quickly went to work, Athena felt as if they were robbing the place. It was dirty and shabby and reeked of liquor and cigarette smoke. There were no walls between the living area and the kitchen. Most of the kitchen drawer fronts sat askew. One of the cabinet doors was missing, exposing mismatched cups and a mousetrap.

"Are you almost done?"

All Lejla had was a big tote bag, and she'd been searching for things around the mattress that was on the floor in the corner. She swept through the bathroom. She carried more hairstyling tools and products, as well as clothes.

"Yes, I'm done."

Athena was surprised that Lejla was cooperating and coming home. Her mother must have been right that she was ready.

They flew down the stairs.

"Run for it!" Athena squealed, and they burst into laughter. After jumping off the last step, their feet slammed as they hit the metal landing.

"Glad you two are having so much fun while I wait out here, trying not to get killed," Anthony said.

Lejla looked at Athena, and they burst out laughing again.

***

As soon as Athena stepped off the bus, the smell of the plant reached her and her stomach tightened into a hard knot. The anticipation of having to turn off her mind for twelve hours, of having to make herself smaller so Richard wouldn't have a reason to fire her, of waiting for the overtime offer she could never turn down but desperately wanted to . . . these things plagued Athena on the fifteen-minute walk into the plant and to her station.

She'd been reassigned to a bush press. She'd been there about four weeks now. It was monotonous and hard on the hands, but once she got going, the stiffness and pain were mostly gone in five minutes. The work area was isolated. Athena brought her own lunch and passed whole days without saying so much as one word to anyone. Today was different, however.

Richard was standing waiting for her to arrive. "Here's your notice."

Athena took the small slip of paper, her face filled with worry.

He was turning to leave.

"Wait. What do you mean?"

"It means you're done in two weeks."

Athena's shoulders sank.

"Look. You shouldn't have even got this job. There's people—men—who need these jobs. We don't need to be givin' 'em to kids who're going back to school and here for a holiday."

Athena didn't speak back or nod in agreement. She wanted to stay on or at least be called back. She stood there watching Richard, a grown-up but out of touch with reality about who needed a job and who didn't. His mouth moved in anger. He talked down to Ivan and Janko too, but they couldn't be fired so he didn't push too hard. Athena knew she was a good worker, but he'd never even told her that once. She studied him and thought, *This is a lesson right here—what not to be like.*

After second break, the man with the clipboard caught Athena's eyes and she nodded to the extra overtime. She then went back to *one piece, two piece, flip, flip, one, two, three, press these buttons, hold.* As her body went through the motions, she imagined owning the company and being careful in how she treated each soul. She would look Ivan and Janko in the eyes and thank them and inspire them. She wouldn't even fire Richard. She would just help him understand that this was not how you treated people.

***

When Lejla's belly got noticeably bigger, she no longer went anywhere. Tilley called Niko's mom and they discussed the "situation."

"If you're going to act like an adult, doing adult things, then you're going to have to accept the consequences," Tilley told Lejla.

Athena wondered how it would have been if she was marrying Niko and her mom was talking with his mom about the bridal shower. It made her hate her sister.

Lejla wasn't sure what she was going to do about the baby. Tilley wanted her to keep it. Athena was afraid she might hurt the baby; she hated it so much. Lejla was sitting at the kitchen table, tapping her fingers. Athena knew she was dying to have a smoke, and as soon as their mom left for work, Lejla pulled a silver package from her purse and removed a cigarette.

"That's not good for the baby," Athena said.

Lejla shrugged. She placed the cigarette between her lips. The back door was open to let the smoke out.

"How could you even consider keeping the baby when you don't care at all? My friends say they saw you drunk or high or both downtown last week." Athena sneered when she spoke.

Lejla didn't answer.

Athena suppressed her anger with all her might. Sometimes she wanted to destroy Lejla. Just the sight of her induced disgust. Her sister mostly spent her days eating, sleeping, and watching television. Amid her mother's protests, she occasionally went to hang out with her friends. As Lejla's stomach grew more prominent, so did Athena's hatred.

One day, Lejla waddled down the stairs and took up her spot on the couch. Athena had just come home from working and had given her mother two hundred dollars for groceries.

As Lejla spooned ice cream into her mouth, Athena's rage boiled over. "Look at you."

Her sister looked up the stairs to the kitchen.

"You're gross, just feeding your face. Getting fat."

Lejla's head turned back to the TV. She didn't argue, protest, or cry.

"You're like a huge pig. You're not a popular teenage girl anymore. You're a pathetic slob who sits around getting fatter and more stupid as the days go on. You get pregnant, but you can't stop getting high?" Athena tried to walk away but couldn't. "You're not just a slut but an idiot as well. You make me *sick*." Athena spat her words out in a venomous stream. There was something so familiar about the sound of it. She walked down the stairs and couldn't resist, stopping and firing at Lejla again. "Your body will never be the same. It's like an old woman's now, all stretched out. You're revolting. I can hardly look at you."

Athena went into her bedroom and shut the door, wondering where she had heard the words before. She broke into a cold sweat from her head to her hands when she realized she sounded just like her father.

***

"No, he's just a jerk, Mom. It's done. I'm not going to report him. It wouldn't matter. All I'm saying is that some people treat others with no respect and dignity. He thinks he's great because he's the middle manager. Big deal. He's got bosses over him and people over them."

"Well, not everyone is as smart as you," Tilley said, smiling while breaking eggs into the hot pan on the stove.

"No, but that shouldn't matter."

"I'm not as smart as my bosses," Tilley said matter-of-factly.

"Yes, you are."

Tilley chuckled softly. "No, I'm not. I'm not book smart."

"You could have been if you wanted, Mom." Athena wondered how many times her father had told her mother she was stupid.

"Don't be crazy." Tilley turned her back to Athena. "I didn't even graduate from high school."

"You didn't?"

"No. The telephone company was hiring, so I got a job as an operator. It was good pay and steady hours. I was only two credits short."

"Well, you have to get them now."

Tilley slid the eggs onto a plate with two pieces of buttered rye toast. "And how exactly would I do that?"

"Easy. They have all kinds of night classes you can do."

"Who has time for that?"

"You do!" Athena opened the Yellow Pages and flipped through it. "'Night school. See Adult Continuing Education.'" She knew by the look on her mother's face that this was something she desperately wanted. "You can take one course at a time."

"How embarrassing, though. At my age?" Tilley was smiling so much, she bit her lip to stop herself. This made Athena happy.

"I'll help you, but you won't need it, Mom. You're smart."

"I don't know about that."

"Well, I do."

"I wish I was as sure about things as you are."

Athena felt something inside her nudging her to say, "Just because Dad told you you're stupid, you don't have to believe it."

"Athena!" Tilley stopped what she was doing and faced her. "I don't like that kind of talk."

"Neither do I. Neither does anyone."

"Listen, your father loves me. Deep down."

"But he says mean things."

"He doesn't mean them."

"Then why do you believe them?"

Tilley turned slowly back to the sink.

"Lejla believes him too. People can say all kinds of things. It doesn't make them true."

"I don't like this conversation. It's not nice talking about your dad. He needs our support right now."

"No, Mom! We need his. And where is he?"

"Athena! Enough!" Tilley smacked the countertop with the wet dishcloth. "I don't want to hear another word."

***

Athena's paycheques went straight to pay the bills. She was always shocked at how much the government took, but she knew she would receive all of it back in a refund. The trouble was, they needed the money now.

"I think we'll have enough until October." Tilley tapped her finger nervously on the table as she stared blankly at the stack of envelopes.

"It's okay, Mom. It's going to be okay. We just need a lower interest rate on the house."

"That was all I could get."

"Well, maybe ask again. Don't you know anyone who could help you?" Athena was thinking someone Serbian in banking.

"No, no, I don't."

Was her mother telling the truth? She thought it silly to be so proud when it came to money. "Money isn't real, you know, Mom? It's just an invention."

"Well, these bills are real, and getting your house taken away is real. When you grow up, you'll see."

But Athena did see that it was money, specifically a lack of it, that caused the most problems. The dilemma was getting your hands on it. All the hours on the bus could be spent working. All the hours in school could be spent working. All the hours sleeping could be spent working. Working by the hour meant that time limited how much you could make. Her mind never rested. She had to free up time.

Chapter 62

"This is something new," said Mrs. Harriet. "What I'm passing around is the answer sheet. Do not write on it anywhere or make any marks other than one answer per line or the computer won't be able to read it. It's called an aptitude test."

Athena looked over the hundred questions in the accompanying handout. They seemed random and repetitive.

"Answering with your first thought is best. Don't overthink it." Mrs. Harriett explained.

Being young and pretty, she was one of the more popular teachers. She was also helpful and forgiving if circumstances prevented you from handing in an assignment on time. This was important. In grade thirteen, lots of the students were already eighteen. Parents who couldn't afford their kids or didn't want them anymore had either already kicked them out or started charging rent. Work could really interfere with quiet reading time.

When Athena was finished, she walked to the front and placed her sheet on top of the pile.

Mrs. Harriet looked up. "Oh, Athena," she whispered so they wouldn't disturb the others. She beckoned with her finger for Athena come closer. "I'm running the public speaking club. I'd love it if you joined. I think you would be a natural."

"Thanks, Mrs. Harriet. I'm not sure . . ."

"You don't have to let me know right away. We only meet once a month. There's a competition in February, but it's here at our school this year, so I really want us to make a good showing."

Athena smiled. She appreciated teachers who made an effort.

"It's just, with being the yearbook editor . . ." Athena said. She really wanted to help her out.

"I understand. You're super busy. Has basketball started?

Athena nodded.

"If you could do it, it would be another great point on your resumé." She smiled, a warm and caring glow surrounding her.

"Sure, Mrs. Harriet. I'll see what I can do, but I can't really promise."

All of the teachers knew Athena. She was conscientious, reliable, and trustworthy.

"Do you have any idea what you want to be, Athena?" Mrs. Harriet tapped the answer sheet before a boy tossed his on top, and sat back down.

"I've always thought about becoming a doctor, I guess."

"Wonderful, yes. We'll see what's in the cards, eh? I'm sure you'll do whatever you put your mind to."

Athena smiled. The truth was that she still dreamed of writing comedy sketches, but that could never happen. She needed to go into something that guaranteed enough money to provide the kind of life for her family that they deserved. Athena had been amassing accomplishments to pad her impressive application for student awards. The grand prize for the student athlete of the year in each school was five thousand dollars, and best in the city was ten thousand. She was a shoo-in for the academic prizes. Athena dreamed of how she would use the money to help her mom so she didn't have to work so hard.

***

"I don't know why you have to do this too." Anthony gestured to the photo layout Athena was spreading out onto the large table in the cafeteria.

Athena had designed the student pictures for each grade to form letters that would spell out *Montcalm S.S.* She was in the process of collecting personal write-ups from all the graduates. She had made an announcement to hand all of them in to the student council office. Athena thought of how badly she needed to win those scholarships.

"The more I do, the better chance I have."

"You're going to win. You play four sports and get the highest average every year."

Athena didn't look up. She twisted the tape into circles to stick the photos down. She made sure that the right name was with the right person, then double-checked the spelling of each person's name against the master list.

"You don't have time for this."

"Do you mean I don't have time for you?" She smiled flirtatiously at her boyfriend.

Athena was officially over one inch taller than Anthony. He never brought it up anymore but its presence was known somehow. Athena looked at the clock on the wall; she still had half an hour until practice started.

"Come on, help me put these away for now," she said.

"No. I have to get going. I have a lot of math homework."

"Just help me!" Athena nudged him as she stacked the large, awkward layouts, careful not to mess up their order.

She fumbled in her purse for her key chain. It was a bright pink rabbit's foot with about six keys on it. "Just a second." She fiddled with the keys until she found the one that opened the darkroom door.

"Step into my office," Athena said in her sexiest voice, smiling.

There was hardly anyone in the hallway. She quickly locked the door behind Anthony and turned the "do not disturb" light on. The switch lit the red light outside the door to indicate that she was developing pictures. The red light shone inside as well. As the yearbook editor, only she and her assistant, Josie, had keys.

"But what if she comes in?" Anthony said, pushing Athena's hands from his body.

"You can't open the door when pictures are being developed. It would ruin them." Athena dove on him.

The small room had countertops on all four sides. There was a space of about two by four feet to stand in. Overhead cabinets ran along one wall, and across from that, white trays sat filled with developer and fixer. A clothesline with pins was strung up for hanging photos to dry.

"We can't take long," Anthony said, then lustily kissed Athena and started to unbutton his jeans.

Athena turned around after doing the same and leaned her elbows on top of the counter at the end where she had put the layouts. Anthony entered her from behind.

"You're always so wet."

"Do you have something?"

"I'll just pull out."

Sex was always such a good release. It took Athena out of her thoughts, out of always worrying, to a place where nothing mattered.

Athena brought her thoughts forward momentarily. "Okay, yeah. I'm going to get my period next week, so we're good."

Anthony got into it. Athena pushed against the counter and felt the deep pressure inside of her build. Anthony was strong and athletic. His pace increased and he came inside of her. Athena could feel it and it made her orgasm. She felt powerful when he couldn't control himself.

"Are you sure it's okay?" he asked.

"Yeah, don't worry."

They were both breathless.

"Do you still think it's not a good thing?" Athena asked.

They laughed as Anthony looked for something to clean himself with and found a paper towel. He pulled up his pants.

"All right, honey bunch. I have to go."

Athena's stomach lurched. She always felt a nagging neediness after sex and hated for him to go right away. Waves of guilt rose and she stayed them with reassurances to God that she would keep her promise and marry Anthony.

"Wait, at least." She motioned to herself and wiped up.

"Make sure no one sees that," he said.

Athena crumpled up the paper towel and ran it under water, then wrapped it in another before throwing it out. "All good." She zipped up and kissed him again.

"Theenie, I gotta go."

"One more time."

"No, listen." He pushed her hands off, but Athena giggled.

"No. Really, I gotta go. We got all year."

A deep loneliness swept over her. She knew Anthony loved her. She loved him too, for all his good qualities and was lucky to have him.

They exited and she locked the darkroom door.

"Where you gonna go?" he said.

"I'm just going to sit in the gym until practice. I have to read some English."

"Why don't you go to the library?"

"I just want to be where there are people," Athena said.

"No. I don't want you to sit in there."

Athena was used to this.

"Are you trying to meet guys or something?"

She sighed. "No, I'm not trying to meet guys," she said in a bored tone.

"But that's what it seems like. I have to go." Anthony was getting irritated. "Can't you just go to the library?"

"Yes. Sure, I guess."

Athena walked with Anthony toward the exit. They kissed in front of the library doors. He opened it for her.

"I'll see you tomorrow," Athena said, smiling.

"Hey," he said, pulling her closer, "you're mine and I don't want any other guys checking you out."

Athena smiled. "I know."

"See you tomorrow." Before he left, Anthony waited until Athena had walked into the library and sat down.

Athena didn't go to the gym before practice. Tomorrow, Anthony would probably ask the guys if they'd seen her there, checking on her like he always did.

Chapter 63

Athena caught the early bus to school. It was a Monday. She wanted to put some finishing touches on the layouts for the senior graduates. She had written her own little blurb, but it seemed incomplete or insincere, maybe both.

"Thanks," Athena said to the driver as he opened the door for her.

As she stepped out of the warmth of the bus, the wind pressed on her. She loved the wind, with its potential to stir things up. When the light changed, Athena crossed the street, watching a miniature tornado of brown leaves swirl around.

There was Teta Nadia's house. Her two front room windows were lit up. The scene reminded Athena of a Beatrix Potter book. The warm light was the colour of a candle. It extended in a globe, trying to touch the sidewalk, beckoning her. Athena thought of the empty hallways of school awaiting her one block farther. She turned up Teta Nadia's front walk.

Athena didn't want to wake the house up. She hesitated, second-guessing her intrusion, when the front door suddenly swung open and Teta Nadia appeared wearing a fuzzy blue robe and a flowered kerchief around her head. She moved as if she was dancing, swinging open the door and ushering Athena in.

"Atheena," she said, stretching and pouring out her name. It was as if her voice had a big smile.

"Good morning," Athena whispered, stepping forward.

"Tea, sweetie? I was just putting the kettle on and I've got some cakes too." A plate of pastries was already on the counter.

"Were you expecting me?" Athena dropped her purse and removed her shoes before she tiptoed to the kitchen three steps away.

"I'm always hoping you visit, darling. You know that you can come here anytime."

Nadia filled the kettle with water, put it on the stove, and turned the gas on. It clicked four or five times before the blue flame jumped.

Nadia squeezed her. "Eat. Eat something. You're so thin."

"It's from basketball. All the running," Athena explained, reaching for a lemon tart.

Nadia placed a small serviette in front of her. "What's on the books for you today?"

Athena filled her in on the yearbook while she took the kettle off before it began to whistle too loudly and then made the tea.

Nadia listened intently. "That's really amazing, my dear. Simply wonderful."

Not fifteen minutes later, a door in the small hallway opened.

"Oh, we must've woken the boys up," Nadia said.

Christopher, the middle boy, stepped out, rubbing his eyes. "Mornin', Mum." He saw Athena, waved, and disappeared into the bathroom.

Athena hadn't wanted to disturb them and felt uncomfortable when Christopher came out. She didn't usually visit outside of her lunch hour. She got up hastily, packing up her napkin and finishing her tea with a gulp.

"You don't have to go if you don't want to do. I love having a girl in the house."

Putting her shoes on, Athena smiled back at her.

"I'm always praying that you or one of your sisters will marry one of my boys."

"You never know, Teta Nadia," Athena said, opening the door.

The dark sky was just beginning to brighten, and the hot tea and tart fortified Athena.

"Have a good day, love." She gave Athena another big hug.

Athena felt comforted knowing that there were other families like hers—imperfect. She thought about marrying one of the Marinkovich boys. If she had to choose, it would probably be Christopher.

When she opened the darkroom, she snapped back to reality.

Athena pulled out the files of student write-ups. *Best known for: Falling asleep in class. Favourite quote: Bueller? Bueller? Future plans: Retire in Tahiti.* Athena felt as if everything she read was fake somehow. People wrote what they thought they should write because they knew others were going to read it. The truth—that most of these kids would struggle to make it and work hard to scratch out a mediocre living—was too painful. Money was definitely the only ticket out.

***

It was almost five o'clock. Athena checked the time on the Swatch watch that Anthony had given her for her birthday. It had come with a dozen red roses and dinner out at Red Lobster. Afterward, they got a room at their usual hotel and she opened a box of Italian chocolates. Each one was individually wrapped, with a different romantic quote printed on it. Athena opened one and read it aloud: *"Il Bacio è un segreto sussurrato a una bocca anzichè ad un orecchio.—E. Rostand."* This translated to "A kiss is secret talk to the mouth instead of the ear." A memory of Niko flashed into her mind. It was too late. Anthony saw her expression change. The night had ended badly.

Athena picked up her binders from the library table. She opened a small notebook and scanned down her list of things to do. *5:00 p.m. Basketball practice.* Athena swung her bag over her shoulder and headed to the gym.

She turned the corner from the library to see Maggie Telfer and her boyfriend, Cole Lanvin. Cole and Maggie were one of the beautiful couples.

Cole grabbed Maggie by the forearm and shoved her hard against the wall. She looked as if she was begging him for something.

Athena walked straight for them. "Hey! Cole! What are you doing?"

The couple stopped and looked at Athena.

"Mind your own business," Cole barked at her.

"This *is* my business."

Cole scoffed.

Athena continued, "Maggie's my friend and you're hurting her."

Cole shook his head.

"Yes, you were. I saw you. It's not okay."

Neither one of them really knew how to react.

"Maggie, he can't put his hands on you like that. It's not right."

"Look, it's not what you think, Athena. He's not hurting me. We're just having a fight," Maggie said quickly.

Athena frowned, staring at them both. "Keep your hands off her, Cole."

"Keep your nose out of our business, bitch." He was facing Athena.

But she was unfazed. She wasn't sure where her newfound courage had come from, but her conviction was unwavering. She stared calmly back at Cole.

He turned to go, obviously annoyed at both girls. Maggie tried to grab his arm and he ripped it away. He turned and said, "Hang with your little buddy. Have fun," and then swaggered away.

Maggie gave Athena a dirty look and ran after him.

***

"We need to get a car, Mom." Athena sat at the table, looking through the newspaper.

"I can't buy a car."

"Why not? We have enough for a cheap one. The bus is a total waste of time. We need to be able to get places."

Tilley bit her lip. She dipped a piece of toast into her coffee and took a bite, thinking. "I don't want to get a lemon. What if there are repairs?"

Athena had thought about that too. "Maybe before you're done at Ford's we should use the employee pricing? That way we could get something with a warranty. That could be an option. We could make the monthly if it was low enough."

"But then there's insurance and gas."

"We live too far out of town not to have a car," Athena insisted. She could tell that her mother was afraid. She'd been offered a retirement package. She would keep her pension and benefits and avoid the risk of layoffs. She would also get a payout. The lawyers wanted her full time anyway. "Then you could drive to work."

"I don't mind taking the bus."

"Well, then I could drive to school." Athena laughed.

"Okay, we'll go look and see what's at the dealer."

Athena knew that she could get her mother to buy it.

They settled on a demo car. It felt like a celebration to see her mother driving. Tilley took Athena, Mitzi, and Max for a drive along the river and they continued all the way down until they found themselves at the turn to their former street.

"Let's go past the old house," Mitzi and Max shouted from the back.

As the hill came into sight, Athena felt distant memories surface. Her childhood, or parts of it, was separate from her now. Thinking about playing on the hill or at the park while they waited for the school bus made her feel nostalgic.

Mitzi pointed. "There it is!"

Tilley blinked back tears. "Ours was the first house built here."

There were no empty lots now, just manicured lawns and two-car garages. They didn't stop.

"Wave," Athena instructed, waving at the house.

They all did it and Tilley pressed her foot on the gas. Athena wondered what everyone thought or felt about that house. "It's just a house," she said as they rounded the corner at the end of the block to head out.

"Yes. It's just a house." Tilley smiled at Athena, her big brown eyes carrying a wistful hint of gratitude. She reached over and held Athena's hand, then gave it a squeeze.

As they drove past the park, Athena took in the emptiness of it. Low, grey clouds sat close to the bare trees she used to climb. The hard yellow grass made her feel thankful she was inside a warm car with the heat turned up. Athena looked at her mother's hand on hers before she lifted it to make the left turn. As the car turned, Athena looked at the water. The lake was grey-brown like everything else. Whitecaps were visible as far out as you could see. It looked cold. Athena took a deep breath and blew it out, thinking about her dad and what he would say if he knew they'd bought a car. It made Athena's stomach nervous.

"It drives really nice." Tilley was smiling.

Athena smiled back at her. "Yeah, it's so cute, Mom. Like you."

Tilley's smile grew bigger.

Athena looked back out at the rough waters that followed them.

***

By law, Lejla had to keep the baby for five days before giving it up for adoption.

"She's so beautiful," Tilley said at the kitchen table. "I hope Lejla will fall in love with her and not be able to give her away."

Athena's repugnance at the conversation seeped out of her pores.

"Aren't you going to go and visit?" her mom said.

"No."

"You should. You're an aunt now."

"No, I'm not," Athena said matter-of-factly.

"Shame on you for saying that."

"Shame on *me*?" Athena yelled back. "Wow, that's rich."

Her mother didn't reply.

Four days later the phone rang. Tilley answered and from downstairs Athena could hear her speaking. She heard her mother's footsteps. Tilley knocked on the door and peeked in.

"It's Lejla on the phone. She says she wants to talk to you. She says she respects you and she'll do whatever you say." Tilley's face was strained.

Athena's struggle about what to say resolved as she followed her mother up the stairs.

"Hey, Theenie," Lejla said.

"Hey."

"You didn't come see the baby."

"No."

"I named her Samantha."

"Good for you."

"Listen, I think you're smart and I trust you. You know what I should do. I'm going to do whatever you think is best."

Athena didn't hesitate. "You can't even take care of yourself. How are you going to take care of a baby? We have no money. You're on drugs. You didn't graduate from high school. You're irresponsible and an unfit mother. There's no question you should give the baby up for adoption."

There was a pause and a deep sigh. "If that's what you think."

"That's what I *know*. Here's Mom."

Athena listened to her mother trying to convince Lejla otherwise. When she hung up the phone, Tilley cried silently. When she looked at Athena, sitting satisfied at the table with her, she clucked her tongue.

"What?" Athena said, challenging her mother.

Tilley just shook her head. "I'm going to bed." She walked upstairs, leaving Athena alone in the kitchen, surrounded by her mother's disappointment. She didn't second-guess her recommendation to Lejla, but she felt dirty for not having been transparent about the real reason she couldn't tolerate having the baby in her life. How could she ever accept that her sister had slept with the boy she'd dreamed of marrying her whole life?

Samantha was given up to a professional couple who couldn't have children. Athena took comfort in the fact that someone's dream had come true. But the comfort couldn't erase the underlying feeling that she had done something irretrievably wrong.

Chapter 64

"How long are you fasting for?" Kat was lying across her bed, flipping through an old copy of *Vogue.*

"I wanted to do the whole time, but I think I'm only going to do two weeks," Athena said.

"Which page do you like better?" Kat held up the spread.

Athena gazed at them a moment and pointed to the right side.

"Me too. We're going to *Badnja Vece* this year. I put my name down to help."

"Yeah, I'm already down for tickets. I'd rather sell tickets, but I'll probably be serving."

"Oh my God. This girl is a skeleton!" Kat showed Athena a picture of an emaciated model. "That's not so healthy. But it's so weird how that's what we're supposed to look like."

"Like we're starving?" Athena laughed. She stood up in front of the long mirror and rotated, flattening her stomach with her hands.

"You're so lucky," Kat said, grabbing her own midsection. "I used to be skinny, but then this."

"We're still perfect."

"If only that were true," Kat said.

***

The Serbian Christmas Eve service was one of Athena's favourites. The church glowed from inside as they approached. The flickering candlelight made it look as though the figures in the stained glass windows were moving. Inside, the incense welcomed her.

"Here, each of you take two of these. Put one underneath for Baba." Her mother offered Athena, Mitzi, and Max the candles with the long wicks Athena loved.

Athena crossed herself, kissed the candle, and thought of her baba. Was she disappointed with the way her daughter's life had turned out? Athena watched her mom softly chatting and smiling with person after person. She was proud of her.

The church lights were on, but the darkness that shrouded the church made the light from the incandescent bulbs and candles barely reach the walls. It was as if the entire congregation was absorbing all the light. They huddled tightly together for warmth.

"Is the heat on?" one of the ladies asked the men on the other side.

One of them walked over to reassure them. "I turned it on, but it hasn't heated up yet."

Athena could feel her toes going numb as her pointy dress shoes slowly cut off the blood supply.

In his golden robes, the priest flung the incense burner and sang incantations in a monotonous drone, which Kat and Roxy often imitated. Thinking about this, Athena stifled a burst of laughter. She crossed herself on cue. Tonight was one of the rare times she would take Communion on a day other than Sunday. People started moving to the middle aisle to line up for confession. Tilley caught her eye and nodded for her to join. Kat was going too. She'd descended from the choir loft. Athena wished she could stand up there too and watch everything.

"What do we say again?" Athena whispered to Kat.

"Just say yes to whatever they ask. I'll go first. Just do what I do."

This priest was new. He had a heavy accent that made his English sound Serbian and a huge mole on the side of his nose, which Kat liked to point out.

When she thought of this, Athena's laughter bubbled up again. She would have to control herself. "I have the giggles," she whispered.

"No," said Kat, recognizing they couldn't go anywhere at the moment.

That was the lid on her laughter that Athena needed. She resumed her sober stance. She glanced at her mom, who was standing with perfect posture, her silvery-white hair standing out among all the dark coats and kerchiefs. With a serene look, she tipped her head when she saw Athena. Athena took a deep breath and looked back. Kat was going up.

Athena watched and listened very carefully. She heard murmurings and saw Kat with her head bowed. The priest was saying incomprehensible words and made the sign of the cross over her. Kat crossed herself and walked past Athena, but not before placing her index finger on the side of her nose and mouthing the word "mole" slowly and precisely for Athena to see. Athena's laughter escaped, and she bent over, coughing into both of her hands as Kat tiptoed quickly out of the way.

Athena stepped up. *Something, something, something* in Serbian.

"Yes." Athena nearly choked on the word and she tried to bottle up the peals of laughter threatening to surface. She waited.

The priest said in her ear, "Vat is your name?"

Athena wanted to laugh for some reason. She pressed her lips together, and her eyes were watering as she bowed her head underneath what looked like a gilded table runner. "Athena." She managed to squeak out her name.

"OK, Ateena." *Something, something, something* in Serbian.

Athena's shoulders shook with the ridiculousness of it all. The pressure to be perfect, to be forgiven, to be standing in front of everyone without a clue as to what was being said . . . it all amounted to an explosion Athena could only barely contain. Light seemed to erupt from the base of her spine. Her laughter contained her own belief that sex wasn't truly a sin, that there was no hell, that none of this mattered and it was all pretend. Athena sputtered and coughed, covering her mouth with her arm and trying to hide her laughter.

The priest wouldn't give up and asked her again what her sins were. Athena bit her lip and held her hands tightly together and nodded. Tears formed in her eyes and ran down her face as her body began to shake as she tried to hold back the tide. Athena was hoping he thought they were tears of remorse. The priest launched into the rest of the blessing and Athena barely breathed, clenching her teeth and wiping the corners of her eyes. She would have to run downstairs immediately or risk disappointing her mother.

As the priest lifted the scarf, she crossed herself with one arm and held the other tightly against her stomach. She turned and walked straight back out to the entrance and then bolted down the stairs to the basement. No one was there to hear her thunderous laugh. Athena howled with childish glee at the insanity of it all. She continued laughing and wiping her eyes as she walked around the room, releasing the pressure.

Athena twirled around. The sound of her shoes on the polished concrete floors sounded almost exactly like the metal plates on tap shoes. She took off her shoe. They used to be Danica's. The metal part of the heels was exposed because the rubber had worn off. No wonder. Athena laughed harder at the poor condition of her shoes. She put one hand on her hip and fluttered the other in the air as she Buffalo-shuffled back to the double doors. As she was about to push through them, the door swung back at her and Niko followed, almost running straight into her.

He grabbed her to keep her from falling back. "Oh, hey," he said, smiling.

Athena jumped and looked at his face. "*Sretna Badnja Vece*," Athena said, and they kissed three times on the cheeks. *One, two, three.* Athena felt his smooth skin and was enveloped in his cologne and the feel of his hands on her arms.

"*Sretna Badnja Vece*," he said. "What are you doing down here?" He didn't move his eyes from hers.

Athena paused, her eyes twinkling. "No, what are *you* doing?" she said.

"I asked first."

"I was escaping from my laughing fit."

"What's so funny?"

It didn't translate as well into hilarity so much as strangeness so Athena didn't try to explain.

"You look great, Theen."

"Yeah, you too, Niko. Anyway, I was just going to head back up."

"Me too, I guess."

Athena smiled. She climbed the stairs slowly, aware of Niko walking behind her. Melancholy draped over her as they ascended back into the familiar realm. They were supposed to have been together.

"Look at you two." An old baba smiled and grabbed at Niko's cheek, looking first at him and then at her. "You Tilley's daughter?"

Athena nodded.

"Eh, Niko?" The baba poked him with her elbow and gestured to Athena with her thumb.

Athena's throat tightened. She squeezed her eyes together and forced out a cute smile for the elderly woman. She walked quickly back into the main part of the church on the girls' side and bowed her head. Hot tears came up and Athena brushed them away, one after the other, unable to make them stop. Laughing was like crying, except in church it was only acceptable to cry. Who made that rule up? Certainly not God.

"I know you're sad about your dad, sweetie. But you're strong for your mom, she tells us. That's what's important." Teta Olga was squeezing her arm.

Athena felt a pang of guilt. She hadn't even thought about her dad except to pray that he never came home.

Athena stopped crying.

The church bells started clanging as though at some distance. *When you hear the bells, you cross yourself*; Athena could hear the instructions as they'd been given to her. She followed them automatically. As she did, her eyes wandered up to the figure of Jesus nailed there. "I'll bet you died laughing," Athena said under her breath.

Chapter 65

After she extracted the long gold chain from the blue velvet box, Athena dangled it in the air. At the bottom of it was a giant heart-shaped locket.

"It's fourteen karat gold," Anthony said as his whole family nodded approvingly. "Put it on."

Athena looked for the clasp.

"No. You don't have to undo it. It's long enough that you can just place it over your head." He grabbed the chain from her and placed it around her neck.

Athena picked up the heart. "Oh, it's so nice."

"Good job, Anthony," said his father.

"Do you like it?" Anthony asked.

"Yes, it's so beautiful. I'm so lucky." She smiled at Anthony, who was sitting next to her on the couch. They leaned in and kissed quickly.

"The lovebirds," his younger brother teased.

Athena felt a wave of shame pass through her and bowed her head, blushing.

"Nothing's too good for my girl. When we're married, I'm gonna build you the biggest house and fill it full o' gold."

With a zap of panic, Athena's stomach clenched. Tensing, she looked down at the locket. On the front was scrolling hearts and roses. She turned it over. The back wasn't engraved. Athena felt relieved. She pried the seam open with her thumbnail.

"I didn't put anything in it. I wanted you to do it."

"It's lovely. Thank you again."

"Do you love it?"

Athena nodded again.

"I want you to love it."

"Yes. Yes, it's perfect. What's not to love?"

"Well, you're kind of quiet, so I don't know."

"No, no, it's absolutely gorgeous. Really. I'm just kind of overwhelmed by it. It's so nice, right?" Athena held it up to the room.

Anthony's father, brother, sister, cousins, and uncle were sitting around the sunken living room, a fire crackling in the fireplace. His mom and aunt were in the kitchen, cooking the Sunday feast. It was almost Valentine's Day.

"I wanted to give it to you in front of everyone."

Anthony's mom came into the room, wiping her hands on her apron. "Lemme see, lemme see."

Athena loved his mom. Luisa made funny remarks under her breath and openly adored Athena.

"You couldn't find anything bigger?" She laughed.

Anthony rolled his eyes. "Only the best for my Athena."

She felt comforted by the fact that she loved Anthony's family. It would all be okay in the end.

"When we have the cutest babies in the world, you can put their pictures in there and carry them with you." Anthony swung his arm around Athena.

Reflexively, she pulled away.

"Hey, what's—?"

"I'm just going to help your mom." Athena forced a wide smile and fine-tuned her tone, making it as sweet as could be.

"Congratulations on making the all-star team," Anthony Sr. said to her as she got off the couch.

Athena started to reply but Anthony interrupted her. "She should have been first team, but the coach didn't put her name in. Said they had better odds on first team if they kept it to two girls. Mariela and Paula got it, but my babe got second. Still good. She doesn't need those girls anyway."

Athena listened like everyone else as she moved plates of food from the kitchen island to the table.

"They dumped her," Anthony continued. "As soon as the season ended, no more friends. Those girls were never your friends."

Athena wanted to argue differently, but it didn't matter. And it was true that Paula and Mariela had stopped speaking to her, as though she were invisible. It made going to school difficult.

"That's no nice. Nobody should be mean to my daughter-in-law. I'mma gonna kill 'em," said Luisa.

Athena laughed. Luisa was as gentle as a lamb. How could she not be part of this family? They all loved her. Athena looked at Anthony. He was watching her.

"C'mere. Let me see that again."

Athena walked over to Anthony and he lifted the locket, which rested between her breasts. "It's heavy. This cost a lot. I hope you love it." He was holding the chain taut so she couldn't move.

"I do. What do I have to do to convince you? It's the nicest gift I've ever received, honestly." Athena smiled and pleaded her case, fighting the desire to pull it over her head and throw it at him. She wished he wasn't like this. She wished she wasn't like this.

"I can take it back, you know?"

Athena sighed and he let it drop. "I love it. Thank you."

Anthony smiled as though sensing she was reaching the end of her patience. "You don't need those dumb girls. You have me. I love you and I don't care who knows it. You're my girl and I'm going to marry you and keep you all to myself." He laughed as he spoke, as though he were joking.

Everyone laughed along with him except Athena. She just nodded and smiled, her fingers climbing the heavy chain around her neck, then feeling the weight of the heart in the middle of her chest.

***

"Congratulations, Athena!" Diana, the school's office secretary, shouted through the window as Athena trudged in from the downpour.

She pulled down the hood on her windbreaker. Her lips had turned slightly blue she was so wet and cold, even though it was almost March. Athena threw open the door to the office.

Athena smiled, confused. "For what?" she asked.

Diana shook open the lifestyle section of the newspaper and folded it back on itself. "Take a look. Montcalm's student of the year."

Athena's student picture stared back at her, accompanied by a glowing write-up.

"Mr. Henrik wrote that himself," Diana said, tapping the article to emphasize its significance.

Athena's heart soared. This indicated the big-money prizes; the student of the year always cleaned up big at graduation.

Athena made a mental note to write Mr. Henrik a thank-you card. "I'll thank him later, Diana." Her eyes roamed over the page, which profiled a student from every high school in the city. She tried not to drip on the newsprint.

"I'm going to cut it out and put it on our board in the lounge." Diana smiled. Athena floated out of the office.

The afternoon came on stormy. Large dark clouds approached and lightning bolts crackled across the sky, followed by rolls of distant thunder. The weather carried an ominous message. Something was off. Athena sat in calculus, watching the trees bend to the will of the wind. A sharp clap of thunder made her jump right at the moment her teacher called her name. Athena looked to the front of the classroom. Mr. Reitman was holding up the article.

The kids took shots at her.

"Keener."

"Kiss-ass."

"Suck-up."

As Mr. Reitman walked the aisle to her desk, his smile changed to a grimace. He decided to give a short lecture about how others could learn from Athena's example. It wasn't going to go well—Athena knew this instinctively. She sat quietly, staring straight ahead and wishing he would be brief, which he was.

Rianne saw Athena emerge from calculus and bolted to her, excited. "Everyone! Everyone, here she is! The best brown-noser in the building!"

"Best in the *city*!" someone shouted.

"Best in show!"

Lots of boys laughed.

Athena walked past them, feeling unsettled and worried about something she couldn't place.

"Well, I'm proud of you. You're the smartest girl here. They're just jealous." Anthony comforted her, but he seemed uncomfortable himself.

"I just don't get why people want some people to win and not others. I always feel as though people would love to see me fail." Athena felt panic.

"That's what jealousy is, sweetie. Don't worry about it. They're a bunch of losers."

Something suddenly coalesced in Athena. "I'm going to go see Ms. Hudson about nominations."

"Why? You're going to be nominated for all the awards, Athena. You've got the highest average, you're student of the year, yearbook editor, and sports. No one comes close."

The lights flickered off for five seconds with a huge boom of thunder and then came back on. Just as quickly, Athena felt a surge of fear when the premonition filled her mind. "Oh my God, Anthony. She's not going to nominate me."

One, two, three, one, two, three. Athena counted her quickened steps to the office of the senior girls' gym teacher. Ms. Hudson's job was to nominate the girls who best exemplified what it meant to be a student athlete. Ms. Hudson liked Paula and Mariela, but Athena didn't share a connection with her. Athena knocked on her door.

"Come on in."

Athena stepped just inside. Ms. Hudson's desk was a study cubby scattered with papers.

"Oh, hi, Athena." Ms. Hudson's toothy grin flashed up at her. "Congratulations on student of the year."

"Thank you, Ms. Hudson." Athena smiled but her heart was pounding. "That's actually the reason I came. Well, part of it."

"Oh?"

"Yes, well, I was wondering if you put in the girls' names for nominations . . . for the scholarship awards." Athena's throat was dry.

Ms. Hudson, who had been reclined in her office chair, slowly leaned forward, and looked squarely at Athena. Her elbows were on her knees. "Well, yes, I have, Athena."

Athena waited.

"So you're wondering if I nominated you?" Ms. Hudson's eyebrows lifted.

"Um, yes. It's important."

Ms. Hudson took in Athena's face and her saccharine expression changed to one of matriarchal condescension.

"Yes, Athena. It *is* important. I can't nominate too many people or the voting will be difficult. I decided this year to keep it to the two students who I thought best fit the criteria. Unfortunately, you weren't one of them."

Athena's mouth fell open. "Ms. Hudson"—her mind was racing—"please."

"As you know, there are other girls in the school who deserve to win as much as you do. Or, dare I say, *more?*" She shrugged.

"But you could still nominate me. I don't understand how I wouldn't at least get nominated."

"My mind is made up, and frankly, this is showing an unattractive side to you. We don't appreciate greedy people, Athena. You've already won student of the year."

"But there's no monetary award with that," Athena argued.

"And every teacher here knows that you'll qualify for a full academic scholarship to the University of Windsor."

Her books and tuition were likely to be covered. But not their mortgage. She had to convince Ms. Hudson.

"You can't win everything, Athena. Other students need it more than you."

Athena's bitterness boiled up into the back of her throat. "But it isn't right, Ms. Hudson. It isn't fair."

"I'm trying to make it fair."

"I have the highest average in the whole school—boys or girls—and I've played more varsity sports than any other girl. Who are you to decide against me? You're not even giving me a chance."

"Athena, this is uncalled for. I've made my decisions, and they're final."

"So Paula and Mariela are going to get the awards at graduation?" Athena's anger flashed.

Ms. Hudson sat smugly and rested her chin on her fist, watching her. "Don't you *want* to see your friends win something?"

There was no chance of convincing Ms. Hudson. She wouldn't admit that what she was doing was unjust. Athena's pride reclaimed her.

"My friends wouldn't want to win something that belongs to me."

"You're a conceited girl, Athena. A little humility would serve you well in life."

Athena stared at Ms. Hudson, who absentmindedly shuffled papers across her desk. The fifteen thousand dollars from the two major awards wouldn't be part of her graduation ceremony or alleviate the financial strain of spending more money than Athena and her mother could make each month. Athena swallowed hard and her tears dried up.

"Thank you for the advice, Ms. Hudson," she said in her best imitation of sincerity.

Athena was halfway out the door, "Oh, Ms. Hudson?"

The gym teacher looked up with a quizzical smile.

"Did you go here?"

Ms. Hudson's face broke out into a grin, and she gushed, "Yes!"

Athena stared into her eyes. "You can tell."

She turned before Ms. Hudson could respond, letting the door slam shut. In frustration, Athena broke into tears and ran down the hallway, through the doors, and out into the pouring rain.

***

Athena sobbed into her pillow. The money situation was like quicksand. If she tried at all to get more, it seemed she sank faster. Athena rolled onto her back and laid her forearm across her head and placed her other hand on her heart. She felt pain in her chest from the struggle.

"No one is going to give you anything, Athena," she told herself. "You have to go and get it. You're smart. You can do this." She sniffled and watched the dance of shadowy shapes on her wall. "Please, God. Help me find a way." Athena watched the light jumping up and down. The moon reflected the sun's rays; it didn't produce any light, so Athena was really seeing the sun, which was on the other side of the Earth. She thought about how the light had travelled all the way around the globe and still encountered obstacles, but somehow it reached her. She just had to keep moving. "I get it—just don't give up." Athena looked at the wall; the light was trying to get through the branches but could only go around them. Athena wrote out her name in the air. "That's why there's a saying, 'It's always darkest before the dawn.' Things get worse before they get better, but they *do* get better."

Athena rolled onto her side and pulled her knees tight to her chest, burying herself in her comforter and tucking it under her feet. The wind moaned, rattling the window and sending a vibration through the covers. Athena listened to her own breath going in and out. Her breath was like a huge wind in a tiny world. She was tiny in the massive universe. She felt herself receding into the middle of her mind, the shapelessness enveloping her. She sucked in air sharply to stop it. "No. Stay here," Athena said, a familiar fear creeping up the back of her neck. She could go insane. When she heard her breath again, it was faster. Athena counted in time to it until she fell asleep.

***

"Mr. Henrik?"

"Yes?"

Mr. Henrik was like a beloved character from fairy tales. The principal stood almost six foot three and strolled around the school with one hand in the pocket of his relaxed trousers. He spoke to all the students in an easygoing way, and he was also a very good listener.

"Oh, hi, Athena. C'mon in."

He smiled, put his pen down, and leaned back, gesturing to one of the two chairs in front of his large mahogany desk. "Have a seat."

Athena balanced on the edge of the chair. "I wanted to thank you, Mr. Henrik, for choosing me for student of the year."

"Well, it was an easy decision."

Athena smiled and bowed her head to accept this high praise.

"It's not often I see a student like you. You're a shining example of what it means to make the most of high school."

Athena's stomach tightened. She didn't feel like she was a part of anything.

"Thank you so much, sir. I need to talk to you about the student athlete awards. I don't know if you know anything about them?"

Mr. Henrik's face clouded and he interlaced his fingers and placed them on the desk. "I do, Athena." He sighed heavily.

Athena waited.

"I'm afraid there's nothing I can do. I can tell you, there's been a lot of discussion about it."

Athena suddenly felt smaller.

"If anyone deserves those awards, it's you. But my hands are tied. It's decided through the school, not the board."

"That's okay. I just thought I'd ask." Athena hadn't raised her hopes so she wouldn't fall far, but she still felt as if she'd been run over. "I better get to class. Thanks again, Mr. Henrik."

"Athena?"

Rising to go, she stopped.

"You're going to be okay."

Athena smiled and nodded as if agreeing. "Yes, I know," she lied. "Thanks again for everything."

Chapter 66

Athena crossed her arms over the desktop and put her head down. She could hear the footsteps of people coming in and the slamming of their bags, purses, and books onto the desks. Girls were talking and laughing. Wet shoes were squeaking on the tiled floor, and she heard the sound of the teacher's heels. Athena felt drained. She wished she could sleep.

The overhead PA system crackled to life. "Please stand for the singing of 'O Canada.'"

The commotion of everyone getting up roused Athena. She pushed herself up and stood with one knee on her chair, clutching the desk with one hand to hold herself up. After the anthem finished, it was announced, "Prom tickets are on sale at the student council office."

Athena sat back down and shut her eyes, resting her forehead on her hands. Anthony had already got their tickets and had made a reservation at the hotel near the auditorium.

The boy and girl doing the announcements droned on about garbage in the student parking lot, swim practices being cancelled due to pool repairs and the boys' basketball win at the tournament on the weekend.

"Finally, the student council has decided to challenge the declaration of valedictorian for our graduating class."

Athena froze.

"As seniors, we'd like to be able to choose the person who best represents our class to speak for us. Historically, the valedictorian is the person with the highest academic average, but the student body will now be able to nominate a representative, and the graduating classes will vote to elect the person who will give the valedictory address. Ballots are available at the student council office. You can nominate yourself. Nominations will close this Friday. The voting will take place next Monday."

Athena's body felt like pins and needles. She kept her head down, unwilling to look up to see what she would face. Paula and Mariela didn't want her to be the valedictorian. They were going to get the athlete awards, and this year, she would not be entitled to give the address at graduation. Athena felt her body fill with shame.

"Too bad for you, eh, Athena?" a boy said.

Athena lifted her head up, the pain releasing from her body. She wouldn't run against anyone. She wouldn't be the valedictorian, not if her own friends didn't want her.

"It's actually good for me. I don't want to worry about giving a speech." Athena was exhausted.

The boy across from her wanted to rub her face in it, but no one really enjoyed giving a speech, so he believed her.

"Besides who's to say I'll get the highest average? It could be Bernadette." She motioned to the girl who still tracked all of Athena's marks to determine if she was in the running.

Bernadette's face said that she knew she wouldn't surpass Athena's grades. "I think I'm going to nominate myself," she announced.

That made Athena, and everyone who heard it, laugh. She laid her head back down and, amid the teacher's droning, fell asleep.

***

"I'm here for my aptitude results." Athena poked her head into the guidance counsellor's office. It brought back the memory of the day she'd started at Montcalm. She hadn't been back to the office since that day.

Mr. Dunlop hadn't changed at all—same beige-yellow shirt, same brown tie. "Yes, come in, Athena. Congratulations on being student of the year," he said.

"Thank you." Athena didn't want this to take too long.

Mr. Dunlop flipped through an accordion folder filed in alphabetical order. "Brkovich," he said, pulling out the paper with her name on it.

"You've got a tie, Athena. Ninety-six percent for either a dentist or a journalist."

"Who makes more money?"

"Well, the average journalist would probably start off at twelve to twenty thousand dollars a year. A dentist could make sixty to seventy, depending on how hard they worked."

She was still for a moment. "How do I become a dentist?"

"Yes, well, you'd need to take sciences and write the dental aptitude test and then apply. Usually, you need a three- or four-year undergraduate degree."

"Do you have to have one?"

"Well, no, but you'd need an exceptional application to get in after only two years."

"I'm already signed up for biology, so that's good," Athena said, getting up to leave.

"Yes, and Athena . . ."

She paused with one foot out the door.

"You could always write once you're a dentist."

***

"Athena! Athena!"

It was Mrs. Harriet, scampering toward her. She was a petite woman with round wire-rimmed glasses. She came up to Athena's shoulder and made her feel big and awkward.

"You have to help me!"

Athena leaned in to listen. She was fond of Mrs. Harriet.

"We don't have anyone for the impromptu."

Athena's eyebrows went up. Mrs. Harriet just stared at her questioningly.

"And you want me to do it?" Athena said.

"Yes, yes. Would you? Oh, please, it would save me. I can't believe we don't have an entry."

"When is it?"

"Now. It's right now. I mean"—she checked her watch—"it will start in probably fifteen minutes."

"Am I even allowed?" Athena didn't really want to do it. Extra activities didn't matter now.

"Yes. You were on my list, remember?"

Athena didn't remember joining. "But I never went to anything, Mrs. Harriet. I don't know how it works."

"I'll explain while we go. Come on. You'll do it, then? For me?"

Athena didn't know how to say no. "Yes, all right."

Mrs. Harriet started walking quickly toward the small auditorium near the office and Athena followed. "You'll be scored on content, originality, and delivery. Points will be deducted for every fifteen seconds you're short, and don't go over three minutes. Don't worry, there's a timer and she'll signal you."

Athena wished she was the timer. "I don't know," She slowed her pace, trying to take in exactly what she was marching toward.

"You can do this, Athena. You'll be great. Oh, it will help me so much! It's so embarrassing. I just messed up . . ."

Athena knew she could help her. Her heart went out to her.

The small auditorium sat about three hundred people. The room was filled; there was hardly an empty seat.

She focused on the boy on stage. His royal blue polo shirt was tucked in, revealing his soft, fat belly, which hung slightly over his pants and was accentuated by the lighting. His hair was greasy. He spoke with a slight lisp. His hands were flat to his sides. He was speaking about tall ships. It was crazy that he'd had the misfortune to pick a topic in which he had to make so many s sounds.

"All the sthipsth . . ."

She shook her head. She couldn't be any worse than this. She stood at the back waiting for the sthtory of the sthipsth to end and then followed Mrs. Harriet quickly to the front.

"I'm missing class right now," Athena said.

"Don't worry." Mrs. Harriet smiled broadly as Athena took the seat in the front row. "You're a lifesaver, Athena. Thank you so much."

Athena sat looking from side to side. Three other people were in the front row beside her. Maggie Telfer was in the seat at the end, and two other people. Maggie waved at Athena, who laughed and shrugged.

"When there's thirty seconds left, I'll hold up this," Maggie said. It was a card with a yellow dot. "At three minutes, I'll hold up the stop sign."

Athena nodded, nervous with excitement.

"Have you ever done this?" Maggie asked.

"No." Athena shook her head.

"I would rather die than go up there."

Athena didn't see it like that.

"Aren't you nervous? I feel like I'm going to throw up for you," Maggie said.

"I'm excited a bit. It will be challenging to write something. I guess I'm nervous about the topic."

"You go into the prep room behind the stage. There are encyclopaedias and books in there, I guess to help you."

She nodded.

"Okay, they're going to start. Good luck," Maggie whispered and smiled.

Athena liked her. She wondered if Cole hit her very much.

"Our third and final contestant in the impromptu open division is Athena Brkovich, a grade thirteen student from Montcalm."

There was a smattering of applause. *So much for the home crowd advantage*, Athena thought. That most of the people were strangers was comforting. Athena reached into the cup and pulled out a slip of paper. It read, *AIDS, acquired immunodeficiency syndrome.*

"Your time starts now," the moderator told her, pointing his finger at her.

Athena looked at her watch. She walked quickly to the prep room. She had heard about AIDS, that it was something gay men caught from having unprotected sex. Some people thought it was God's way to punish them. How could she talk for three minutes about something that wasn't even in an encyclopedia? Her heart started to pound. A paper and pen sat on the table, as well as a stack of magazines. As Athena rifled through the cover stories, she saw an article on AIDS; it was two pages long. Athena put her head in her hands. She needed a good opening and would make up the rest.

The stage seemed very large once the moderator left. The glare from the lights obscured her ability to see the audience, except for the first two rows. Athena looked at Maggie, who nodded encouragingly with a sympathetic smile, giving her a thumbs-up. Athena cleared her throat and licked her lips. *Deep breath, speak slowly, project loudly*, Athena thought.

She began, "Mr. Johnson, we got your test results back. You've got AIDS . . . But I'm not gay . . . Sure you're not."

The Eddie Murphy joke landed and a wave of laughter spread through the room.

She felt electrified as she spoke on stage. Using the content gleaned from the short article, Athena continued with great candour about the disease. She tried her best to stretch out her speech but came in just under the three-minute mark.

"That was amazing, Athena!" Mrs. Harriet gushed, hugging her after she got off the stage.

"I wasn't sure at the end. I was just making stuff up to keep going."

"You looked so natural up there," Mrs. Harriet said.

"Yeah, you didn't seem nervous at all," Maggie said.

She felt a rush, better than drugs, flowing through her body like a powerful energy source. She felt very sexy. She suddenly wanted to see Anthony. As everyone filed out, she stopped to get another hug and more praise from Mrs. Harriet.

"I wish I'd known you were so good, Athena. You'd have been my star speaker."

She turned and went to the business wing. Class would be letting out in ten minutes, so Athena waited by the door. Anthony noticed her in the hallway and he lifted a finger, indicating that she should wait. When the bell rang, Anthony talked to Duncan, who was in that class as well. They were taking their time packing their books up, so to get to them she pushed past the people trying to leave.

"Hey, what are you doing here?" Anthony asked.

"I just did the public speaking thing. It was crazy."

"Okay, well, I'll talk to you later about it." He turned his back toward her and Duncan continued his story about something on TV. They were walking out ahead of her.

Athena stood, flabbergasted. Hadn't she done as she was supposed to and abandoned all of her friends to be the best girlfriend?

"Excuse me?" Athena asked, not moving.

The two boys turned.

"Girls!" Duncan yelled back at her.

"Cut the drama, okay?" Anthony told her, and the boys high-fived. At the door he looked back and said, "Come on, sweetie. I'm just walking with my best friend. Don't make it weird." He nodded for her to come along.

Athena's energy had gone from high to low in a five-minute span. Now all she could think about was struggling through the last thirty seconds of her speech. *So the thing is . . . what we want to remember . . . is that AIDS, acquired . . .* She cringed. She wanted to cry and scream. She would not follow them. She walked out of the classroom slowly in time to see Anthony and Duncan disappear around the corner at the end of the hallway.

When she caught up with him later, she said, "I just thought *I* was your best friend."

"You're my girlfriend." Anthony looked at Athena, frowning. "I don't know why you have to do this."

"Do what?"

"This." Anthony waved his hands between them. "Everything's fine and you have to make problems up."

"Me missing you or wanting to tell you something is a *problem*?"

"You can do that, but I can still have my friends."

"I didn't say you couldn't." Athena hesitated and then added, "But *you* say I can't."

"I'm done with this."

She reached out to touch him and he pulled away, grabbing his gym bag. "Wait. Anthony, please." She ran after him. "What do you mean, you're done?"

Anthony turned abruptly and faced Athena. "Look, everything could be nice if you wanted it to be. Stop making problems. I booked us a limo and a hotel room. I paid for the prom tickets and got the stupid tuxedo to match your dress. Do you know how much all that costs? Isn't that being a good boyfriend?"

"It is. It is." Athena was contrite. He was a good boyfriend. "I'm sorry."

"Yeah, well, I'm trying my best to make things special and you're cutting me up."

"No, I'm not, I was just—"

"You were just trying to make me feel small, which is what you do. You know how to be mean."

Athena's heart sank. She had confided in Anthony that she'd been mean when she was younger and wished she hadn't. Now she regretted telling him.

"I said I was sorry."

He paused and inspected her face. "Hey, don't cry. There's people around."

Athena stopped. "Everything's okay, then?" she asked, looking through blurry eyes.

"Yes, I love you." Anthony squeezed her hip and gave her a quick kiss.

Chapter 67

"I'm going to wear one of Dani's old dresses. She wore it to prom at her other school so I'm sure no one's seen it. It's chiffon and cut really low in the back and has a short hemline at the front. You can't wear a bra with it. A wide blue satin sash wraps around the waist."

"Oh, that sounds sexy," Kat said.

Athena was sitting on the floor. Kat and Roxy were draped across Kat's bed.

"What shoes are you wearing?" Roxy asked.

"Just my black ballet flats."

The friends nodded, knowing that the height issue loomed large.

"Do something like this with your hair." Kat turned the page of her magazine around to show her a big romantic updo.

"You're having a pre-party? Is that what I heard?" Roxy asked Athena as she rummaged through Kat's lipsticks and finally settled on a dark red. She started applying it.

"Yeah, my mom said it was okay, and I thought it would be cool to use the limo. Anthony had to pay for half a day anyway because it's picking us up at the end of the night to *take us to the hotel*." Athena sang the last five words.

Kat and Roxy didn't comment on that, but Kat asked, "So who's coming?"

Athena ran down the guest list. Everyone liked Anthony, and with Duncan being his best friend and as popular as he was, the girls agreed it would be a great party. Even with Paula and Mariela there.

"I'm going to have some trays of hors d'oeuvres. My mom wants lots of pictures."

***

Athena waited nervously at her house. She'd spent the last three hours getting ready. She took a bath to shave her legs. She'd put her hair into hot rollers and used almost sixty bobby pins and a bottle of firm-hold hairspray to make something that resembled the romantic updo she was trying to copy. Athena put the slip of a dress on and her mom helped her tie the sash tightly in the back.

"You're so tiny," Tilley said.

Athena had hardly eaten that week. She wanted to look as skinny as possible. "That's what I was going for."

"Not too much makeup," her mother said.

The house looked nice. There were two shrimp rings with cocktail sauce and a cheese and crackers tray, with cans of different pop next to them. The limo was supposed to arrive at four o'clock. Athena figured they would have an hour at her house and then drive to the prom to arrive for six. It was almost five o'clock when the limo pulled up slowly at the front of the house. Athena's agitation, which had been mounting an assault on her senses, disappeared as the four couples spilled out onto the front lawn. They were all laughing and assembling themselves into appropriate pairs. They'd been partying, drunk or high or both. Paula's mom had gifted them a few bottles of champagne, but that was long gone.

Athena skipped out onto the driveway. "Hi!" She made a beeline for Anthony, anxious to feel included, suddenly self-conscious that she wasn't really part of this group. "What took you?" she asked in the cheeriest tone she could muster, then told everyone to go in and help themselves. "There's food."

"Is there a bathroom?" someone said, and laughter followed.

Anthony grabbed Athena by the elbow and held her back from leading the way. "What the hell?" He looked as if he was in physical pain.

"Are you okay? What's wrong?"

"What's wrong? *What's wrong?*" he kept repeating. Horrified, he stared at her.

The familiar feeling of failure rose in her chest.

"Your hair! Why the hell did you wear your hair up? You're not friggin' tall enough? Do you have to do that? Take it down."

"I can't," Athena said plaintively.

"You have to."

"I can't. I'd have to take a shower. It's done."

"Well, thanks for ruining my night." He stormed past her into the house.

Athena tipped her chin up, not wanting anyone to know. She put on a smile as sounds of the intoxicated revellers reached her on the front step, which had already started to sink into the earth on one side. A single pink rose was in full bloom where Tilley had planted two thorny rose bushes. Inside the sparkle of satin in all different colours met her eyes. Ten people made the room feel completely full. Everyone's parents wanted pictures at every stop, but so far Athena wasn't in any of them. Tilley had her Kodak camera ready. "Let's get some pictures. You all look so nice."

Everyone was excited.

"Thanks for having us, Mrs. Brkovich," said Paula.

"Be careful tonight. You're staying at Paula's?" Tilley asked.

"Yeah." Athena lied and gave her a kiss.

They had to leave quickly. The dinner tickets had cost forty dollars apiece, so no one wanted to miss it. The boys had bottles of beer waiting for them in the limo. Everyone lined up along the car in couples.

"Boy, girl, boy, girl," Tilley said, standing almost on the porch to fit everyone in.

Anthony had hardly spoken to Athena. She grabbed his hand and tried to pull him closer but he resisted, talking loudly to her mom and the driver and the other couples. Athena stepped back down into the gutter and moved behind him.

He turned and saw her. "Hey, bighead." He threw his arm around her neck as she leaned in awkwardly, bending her knees to shorten herself more.

"I don't know if you'll fit in the car with that big head of yours," he joked when she was climbing in.

Everyone laughed.

Feeling the heat rise to her face, Athena realized she didn't need fake blush. She laughed as if she was perfectly fine. No point in bringing everyone down.

But Athena had already ruined it for herself. Anthony refused to dance with her all night because her hair made her taller than him.

She danced alone to all the fast songs. The music filled her body and she moved, not caring which group of people she was with, just gliding across the dance floor as though she was looking for people she'd come with and then moving on.

Not wanting to make Anthony angry, Athena had trained herself to avoid looking at Niko if he was in the room, but the flash of his blonde hair caught her eyes as he strode onto the dance floor straight to her.

"Hey, you look great," he said loudly, leaning in to speak over the music.

"Thanks. You too."

He did look very handsome in a tailored tuxedo. Athena leaned closer to him, his proximity triggering a jolt in her body.

"Can you believe we made it?" He grinned.

"Just barely."

They smiled at each other.

Athena looked away. *This will never end well*, she thought. "Well, I gotta go."

"Yeah, I figured." He motioned to her table.

Anthony had just seen her and was making his way through the throng of students whose formalwear was growing limp from the sweat and heat. Athena danced toward Anthony and left Niko behind. The remainder of the night was a rundown of her poor choices and how this had ruined things. Anthony didn't want to have sex with her and he complained about it, having wasted all that money on a fancy room for nothing.

At the hotel, Athena rewound the night in her mind as she lay staring at the strange ceiling. She visualized everyone all dressed up in her living room, laughing and eating, twirling around and posing for pictures. Surrounded by strangers she pretended were her friends or lying next to a boy she pretended to love, she had never felt more alone.

Chapter 68

Tilley was the only one who attended Athena's graduation ceremony. Athena watched as some of the students cried and hugged others and spoke dramatically about the significance of the moment. Athena felt as if this was just another season ending. Seasons came and went; they couldn't last forever. Change was inevitable, and it was pointless to be surprised by it or saddened by it. Death was inevitable too, and it wasn't worth crying over either, but it seemed to her that no one realized this.

Things had been strained between Athena and Anthony for the week or so since prom. Athena had French braided her hair for graduation.

The students sat in alphabetical order, as they would be called across the stage. Athena got to go early, which she was thankful for. Her Ontario Scholar and highest average award were announced as well. There were no big cheers, the hallmark of popularity, but she had prepared herself for that. Even her siblings hadn't thought to show up.

"Niko Jovanovich."

As Niko strode across the stage, a huge cheer went up from his clan, who had shown up in droves. Even all the girls who had forgotten that they didn't like him for dumping them hooted.

Ms. Hudson, who wore a teal pantsuit with big shoulder pads, raved about how Paula and Mariela were like daughters to her, read off their impressive resumés, and handed them their life-changing envelopes. Duncan, who had been chosen over Athena as valedictorian, gave the address, which was uninspired.

The principal stood behind the podium to draw the ceremony to a close. "Before I share with you my final thoughts, I want to acknowledge one of the graduating students. To me, she's an inspiration. She's only been on the stage once, to receive her diploma, yet I can't recollect ever seeing someone like her pass through our hallways."

Athena was listening but didn't realize Mr. Henrik was speaking about her until he said her name.

"Athena Brkovich is one of the most outstanding people I've had the pleasure of teaching. Not only has she consistently won top honours, but she's also played every sport imaginable and headed up the yearbook committee, all while holding two jobs outside of school. She's an example of hard work, effort, and grace. In all my years I haven't come across this rare combination of exceptional talent and diligent work ethic. Although I don't have another award to give her, I'd like to congratulate and acknowledge the person who raised this fine young lady."

Mr. Henrik bent down, reached under the podium, and pulled out a bouquet of colourful flowers wrapped in cellophane. "Mrs. Tilley Brkovich, would you please come up on stage and accept these, along with my sincere admiration for having raised such a wonderful daughter."

Athena wasn't sure how she felt. At first mention, she'd felt a rush of excitement and gratitude for Mr. Henrik's words, which then changed to embarrassment over the unexpected attention. It wasn't an award, just a statement.

Her mother, always graceful and likeable, made Athena bounce back when she graciously accepted the tribute to a great deal of applause. It was as if all the other parents were happy that one of their own had been acknowledged. Athena hoped her mother was filled with pride. As Tilley stepped down from the stage, Athena felt humbled by all her mother had done for her—and she had received only flowers.

As the applause died down, a boy sitting two rows behind her said loudly, "Rich bitch didn't get the money prize, though," and everyone laughed.

Athena didn't turn around to see who it was. She simply sat up straighter.

She looked down at the big heart locket dangling from the end of the long gold chain. She picked it up and turned it around in her fingers. She could feel the weight of it around her neck. Athena couldn't pretend any longer. She was done with the tediousness of high school. She wanted to be free. Everything would change. This was her chance.

Mr. Henrik gave his final speech, comparing life to a train ride. You think about the final stop, but that only comes when life is over. It's what you do along the way that counts. Athena listened intently, understanding this already. Death was the final destination. The next part of her journey was about to begin.

Book I: Windsor

Book II: London

Book III: Dorchester

Book IV: Woodstock

soniapalleck.com

windsor

SCAN ME

CPSIA information can be obtained
at www.ICGtesting.com
Printed in the USA
LVHW030413170323
741829LV00002B/339

9 781039 162389